BRIDGE

Also by Lauren Beukes

Afterland
Broken Monsters
The Shining Girls
Zoo City
Moxyland
Slipping: Short Stories, Essays, and Other Writing
Maverick: Extraordinary Women from South Africa's Past
Survivors' Club
(with Dale Halvorsen and Ryan Kelly)
Fairest: The Hidden Kingdom
(with Inaki)
Wonder Woman: The Trouble with Cars
(with Mike Maihach)

BRIDGE

A NOVEL OF SUSPENSE

LAUREN BEUKES

MULHOLLAND BOOKS
LITTLE, BROWN AND COMPANY
NEW YORK BOSTON LONDON

Mulholland Books / Little, Brown and Company
Hachette Book Group
1290 Avenue of the Americas, New York, NY 10104
mulhollandbooks.com

First Edition: August 2023

Mulholland Books is an imprint of Little, Brown and Company, a division of Hachette Book Group, Inc. The Mulholland Books name and logo are trademarks of Hachette Book Group, Inc.

ISBN 9780316267885
Library of Congress Control Number: 2023936010

Printing 1, 2023

LSC-C

Printed in the United States of America

BRIDGE

BRIDGE

Portrait of a Kidnapping

April 2006

On the long stretches of highway, her mom lets her sit up front next to her, although Bridge has to slouch down when they pass a police car, because they are being a little bit naughty and seven-year-olds are supposed to sit in the back. The road is a dark ribbon through the trees, like in the story about the little girl escaping from the witch Baba Yaga and her chicken-footed house.

You don't have to think like that, Mom says. *There's no one chasing us.* But her eyes flick to the mirror again and again, and when she has to pull over at the gas station to take her pills so she doesn't get fits, she sits waiting in the car, watching the parking lot, before she goes inside, and Bridge can't stay behind because *I need you to pick the best doughnuts.*

"Isn't this nice, the two of us getting away? Surprise vacation!"

"I miss Bear," Bridge says. "And also Daddy." Her dad is a very busy guy. And motels don't allow galumphing Labradors. But it doesn't *feel* like a vacation. It's not very fun. And she thinks maybe this is her fault because of what happened at her mom's lab, which isn't really her lab, but the professor lets her come there to do her studies and sneak Bridge in. It's boring there. She is not allowed to climb the high wooden shelves or roll down the corridors on one of the wheelie chairs or play with the plush toy of a brown worm with a knot tied in its tail that sits on top of the filing cabinet, and *I'm not sure how your dad would feel about you playing with Ebola.* Bridge does know. He would not approve.

Mostly, she sits at Mom's desk reading comic books or doing her puzzle, which has five hundred pieces, but she lost four of them, so there is a hole in the unicorn's butt like a tiger took a bite out of it. But one day she did something bad while Mom was busy talking to the other brain scientists. So much talking! She didn't mean to. The rats were so cute and she just wanted to let them out so she could play with them, and she didn't even really manage to open the door to any of their cages, which aren't really cages but kind of glass nests.

Mom got in so much trouble with her boss and with Daddy.

She shouldn't have been there unsupervised, her dad said, talking through his teeth, and *What were you thinking* and *This is why*—and he caught her looking and pulled Mom into their bedroom by the elbow and slammed the door and their voices were soft and spitty like cobras and then suddenly loud and high like yappy dogs, and Bridge could hear the words *What do you expect me to do* and *I can't live like this* and *Ungrateful is what you are, I didn't even want*—and Bridge just turned up the TV because it was her fault they were fighting because of the rats. So maybe it's also her fault they need some girl time now, her and Mom.

They find a youth hostel near Bourbon Street, which smells gross on Sunday morning, like wet garbage and sick. Jo does card tricks for the backpackers from South Africa and New Zealand and Ireland and tells them how she used to live here, in New Orleans, but not in the tourist part, when she was their age, or younger, actually, fourteen when she ran away from home—and for the first time, Bridge thinks: *Oh, is that what we're doing?*

They drive all around the city, past old-fashioned houses and under twists of highway near the stadium, past the cemetery with white marble tombs like a Lego city for ghosts. They visit a broken house with graffiti and holes in the floor and Mom says this was her home when she was a runaway, but Bridge doesn't want to go inside because it's creepy and there are spiky thistles everywhere and what if the roof falls down?

They stop at restaurants and bookstores, Mom always asking around for people she used to know. Once a man followed them back to the car. *Hey, pretty lady, I can help with that, maybe you can help me, know what I'm saying* and Mom snarled, *Fuck off,* and that only made him mad, so they had to run and jump into the car, and he came after them and slapped the back windshield as they drove off.

Her mom says they're trying to find a rabbit, but they find a witch instead, with curly hair and tattoos of stars and not scary like Baba Yaga. Her name is Mina and she knows her mom from *back in the day*, and Bridge is impressed at how she is grubby and glamorous at the same time in a short black dress and big army boots with the laces undone so she might trip at any moment.

She lives up a flight of rickety metal stairs in an old warehouse, and as she climbs, Bridge has to hold the railing really tight and not look down at the gaps where the sky shines through. Everything is in one room, the rumpled and crumpled bed and the kitchen, full of plants and glass bottles and things you might find washed up on the beach, old bones, and antlers and bits of coral, still pinky red, with skinny twisted fingers. There are string lights hanging from the ceiling and the skeleton of a huge bird with its wings spread wide and some of the feathers still attached, kinda ratty, but still determined to fly. She has dreams about that dead bird afterward, but she has a lot of weird dreams that year.

Mina and her mom talk and talk and talk and cry and Bridge gets bored and embarrassed. Then she must have dozed off on the couch, because it is evening and Mina is unlocking one of the display cases and lifting out something wrapped in a creamy cloth like an Egyptian mummy.

Mina keeps saying the rabbit is dead and, maybe that's what it is, all wrapped in cloth—a dead baby bunny—also Mina doesn't want to give the mummy to her mom, but her mom keeps saying she needs it. More than anything. Please.

And Mina says, *I hope you know what you're doing.*

And her mom says, *I don't have a choice.*

BRIDGE

So Barve RN

This is not where Bridge is supposed to be. Story of her life. But here especially, standing on the threshold of her dead mother's home—this most haunted of houses. *Reality is not real,* her mom used to say. *Your perception is a lie your mind tells you.* It's only that Jo's brain told her grander and more dangerous lies than most people's—that the world was more than it was—and for a time after they got back from being on the run, Bridge believed it too.

"It's not your fault," her therapist, Monica, told her repeatedly. She was a little kid, seven years old; her mom had a brain tumor that made her delusional, and she brought Bridge into her dreamworld for a little while. She was better afterward, didn't mention it for years and years, but then she got sick again, and it all came rushing back. The absurd, desperate fantasy. And now she is dead.

This is a raw physical fact; incontrovertible.

This is *real,* like the cold metal of the key in her hand on this quiet street in Mount Scott–Arleta, the cicadas ratcheting in the trees, and the Grand Am's engine clicking accompaniment. Dom drove it here all the way from Austin to help her, and it broke down only once. Or so they claim.

Dom is wearing a blue jumpsuit and puffy Day-Glo sneakers—"Manual labor, but make it fashion," they quipped when they picked her up this morning from that hateful anonymous apartment two blocks over from the OHSU Hospital in Marquam Hill.

By contrast, Bridge is wearing leggings and a black T-shirt. Grief, but make it entropy. It's been her uniform for the past few days, since her mom took a sharp, sudden downturn and she flew here, too late. Jo was in no state to even recognize her. *You're not my daughter.* Chemo-induced dementia, the doctor said, or the tumor pressing on her brain. Again. Jo was fifty-one years old, but the cancer had been trying to kill her for almost forty years. Once, twice, third time's the charm. Joke the pain away, she thinks.

Dom has brought supplies: cardboard boxes, folders, labels, stickers, packing tape, groceries, a bottle of tequila—all the essentials needed to deal with your dead mother's estate. And doesn't that word *estate* imply a mansion in the countryside with secret passages for the servants and hidden treasures in the attic rather than this modest boho cottage, cycling distance to Everard University? Sure, her mom had sent her a cryptic e-mail about "frozen assets," adding that she'd provide further instructions when they next saw each other, but in the hospital she was too out of it to talk, and her lawyer didn't know anything about it. Wouldn't it be great if there was a secret inheritance: gold bullion, a lost Dora Maar portrait, or, ya know, answers, closure? All the things left unsaid.

I don't know you.

She didn't get to say goodbye, not properly, not in those circumstances, with Jo turned to face the curtain, her scrawny shoulders hitching, flinching away from Bridge when she tried to touch her, tried to tell her she loved her. The uncrossable gap between them stretching wider.

I want to go home.

Bridge thought she only had to wait it out, that it would run its course like Jo's epileptic seizures, and her mother would emerge on the other side, and they could talk. But she didn't. And now all that's left of Jo is cremains in a plastic bag inside a wooden box shoved in a cheap wheelie suitcase.

Dom is mucking about, holding a blue plastic label printer like a gun and sweeping it across the neat houses of Portland, with their neat lawns and their neat curtains and neat lives inside, acting as if they are in an over-the-top action movie with assassins ready to descend instead of in another chapter of Bridget Kittinger-Harris's so-far-pretty-pointless existence.

"Coast is clear," they announce and Bridge manages a smile. Trying for okay.

"How about it," Dom prompts again. "You ready to do... *the thing?*"

"Fuck no." Bridge sighs. The dread is like someone stuck a feeding tube in her throat and poured concrete down it, and now it is sitting thick and heavy behind her rib cage. "Are you sure we can't just burn it all down?"

"Hmm." Dom is fiddling with the label maker, jabbing at the buttons. "Well, you'd be the first suspect. And the landlord would be pissed."

"The landlord could file an insurance claim," she protests.

"Bridge, my love, we are going into that house and we are doing *the thing* if it kills us."

"It might, though," she pleads. The label gun makes a grinding chirp as it prints something out.

"Here." Dom peels off the new label and sticks it on Bridge's shirt upside down, so she can read it.

SO BARVE RN

"Barve?"

"Flying fingers, bonus typos." Dom shrugs.

"Yeah, well, that solves everything."

"Like magic. Language has power. Feel the courage."

"All right, all right." Smiling despite herself and the cat's cradle of emotion, all the tangled anguish and despair, along with the rage. She is goddamn *furious* with Jo for leaving her, for being right about the brain cancer, for not calling her sooner. And furious with herself. The guilt that she didn't come sooner, when Jo told her, three weeks ago. And in general, that she didn't visit more, call more, pick up on her mom's erratic behavior: her new squirrelly evasiveness, the trip to Argentina, the dramatic breakup with Stasia, losing her job. But Bridge had been caught up in her own life, her own problems, now minor and stupid in comparison. She'd thought she would have more time. Her mother wasn't supposed to *die*.

She slides the key into the scuffed lock, turns it with a click, and pushes the door open, drawing a jangle of protest from the squared-off antique Chinese bell hanging above it that is supposed to summon blessings or whatever. Dom steps in behind her and taps the doorframe twice, murmuring something in Spanish—a Puerto Rican benediction for the dead.

"That's really kind," she says, trying to mean it. She's not ready for this: Acknowledging the dead. Making a peace offering. Death is pretty fucking *real*, it turns out. A whole set of realities, all uniquely awful. And now the infuriating bureaucracy that comes after. Sadmin, Dom calls it.

Her dad has already offered to pay for an agency to deal with Jo's junk, once Bridge has gone through it, and for the memorial service, when she's ready, and for more therapy. But he can't be there in person. Unfortunately. Solving everything with money. Solving nothing. She hasn't told him she dropped out of the business-degree program he's paying for and is now working full-time at Wyvern Books.

Does she even want a memorial? It would have to be in Cincinnati, for her very elderly grandparents, and maybe her uncle would show, and the cousins she hasn't spoken to in years. But Jo's students? Her colleagues? There are scores of heartfelt posts on Jo's Lifebook wall, regrets and blandishments that all run together. Bridge stopped reading them, mechanically clicking Like, Like, Like, so she didn't have to respond to these strangers who thought they knew Jo but who saw only one version of her. Would anyone come to mourn her life in person? Jo had nuked all her bridges once she got her diagnosis.

Standing in the entry hall, half blocked by the antique desk with its drawer hanging slack-jawed, Bridge tries to shift gears, to be *barve.* She puts on her best poncey British decorating-show-host voice and gestures grandly around the shabby interior, at the mismatched picture frames, the bookshelf running the length of the hall. "As you can see, what we have here is a classic take on absent-minded adjunct-professor chic." Always playing the clown. Distract, deflect.

Dom takes in the details, deadpans: "I was expecting more beakers."

"Beakers is chemistry." She moves to help them haul in their bags. There's the reassuring clink of the tequila bottle—because no one should have to do this sober. "Neuroscience is all about electron microscopes and patch clamps and oscillatory...majigs. Actual technical terms. And that would all be at her lab at the university."

"How about disgusting specimens decaying in jars of formaldehyde?"

"Also at the university. We'll probably need to go clear

out Jo's things there too. There's a creepy surgery museum you'll love."

"Diablo," Dom says. "You know I'm always down for gruesome medical historia."

She's been to the lab here only once, when she visited before Thanksgiving. It was a fusty old building glommed on to the side of the shiny new medical wing, and it looked like every other lab Jo had worked in except this one had her name on the laboratory door and she was so proud to show it off.

The desk drawer isn't closed all the way, revealing unopened bills (add those to the sadmin pile), and she nudges it shut with her hip, runs her hand over the scuffed green leather desktop with an untrained evaluator's eye. A hundred bucks? A thousand? Yard sale or online auction?

"Bad breakup or bad case of the poltergeists?" Dom says, tilting their head at the books scattered across the floor.

"Oof," Bridge says, picking up a copy of *The Physics of God* haphazardly spatchcocked on the worn-out runner. She's still doing the cataloging, the arithmetic. Fifty cents a book? Two dollars? She slides it between *Being You: The Neuroscience of Consciousness* and *Swamplandia!*, which seems a fitting title for what she's going through.

But the mess makes her uneasy. It could have been someone throwing things in anger or her mom having a seizure and grabbing at the shelves. But it doesn't look scattershot; it looks deliberate, as if someone was searching for something, sweeping books out of the way, rifling through desk drawers. Her heart free-falls.

"Burglary?" Dom offers.

The state of the bedroom confirms the diagnosis. It's been tossed; the closets are gaping, all of Jo's signature black clothing yanked off the hangers. The mattress has been heaved aside; the storage bench of the window seat yawns open. The little desk in the corner is strewn with papers, some spilling onto the floor, a laptop cable dangling uselessly among the stacks.

"¡Coño!" Dom says, whistling.

"Fuck," Bridge agrees.

The living room is in the same state: the sofa knocked on its ass, pillows tossed, art removed from the wall, revealing only ghost impressions instead of hidden safes.

And, yeah, undeniable: In the kitchen, the window by the back door is broken. Glass jags on the earthy red tiles and leaves blown in through the gap. Ransacked cupboards and drawers. The washing machine is open, and the toilet cistern lid has been removed. Like they were looking for hidden cash or drugs?

"Fuck," she says again, more softly.

"Do you want to call the cops?" Dom says, not meaning it for a millisecond. But she appreciates them saying it out loud, especially considering their whole brown-queer-from-out-of-town thing. The police in Portland have a reputation.

"What are they going to do? Not like my mom had any valuables. Or insurance." Hope is a small and brittle thing—she hadn't realized she'd genuinely been holding out for secret treasure. "Probably stupid teenagers." At least it's not squatters. She wraps her fingers around her ponytail, tugs it hard.

Dom pretends not to notice she's on the verge of a panic attack, taps the label printer against their cheek. "Look, I can fix this window, easy. Landlord won't know a thing. But you have a critical job."

"Keeping it together?"

"That," Dom agrees. "But also CSI. Go room to room, see if there are any other damages you might be liable for. Make a note of anything important or valuable that's been stolen so we can decide if you want to call the police or hit up pawnshops after we do the hardware store."

"What are you going to do?"

"Well, baby, I'm going to take care of the *really* ugly stuff. You smell that?" Dom wafts their hand in front of their face, sommelier-style. "That might just be a dead body." Dom tiptoes over to the refrigerator, which is clearly the source of all evil. "Possibly several. Was your mom killing people and harvesting their brains?"

They fling the door open and Bridge reels back, choking on the odor of rotten food. There's soft mold fuzzing over a mush of old strawberries, recognizable only by their label, milk that expired a week ago, desiccated leeks, and wilted greens turning liquid in their bags. The power is off, she realizes. Add that to the list.

She hadn't been able to face coming to the house while Jo was in the hospital. Not alone. Not even to pick up a fresh pair of underwear for her mom. She'd bought them brand-new from Pioneer Place instead. But now, my God, she wishes she'd come sooner and dealt with this before it became a biohazard. Bridge shoves the door shut, mock gagging. "Can I burn it all down yet?"

Dom shakes their head. Their thumbs do tippy-taps over the label printer. It grinds out a new message, another typo:

BEWARE!!!!!!!!!
BAGD SMELL LIVES HERE

They slap it on the refrigerator door beneath a shopping list stuck on with a magnet advertising a talk about the science of dreams. And then they print out another:

LEAVE IT TO DOM

"We can trade? I'll do this if—" Bridge would rather scrub out a thousand refrigerators than sift through the ghosts of her mom's possessions. Possessed-sions.

"No chance. I'm not qualified to do your job, so leave me. Leave me here!" Hand to their forehead, sacrifice face. "Go! Before I change my mind!"

"Ugh, fine!" She stomps away to find the circuit breaker and restore electricity to the land. Nosing in to the living room, she rights the sofa turned turtle and replaces the cushions, threadbare and wine-stained. Probably from the pre-Thanksgiving potluck Jo held for the students still on campus, her and Stasia's coterie combined—the neuro kids and lit majors—and Bridge, the dull daughter, half-assing her way through a business degree when she really wants to do film studies. The guests/students draped themselves over the furniture and spilled into the kitchen and the little garden, the conversation bright and intent, and her mom and Stasia kept touching each other, which was really cute and also embarrassing. Jo seemed so different from her usual spiky self. Playful, happy. Bridge couldn't remember the last time she'd seen her mom like that.

Stasia hadn't come to the hospital. It was that kind of breakup, although Bridge is uncertain of the details. Stasia was already at her new job in Baltimore, a million miles away, but she'd sent Bridge an e-mail with her condolences, something about Jo's defiance, her fire, how much they'd loved each other. Past tense. *The problem with fires,* Bridge thinks, *is you can't really contain them. They burn you up, burn you out.*

This is a lost cause. How is Bridge supposed to tell the difference between a something-that-has-been-stolen vacancy and Stasia's-shit-that-she-took-when-she-moved-out one? She needs a before-and-after, a spot-the-difference. Playing detective. She could e-mail Stasia, she supposes, the same way she is going to have to track down and mail a few of Jo's grad students to help her go through her mom's papers.

The shelves are full of photos turned facedown, which she leaves right where they are. If Jo couldn't bear to look at them, Bridge isn't ready yet either. Assorted tchotchkes, including a vivid emerald vase; a rough wooden carving of a man with one glass eye holding a snake ribbed with nails like a giant studded penis (gross); a small brown rubber fetus (more gross). And, up on the top shelf, her mom's musical instruments: an African thumb piano with double-stacked metal tines inside a gourd and a sitar with a long neck, tall as the wooden statues. "Giraffe guitar" she used to call it when she was a kid, and her mom used to play it for her, sitting on the floor next to her bed. She tried to teach her how to play, but Bridge could only manage the thumb piano. A marimba? *No, mbira,* she remembers. She reaches up on tiptoe to get the sitar down. As she lifts it, a silver key drops out from where it was tucked under the bridge; attached is a plastic tag that reads STASHER4U K-551. She palms it together with the fetus and goes to show Dom.

They are deep in the refrigerator, wearing yellow gloves and a face mask they've found somewhere like it's the peak of Lord Corona all over again, an industrial-strength black garbage bag emitting a sickly breath at their feet.

"Found your corpse," Bridge says, holding out the rubber doll, nestled in her palm.

"Ugh!" Dom's brow furrows in disgust. "What the hell is that?"

"Stasia got Mom into volunteering as an escort at abortion clinics. The pro-lifers try to hand these to people going in. 'Look, this is your baby! This is what you're killing.' It was an intervention. The more dolls they collected, the fewer the assholes had to terrorize people with."

"Hmm. Or... consider that your mom and Stasia might have been in the pay of Big Rubber Fetus. Maximizing profits by ensuring the lunatics had to go buy even more squeezy embryos."

"And something else." She opens her other hand.

"What's that?"

"Key for a storage locker, I think? Maybe that's where the buried treasure is."

"Or corpses. We can go check it out tomorrow. Once I'm done with this horror show." They grab a pile of Tupperware from the freezer and start lugging it over to the sink. All Jo's prepped meals turned to soggy defrosted mush.

Bridge makes a face. The rotten smell is still lingering. She notices Dom has set out a bowl of fruit and placed a vanilla candle on the windowsill in front of the broken pane of glass. Another peace offering for the spirits. Bridge wishes she had any kind of faith or tradition right now—ritual as a life raft.

"Don't think I haven't noticed you're avoiding the tough stuff. Go, scoot, back to your job." They tap the upside-down label on Bridge's chest. SO BARVE RN.

The bedroom draws her in with a terrible gravitational suck. It's dim with the rattan blinds down, allowing only a narrow band of light to slice across the floorboards.

She rolls up the blinds, revealing a milky fog of condensation rising halfway up the glass and, beyond it, a moonflower tree drooping its pretty poison bells. It takes her a moment to realize there is someone with a bicycle standing across the street, staring at the house. Red hoodie, dark hair, no helmet. *Fucking genius over there*, she thinks. Head injuries are a serious business. Kill you just as effectively as brain tumors. He raises his hand, less greeting, more *Professor, I have a question.* She makes like she hasn't seen him and drops the blinds. A few moments later, the doorbell rings. Tinny and electronic and too loud. Her mom would have bought the first one she saw at the hardware store, left it on the pre-set tone.

"Ignore it!" she yells to Dom.

"I am elbow-deep in some very bad things. If you think I got time to worry about the damn doorbell—"

It goes off again. And then a sonorous jangle of the Chinese bell. *Fuck off*, she thinks. Tinker, tailor, bill collector, or worse—someone wanting to offer their condolences. The emotional capacity to hold someone else's hand is not something she has right now. She wills whoever it is gone, gone, gone, and, finally, the shadow undarkens the door.

Back to the bedroom.

Picking up papers, trying to decide how to sort them. Documents have colonized the whole surface of the desk in unruly stacks. *Leave it another month,* Bridge thinks, *and the piles will take over the entire house, fill every room, splicing and multiplying like slime mold, the weight bursting the doors and windows, spreading into the street. Wouldn't that be something?*

Most of the stacks are undisturbed, which tells her the robber wasn't looking for top secret research. She scans the visible pages, but it's all the same shit Jo had spent her life on. So obsessed with her own epilepsy, she'd made it her specialty: "Inhibitory synaptic transmission and neuroinflammatory responses in the emergence and termination of seizures."

If Bridge were to collect all these documents and her mom's notebooks into a great pile and set them alight, would the world really be any worse for it? There she goes again with the arson fantasies. It's a kink of her generation, wanting to burn it all down.

Oh, and here's the laptop, buried under a folder of student

papers. *Really* incompetent burglars. Or an indication of how out-of-date this clunker is—an ancient Mac circa 2015.

"Hey, Bridge?" Dom calls. Something's off in their voice, like maybe they did find a damn corpse after all.

"Is it sentient mold?" She heads back to the kitchen. Dom has taken off the mask and is wearing their best what-the-hell-is-this-shit face, which, to be fair, they use quite often. In the sink, several recently decontaminated Tupperware containers are piled up. One is laid out on the table, although even from here, Bridge can tell those tomato stains on the side are never coming out. *Like blood,* she thinks, but of course it's not. It's her mom's ratatouille. Zucchini and eggplant and onion and vegan chorizo and a shit-ton of tomato and garlic. Her favorite when she was a kid.

There's something inside it. You can see the shape through the stained plastic, and it's somehow *off.* About the size of an avocado, but saggy, malformed. Familiar. Foreboding.

"What is it?" she says.

"Fucked if I know. It was buried under the leftovers, emerged like ancient anthrax from the melting permafrost."

"Frozen assets," Bridge says, realizing. How cryptic, how unnecessary, how freaking typical of her mom. A breeze through the broken window tugs at the candle flame, wafting vanilla and unease across the room.

Dom comes to stand beside her, rubber gloves drip-drip-dripping dirty dishwater onto the floor. Bridge's hands reach for the lid even though she doesn't want to open it, would in fact much rather do all the paper sorting in the world right now, deal with all the accounts in arrears.

She lifts away the lid. No ceremony. Get it over with. Reveals a lumpen yarn-y cocoon. It's grayish yellow, bulbous, and striated, like a spindle wrapped in rotting elastic bands.

Dom leans over her shoulder. "Some kind of disgusting German delicacy? Schmorgenborst?"

But Bridge knows. She recognizes it. From a lifetime ago. From a witch woman in New Orleans. From sitting on the bed in her room while Daddy was at work and her mom strummed dreamy chords on that sitar, and they watched the spinning toy, around and around, and Jo kissed the top of her head and said, *Don't forget to come home.*

She'd forgotten. Willfully repressed it, burned through the memory, curled black edges around the hole. Didn't want to deal with the implications. Which she is reeling away from now, thank you. *A fantasy. Make-believe.*

"What is it?" Dom says again.

"The dreamworm," Bridge says and eases her fingers underneath the finely bound mesh of the carapace. It's brittle and somehow *warm,* and a strand comes right off in her hand, as easy as if it belonged there—and maybe it does. Gold in the light, not moldy yellow. This is also familiar.

"Am I supposed to know what that is?" Dom asks.

"It opens doors to other worlds." And before she can think about it, before Dom can stop her, Bridge puts the strand in her mouth—*baby bird*—and swallows it whole.

DOM

Bad Life Choices

"Oh no, don't—" Dom starts in dismay, but it's too late. Bridge is choking and gagging. She drops the crusty stringy chrysalis thing that no one in their right goddamn mind would bring anywhere near their mouth and throws herself across the room to the kitchen sink. She's doubled over retching—or trying to—and Dom is raiding the archives of their brain for the first-aid course they did once upon a time. Trying to evaluate the dangers. There's a script for this. Most urgent: blocked airway.

"Can you talk? Can you breathe?"

"Yeah, I'm fine."

"Spit it out."

Moving on: Is it a toxin or bacteria? Making a little song up in their head: *E. coli, staph, listeria.* What are the chances there's activated charcoal somewhere in the house? A medical kit? Can they run to the neighbors to borrow a gallon of milk? What if they're vegan; would soy milk do the trick? At what point do they need to go to the hospital?

"Ugh." Bridge spits into the sink.

"Properly."

"I swallowed it already. I could try..." She mimes sticking her fingers down her throat.

"Definitely don't do that! Vomiting might make it worse."

Bridge downs a glass of water. Pours another one, shaking her head. "It's not poisonous. It's the dreamworm." She looks terrible—sallow, unwashed hair, grief-sodden, and somehow brittle, as if she is a girl made of sticks instead of bone.

"Right. Of course. I mean, obviously," Dom says. They're examining her for symptoms: dilated pupils, flushed skin, facial swelling, airway closing up, signs of anaphylactic shock. There's none of that. Not yet, anyway.

Bridge wipes her mouth with the back of her hand, but her fingers linger against her lips like she's just been kissed by her crush. She comes back to the table and picks up the lump with something like reverence, and, hoo, boy... whatever it is, it can't come on this fast. Can it?

"You okay?" Dom says.

"She left it for me. I was supposed to find it. But she said there would be instructions..."

"On a scale of ten years' straight to sliding down gravity's rainbow, how high are you right now?"

"Sober as a church mouse. It won't work without music and the—shit, the old-fashioned whirligig animation thing? Have you seen anything like that?" Buoyed up on this new quest, she is opening cupboards, scouring shelves.

"A zoetrope?" Dom follows her. "I would have remembered." Honestly, they're impressed. Between the rubber fetus, unusual musical instruments, unknown substances, and now early-cinema gadgetry, they're thinking Jo is more interesting than Bridge ever let on. But then, it's always much easier to appreciate other people's parents.

"Can we back up, though?" They already have their phone out and they're typing into the search box. "What is the dreamworm? What's it made of, what does it do, at what point do I need to drive you to the ER to get your stomach pumped?"

"It's a psychedelic, a really rare one. It helped my mom when she was sick. Before, when she had cancer the first two times. It opens other worlds, places where she found a cure or, rather, the information she needed to save her life, because no one believed her."

Desperate times, magical thinking. Dom has some experience in clutching for meaning in the dark, full of knives. Also in recreational psychedelics. And, hey, it's possible, right? "Cool. So, tapping into her bodily intuition, her subconscious, she got some deep revelations?"

"Yeah," Bridge says. But she's being shady. "She had a neuroscience degree, so it's not such a stretch that she figured out where the tumor was when the doctors couldn't."

"So not *technically* other worlds."

"One way to find out." Bridge grins and proffers the spindle chrysalis thing. She looks so damn hopeful. "Will you do it with me?"

"Oof." They've tripped balls a bunch of times, the pair of them laughing their asses off at Pedernales Falls on shrooms or rebooting their brains on LSD at home, watching videos of Bob Ross and that guy who makes blades out of cucumbers and smoke and rubber flip-flops; they did ketamine in a tent hung with LED lights in fractal patterns on the playa at Burning Flipside with a sweet boy in a pink fur coat sitting beside them and holding their hands. Dom made out with him later and, maybe coincidentally, caught the gastro going around.

"Let's see what the internet has to say." Dom stalls, reading from their phone. "I have a bunch of hits on how to interpret your dreams *about* worms: You need to 'protect yourself from toxicity,' 'guard your good intentions,' and, ahem, case in point, 'prioritize self-care.' The dreamworm is also the monster in one episode of an obscure anime and the title of a babymetal song by a band called Magna Kafka. The lyrics would suggest the dreamworm in question is a penis that shoots out squiggly dreamworms of its own 'deep into your fertile womb cave, baby.' There is not a single result on hallucinogens, street or otherwise, by that name."

"I did mention it was really rare, right? My mom spent years looking for it. I thought she'd made it up." A twist of guilt across her face. "I didn't believe her. Fuck. All those years." She gestures at the house, the boxes. "Please, Dom. I have to get out of my head. Even if it's for a couple of hours. I need this. I don't want to do it alone."

Dom sighs. They know a no-good-very-bad situation when it's right in front of them, and this stringy yellow artifact is not what Bridge wants it to be—an inheritance, a great mystery, a secret message in leftovers. But, hey, if it *is* a cousin to peyote or acid, maybe this could help Bridge access complex revelations about her relationship with her mother, and this is *exactly* the time and the place. Besides, (a) that ship has sunk, since she's already taken it, and (b) they have real trouble saying no to her. They're working on this.

"It better not be poisonous."

"We always said we'd go out together."

"Fighting the zombies! Or in a suicide pact at ninety-nine years old, riding the euthanasia coaster to terminal g-force!"

"I know what this is, Dom. Trust me. My mom left it for me. She wanted me to do this. It's safe, I promise."

"Oh my god." Dom digs in their grocery bag, gets out the tequila.

"Is that a yes?"

"I'm sure I've done more ill-advised things in my life." They definitely have.

Bridge breaks off a piece, a thumb-length slender strand, and holds it up to the light. It glints golden, and they don't know how they could ever have mistaken it for moldy yellow. They take it from her. *Rapunzel, Rapunzel,* Dom thinks, and washes it down with a swig of tequila.

Bridge searched up a zoetrope-style animation of ballroom-dancing skeletons twirling around through hypnotic repetitions, and they're watching it on Dom's iPad, curled up together in the nest of cushions they've piled in the living room, to the accompaniment of traditional sitar songs playing on Bridge's phone, soaring and strange with a resonant fuzziness that lingers after every note—or maybe that's her busted-up speaker, tinny from all the times she's dropped her cell.

Trip*py*, for sure, but they're not feeling anything that would qualify as trip*ping*. Dom lies back, folds their hands over their chest, and takes deep breaths. Beyond the music, they can hear the cicadas in the trees outside, the soft thrum of a car passing, a lawn mower in the distance. Somewhere a woodpecker is drilling a tree in fluttering staccato.

"It's not working." Bridge sighs, startling Dom awake.

"Give it time." Dom blinks and wriggles their arms above their head. "You are one with the dreamworm, the dreamworm is you."

"It's been over an hour."

"Barely. Give it another half an hour. What's supposed to happen?"

"I can't really remember," she says, but she's cagey. "It feels like you're falling and then you're somewhere else. It's kinda instant."

Dom rolls onto their elbows. "You've done it before." Not a question.

"I thought I hadn't." Defensive. "I thought it wasn't real, that it was part of my mom's sickness. That's what Monica says—my therapist."

"I know who Monica is." All those late-night chats on the roof of Dom's crappy apartment building, drinking beer and peeling lychees and spilling their darkest and deepest: Bridge's mental-health vacations, when her dad had her committed; Dom coming out to their parents twice, first as nonbinary and then as an atheist, which was almost harder for their folks to get their heads around. Bridge's string of bad-news boyfriends right up until the lovely Sam and the total heartbreak that derailed her when he got a job abroad, and she said she was never going to love anyone again. And lots of perspective, thanks to Monica the perspicacious.

"You never mentioned any dreamworm before, I'm just saying."

"Because it wasn't real." Bridge sits up, pulls her hair loose, and combs her fingers impatiently through the tangles. "It was a dumb game. My mom played the music and spun the zoetrope and we'd close our eyes and imagine we were somewhere else, and I wanted to believe it so much because she was *my mom*. But it was me buying into her delusion."

"Hang on. How old were you? Was your mom giving you *hallucinogens?*"

"Or sour worm candy or a gnarly herb. Obviously it was all hot garbage." Bridge scrambles up from the nest of cushions. "She made it up. Stockholm syndrome, Narnia edition. We should toss that thing in the compost heap." She offers her hand to Dom to pull them up. "I'm sorry I dragged you into this. Glad it wasn't poison." Playing it cool to hide how mad she is.

Dom has believed in worse things than dreamworms. Fifteen and confused and angry and living online, falling in with Lulzchan, high on their own self-loathing and denial and wanting other people to hurt as much as they did, trollololling until Papa found out and took away their phone and their laptop. He sent them to Aunt Yolanda in New York for the summer, where it was so humid Dom felt like they wanted to grow gills, and their thighs got sore and chafed from wearing short shorts and all the damn walking everywhere.

Yolanda *could* have left them to their own devices to prowl the Lower East Side with the other summertime teens, but every day she dragged Dom into the sweltering office where she worked as a legal secretary and plonked them in the corner by the air-con, which periodically gave you twenty minutes of rattling hope, then died again for long sticky hours.

Dom wasn't allowed near a computer, so there was nothing to do except draw on the back of printer paper rescued from the recycling bin and read legal files. Papa hoped the law would rub off on them, and it did. The piles and piles of immigration cases of people who'd left terrible situations with all the hope in the world, fleeing narco-violence and governments that killed journalists, really, *really* put their shit in perspective. But Papa had also taught them to draw, and with the chance to practice, it was the art that stuck.

What Dom really wants is to be a full-time comic artist—indie, not superheroes, thank you, although maybe they could cut their teeth on some mainstream Marvel or even Wonder titles. They can see themselves doing a distinctive take on Dark Girl, that lawyer by day, crime-busting sorceress by night. Learn the ropes (and the tropes), build an audience before they launch their own thing. After their design and tech degree, of course—setting themselves up for a more practical art career. They're not like Bridge with an absentee dad who is willing to bail her out as long as it's just money, although they recognize that's its own kind of fucked up. Too much rope to tie yourself in knots with. Their parents may be annoying and suffocating and can't get their pronouns right (to be fair, Spanish isn't built for it), but they've never doubted their love.

"Okay, so that's a bust. Ready to get into the great packening?" Bridge says, too chipper.

"Or we could go for a walk? Shake it off? Do some tourist shit, pick up Arcana doughnuts, ride the aerial tramway, maybe even drive out to the Timberline Lodge, which is only like an hour away and was the location for—"

"*The Brightness*, I know. You're not the only true horror fan here. Maybe tomorrow. My mom's shit isn't"—her voice cracks—"it isn't going to pack itself." Bridge covers her face with her hands, and Dom envelops her in a bear hug.

"She was pretty sick, Bridge. It's not her fault. Or yours either."

"I know," she manages.

"Déjalo salir. Let it out, baby. It's okay."

"God. Don't be kind to me! That's the worst." She breaks down and buries her head against them. But she only gives herself an instant. Suppress, repress. Can't be having feelings. Dom knows how scary it is to let go, to let yourself feel.

"You better not be snotting on me."

Bridge gives a herky-jerky snort. "Too late."

"Oh, well. At least it's not vomit."

"Do you think there's still a chance we'll find treasure?" Bridge mumbles against their shoulder.

"Not in the freezer. All the other 'frozen assets' are mush."

"We still have a mystery storage locker to explore."

"And I've started an inventory spreadsheet, already sent the link to your phone. I reckon if that desk is real mahogany, it might be worth fifteen hundred dollars or more, and maybe there's a collectibles market for rubber fetuses."

"I don't deserve you."

"No one does, baby. No one does. Ay!" they complain as

Bridge sags against them. "Stand on your own two feet, for God's sake, woman!" She flops her full weight onto them, and Dom staggers, clowning, but then does go down. "No, ugh!"

"Sorry," Bridge says. Not sorry at all, sprawled across their chest.

"Oof," Dom grumbles from under her. "Of all the difficult bitches in the world, I had to choose you."

"Think you'll find we chose each other," Bridge says.

BRIDGE

Not the Real-Real

June 2, 2006

Bridge loves this part of the magic game. Mom playing the music, and then the lights in big circles, and the colors, more and more of them, like double rainbows, and it feels like when you're on the spinning shells at the amusement park, and there's a really loud wind, and *whoosh!*

Bridge is wearing a dress she doesn't own, white and scratchy with silver sequins that sparkle like snowflakes. But it's not chilly Seattle fake summer here. It's hot, and the heat makes Bridge's long hair stick to the back of her neck. This is exactly why she doesn't *have* long hair, she thinks, irritated. There are two old people looking down at her, older than her mom and dad but not as old as her granny. They seem to be waiting for her to say something amazing, and she wishes she didn't always land in the middle of things and need to figure stuff out.

"Um. Maybe a vet?" she says, because this is something boring grown-ups always ask when they don't know how to talk to kids: And what are *you* going to be when you grow up? But they look confused, so she smiles, showing all her teeth, and curtsies, which is not something she would ever, ever normally do, but being polite is a good disguise. "Please excuse me," she says and skips away.

"Ah," the old lady says, but Bridge is already crossing the lawn, darting between the grown-ups, who are all wearing fancy clothes and holding glasses of wine or fruity drinks with flowers in them. Bridge is a spy and a detective, and these are important clues.

The sky has gone the color inside a snail shell, pale and pearly. Shadows are stretching themselves out across the lawn. Paper lanterns have been lit around the deck of the house, which is not her house, even though she has been here before. The girl reflected in the windows as she runs up the stairs looks like her only because this is a dream. Her own private dreamworld.

A woman shrieks, too bright and sharp, like the last fading notes of music she can still hear. But it's a something's-funny scream, not a scared one, because her high heels have sunk into the grass, and she's spilled her drink over a man and is clinging to his shoulder.

"Yikes," she says. "I'm such a klutz." Bridge rolls her eyes like her mom does, because *Drunk people are ridiculous.* (Also: *Your dad sure does like his beer.*) That's another difference in the dreamworld. Her parents don't fight here. And they live in Florida! They also have a big house with big glass doors and a tree house in the garden and a trampoline and a swimming pool! It's huge and round with a mermaid mosaic on the top step that looks like blurry blocks when you look at it underwater, but when you stand outside the pool, you can see how all the different-colored tiles come together to make up her long flowing hair and the scales on her tail.

You can't see it today, because there is a woman sitting on the edge of the pool with her bare feet in the water, legs like pale stumpy logs. Bridge doesn't recognize her, but she doesn't recognize any of these people anyway, and she's paying attention to her only because she's sitting with her dirty feet in her pool! The woman has hair that is too yellow, like a bruise that's done being purple, and a T-shirt that's also yellow and says SUNSHINE PETE'S TACKLESHACK with a drawing of a fish leaping out of the water wearing sunglasses. Even Bridge knows that's not what you're supposed to wear to a party with flowers in the drinks. She frowns at her, and the woman raises her eyebrows and pats the tiles next to her in invitation.

Bridge scowls harder and slips into the living room. There aren't any kids her age here and she's hoping to sneak past all the chattering grown-ups and up the stairs to her room so she can play with the toys she doesn't own. There's a fuzzy blue octopus and a bright pink plastic dollhouse with a claw-foot bathtub and a bed with a pink mosquito net you can pull around it like your Barbie is dead and it's her funeral. But the living room is thick with adults talking too loud, their voices echoing, and the growling zing of the blender in the kitchen and the clatter of plates, and Bridge turns around and marches right back out. The woman is still sitting by the pool with her bare feet and rolled-up cargo pants. She stands over her, hands on her hips, like when Mom is mad, but her heart is racing.

"You're not supposed to be here," she challenges.

"Neither are you, I think," the woman says, not bothered. "You wanna see something cool?" She stands up out of the water and lifts one leg to show off four ridged scars striped down her calf just below her knee.

"Did you get attacked by a tiger?" She's impressed.

"Alligator. Sunk its teeth in and then tried to roll me, which is why it's all dragged out instead of neat tooth marks."

"Look, I also got hurt!" Bridge holds up her arm, which has a long scar down the middle with little dots beside it from when dream-her fell out of a tree and she had to get a metal pin put in the bone. Not as cool as an alligator bite.

"You want to be careful *here*, kid," the lady says, taking her elbow and squeezing it, and her voice is like gravel that scrapes her skin. And her arm is itchy, she notices, like she is getting a rash where the lady touched her. "You don't want to get more hurt. I don't want to have to fix this. Who is giving it to you? Your daddy? Your mommy? I need to have a talk with them. This isn't a game. You need to stop."

Bridge yanks her arm away. "Leave me alone!" It comes out small and stupid, but enough people turn to look that the woman backs off.

And right then, her not-mom comes out of the house. "There you are, Birdie!" her not-mom says, beaming. Her face is flushed pink, like the sky, and she's wearing a red dress with lace sleeves and a fake rose pinned in her dark hair, which is long and wavy over her shoulders. Not at all like her real mom, who only wears black and jeans and whose hair is always, always tied up in a ponytail to keep it out of her face. "Where have you been, my little bird?" she says. The lady in the yellow T-shirt is already moving away into the crowd, but she looks back, once, like don't-forget-what-I-said (or just don't forget me).

"Oh!" her not-mom exclaims in dismay. "What have you done to your shoes?"

Bridge looks down at the white slippers that match the dress, with pretty sequined straps at the ankles, now stained with grass and mud. A mosquito lands on Bridge's cheek, and she swats at it, and her hand comes away streaked with her blood and a black splatter of bug.

Bridge holds up her bloody palm. "I got bit," she says.

"Aw." Her not-mom kisses the top of her head just like her real mom. "Sorry, my little budgerigar. Come on, we were waiting for you to cut the cake. Never mind the shoes."

"Gather in, could everyone gather in," says a man she

doesn't know. He's standing on the deck, circling his arms. "Come on, then, gather in!" and the people come waddling across the grass like when you throw bread to the ducks, and she looks for the woman with the alligator bite, but she's gone.

On the marble island in the middle of the kitchen is a giant chocolate cake with roses made of red frosting to match her mother's dress and a candle in the shape of a 3 and another in the shape of a 0, waiting to be lit. The people crowd around, and her not-dad calls for a lighter, and everyone is smiling and laughing.

"But I don't even like chocolate," Bridge says, though she says it under her breath. She doesn't want to hurt her not-mom's feelings. Even when it's not the real-real.

From: Caden Lyall
To: Jo Kittinger (private)
Date: Monday, August 9
Subject: You okay?

Hi, Jo,

Checking up on you. You haven't answered any of my e-mails. Your phone goes straight to voice mail.

I went to visit you in the hospital but the ICU is family only. Please tell them to let me see you.

I tried to explain, but how could I, really? I saw your daughter going in. She looks like you. I wanted to leave a note for her, but the receptionist said she wasn't a secretary. Let her know I'm on the approved list, okay?

I can help. You know I can. You owe me that much, Jo.

—C

BRIDGE

No Undo

Bridge rouses from the sweet dark depths of sleep at ungodly o'clock. It's her body punishing her for drinking too much, pinging her brain: *Yo, wake up, you poisoned us, now you have to suffer too.* The whole damn bottle of tequila, she thinks with great regret, and glances over to where Dom is cocooned in all the blankets, snoring softly on the other side of Jo's modest Ikea double bed.

She lies there with her eyes closed, willing herself back to sleep. But it's gone. *Poisoned!* her body complains, her throat burning with dehydration. *Yeah, yeah, okay.* She checks her phone. Six eighteen in the A dot M.

There's a glass of water and an aspirin on the bedside table next to a note in the professional font of Dom's handwriting with an illustration of a happy little glass beaming rays of sunshine. *Eat me! Drink me! Thank your guardian angel of hangovers later.*

She really doesn't deserve them.

And then the loss kicks in all over again, and she has to shove it down deep where she can't feel it—or at least pretend she doesn't. Focus on the hangover. On what they accomplished yesterday: two whole rooms.

Dom stuck up poster-size sheets of paper in the living room with various to-do lists and started piling movable objects beneath their respective categories: Things to Sell, Keep, Donate, Chuck, Get Professionally Valued. A lot of manual labor, sorting, and studiously avoiding talking more about her mom or the stupid fucking dreamworm.

She was grateful Dom didn't press the subject. They ordered in Thai and talked about everything but. Dom held forth about internet esoterica, like the sheer number of serial killers in Oregon, for example, and how ninjas wear black because that's how stagehands dressed in Japanese theater, and one day, one ingenious playwright had a stagehand (who was literally part of the furniture, or, rather, the mechanic who moved the furniture, but the point is, everyone agreed he was invisible) step forward and commit the murder, which blew the audience's mind. The conversation segued into Victorian kinks and a horrifying ye olde treatment of applying leeches to the cervix, and Dom said maybe the dreamworm was a leech and had they tried to feed it blood yet? She playfully punched their arm, but with the half-hearted strike of the desperately tired, and Dom hauled her up and shoved her down the book-cramped hallway to her mom's bed.

Now, Bridge swallows the store-brand pill (because "Big Pharma is a sack of dicks") and a whole damn pint of water. She lies back down, but her head is in some kind of hell vise, and her brain is whirring through the fog, and let's face it, there is zero chance of her going back to sleep. Reluctantly, she gets up and pads through the hushed rooms of the house on bare feet. It's somehow less haunted at six a.m. In the gray dawn, it becomes anyhouse. Like the acetaminophen: generic.

The Tupperware is still sitting on the kitchen table. She considers tossing the ugly useless thing inside it, shoving it down the disposal unit, grinding it to dust. But maybe it's the apotheosis of her mom's work. She could get it tested. One of the grad students, a colleague? She'll need to find someone, slip it in there while she's asking about what to do with her mom's papers. *Hey, know anything about her research on the dreamworm? Totally fake, waste of time, but I thought maybe I could dump it on you just in case?*

It *felt* so real. The grass under her bare feet. A scar on her arm. Not magical. No unicorns or dragons or kingdoms in the clouds. Perfectly normal; banal, even. Monica helped her realize these were false memories, maybe even suggestions her mom had made so she'd be able to imagine a different life, prepping her for the divorce and how things could change. A kind of hypnosis, using the zoetrope and the sitar.

That tracks, she hates to admit it. She remembers pretending she was somewhere else, somewhere nice, with a big house and toys and a huge garden and a pool in Florida where her dad's folks live, and there was a party one time, and her parents were her parents but also not. Or she was standing on a beach, looking out over fir-topped coastal islands, the wind rippling the grasses, and her mom holding her hand and saying, *Isn't this lovely?* She imagined bad times too. Her parents yelling worse than they ever did in real life, smashing things. Her mom and her living in a car, snuggled up on the back seat among all their worldly possessions. Part of her processing, according to Monica.

Bridge pours herself another glass of water and goes to her mom's desk. Might as well try to be productive. Taking a note from Dom's mad organizational skills, she creates five new folders on the laptop: Mom's Work, Personal Shit, Admin to Sort Out Now, Admin to Sort Out Later, and WhateventhefuckdoIdowiththis, and abandons them all to comb through her mom's photo albums. There's a folder labeled TO PRINT, which she obviously never got around to, because whoever does?

Here are Jo and Stasia, happy and swaddled up on a frozen pier on vacation in Copenhagen, their cheeks red from the cold. Jo with her students in front of the lab, fresh-faced science babies, one of them, a girl with soft pink hair and glasses, performing fire poi. A portrait of Stasia curled up in the window seat reading, caught as she's looking up at the camera, features curved in tender surprise.

She quick-scrolls through the others, pauses on a shot of a skull painted red nestled in a sculpture of plastic dolls and tangled with wood and wires, which is fucking weird. Jo standing next to a motorcycle on a hilltop, squinting into the sun and holding out a small battered tobacco tin like a prize. Was that Haiti? Everyone told her she'd been lucky not to get kidnapped. An unsmiling Black man with dreadlocks and Ray-Bans leaning on a filigreed balcony. What was Jo even doing there?

Back further. A photograph of Bridge at her high-school graduation standing between Jo and her dad, one of the few post-divorce occasions they'd managed to tolerate each other, all of them smiling too hard. Sixteen-year-old baby-goth Bridge with purple hair, phone dangling from one hand, slouching in a long-sleeved black shirt and jeans in front of piles of rocks at Chiricahua because the Grand Canyon was too misty for them to see anything. Only pretending to hate it, because hiking was the one activity where she and Jo seemed to relax around each other.

Bridge goofing around in drama club, dressed in black again (like Dom's ninjas); at fourteen, heading off to Bible camp, acting so devout to hide that she was full of hormones and turmoil. At eleven, at a Katy Perry concert with her best friend, Maya, both of them losing their minds; at nine or ten, her mouth smeared with marshmallow and chocolate, camping in Deception Pass with her mom, who was trying too hard to make up for how busy she was with her PhD, all the times she wasn't there. At eight years old at the Big Fun theme park, where she started crying after the first roller coaster and wanted to go home. Jo was furious because she'd spent so much money on their entry tickets, called her "a little scaredy-cat." *Nice, Mom.* But Bridge remembers being illogically terrified of falling out. No, more than that—of falling away and never being able to find her way home and losing her mom forever and ever.

She stops prowling through the pictures and, against her better judgment, clicks on the "hidden" folder. Someone has to scrub her mom's sex tapes from the Cloud, and it might as well be her. There are a bunch of videos with cryptic names, all variations of numbers and letters, like FJ_Key4h, and ominous black thumbnails. They fill her with a different kind of dread—a squicky slurry rather than concrete.

She *could* ask Dom to do this, especially after the New Year's Eve incident. The pair of them skipped the parties and were mainlining gin and tonics and episodes of *The Golden Girls* on her roommate's ridiculously expensive white couch, which didn't even make sense to have in a shared student house, and Dom abruptly declared they were going to hurl, and Bridge...caught it in her cupped hands. On the exchange rate of friends-saving-the-day-no-questions-asked, a double-handed couch-saving puke catch has to be worth skimming through DIY Mom porn. But even though she knows Dom would handle it with stoic efficiency and never speak of it again, she can't do that to Jo.

Bridge cowgirls up and clicks on the first one, labeled ZC_12M. The video begins with bands of color, like a test signal, and then a familiar zoetrope pattern starts, the horses running, and the sultry notes of a sitar but stranger, somehow. She pauses it. Glances over at the bed, where Dom is dead to the world, starfished across the mattress.

Absurd to feel guilty but she does as she tiptoes into the

kitchen, where it's waiting for her. She pries the lid off the Tupperware, looks down at the dreamworm, which is pale and iridescent. She should wake Dom, let them know she's doing this. That would be the responsible and considerate thing to do. And then Dom would considerately and responsibly talk her right out of it.

Bridge breaks off a spaghetti-like thread and carries it back, lightly cupped in her palm. It's only her imagination that it's warm. She sits down in front of the laptop, takes another look at Dom, who has rolled over, cocooned in the covers, so she couldn't abandon this and get back into bed even if she wanted to. But they'll be right there if anything goes wrong...

Bridge untangles the headphones with one hand and plugs them into the laptop. The snag of dreamworm in her palm has curled up; from her body temperature, obviously, like one of those fortune-telling fish you get in party crackers. It's not magic. It's not alive. It's not going to give her brain cancer.

Her mouth is dry as an Arizona desert thanks to the hangover and the anticipation. She takes a swig of water and holds it so she doesn't have to feel the slimy texture, the sweet beetroot-y-taste of dirt, as she puts the worm in her mouth. She swallows it whole. It doesn't wriggle. Too late now. Before she can hesitate, she leans over to press Play on the video.

The music swells through the headphones, the strange familiar sound of the sitar, and the black-and-white animation loop goes faster and faster, the zoetrope horses running and running until they are a blur, no longer individuals but a centipede of stallions, and there are colors, a whole damn Pantone catalog in kaleidoscope, swirling fractals, and a whooshing rushes up to fill her head and there's a terrible pressure and then...

BUDGIE

The Moment You've Been Waiting For

This is not the first time Budgie has woken up on the floor. Not by half. But this isn't her carpet; it's not her room. Which means it's happened. A small, relieved part of her thinks: *Finally.* Hasn't she been anticipating this her whole life? The inconspicuous white van, the man's gloved hand over her mouth, blade against her throat, his breath against her ear, hot and foul, his voice raspy, disguised. *Don't scream or I'll fucking kill you* is what he would have said. Or some variation.

And Budgie, knowing what she knows — that you cannot let the serial killer take you, no matter what — would have fought like a demon or, worse/better, a mom, because she has her two babies at home, and she would have bitten down on the fingers pressed against her mouth, twisting her body at the same time to ram her elbow into his gut.

And if he'd released her for an instant in surprise and pain, she would've slammed the back of her skull into the cartilage of his nose, although she is only five foot five, and he would have been bigger, but skulls are hard, and getting hit in the face is shocking, deeply shocking, she can tell you, especially when the fist that breaks your cheekbone is attached to the man who fathered your children, the man you once loved. Still do, in some small part of your heart and your brain — the same parts that are fucking relieved that the worst has now happened, *Because you were kind of asking for it, Bridgie Budgie Budgerigar.*

This part of her speaks in Franco's voice. The same easy cruelty, twisting that affectionate childhood nickname. But *fuck you*, because she *is* here, still alive, still fighting. Wherever *here* is. A bedroom, she thinks, her eyes adjusting to the dimness. She's on the floor beside a desk, the faint glow of a computer screen above her. Double bed against the wall. Light leaking in beneath the closed bedroom door. Should she crawl over and open it, slip away through the unknown house?

But why can't she remember anything? She can imagine the man coming up behind her, his voice softened, abashed: *Excuse me, ma'am?* Hitting her with his crutch, dragging her into the van. No. That's Bundy.

All that true crime rots your brain, Bridgie, Franco always said. *No serial killer would waste his time on you.* As if he weren't the one who gave her a concussion, slamming her head into the kitchen wall as casually as he used to come up behind her in the good days and lift away her hair and kiss the nape of her neck. Marlon watching with his big thoughtful eyes. She hadn't even *done* anything to deserve it. Not that time. *But you would have*, he said. *I know you.*

This dim room. Stolen from her babies. The absolute worst that could happen. (No, that's something else, something *really* unthinkable: a car accident, a fire, little bodies under sheets.) *But you don't know that didn't happen, do you, Budgie? Because my sweet li'l dum-dum can't remember how you got here. Maybe your big bad serial killer snuck into the house and held the little ones down with pillows over their faces before he simply carried you off over his shoulder, like a princess to lock in his tower? And you didn't even hear him, let alone put up a fight, because you were passed-out drunk, but hey, Budgie, at least you kicked the fentanyl.*

Fuck you, Franco, she thinks. *Fuck you to hell.*

Maybe it was me, dum-dum. Ever think of that?

Impossible. He doesn't know where she lives now. She drove hundreds of miles to Boulder in that shitty Honda with nothing, absolutely nothing, except her kids and the clothes on their backs, the miles slipping away behind them. Far enough. Hopefully. He'd never suspect she'd go anywhere near where her mother lives. Not after the custody battle, violent as the brick through the window, Franco smearing shit on her mom's windshield.

But here, now. *Focus, Budgie.* She's wearing panties and an oversize T-shirt that's not hers. Which makes sense. The killer would have cut off her clothes to...you know. Her brain skids away from the word. *It doesn't matter,* she thinks. *What matters is getting home.* First: the door.

But why would he leave her in a room with a computer? Unless he's using it to watch her, film her for the dark web. She shifts onto her knees, realizes she's tangled in headphones. She slides them off and shuffles, still on her knees, toward the door, staying low in case the camera on the laptop is on and this is a horrible game.

And then something terrible: *Someone* stirs in that double bed. She screams, only it's not a scream, it's more a sharp yip of fear that she cuts off, her hands to her mouth, her throat. It's *him*. Franco. No. The serial killer.

Or a one-night stand, you filthy li'l slut. Got so drunk you don't even remember, didn't make it home, and the babysitter was ready to call child protective services.

No. That was before. That was over a year ago. And it wasn't a one-night stand with some stranger. She was with Franco, and she hadn't meant to go back to him, but he'd pleaded with her to meet him at the Firebird—*C'mon, Budgie, for old times' sake*—and they had a beer and it was like old times, and then he said it would be quieter for them to talk, really talk, if she could come back to his place, and it was just around the corner, the apartment he was renting since he moved out, and he had a bottle of bourbon and a pipe, and it would make it easier for them to be honest with each other, profoundly honest, and the way their bodies spoke to each other, that was honest too, that was the way they'd always communicated best and he was so repentant and so loving and so kind and didn't he know her the best, better than anyone in the whole world, and didn't the kids need their dad?

She knows it's been more than a year because that's how long since she left to take Marlon to preschool with Jess strapped into her car seat, grumbling at being roused from her cot, and she drove away from Franco and the drugs and the booze and didn't look back, and she's got a plastic AA chip to prove it.

Budgie knows that's not Franco in the bed. She knows the shape of him, the sounds he makes in his sleep. This is someone broader and softer, and she looks longingly toward the door. But if the killer wakes, if he follows her, pulls her back by the hair, knocks her to the ground, gets on top of her, his weight pushing down on her, crushing her ribs... she knows that feeling already. It's not a good feeling.

So she picks up the only thing in range—the ceramic lamp beside the bed, clunky and heavy—and prays it will be enough if she brings it down hard and repeatedly.

DOM

Shower Scene

"¡Carajo!" The terror of waking up to find their best friend looming over them, her face contorted in hate, teeth bared, eyes huge and glinting, bringing something down straight at Dom's face.

Total instinct. Rolling away, kicking out. They hit Bridge in the side, but what saves them from imminent concussion is the cord attached to the lamp she is trying to brain them with. She hasn't unplugged it, and it pulls taut, arresting the trajectory, and the lamp thumps uselessly onto the wooden floor. No tinkle of broken glass, thank God.

They lurch to their feet, half tangled in the sheets. Bridge is hunched over, clutching at her ribs, snarling like a possessed girl: "Fuck you, fuck you, fuck you, you won't take me."

It's so weird, so ludicrous, Dom nearly laughs. But then Bridge lunges for the bedroom door, and Dom grabs at her arm—not to hurt her but to catch her.

Bridge twists in toward them, turning their wrist in on itself, and where the hell did she learn that nifty Krav Maga move? Dom lets go but manages to get between her and the bedroom door, arms outstretched like a goalie in the worst game of soccer ever.

"Tranquila," they say, trying to calm her. "You had a bad dream. It's me. It's Dom. Everything is okay."

Her eyes roll, spooked horse, searching the room for another weapon, Dom realizes. They both go for the laptop at the same time.

"Put it down, Bridget. I'm not fucking kidding."

Her eyes go wide and she gives a half moan, half sob, knees sagging. She thrusts the computer at them and dashes for the bathroom door.

By the time they've tossed the laptop onto the bed and crossed the room after her, the door is locked. The shower is gushing and they can hear her sobbing inside, hysterical.

"Come on, Bridge. It's me. It's okay. Let me in."

"Don't call me that!" she screams. Dom is trying to remember how big the window is above the toilet. Too small for an adult human—that's why the burglar came in through the kitchen window.

Knocking softly. "Stop messing around. You're scaring me."

"Fuck you! Let me go!"

"I will if you come out. We can talk, just talk. How does that sound?" They're raising their voice to hide that they're moving away from the door, going for their phone on the bedside table. They nearly trip on the damn lamp cord. Hands shaking and of course it's too dark for face ID. They key in their code, scroll to their in-case-of-emergency notes.

"You're not going to kill me!"

"No one's going to kill you, you idiot!" The wrong thing to say. They always thought Bridge's dad exaggerated her breakdown. Here in the note is all Bridge's essential information: Jo's number—fat lot of good that will do. Her dad's number, Sam's number—they hesitate over it for a second, but he's a whole ocean away, out of the picture, not even in the storybook. Bridge's Social Security number; her blood type, O negative—that might be important. Please not. "I didn't mean to call you an idiot. Please come out, we can talk."

They copy-paste her dad's number. Hit Call. It rings. Dom's knocking on the door. "Hey, come on, please let me in."

"Get away from me!" she screams. "Leave me alone!" More sobbing.

The phone rings and rings and rings and rings, then goes to voice mail. A friendly, professional baritone: "You've reached Dave Harris, I'm unavailable at the moment, please send a text or try again later." They hit Call again. Same story. And again. Fumble a text. Still knocking, but softer, less intimidating, they hope.

Muffled sobbing under the sound of rushing water.

"Please, Bridge. Please let me in."

Hi, Mr. Harris, it's Bridge's friend Dom. She's

How the hell do they describe this.

in a bad state. Please call me urgently.

They sink down, back against the door, repeating a litany: "It's okay. It was a bad dream. Let me in, please. Let me help you. I'm not going to hurt you. You're upset. It's okay. Can you talk to me? Please, Bridge." Thumb hovering over the keypad. "Bridge, if you don't come out, I'm calling the cops. You need to come out."

Screw it, they're calling 911. They get to their feet—for some reason, that's important to be able to call emergency properly, to be able to convey the seriousness of this.

The shower turns off, abruptly. "Dom?" Bridge calls out cautiously. Her own voice.

BRIDGE

Refresh

A freezing shock of water over her head. For an instant of sheer terror, Bridge thinks it's an avalanche—the snow-flecked mountains outside the grocery store bearing down on her—but no, she's sitting hunched up in the bathtub wearing the T-shirt she went to bed in, soaked through and shivering, with the shower set on cold and going full blast.

Her mother's house. She recognizes the bland blond frame of the mirror, the actual sea sponge Jo always insisted on using; it's right beside her hand as she grips the edge of the tub and levers herself toward the faucet to turn it to hot. Please, sweet hot. Not too hot, though, in case she has hypothermia. Can you get shower-inflicted hypothermia?

She peels off her sodden T-shirt and underwear. Her teeth are chattering, her skin is pricked to goose bumps, but slowly, slowly, she starts to thaw. How long has she been sitting here? You can die of hypothermia in as little as fifteen minutes. It can make you confused, cause actual brain damage. Mix that with hallucinogens of dubious provenance, and maybe that's how you get to have vivid experiences of wandering through the toiletries aisle of a shitty supermarket you've never been in before.

It felt so real. So ordinary. Caught mid-action, reaching for something on the shelf. She didn't know what, though.

Deodorant or toothpaste or two-in-one anti-dandruff shampoo?

Looking down, she saw she was wearing punky crocheted fingerless gloves with a black-and-red pattern that she'd never seen before and would never have worn in a million trillion years.

She'd let her hand drop, following its trajectory, plucked a floral antiperspirant spray, Extravagant Orchid, from the shelf, and went to put it in her basket—but she didn't have one. She had vague memories of having to play detective, dumped in the middle of unknown circumstances. Part of the game, having to figure it out.

The Muzak over the store speakers was interrupted by a man's voice, deep and smooth: "Have you signed up for our value card yet? Super savings, super rewards." Someone's toddler was fussing in the shopping cart across the aisle while a little boy waggled a very bedraggled fluffy blue octopus toy to placate her. *Where were the parents? Jeez.*

Bridge started walking toward the cashiers, trying to look as if she knew what she was doing, sneaking in details. She was wearing denim dungarees, a black crop top that made her boobs look enormous, scuffed Doc Martens, and a huge yellow purse over her shoulder, the fake leather starting to fray. She flipped it open, one-handed, to find a phone, a zip-up travel purse, wet wipes, a squeaky dinosaur—for a dog, maybe? She had always wanted a dog. Eight dollars and sixty cents. A debit card, but she didn't know the PIN.

Losing her nerve, she set down the Extravagant Orchid spray at the end of the cereal aisle and quick-walked for the glass doors of the exit. She needed air; she needed to feel like she wasn't dreaming this.

Bridge stepped out into a strip-mall parking lot. Overcast skies and, through the haze, a ring of mountains, slate-colored and etched with snow. Not Portland or Seattle or anywhere she has ever been before.

Someone was calling after her, *Ma'am, ma'am,* with anxious urgency, and when she turned, there was a man in the entrance, soft in the middle under his red staff apron, expression of baffled concern, holding the red plastic handle of the cart with the bawling toddler. Her hands were opening and closing like sea anemones. Behind him was the somber little boy still holding the octopus—was he three, five? She can't tell children's ages—looking at her from an uncanny echo of her own face.

"Ma'am," the supermarket guy said, cross, confused. "Are these your kids?"

Bridge laughed in astonishment and shook her head, *No, no, no, impossible,* which only made the little girl howl louder. As the glass doors closed behind the guy, the reflection showed a woman with dyed red hair also shaking her head, but when Bridge turned to look, there was no one else there. Blue dungarees, huge yellow purse. It took her far too long to realize... and then the sound of the ocean, waves crashing against rocks, the showerhead blasting against the porcelain.

Steam is rising up around her now, smogging up the glass, her limbs thawing. Under the hiss of the hot water is another sound that has been going on for a while, it seems: someone talking through the door.

"Dom?" Bridge calls out, uncertain, because maybe this isn't real either. Maybe she's still somewhere else. (Some*one* else.)

"Bridge!" The relief in their voice. "Let me in, for fuck's sake."

"Okay, okay, hang on." She turns off the shower, wraps herself up in one of her mother's white towels. She drips over to unlock the door, and as soon as the latch clicks, Dom barges in.

"Holy Christ on toast, what the crap were you doing? I was worried sick!"

"Dom, it works." She's delirious. "I went somewhere else, a town in the mountains. Canada or Colorado, maybe. I had these stupid gloves on. And I had kids. And boobs." It's a wonder and a delight and a nauseating confusion, this might-have-been Bridge, this rebel redhead mom. "I've never even wanted kids."

Dom is incandescent. "I literally could not give a single fuck about your trip. You tried to club me with a lamp. With a *lamp*, Bridge. Do you know how sharp broken light bulbs are? And then you barricaded yourself in the bathroom and you were screaming, and I thought you were having a psychotic episode. I didn't know what you were doing in there for fifteen minutes. Fifteen minutes! I don't know anyone in this stupid city, and I don't have your insurance info, and I was trying to message your dad and—"

"My dad?" Bridge's heart tanks. "Please tell me you didn't." The always-threat hanging over her, that he'll have her committed again. Crazy like her mother. He never said that—he didn't have to. *Sometimes everyone needs a time-out* was the way he explained it the first time, like she was five. He's done it to her twice: When she was fifteen and cutting herself. Again several years later, after Kyle ripped out her heart and stepped on it like so much trash, and she'd crashed her car because she was crying so hard, and her dad read it as a suicide attempt.

"He didn't answer. But you scared the pants off me. You were freaking out. You didn't recognize me. And you tried to kill me. Did I mention? Pendejo." They're crying as they swat at Bridge's shoulder. "You fucking asshole."

"I'm sorry. I'm so sorry!" She tries to hug them, but Dom shrugs her off.

"You should be. God." They backhand their tears away. "I'm so mad at you and I was so fucking worried. And don't you ever, *ever* do that to me again."

"I won't," Bridge says. "I'm sorry."

"It's okay," they grumble. "I'll add it to the list of things I'm never going to let you live down."

But in her mind are thoughts like clouds racing over mountain crags. Because she'd nearly gotten pregnant before, once. With Kyle. The condom broke and the pharmacist at the drugstore where she went for the morning-after pill had given her a sneering look that said *Slut.* Kyle told her she'd been imagining it, but the pill made her so sick, and the packaging warned it was only 99 percent effective, which meant it didn't work one out of a hundred times. Maybe that other Bridge was unlucky. Maybe she'd married young (was she wearing a ring?), popped two kids out, one after the other. Moved to Nowheresville. What a waste of her whole damn life. But then, it's not like she's done any better here. Doesn't even have genetic offshoots to show for her not quite quarter century on this earth.

It *was* real. She manages not to say this out loud and upset Dom further. But she's thinking it. Like before, when she was a little kid and she and Jo used to do this together. Another reality. Another version of her. A different life. Different choices.

She has no idea what to do with any of this.

AMBER

Group Work

The sign on the door of the Parkside church hall reads TOMESIANS SUPPORT GROUP ALL WELCOME. And that's the problem, really, Amber thinks as Lonny holds forth about his new grandchild: all these pretenders. She drove up to Charleston only because there was a potential, a newcomer asking interesting questions on the forums, but so far he's a no-show.

"With tears in my eyes," Lonny says, having worked himself up so much that his eyes are glinting, and his whole face is ruddy, cheeks and nose striated with broken blood vessels from drinking, which is more likely to be the cause of his various symptoms and maladies—the shaking hands, the memory loss—than any "alien infestation."

"I don't know how to convince them," he says. "They know there's a genetic susceptibility, and Diane's lucky it skipped her..." He pauses before he says, as if they haven't been paying attention: "That's my daughter, Diane, but little Johnny, that's my grandson, not even six months old..."

"Such a baby," Marta agrees. "Tiny thing."

"I told her that he's showing the signs. I found fibers in the cot where he sleeps, but Diane says it's from the blanket, and she won't let me put matchboxes in the crib with him. She says she's getting real tired of this, and Mark doesn't want me to come around there anymore if I'm going to be *this way*." He yelps in indignation. "This way!"

"Mm-hmm," Marta says, shaking her head in sympathy and scratching at her arm, dotted with little round Band-Aids where she has pulled out Tomesians threads she says were wriggling under her skin. She claims it gets real bad with the change of the weather. This is not accurate, Amber knows. Because she is the only real expert here, the only one with real experience. Marta probably has a bad allergy or an attack of the scabies, but she won't go to the doctor because the doctors don't believe her. Or any of them.

Marta, like many of the group attendees, is wearing thin latex gloves, ostensibly to prevent the infection from getting under their fingernails and spreading. Amber wears gloves for another reason entirely, but she's happy to fit right in with these poor would-be sufferers who couldn't possibly believe what she is capable of. She uses a fake name in her videos, a long wig with bangs she can hide behind. Same one she's wearing now.

Knox chips in: "They don't want to hear it, they can't handle the truth."

"That's right. I know, we have to be patient, that's the way through, but excuse me if I'm concerned for my own grandson! After everything I've been through! I'm trying to protect that little man, the way no one ever protected me." How many times has she heard variations of this? The same simpatico circle jerk of sad sacks bleating at one another for an hour and a half before clearing out for the Bereaved Parents and Siblings group that comes in afterward.

"We're here for you, Lonny." Marta smiles without showing her teeth because she is shy about how snaggled and rotten they are—another problem she's blamed on Tomesians and its too-many-to-count side effects. But bad teeth is also not a thing. Amber could educate them, tell them the real signs, but that would make her job more difficult. More tourists, more wannabes. You load the lure with enough information to reel them in but not with the truth, not all the details. The true sufferers will reveal themselves.

She doesn't come to meetings often, only when there is a new attendee who seems promising. Mainly she lurks on the forums, keeping up with the comments and the groups in Charleston and New Orleans and Fayetteville and farther afield too: Kuala Lumpur and Glasgow and Turku and Krugersdorp, anywhere the sad conspiracy theorists have found one another.

All along the watchtowers. They keep guard, lay their snares. But there hasn't been a peep in two and a half years, not since that pasty noodle of a man who worked in the mobile phone shop in England who was very much the Real Deal, and she'd had to fly out to solve the problem. She hates airports—the lines and the security checks and everyone rushing to squeeze into the cramped metal tube. You can't bring guns on planes, not without paperwork.

Two and a half years. Some of the others have argued this means they're done, they're safe, they can give it up, get on with living their lives. Finally. *Haven't we earned it?* Sixty is too old for this line of work. But they all know it happens in clusters. Two and a half years is nothing. Besides, Amber has been feeling *scritchy* lately. Something is stirring. The others feel it too.

She doesn't like it. "Not one little bit," she whispers to Mr. Floof II, who is sitting upright and attentive with his paws over the edge of his carrier, an active participant, wagging his tail to the sob stories. Everyone loves Mr. Floof II.

He's the draw in the little videos she makes to lure people in, shiny, shiny, in the dark of the internet, like an anglerfish. She plays older, more pathetic, hunching her shoulders under baggy T-shirts and sweaters featuring pictures of Maltese poodles, and she talks in a girlie high-pitched voice about the symptoms that affect her and Mr. Floof II. Pets are great for making someone look harmless, wholesome, a little or a lot crazy or lonesome; one of the others makes videos with her cat on her lap.

Her channel gets only a couple of hundred views a month unless one of those scoffing young men decide to make a reaction video or a roundup of "weirdest of the week." They bring in more viewers than she could ever hope to reach on her own; thousands, sometimes tens of thousands of views and comments, most along the lines of *LOLOLOLOL* or *Fucking freek* or *Someone needs to rape some sense into this fat old crazy bitch, And her little dog too,* their fury and impotence spilling out in typos and emojis.

They can try. See how that goes down.

Sometimes the lures work exactly as she intended—the Belgian man found her on the forums via her videos—and she had to persuade him to fly out so she could help him. Sometimes it's luck. A feeling. Like calls out to like. Sometimes it's old-fashioned police work, what she did for years in the force before she retired to Florence, where no one knows her. Not anymore. Not since Chris died. She doesn't mention that in her videos, or her military history, or why she is the true expert here.

Unfortunately, the bullying trolls occasionally come looking to make content in the offline world. That's the problem with *All welcome.* In Fresno in 2019, a bright-eyed "journalist" came in all sympathetic and asked all the right questions, then wrote an essay overflowing with patronizing empathy for the "delusion of community," which she twisted around so it was about her miscarriage and how alone she felt. Self-indulgent, like everyone here.

Last year they had a TikTok person show up right here in Charleston, someone full of glossy teen sincerity, appealing to their vanity and heroism, saying they should speak up about the condition they were living with, how more people needed to know about it. Amber wasn't in town for that one, but she saw the videos afterward. Mr. TikTok examined the wounds on their arms and legs where they'd been digging around with tweezers, asked them about the fibers they'd pulled out, how people could identify them as legit Tomesians. Why did they keep the strands in matchboxes? He'd heard it was the red phosphorus, and Lonny, beaming, explained that yes, the chemical in the strip on the side of matchboxes made Tomesians inert, but it was hard to get it in any kind of meaningful quantities.

Then the little prick and his camera crew asked if they could help him identify some things he'd extracted from his own skin. He hauled out his own matchbox to show them, but instead of fibers, he had red licorice twists and a dead cockroach. "They were under my skin, bro, crawling. I could see them moving," he said, jiggling the matchbox so the contents twitched around. "Look, they're moving now!" Then he threw the contents in Marta's face and ran off giggling, shouting, "Freaks!" and more insults: "Tomesians doesn't exist, you fucking pathetic weirdos!"

It does exist. Amber knows. But not in this little crowd of regulars. Knox is a human misery sponge who comes to all the groups, whether it's Alcoholics Anonymous or the parents-of-dead-kids meeting, mumbling behind the thin scruff of facial hair that doesn't quite disguise the ravages of meth and alcoholism and who knows what else. Perhaps he does qualify for all those other groups.

Marta Herrara is the part-time flamenco instructor who has lost a series of boyfriends to her Tomesians piety; a good student, but not a true sufferer. Lonny Vermeulen is a former autoworker drunk on alcohol and his own simmering impotence, just like those vicious boys on the internet. Tomesians gives him somewhere to be, someone to be, and as the de facto leader of the group, he hogs the spotlight, which is good for her.

Amber was suspicious about Philippa Rathgood, who joined seven or eight months ago, but after she followed her home to her shitty apartment, where everything was wrapped in plastic, including her cutlery and her plates, she had to concede that she was only schizophrenic and desperately alone, not one of the ones Amber was looking for. She was not a Nest.

Amber is ready to call it a day; the newcomer who has been saying such interesting things on the forums is a no-show, and she's wasting her time. But then she feels it, a deep twist inside. Mr. Floof II does too—he jumps up, barking his fluffy little head off at the scrawny white boy with floppy dark hair who has appeared at the door.

"Oh no, my boy. Oh no, oh no." She has to hold him, because he's turned into a spitball of fury. "What's up with you, Mr. Grumpy Face?" Trying to calm him down but also cover the sudden attack she's having. Because something has stirred inside her. More than stirred. "You're upset that Lonny's family won't listen to him? Yes, that's terrible, isn't it, my baby. Yes, it is. Yes, it is!"

"It's shameful is what it is," Lonny says, raising his voice over the yapping. He gestures at the newcomer, impatient: "Come in, come in, don't be lurking out there."

The boy—man, really, late twenties, early thirties, with a long nose and wide-set eyes and a stupid little mustache—hesitates. She recognizes his profile picture from the forum. *Shiny-shiny*. He gives an uncertain smile. "Uh, Tomesians?"

"Yes, yes, come in! You're in the right place," Lonny bellows and glares at the one-dog cacophony.

"I'm so sorry, he needs his medicine." She reaches into

her bag, rubs a little calming paste on Mr. Floof II's teeth. He gets like this when she has particularly bad days, reacting to the stirring inside her. "Stop it, you silly thing," she scolds Mr. Floof II, although who can blame him. It's been so long—and now one waltzes through the door.

He pulls out a chair, the metal legs scraping against the linoleum, raises a hand, self-deprecating. Expensive jeans, Amber notes, fancy sneakers. His hair looks scruffy, but it's deliberately cut that way.

"Hi, I'm, uh, Aiden. I'm a musician but not in a band or anything. Mostly TV and commercials."

"Big industry." Lonny nods, showing off. He knows a little about a lot. And nothing, truly, about this.

"You're among friends," Marta says. "Would you like a cookie?" They're all watching this Aiden intently to see if he will go for anything on the table, which is set with polystyrene cups and instant coffee, powdered creamer, a Brita jug of water, and a plateful of Oreos that are a trap (one of many) that the "real" sufferers know to avoid, lest the processed sugar exacerbate their condition.

"No, thank you." Aiden holds up a steel flask. "I brought my own water. Filtered." There's a ripple of approval through the group. This means he's done his research, isn't a know-nothing newbie or a tourist or a "content producer."

"So what brings you to our circle, Mr. Aiden?" Lonny says. "You got something you want to show us?"

Aiden falters, then reaches into his denim jacket. "Yes. I, uh, flew from LA for this. I brought the matchbox. I read that was something you should do."

"Oh, yes, show us," Marta says, eager for affirmation.

Aiden clears his throat, self-conscious, and slides open the matchbox. He looks so hopeful, so desperate.

Everyone leans in to see. "Not too close," Knox warns.

"You don't want it to burrow into your retina. That can happen."

But the contents of the box are disappointing. Marta curls her lip, leaning back in her chair, her long dancer's legs stretched out like she is trying to get as far away as possible from this charlatan. Knox wilts, and Philippa looks to the rest of them to calculate her own reaction.

"Eh. That's not Tomesians, my friend." Lonny chucks him on the back. "Sorry to be the bad-news bear."

Amber keeps perfectly still. Contains herself. The pull of it, like the ticks she would burn off her ankles as a child. *And what exactly are we going to do about this?*

"But they came out from under my skin. Right here." Aiden runs his long pianist fingers along the inside of his wrist. This is accurate, both for fake Tomesians and the real McCoy.

"Let's review the qualities of Tomesians, shall we?" Lonny says. "Number one: Thin *red* fibers; some people think they are worms, but they're alien technology that's been implanted."

"Not alien," Philippa corrects darkly. "It's the Chinese government."

"Some of us disagree on the provenance," Lonny says. "But they're fiber-optic cables wired into your nervous system to control you."

"Control your thoughts, make you feel good if there's something they want you to feel good about—like a certain political candidate, for example," Knox says. "Or make you feel bad, fuck up your whole immune system to keep you down, make sure you don't interfere. It's a war. We're in a war here."

"Thank you, Knox. Mr. Aiden, do these look like red fibers to you?"

"No," Aiden says, peering down at the pale yellow threads. "They're not red, but they came out of me, and something else—"

"Have you had any of the following symptoms?" Lonny ticks them off on his fingers. "Migraines, skin rashes, a feeling of heaviness in your body, brain fog, sinus issues, gastric problems?"

"Yes, some of those, but—"

"All of them," Marta says. "I get all of them every day. Try running a dance studio when you're riddled with Tomesians. Some days I can't bear to listen to music, can't bring myself to raise my feet. It burrows right in here"—she taps her head—"makes it all worse."

"Yes, I feel that," Aiden says, "the pressure inside my head. It's like being in a wind tunnel or lying under a train. Roaring, whooshing wind."

"No." Marta shakes her head, but not unkindly. "No, no, no, not like that. It's a drill, whining, right into your temple."

"Yes," Lonny says, toeing the company line. They are all the best students of their fictional disease. "It's a sharp pain, needles behind your eyes."

But Aiden is desperate to continue, despite the eye rolls, their casual dismissal. "There's something else. It's not on any of the discussion boards. But I had an out-of-body experience. The realest dream I've ever had."

Lonny harrumphs. "Sounds like someone's been smoking the wacky baccy. Just because it's legal in California..."

Marta pats Aiden's hand. "You should probably see a doctor, dear. Or maybe a psychologist. Oh!" She beams. "I believe there are sleep studies if you're having bad dreams."

"It's all right." Knox gently closes the matchbox for him. "Not everyone is infected. You can still come to the meetings if you want."

"Hi there, remember me?" Amber leans out the window of her anonymous white van. It's even more invisible than a postmenopausal lady in a cutesy dog sweater, especially if she puts the decals on the side. She switches them up when she needs to: one for Amazon and two for nonexistent companies, one for delivering food, one for courier services. She also has a film over the plates that reflects the light and hides them from the prying lenses of security cameras. There are none on this corner, she knows, because she pays the same kind of shitty boys on the internet who love to mock her videos for maps of security cameras, the same way she pays for medical records and for others to comb through data for her.

"Oh, it's you," Aiden says. He looks haggard, disconsolate. "With the dog."

"Do you need a ride?"

"No. I was going to go for a beer, get an Uber back to my hotel. Maybe change my flight to first thing tomorrow. This all seems to have been a huge waste of time. But the doctors don't believe me, and my girlfriend—well, I don't know if she's my girlfriend anymore..."

"Oh, yes, where was it you came from?"

"Los Angeles." He looks tired. "I was hoping for..." He flicks his hand. "More than this."

"Why don't you come have an iced tea at my place, and we can talk more. Those people in there, they don't know what you're going through. But I do." She really does. "You fell through a door into someone else."

He sharpens, a wire jerked through his spine. "That's exactly it. How do you—"

"Get in." She leans over and opens the passenger door, an invitation, that most irresistible lure—someone who understands. "We'll talk."

What are we going to do? Take care of it.

BRIDGE

Great Pretenders

The Willamette River is a sullen gray slash between the trees as they crawl up through the traffic on 99 east and then the view opens up to reveal the skyline above the water, the crosshatched girders of the Ross Island Bridge.

There are three Stasher4U locations in the greater Portland area. She'd phoned the 800 number to find out which location would match this particular key, but the customer service agent cheerfully informed her he couldn't disclose that information without a letter of authorization from the original customer. Or a warrant. Which says something about their clientele. So now they are trying all three locations, in order of proximity.

Dom is driving and singing along to their greatest divas playlist, Britney segueing into Lady Misfit into Beyoncé, and Bridge is navigating, or trying to, because getting through downtown is a morass of one-ways and she was never any good at reading maps, and the speaker on her phone is crap, and Dom doesn't have data.

There's a double layer of civilization happening along the wide boulevards lined with office buildings and chain coffee shops, because there are also tents all along the sidewalk. They are blue and red and yellow, like banners fallen from the trees, some fresh and new, others spattered by rain and city grime. Some have been built out with plywood and cardboard.

"It reminds me of the blanket forts I used to make with my mom," Bridge says. *See, not all bad memories.* Followed by instant guilt and a reminder why they're doing this: Because Jo left so many questions behind. And, holy shit, alternate realities! "Not like this is the same thing at all."

"Okay, so this," Dom says, "is actually really interesting. It's obviously a huge system failure of capitalism: economic downturn, lack of social care, community and mental-health facilities being shut down and shoving patients out on the street. But there are also young activists trying to live their ideals, resist, overturn the system, getting involved in protests, trying to build a different way of being. And there are also some trust-fund kids cosplaying poverty. I am coining the term *blanketforters*, thank you for that. And maybe some of these rich kids were trying to teach their parents a lesson or they *thought* they could live by their ideals, but they miss central heating and flushing toilets and being able to walk downstairs and get a cold brewski out of the refrigerator, so they give up and head home."

"Of course you researched this."

"How do you know me? I can also tell you why Blue Moon doughnuts are superior to the world-famous Arcana doughnuts."

Bridge glances into an unzipped faded blue tent and makes accidental eye contact with a man in his fifties, denim shorts, pigeon-chested, brushing his long hair, black and threaded with gray. He holds her look, challenging and unabashed. She smiles and he gives her a thumbs-up, an ironic one, she thinks, a little fuck-you, and he turns away, back to his life, his home.

The light changes and the Grand Am surges forward,

poor dumb car, so overpowered and enthusiastic and oblivious of the heavy traffic.

"Did I ever tell you about Bad Bridge?" she says, still gazing out the window.

"Oh, I think I've met that bitch. Comes out after too many shots?"

"This was when I was a kid. I used to blame things on her. It was after everything that happened with my mom, you know, with the dreamworm..." She sees how Dom flinches at the word and hurries on: "She got divorced in the middle of her second bout with cancer and we had to go live with my grandparents in Cincinnati for a year, in this big old house they couldn't maintain properly. Creaky floorboards, mildew coming up the walls. It was horrible. And my mom didn't seem like my mom. She was so frail." Like a skeleton, Bridge had thought, a skeleton with a bald head and a red snake of a scar across her skull where they'd cut into her, and all her eyelashes and her eyebrows had fallen out, and she was so ugly Bridge didn't want to hug her or watch TV with her, and Bridge didn't even have any of her own toys or books, and Grandma was always fussing, and the house smelled of butternut soup. "It was really difficult, and I was so angry with her because my dad said she was the one who wanted the divorce."

"Wow. What a cabrón."

"And my dog had died. I told you, right?"

"Bear? Yeah, from a stroke."

"It was in the middle of all this. I was angry and I was sad and I was scared out of my mind that maybe my mom would die. So I started acting out."

"Of course you did."

"I broke my grandma's heirloom casserole dish. On purpose. I remember standing among the blue ceramic fragments, feeling so shocked and powerful. And then my granddad grabbed my arm and he was so mad because it was a wedding present from my great-grandma, and I knew how special it was, how precious, and it couldn't have just fallen. And then he stopped. Started apologizing—it was just a pot, it didn't matter."

"That's good."

"Except I knew, even then—I must have been around seven, eight—that it was because he felt sorry for me. Everyone was always tiptoeing around me. Poor Bridge."

"Bad Bridge was easier."

"Except it wasn't real. I was pretending. It was Bad Bridge who called Keri Becker the B-word at school and shoved her down the stairs. I was lucky she only twisted her ankle. My dad got called in and the principal said it was understandable, considering the circumstances and everything our family was going through. More pity. My dad sent me for a million tests in case the cancer was hereditary, even though they already knew it wasn't. My mom was capital-*S Sick* and I was merely *troubled*."

"That sounds awful."

Bridge shrugs. "The cancer went into remission, and she made a plan to move back to Seattle, joint-custody nightmare. My dad said she was unstable after the whole kidnapping thing, would only let me see her weekends, but then he got a girlfriend who was unthrilled about a young kid hanging around, so he relented."

It was uglier than that. Bridge had had to talk to a mediator about who she wanted to be with, and she'd said both because she'd thought that meant they would get back together, not that she would be caught *between* them, schedules changing, moving between the houses. Jo kept downsizing to smaller and smaller apartments, each one farther away from Bridge's school. Her mom was always busy with a parade of basic jobs to pay her tuition and working on her studies when she should have been spending time with her kid, especially when she had her only every other week.

In hindsight, Bridge gets it. Jo didn't have money, she was trying her best, but it felt like her mom was always abandoning her, always leaving her behind. And now, the ultimate abandonment.

"What happened to Bad Bridge?"

"She didn't exist. I'd made her up. Monica helped me understand that. It was me the whole time. Acting out."

Dom glances at her, wary, hopeful. As if she's going to confess that she made up everything else too, that the bathroom incident *was* a bad dream, that she was briefly out of her mind with grief.

"I *knew* I was pretending, of course. It wasn't like when I took the dreamworm. Because *I* was still *there*. I wasn't somewhere else or *someone* else, and they weren't me. There wasn't a swap. And you can't do it out of nowhere—you need the dreamworm and the music and the visuals."

"Ah," Dom says unhappily. Back here again.

"Which is how I know it's real. Because I know the difference. I did then and I do now. And I need to do it again."

"Baby, do you remember the time not so long ago, last summer, when we dropped acid and you became one with the couch and you thought you were all-powerful and could move objects with your mind and control the flight of birds?"

Bridge groans. "This wasn't anything like that."

"You're a thousand percent right." Dom glowers. "Couch God would never have attempted to brain me with a lamp."

"If you'd just try it."

"I already did. Nothing happened."

"Because you were watching the wrong video, listening

to the wrong music. I think it's specific keys and doors. My mom used to play different chords. She said we had to try new music. What if she had a code? The file I found on her computer—"

"Bridge. I love you. You're going through the most. We should never have experimented with calcified psychedelic bugs under the current circumstances, and you had a bad trip. Same as Couch God. Nothing more, nothing less."

"It wasn't like—"

"Nope."

"What about the times as a kid? It felt exactly the same."

"*Nope* holds."

"It was real. I was there. I was someone else. They were me. We changed bodies—"

"Let me think about this. Wait...hang on. Yeah, sticking with *nope*. And come on, infinite universes? Where were the spider-pigs or googly-eyed rocks, the pickle in a rat mecha suit, buildings bending into fractals? Sounds like a very bland and ordinary alternate reality."

"I would have liked to be a spider-pig," Bridge admits.

"I'm no neuroscientist over here, but I am your *most* sensible and pragmatic and well-dressed friend. It seems entirely probable that your poor brain, fried on dubious psychedelics and insomnia and ethanol poisoning from a whole bottle of tequila and grief, for sure, big grief, went right back to the fantasy world of your childhood—"

"I've been thinking about what my mom said in the hospital," Bridge interrupts.

"Mmm." Noncommittal.

"She was crying all the time, saying she didn't know where she was. The doctors said she was confused. I mean, you know this, you were basically there."

Dom kept her sane in those interminable visiting hours

when Jo wouldn't talk to her or look at her. They traded memes and gossip and dumb videos, played Scrabble online. Dom sent her doodles they'd drawn, cute animal videos, ridiculous real estate listings of overwrought mansions with gold sinks and indoor swimming pools: *Look, this is where we'll live when we're both stupid-rich. Show your mom.*

She tried, but Jo didn't want to look.

The doctors' advice was to keep talking to her; they said Jo could hear her, and she could provide comfort. Bridge tried to fill the empty space, invoking memories of her childhood, like when she was too scared to swim in the lake because she was convinced there were shark mermaids in there, and Jo got her to invent a taxonomy for them—so proud of her when she came up with the name *Carcharodon sirenia*. When Jo didn't respond to nostalgia, Bridge tried telling her about her life, about Austin and the goings-on at the bookstore, like the customers who came in asking for "the one with the green cover."

It was easier to confess to someone who had her back turned, who wasn't listening, and she found herself confiding about dropping out and how she really wanted to make films, maybe documentaries, and about the boyfriend she'd never told her parents about: Sam, a biomedical engineer with a septum piercing, calm and quiet and kind, about how they'd been planning to move in together, but then he got a job offer in Cambridge, England, and Bridge didn't have a passport, let alone a work/study visa, and he wanted to do long-distance, but she couldn't handle it, and how the pain was a living, breathing thing, and they hadn't really spoken in six months. "He basically abandoned me," she said, lighthearted to cover the hurt.

And that's when Jo, who had been listening all along, finally responded.

No, no, no, no, no. A litany of denial that devolved into fresh sobbing. *I never abandoned you. I never. I fought for you! All of you. Even with everything he put me through.*

"Huh? Are you talking about Dad?" Chemo-induced dementia, she reminded herself.

I want to go home.

"You can't, Mom," she'd said, trying to calm her. "You're really sick. You need to stay here. Everyone's looking after you the best they can."

I don't belong here.

"No one wants to be in the hospital."

I don't want you.

That cut deep.

Then she started screaming.

I don't know who this is. Get her away from me.

As if we can really know anyone.

I want to go home! Why won't you let me?

The nurses offered to sedate Jo, apologetic, saying it would be best for all involved. But maybe if they hadn't... there's something there, eluding Bridge. She can't quite wrap her head around it. Doesn't want to, maybe.

"Yeah?" Dom asks, yanking her back to the present.

"I wish they hadn't sedated her. That I'd gotten to talk to her more. Closure, you know?"

Answers to the really big questions, like *Hey, did you drug me? Did we go to other realities? Was that real this whole time?* And the gnawing feeling that there was more Jo wanted her to know. The dreamworm in the freezer, the promised instructions she hasn't found yet, the key to a storage locker...

DOM

Chain Mail

Their first stop is Slabtown. This Stasher4U, next to a paint factory and across from a yellow billboard advertising Easy Liquidators, is in a part of town populated by eighteen-wheelers and stretches of warehouses, some of them boarded up. But as they're pulling into the parking lot, Bridge's phone vibrates in her lap, startling them both. She groans when she sees the name on the screen.

"Dreamworm police?" Dom asks. They feel bad about the argument earlier. They have a ton of sympathy for Bridge getting caught up in the notion that there are hidden secrets to the world that make it more complex than you could ever have imagined but that also reduce it to something as simple as a grand plan with someone behind it all, and that explains why everything is so awful and your life hasn't gone the way you'd hoped, and it's not your fault.

Those embarrassingly long months on the hate-boards with the rookie fascists and thwarted man-babies and conspiracy freaks made them feel less alone, even as they isolated from real life, real people. Denial is edgelord armor. Can't hate yourself if you're busy hating on everyone else. So they understand where Bridge is coming from, they do; why she's wanting answers, an externalized explanation—it would be such a *relief*.

Bridge shakes her head, glaring at the phone. "Worse. My dad. Don't worry, you did the right thing. I should have called him earlier." She turns toward the window, hunches over. "Hi, Dad? No, everything's fine. False alarm. Sorry. No, it wasn't a breakdown. Jesus, Dad. I just lost my mother. I was in her house with all her things, her whole life, and it was overwhelming. That's how grief works. Dom freaked out because they're my friend and they were worried, and I didn't hear them banging on the door."

Dom parks the car, mimes opening the car door, and points at the Stasher4U to indicate they're heading inside, so long, giving her some privacy. She nods tightly.

"Because I was sobbing my guts out and the shower was on. I said I'm sorry. No, you don't need to fly down."

They shut the car door and head for the entrance. It doesn't look promising. The doorbell jangles, and the guy behind the counter in a black T-shirt, fluff on his chin like a bloom of soft gray mold, doesn't look up from his phone. He's clearly watching porn, based on the symphony of fake feminine moans.

"Hate to interrupt," Dom says, and he sighs and turns the phone facedown. Doesn't kill the audio, though. *Uh-uh-uh. Oh, yaaaaaaa.*

They dangle the key in front of him. "This yours?"

"Uh?"

Slower for the people in the back. "Is *this* key for a locker *here*? Do you have a box at *this* facility numbered K-five-five-one?"

He takes the key and holds it up like it's a rare specimen of bug, then hands it back. "Not this facility. Looks like one of the smaller lockers to me. We do that too. But not here. You wanna head out to the Beaverton location."

"It's been a pleasure," Dom says. "Really."

Bridge is still on the phone, so they lurk outside, tie their shoelaces, take in the view of derelict industria. It's creeping on to lunchtime, and it's hot as balls. The Grand Am's air-con has only two functional settings: Arctic frostbite and off. This is something Dom is going to have to fix when they get back to Austin, a day later than planned. Or several, let's be real. As long as they're back by next Thursday. Dom has an interview with an architect looking for a part-time assistant, a job that will help them pay their bills, bills, bills, and interest *on the interest* of their student loan.

Bridge helped them write the application letter with a big focus on all those years building houses with their papa. He'd never had the opportunity to study formally. But hey, neither did Gaudí. Dom's father had big ambitions and never enough budget, which meant the whole family chased opportunities around the country, whether that was building a backpackers' lodge or mud-baked eco-houses for an off-the-grid spiritual retreat. Dom learned to draw by sitting next to him at his drafting table and later tried to return the favor by teaching him LibreCAD on their PC. It didn't go great. Papa peered at the monitor over his glasses, dragging the mouse around like a scrub brush, and eventually threw up his hands and went back to designing on paper. They know he'll be pleased if they get the job; hopefully they won't get too delayed with this quest.

Meanwhile it sounds like the phone call is winding down. "That's not necessary. I've got this. Yes, I'm taking my meds. Please. Seriously. This is how grieving people act. I am not taking a tone. Okay. I love you too. Yes, I'll call if I need anything. Love you. Thanks, Dad. Love to Petra and the dogs too."

She sags back against the headrest and indicates it's safe to reenter the vehicle.

"Let me guess," Dom says. "He wants to solve it with money."

"Send in the pros like he wanted to do in the beginning—appraisers, packers, charity-store pickups—to alleviate the terrible stress I'm under, and maybe I need to take a rest so he knows where I am, doesn't have to worry so much. I don't have to shoulder this on my own, blah-blah-blah. Misgendered you throughout, obviously. Although I nearly called Petra 'Isabel,' which was the girlfriend before this one. Oh, no, wait, there was Felicity in between."

"Your dad." Dom shakes their head. "But you *are* under a lot of stress."

"Oh my God, him sending in strangers would make it a million times worse. I couldn't face it. All those people."

"You still have me."

"I know. Thank you. And I'm sorry. I hate fighting with you."

"'Cause I tend to win."

"No, it's because you're insufferable when you do." Bridge slaps playfully at their arm.

"Excuse me! Driving!"

They take U.S. 26 out of town and wind toward Beaverton through lush tree-lined burbs with big houses and then through progressively more run-down neighborhoods. Someone's crappy boat is parked in the driveway, covered in sun-faded tarp. Mixed housing with neglected lawns and low cast-concrete walls. More tents along the side of the road edging the forest. RVs that are never going to roll again, tires blown. Some have modifications: a little portico built from reed fencing, a second story patched onto the top of a camper van. There's congealed trash, broken bottles, but they're interspersed with little veggie gardens, flower boxes on bright display. People trying to make a home. Papa would have a field day trying to design better solutions, would get right in there with the housing projects already under way, would kick and yell about the bureaucratic tangles holding everything up.

A left turn takes them into a para-industrial area with warehouses and rows of small one-story offices, including Cakey Bakey ("Delish homemade goodies and everything you need to DIY your own"), Brite Smile! Dentistry, with a faded mural of a nightmarish cartoon duck with too many teeth, and, yep, a whole bunch of storage facilities.

Stasher4U stands alone in the middle of a parking lot behind a black gate. One of those metal swivel signs announcing they're at the right location is set up in the street outside, barely moving thanks to the complete absence of breeze. If they wanted to melt their face off, they could have stayed in Texas, Dom thinks as they step out into the turgid heat. Also a compelling argument to shave their head again, as much as they love their undercut.

"Ominous," they say as the two of them head toward the flat building. The woman at the front desk in the red shirt is reading a shopping catalog like you get on airplanes and barely looks up when Bridge asks her about unit K-551.

"Yeah. Lockers, around the back."

They walk between the rows of undistinguished storage units with red roller doors. There could be anything behind them, whole lives locked away, a lost Basquiat, dead bodies. Actual fetuses.

At the very end is another building with smaller units, half a warehouse's worth of corridors of tight-packed red metal lockers piled three-high under a low ceiling and fluorescent lights. It's not entirely unlike a memorial wall for cremains, if you were using battered steel, say, instead of lofty marble with bronze plates.

"Like a mausoleum, right?" Bridge says sotto voce as if out of respect for the dead or maybe to avoid summoning monsters, because this maze of battered lockers on the edge of town feels suburban-malevolent, and they can imagine Bridge's dead mom coming around the corner with wide arms, but when she opens her mouth to speak, she'd have a dreamworm instead of a tongue, thick and yellow and dripping mucus. Dom's overactive imagination is a blessing and a curse. Great for drawing comics, terrible for being home alone at night.

"Totally a mausoleum," Dom says, keeping that nasty little fantasy to themselves. "But a practical one for ordinary people. When I die, please skip the ostentation."

"No ebony coffin with gold inlay and your name spelled out in precious gems on the top?" Bridge teases, but Dom can tell she's also a little creeped out. It doesn't help that the letters aren't sequential and row K does not follow J.

"I want one of those fantasy Ghanaian coffins, the ones hand-carved to look like a tropical fish or a chili pepper or a soccer shoe. But I want it cheap, DIY. Papier-mâché, ideally. A giant papier-mâché pineapple containing my human remains."

"So, more like a piñata, then?" Bridge jokes.

"Stuff my cremains among the candy, shower them down on my loved ones' heads! No, wait, that sounds like a terrible idea. I'd like to go back to my storage-locker mausoleum, please. How about you?"

"Me? I want to disappear. Vaporize me. No trace."

"Not even a commemorative plaque on the street outside Lala's?" Their favorite bar in Austin for a while, until the cool kids found it and ruined it.

"Nothing. It doesn't matter anyway. You're here, you're gone, your life is such a tiny meaningless blip, like all the lives of all the billions of other people who came before—" She stops, touches the number. "Oh, hey, I got it."

"Not so meaningless after all, huh?" Dom says, trying to prevent the swerve to melancholy.

The key clicks, and Bridge swings the scuffed steel door open.

It does not contain Jo Kittinger's head, at least. Or any more fucking dreamworms. Dom is hoping for evidence proving it's not what Bridge thinks. A nice typewritten explanation about how the dreamworm is a very heady hallucinogen and Jo didn't mean for Bridge to take it and please destroy it, thank you. But it's a shoebox stuffed with notebooks and photographs and another three keys, these for boxes A-188, F-12, K-243.

"This is why people rent the big units," Dom grumbles as they hunt each one down, excavating more journals and letters and photo albums and articles clipped from magazines or printed off the web, piling them up in the car. Most of the trunk is full by the time they're through.

But they can see Bridge is struggling. In a way, it is exactly a mausoleum. These boxes contain all that's left of her mother. And now she has to try to make sense of it all.

Bridge

From: Stasia Tecuceanu
To: Bridge Kittinger-Harris
Subject: RE: Dreamworm

Dear Bridget, I'm so sorry for your loss and I understand that you're looking for answers.

Your mother, even at the height of her delusion, would never have wanted you to follow in her footsteps on this. If you've found something strange, my best possible advice is that you throw it away.

I loved your mother with all my heart even after she took our savings and ran away to Argentina. I've forgiven her. She was a complex, beautiful, challenging person—and, in the end, very afraid and very sick.

I hold the best version of her in my memories. I hope you can do the same.

I also hope you understand that I can't engage with this anymore.

Stasia

BRIDGE

Due Process

Reap the whirlwind, Bridge thinks, sitting amid the chaos of her mother's journals with takeout she and Dom picked up on their way back to the house and listening to the somehow comforting *bang-bang-bang* of Dom repairing the broken window like a pro.

It reminds her of helping Dom sort out their art portfolio for submission for the dean's list. Dom was in despair at the pressure of having to choose, Bridge holding up one painting after another for them to assign to the Yes, No, Maybe piles, then pitting the finalists in combat against each other in the style of a wrestling commentator: *Only one art will emerge alive from this epic fight to the death! Will it be the illustration of the Grecian vase flowering with hands, which has death-grip fingers but is also very breakable? Or the painting of the naked hippo-headed boys showing their teeth, but with their vulnerable dangly bits exposed?*

But Dom is the organizing badass and Jo was...not. There's no fucking sense to anything, just a slew of generic black Moleskines that Jo seemed to have plucked up at random to write in. Personal and professional, all tumbled together. Here's most of a notebook from 2008 filled with notes from a conference on the role of gut bacteria and mental health; a few blank pages later, there's a series of morning pages from 2011 with affirmations that quickly regress to disappointments and irritations, then at the very back, upside down, a bit about a parasitology conference in Greece. There is no envelope containing instructions labeled WHAT TO DO IN THE EVENT OF MY DEATH. No binder marked DREAMWORM OPERATION MANUAL. Bridge digs into a diary, which is what she's reading when Dom comes back to flop down next to her.

"Window's all done. You can thank me with beer." They offer her a fortune cookie. "Find anything useful?" They're trying to maintain their usual easy banter, but there's a new caution just beneath the skin, like she is one of Dom's handsy Grecian vases and apt to break. They still don't believe her. Stasia's e-mail didn't help. All on her own, she's trying to figure this out.

"There's this. Her diary growing up." She shows them the yellow book she's been reading, with Sanrio's Hi! Hi! Bun-Bun on it, with her floppy ears and skewed pink bow.

"Cute?"

"It starts off with kid stuff: 'Dear Diary, how are you, I am fine,' a list of her best friends, how Danny—that's my uncle—is sooo annoying and won't let her touch his Battle-Mans 'cause they're for boys, but Kev is teaching her how to take a watch apart and put it back together. There are twelve pages filled with one sentence, over and over: 'Please God, make Mommy and Daddy get me a kitten.'"

"I didn't know your mom was religious."

"Grew up that way, grew out of it. After her brother Kev died in a motorcycle accident. I think I went through my super-evangelical phase mainly to piss her off."

"Did it work?"

"Hell no. She drove me and Audrey Ingram to Celebration Church every Sunday and sat in on the services, sang all the hymns, even the ones she didn't know, bought me a tiny gold cross like Audrey's. For two *years*."

"I admire her long game."

"I knew she was just playing along, thinking I would grow out of it like she did, but I swore on my Bible that I was never, ever, ever going to forsake the Lord, and if my mom ended up following me by accident, that would be another soul saved. I was quite worried about her going to hell. But also—puberty. Audrey and I were always going on about how 'vivacious' Pastor Mark was, and Jo would agree without even cracking a smile. I'm having a full-body cringe thinking about it."

"You meant *sexy*."

"*Dreamy*, really. I would never have used that other word at the time. Sex was gross. But he had blond hair, blue eyes, and he'd stride the stage like a rock star and call out questions, and if you got the answer right, he would punch the air and shout 'Yes!' or 'That's what I'm talking about!' We thought his wife wasn't good enough for him. Obviously."

She remembers Jo absorbed in her studies—always studying, studying, studying, about to hand in her PhD dissertation and "defend it," like a Christian soldier facing the heathen hordes. They'd had to move, again, to a smaller apartment, where the Hindu neighbors were always cooking weird-smelling food. Bridge had knocked on their door once, very sweetly, to ask them if they'd been saved. When she'd told Jo, bent over her laptop screen, her mom had laughed in shock and then swore: "Jesus fucking Christ." She marched right out of the apartment, still in her slippers and her mussed-up hair and reading glasses, and knocked on the Naickers' door. Bridge caught enough of it—*I'm so sorry, I hope it wasn't disrespectful, going through a phase*—to make her despise her mom even more. What a sanctimonious little prick she was.

"Your poor mom." Dom shakes their head.

"That's the diary from 1980 through 1984." She flips through the pages of little-girl scrawl. "And then she abandons it for years and picks up again here, in 1987." A more confident hand, looping letters, but messy as Bridge's own handwriting.

Dom mugs. "Glad you can read that."

"It's the year she ran away to New Orleans."

"How old was she?"

"Fourteen."

Dom whistles.

"Also the year she got her first cancer diagnosis. There's the medical report. It fell out when I opened it. And you're not going to like this."

"What?"

"The diary mentions the dreamworm." Also other things that she recognizes. Names: Mina. Rabbit, which at seven she'd thought was a real bunny but who seems to have been a person. The abandoned squat where Jo'd stayed with the other gutter punks and teen runaways.

"Can I read it?" Looking worried again. *Protecc bear protecc,* she thinks, but Bridge doesn't need protecting. She needs them to believe her.

"Only if you promise not to rip it up." Holding it back, as if that's actually a thing they might do.

Dom sighs. "I don't like it because it's clearly hurting you. You're already dealing with grief, and I'm worried about what you're going to find."

"That I'm going to be proven right."

"Sure. Or wrong. Or somewhere fucked up in the middle because people are complicated and messy, and truth is a construct. What if you wade through all this and it turns out to be an extra layer of shit on what is already a pretty shitty sandwich?" She rolls her eyes and Dom frowns. "I'm trying to be serious. We can pack all this up in a big box or—let's be real—several, ship them back to Austin, and you can go through everything in your own time and with professional support."

"You want me to wait? Till after we've packed everything up? Could you?"

"Stubborn and impatient, worst combo."

She can't stand the concern in their eyes.

November 12, 1987

Cher journal,

C'est moi, Jo. In case you were expecting someone else. Sorry to leave you sitting here under the pillow with the smell of rat piss and mildew. Hope it's not black mold. Rabbit says it's definitely not, but what does he know? He's a musician who grew up in Finland and Argentina, but he says he's from much farther away than that and he winks, which is sooo annoying and I wish he'd just tell me. He's teaching me to play the sarod, which is from India and most Westerners haven't heard of it, but it's like a sitar, only cooler and richer and deeper. It's really tricky, not like the mbira, which is used by the Shona people in religious ceremonies to summon spirits.

He's ancient, like twenty-eight, and Mama Capitane doesn't like me and Mina being in his room even though she thinks I'm eighteen. She told him, "Leave that girl alone or I'll sucker-punch you into next week." MC is den mother at the Leftfield place, a big old abandoned house on the edge of the Seventh Ward, but I'm not going to say exactly where in case the pigs get hold of this and use it as evidence for eviction. Fuck you, pigs!

No real names here! Except mine, I guess, but that's already written on the front page of you, cher journal. MC calls me Tic Tac because I'm small and straight up and down and pasty white from growing up in Ohio. Gobi wants to know where my farmer's tan is, but I'm working on it, spending time with the chickens and planting veggies because we have to be self-sufficient.

I like getting my hands dirty, planting seeds, not knowing what they'll grow into because MC gets them unlabeled from Ant Nest House (which some of us have nicknamed

Rightfield because they're so self-righteous up there, like they're the only people who are real gutter punks and anarchists). It feels real, putting your hands into the guts of the Earth.

But the chickens are the best. They don't have time for your problems. I'm a little obsessed. They all have their own personalities and they can recognize your face and hold grudges against people they don't like, including Gobi, who lives in the storage shed on the roof and is a grade A asshole who kicks out at them when he's walking through the backyard to check on his pot plants. Did you know hens have hierarchies? That's where "pecking order" comes from, and being broody is the worst thing in the world. We use it like a joke, but chickens can die from broodiness, they can starve themselves to death because it's all they can think about. You need to give them something to sit on to try and hatch—a boiled egg, a squash ball. I know how that feels. Not wanting to hatch something, but needing something—okay, okay, someone (I'm not going to say who in case Gobi is reading this, fuck you, Gobi, I told you to stay out of my stuff). It feels like I'm on fire inside, like one of those underground coal fires that destroy whole towns and that you can never, ever put out. That's how brooding feels. And love.

Because this is love, okay? You can't tell me it's not, cher journal, because you don't know what it's like to be alive. You're just dumb pages made of a dead tree, and the sentences my brain is putting down on the pages are useless, because words can't catch all of how someone feels.

This part is going to be hard to explain, so pay attention, okay? We're staying in an old house that's trying its best to keep itself together, and we do a lot of patching too. The only rules are you have to respect one another and care for one another, and everyone pitches in. And no drugs. I share a room with Mina, with mattresses on the floor, and we tried to spray-paint an anarchy sign on the wall, but the paint ran. Mina's a bit spooky. She loves picking up feathers and bits of animal bone and shells, but not like vodou, which is a faith she respects. Mina is mixed and she really is eighteen, from Baton Rouge. We ran away for different reasons but also for the same one—wanting more from life, which is the most punk thing you can do. Her mom used to beat her, and I was so sick of the nothing of Cincinnati. I always wanted to see New Orleans and New York, all the News, basically. Mina spotted me sleeping on the steps by the fountain and told me to come back to Leftfield.

It's all a bit ramshackle. Almost no one has a real bed except MC, and the kitchen is full of pots and pans that don't match and plastic cutlery, and there's electricity only sometimes, although it always works in Gobi's room, where he has an Amiga computer he sometimes lets me play video games on and an electric stove top so he can make green tea because that's what he powers through on. No one can really complain because he's the one who figured out how to steal power from next door. Gobi's irrelevant anyway because he's not in on the secret and he definitely can't find out.

Now I'm worried he might find this. I could write it in code but that seems like a lot of work for someone who doesn't deserve it. None of the rooms have locks, and mine is right next to Mama Capitane's, so it should be safe, but just in case I'm going to start putting a used sanitary pad on top of this journal like an evil eye to ward off the assholeness of Gobi. Don't worry, I'll use brown food coloring or something, not actual period blood, because we already have a problem with rats, although it's much better since we got Rose and Elliot, who are two rescue cats.

Okay, security taken care of. Gobi-deterrent ready. So here's the truth: This place looks like a run-down house, and it is, but it is also a door to another world. Or we are the doors—it all happens inside our heads, there's no actual door involved. Rabbit calls it phasing, as in: out of our reality and into another one. He gives us a special medicine. No, it's not drugs, okay? I'm not stupid. It's part of a cocoon that is very rare and hard to get hold of and definitely illegal and probably the government would be after us if they knew about it. He says it lets us un-cocoon from ourselves, open our minds and become more than we are. Mina says it reminds her of being in Catholic school and taking Communion, a "This is the body of Christ"–type thing. Except that sacrament never astral-phased her into another dimension. I don't want you to think of this the wrong way. It's not some magical land like Oz. It looks like our world, only different in small ways and sometimes really big ones.

So we peel a bit of thread off the cocoon and eat it.

Rabbit plays music on the sarod and sometimes the mbira, and we all take turns looking into either a zoetrope or a kaleidoscope. The others keep watch in case anyone comes to interrupt. And then there's a whooshing inside your skull, like sticking your head out the window of the car when it's going eighty miles an hour, and a million colors you've never seen before, spinning and spinning. And then pow. You're somewhere else and someone else. But still you, if that makes sense? Only different.

You're them and they're you, and the best one is Jo-Anne in Cincinnati, not just because Jo-Anne is a better name than Joanne or Jo but because that's where Damien Anastaspolous is. He lives next door to her and I love him, I love him, I love him, and I wish I could tell him, but Rabbit says that's not allowed and he won't let me take any more if I'm going to be like this.

It's been agonizingly short. Only four times. Ten minutes and ten minutes and fifteen minutes, and ten, then I begged and begged Rabbit to let me stay longer, but he says there are side effects, and he shouldn't even have let me try it in the first place.

The second time, when Damien and I were making out in his bedroom, I asked him if he noticed anything different about me, and he said yes! So I think he knows when it's me and when it's her, and I asked Rabbit if I could stay there forever or find a way for him to come here, and Rabbit got really mad and said that's not how it works and I must never ask that again.

So obviously there <u>is</u> a way because he was soooo defensive.

I've tried to find Damien in this world, but he's not in the phone book and I can't exactly write home to ask my parents to look him up in the Cincinnati directory. He probably lives there, because <u>my</u> Damien lives there, next door to Jo-Anne, who is so lucky. (Jo-Anne's father doesn't pretend to go to work and then sit in his parked truck behind Solomon's garage where he thinks no one will see him, but the school bus goes right past and I see him basically every day.)

Damien strokes my hair, even though it's really Jo-Anne's hair, when I lay my head in his lap. He listens to me talk, and he says I'm really funny and I've got such an imagination, but then I remember we're running out of time and I wish we had more.

The fourth time, his hand was under my shirt, and I swear his fingerprints are burned into my skin, my real skin across dimensions, not Jo-Anne's. I was touching him through his jeans and he shivered, gasping into my mouth, and I could feel his heart fluttering in his chest, and I felt giddy with the power, because he was mine, mine, mine, mine, and I was doing this to him. And even though it's her lips, her tongue, I have explained to him that we are not our physical bodies but our immortal souls. Our souls have connected across time and space and I love him. I love him, I love him, I love him.

We're going to find a way to be together.

November 15, 1987

I am bereft. Full of rage and despair at the unfairness of the world(s). First I had to beg and beg Rabbit to let me go back. He's so selfish with the dreamworm! And then when I got there, I found out Jo-Anne's parents said she (I) can't see him anymore and she (I) need to stay home and rest.

Try explaining love and fate and the forces that have drawn you together and how you will die without this. Literally die. Like a broody chicken. Mina says I'm overdramatic, but she doesn't want to do it anymore. I don't know if she saw a version of herself she didn't like or something.

She has to babysit Jo-Anne in my body while I'm gone and in hers, and she tells me Jo-Anne says she would swap lives with me in a heartbeat if she could! She thinks living in an abandoned house is really glamorous and cool and her life is boring.

November 16, 1987

Rabbit has gone away for a few days to visit friends and he's locked up all his stuff, even though private possessions are supposed to be a figment of the capitalist system or something. I've been spending more time with the chickens. They're the only ones who know how I feel. Mina dragged me out because we needed money and I'm cuter than her (I have an innocent face, apparently, plus, she says, I'm white) and the tourists feel sorry for me. She's teaching me to do magic—not the real kind, like phasing, but sleight of hand. I'm counting the days till Rabbit is back.

November 20, 1987

Rabbit has returned! But Mama Capitane has us doing repairs because one of her friends is coming to stay with us, Travis. He is sick with AIDS and she's going to look after him. We cleaned up the room on the first floor because he can't manage stairs.

November 21, 1987

Mina says Jo-Anne is sick. She told her the last time I was there and she was here, and that's why she needs to stay home and rest. I don't believe her. She's lying. She's jealous. She knows Damien loves me more and wants to keep us apart. Jo-Anne can't stand that I'm better and more interesting than her in every way. Can you believe she actually told Mina she is dying?!?!!!?!?!?!?!?!?!?! It's pathetic. I can't believe she would make up such a terrible lie, especially when there are people dying for real. The AIDS epidemic is affecting our community! I'm going to use a really bad word now, so please forgive me. She's a "cunt"!!!!!!!

Mama Capitane thought I was crying on the fire escape,

but it was because of dust mites. All these old houses have mites. Probably asbestos too, and I'm going to die at like twenty-five from lung cancer. Real die, not fake die like stupid faking Jo-Anne.

November 23, 1987

Rabbit refuses to play the song that will take me to Damien. He wants us to give it a rest. Now that Travis is here, we all have to help out more, and he doesn't want Mama Capitane to know what we're doing.

Like I don't know Jo-Anne hasn't been trying to turn them all against me. It's so unfair. She's literally stealing my only chance at happiness. How selfish do you have to be?

November 26, 1987

I couldn't do it. I can't get the music right. I'm not good enough. Rabbit found me in his room and he snatched the sarod out of my hands and pushed me hard in my chest. He was screaming at me, calling me a little bitch. But he's the one being a selfish asshole! He's ruining my whole life! I screamed right back at him, and I laughed at him when he raised his hand like he was going to slap me. I yelled in his face, "Do it! Do it, do it, do it!" He got all ashamed and guilty.

We had to have a house meeting—on Thanksgiving (which doesn't matter because it's a racist holiday anyway)—and Mina tried to explain without betraying us, but Mama Capitane said we know her policy on drugs in Leftfield. Weed is fine, but anything heavier, including booze, is a one-way ticket out the door. I thought she was going to make us all leave, and Mina was sobbing and kept saying she was so sorry. I kept my mouth shut. MC doesn't need to know everything.

She came and found me behind the chicken coop and she said she couldn't have this kind of trouble here because if the social worker helping Travis found out that people in the house were giving drugs to a fourteen-year-old runaway (she knew!!! This whole time!), they'd send the cops and shut the whole house down and probably arrest a bunch of people including her, and then who would look after Travis? She has responsibilities blah-blah-blah.

She said she'd give me one last chance but with all these rules and conditions. I'm not allowed to be in Rabbit's room or anyone else's. I'm not allowed to smoke cigarettes or weed, and if she finds a beer in my hand, let alone drugs, she'll call my parents. She made Rabbit burn the cocoon.

She thinks she knows what my life is like because she also ran away from home when she was a teenager and had it harder because she was on the streets and didn't have a cozy place to stay with someone to take her in. I know she wants to connect on this deep soul level, like we're the same or she's my mother or whatever. I wanted to laugh in her face and tell her I already have two mothers, mine and Jo-Anne's, but I knew that would cause more shit.

November 30, 1987

Mina dyed my hair with gentian violent, which is what I thought it was called, and cut it for me. She used Gobi's electric razor—I left it on his bed with some of the purple hairs still sticking to it so he'd know I used it without his permission. My hair is jagged and ugly now, all different lengths. I want to be ugly. I want to be violent.

December 2, 1987

Cher journal!

The best news. The best.

Rabbit didn't burn the cocoon! He made a fake one out of string wound around one of the rubber balls he stole from the chickens and tossed the dummy in the firepit outside. He made a big deal out of it too, like a Shakespeare performance. Parting is such sweet sorrow etcetera.

He could see how much I was hurting and we made a plan. He's not going to risk getting kicked out, but he wanted to give me a chance to say goodbye in a few days when MC is out because she's borrowing a car to take Travis to his doctor's appointment.

I can't wait.

December 5, 1987

It's bad, cher journal. It's so bad I can't even write about it.

I can't breathe. I can't. I can't. I CAN'T.

What if I have <u>that</u> inside me?

I'm so scared.

I didn't even get to see him.

December 6, 1987

I cut the strings on Rabbit's sarod and stomped on the zoetrope until it was crumpled wire and cardboard and I smashed the kaleidoscope. I went outside and threw pieces of broken bricks at the windows. Mina caught me and held me tight like I was drowning and said, "Don't cry, it's okay," even though it <u>isn't.</u> MC says it's the last straw.

December 9, 1987

My parents know. MC told them. They are not going to press charges. My dad is driving down and they're praying for me. MC and the others guard me like I'm a wild horse about to bolt. She made Rabbit pack his things and leave.

MC tried to tell me I don't have cancer. But she wasn't inside that horrible magnetic metal tube that scans your brain and it's so tight you can't move and it sounds like really bad static going ra-ra-ra-ra-ra so loud you think you're going mad. And how would I be able to describe it if I didn't know? Huh? She said I'm a smart kid, I read, I pick things up, things I'm not supposed to. I must have heard it somewhere or seen it on TV, and my parents are going to take me to a doctor, but she promises, promises, promises I don't have a brain tumor like Jo-Anne does, and also Jo-Anne was never real. It was the drugs Rabbit gave me, and he's lucky she doesn't turn him in to the cops.

December 11, 1987

I'm hiding this inside a box of sanitary pads and underwear. My dad won't look here. I thought about burning you, Diary, like Rabbit should have done with the cocoon. Why didn't he? Why the fuck didn't he? I caught it from her. I must have.

Dr. B. Schulder
Pediatric Oncology
Cincinnati Children's Hospital Medical Center

December 17, 1987

Medical report re: Jo-Anne Kittinger

Diagnosis: Somatosensory seizures secondary to left parietal tumor (suspected low-grade glioma)

This right-handed fourteen-year-old young woman exhibiting severe anxiety was referred to me with a three-month history of tingling sensations in her left hand, spreading on occasion to her left arm, face, and leg.

These occur several times a week. There is no clear trigger.

Schooling and education are at a normal baseline thus far. Her seizures have not interfered with her grades.

Her birth, developmental, and previous medical history are all unremarkable. She has no known allergies or medical conditions.

There is no family history of note, and no family history of epilepsy. She has never sustained a traumatic brain injury.

Notable that she may have been exposed to illegal drugs or toxins (including a substance of unknown origin known as "dreamworm") in mid-November 1987 in New Orleans during a six-week period when she ran away from home. Patient is unable to provide more detail on this.

Patient is insistent she has brain cancer and repeats the phrase "It's a glioblastoma invading the medulla. It's inoperable and terminal." She says she knows this from another life. Mother believes she read it in a book.

On examination:

Height 5 foot 4, weight 110 pounds

BP 120/85, resting HR 64, sinus rhythm. No postural drop to blood pressure.

Cardiovascular and respiratory exam normal. Abdomen soft, nontender.

CNS: No detectable focal neurological deficit, no motor weakness; sensation is intact bilaterally to light touch, pinprick. All other parameters of neurological exam within normal limits.

Basic hematology, electrolyte, and endocrine blood panel normal.

MRI brain: There is a 20x20x30 mm area of FLAIR signal change in the right parietal cortex just posterior to the central sulcus. This corresponds to a similar area of T1 hypointensity with no contrast enhancement.

Differential diagnosis includes low-grade glioma.

Recommend referral to pediatric neurosurgery.

AMBER

Unhappy Camper

Like always, it's messy.

It had taken some work to convince Aiden to come all the way back to her place in Florence instead of returning to his hotel room. *We hate hotels.* There are cameras. There are witnesses. This has gone badly before.

He could catch a flight from FLO to Charlotte and from there to LA, she'd assured him. She'd drop him off at the airport. He'd come all this way already looking for answers; what were a few more hours? They needed to talk in private—who knew who was listening?—and she had something to show him. The others, those desperate pretenders, they wouldn't understand. Everyone wants to believe they're the chosen ones, that they alone have stumbled on an earth-shattering truth. Sometimes—rarely—they genuinely have. More's the pity.

Young Aiden does get nervous when she turns down the dirt road along one of the tributaries of the Great Pee Dee and drives to her squat little house, so isolated, far from civilization. He sits on her floral couch, covered in plastic—easier to clean—and tells her what happened to him. And he drinks down the sweet peach iced tea she gave him, spiked with a little bourbon, a little something else. He asks about the Frequency Machine, wonders whether it's some kind of old-fashioned radio.

"Some kind," Amber says in her little-girl voice. She built it decades ago, after Chris died. She had hunted down the man who'd infected him on purpose and tortured the plans for it out of him.

You get used to death. Especially if you've been behind the wheel of a Bradley following the Abrams tanks that churned the Iraqi trenches into bloody ridges and furrows sown with corpses, arms and legs sticking out willy-nilly, machine guns stuttering like sewing machines.

You get over that real quick, even the up-close ones. Shut it like a door. You have to if you want to live, and she did, desperately. War does that to a person. Makes killing easier. And there are worse things than war. Like torture. Although she tries to do only the necessary, make the Extraction as quick as possible. It's not their fault they get infected. If there were a way to neutralize it, like pouring borax on your mattress to suffocate the bed bugs, she would do that. *We would.*

The boy looks frightened when he realizes he's slurring his words, that he can't get up. Even more frightened when she peels off the wig, dons her disposable rain poncho, and starts laying out the essential tools: The scalpel. The culinary torch meant for crème brûlée she bought online, the tweezers for the Extraction, and the saw and the hammer for what comes after. All those years as a cop means she understands, intimately, all the ways people get things wrong, are lazy and stupid and disorganized and leave evidence behind.

"It's not your fault," she explains while she tunes the Frequency Machine to the appropriate bandwidth that causes the threads to surface. He's slumped on the couch now, his eyes wild and tearing, while Mr. Floof II gnaws on his cow hoof in his basket.

"I'm sorry you have to be awake for this. But I need your attention to make the Extraction, and pain is an amazing focus." He can't reply. His tongue isn't working anymore. Amber feels sorry for these people. But by the time they're showing the signs, it's too late.

It helps to think of them as no longer human. The exterminator does not show concern for the cockroaches and the rats. The surgeon cannot empathize with the tumors she has to excise. Once people are infected, there is no way to salvage them. Oh, they might try to prove to her all the ways they are individuals; they are making a difference, they plead, or they have people who love them, who need them. Don't we all. Chris needed her. And he died because someone did this to him all those years ago.

The voices in her head are clear, present. *We are with you. Always. We're doing what we have to.*

Aiden is twenty-eight forever now. With his arms shredded to ribbons, drugs in his blood: scopolamine to make him docile, make him talk, and fentanyl to cover it up, kill him dead, and a fresh harvest in her freezer compartment to fortify herself and the connections. His broken teeth are in a jar and she will scatter them along the highway.

Later, when it is dark, she will put the dead boy on her boat and take him into the swamp, a hundred pairs of alligator eyes catching demonic bright in the sweep of her flashlight. She will heave his body over the side, and they will take care of the cleanup. No matching dental records. No identifying marks. He'll end up wedged under a log to rot among the mangroves beneath the veneer of algae, catfish, and crabs bothering at the flesh that remains.

The swamp owes her. For her scars on her leg, for the first Mr. Floof. In 2002, a juvenile gator snatched her little dog right off her deck. She likes being all on her own out here, but it meant there was no one to help. She waded in punching and jabbing, gouged out its eye with her thumb, wedged open its jaw with her boot, and yanked Mr. Floof free, not thinking. The gator snapped its jaws shut on her leg. The voices inside her head were screaming, some of them more useful than others: *Don't die! Don't you dare fucking die!* But also: *Stay calm. Go for the eyes. Get your gun. Your gun. The gun.*

As Mr. Floof was paddling for the shore, she twisted away from the beast, reached under her arm for her service weapon, which she always wore strapped to her, because old habits die hard and she had seen enough of the world to keep it close. She jammed the HK45 right against the animal's skull and pulled the trigger. Miracle she didn't blow her own damn leg off.

Got through two tours of duty without a scratch, but damn gator in her own backyard... the scar makes for a good story when she's of a mind to tell it, worth a round of drinks back in the day when she would venture down to Sunshine Pete's Tackleshack. Before the work drove her to be more and more isolated, before she had to lie low. Alone, but not lonely.

Mr. Floof didn't make it. Rest in peace, doggy friend.

The teeth marks on her leg are as much a part of her as the thing that lives inside her. She knows it would destroy her if it could, grow and twist and fill her, kill her, if she hadn't taught herself the tools, learned the frequencies. Her infection makes her (all of them) a weapon, an avenging angel, the monster killer who is part monster herself.

As long as we keep it UNDER CONTROL.

Maybe she could have explained that to the dead boy while he was still alive but unable to move, the machine doing its work. She could have told him about the things she's seen, how she got like this.

But in her experience over these thirty years, this only makes them more frightened, more angry, more desperate.

More tears, more pleading and shouting, and none of it changes the outcome. She still has to kill them, because if she doesn't, it will be worse. Much worse, for everyone.

We don't have to enjoy the job to do it.

Although out of all of them, she does it best. She sometimes has to help the others along when they are discouraged or frightened or letting their emotions get the better of them. She has a moral responsibility.

We all do.

DOM

Occam's Razor Burn

Dom spoons up their breakfast, some chia-coconut concoction, enjoying the soft globules popping between their teeth. They're sitting in a Brazilian café on Mississippi, walls painted lime and lemon, a crush of students and cool young professionals sharing tables and eating way-too-healthy breakfast bowls and talking about normal-people things that do not involve magic worms that let you body-swap realities, *Freaky Friday*–style.

"It's a comic-book plot. Get that down on paper."

"My mom already did," Bridge counters. She stirs her beans into her tofu and avocado scramble so it's all a big mess. Like the mass of papers and journals and notebooks they are going to have to dig through to solve this thing.

The coffee machine behind the counter grinds and hisses beneath the capable hands of the barista who is goddamn adorable in her pinafore with blue and silver braids. She calls out another name in the ever-changing chorus: "Eden? Got your matcha latte."

"I'll admit there are consistencies," Dom says.

"Uh-huh."

"And I'll admit, okay, fine, I'm kinda into this. In a purely intellectual way. Like a puzzle to be solved." Not ready to be a new convert. They're supposed to be the practical one.

"Matcha latte, no sugar!"

"Wow." Bridge flicks a chunk of avo-tofu at them. "Way to dismiss my lived experience, one that might shake the foundation of how we understand reality, and, oh yeah, my whole life up until now?" She's kidding, but there's a spike of pain there. The great dreamworm mystery is weird and enticing, but there's still her dead mom at the heart of this. Maybe this is the process of unpacking your baggage to see what's in there.

"We're going to have to catalog everything. Your mom's system is..."

"Total chaos, I know."

"Yo! Eden," the barista calls, irritated.

A guy in a red hoodie shuffles up to the counter. He's got that Adam Driver thing, just ugly enough to be awkwardly attractive, slightly buggy gray eyes, dark mussed hair, skinny, mustache. And didn't they see him on the street earlier? "Hi, it's Caden. Caden, not Eden."

"Sorry, man." She shrugs. "It's loud in here."

He moves to lurk by the sugars and syrups, scrolling through his phone. He catches Dom watching him and dips his head, a nervous acknowledgment, but he doesn't move.

Dom, not keen on entertaining randos, lowers their voice. "We have to get the journals in order, work out the timeline, the players involved. This Rabbit guy. And you said Mina was the name of the woman you met in New Orleans? We should try to find her. And Stasia said Jo had run off to Argentina. Wasn't Rabbit Argentinean?"

"And Finnish."

"Right. And we're thinking the thing inside Jo was the tumor, not the dreamworm, yes?"

"Because the other Jo—Jo-Anne—had cancer. That was obviously an MRI, the loud metal tube? Finding myself in a supermarket was dislocating enough—it must have been terrifying dropping into that experience."

Dom pushes aside the sriracha sauce and their empty coffee cup to make space for the 1987 notes from Dr. Schulder that Bridge has brought out of her bag. "And there's this in the medical report, about the patient insisting she has brain cancer and repeating the phrase 'It's a glioblastoma invading the medulla. It's inoperable and terminal,' and saying she knows this from another life. Although Dr. S. fails to mention that she might have been right. Is a low-grade glioma the same thing?"

"I know she had a tumor removed from her brain when she was a teenager."

"We're going to need an expert to decipher the medicalese. Maybe one of your mom's grad students? The question is, and please understand I'm still super-skeptical here, do you think your mom caught the tumor from Jo-Anne and brought it back with her? Can you carry things between worlds?"

"I didn't bring back Supermarket Girl's boobs, alas, or her red hair. But I also can't tell you anything about her. No memories, no knowledge, what the kids' names were. Like I said, I was *me*."

"So we don't know why she gotta be so violent."

"Or if her mom is still alive."

"So no transference of memory. Unless it requires repeat exposure? But maybe brain cancer can be transferred?"

"Except..." Bridge points to the paragraph on the medical report. "'A three-month history of tingling sensations in her left hand, spreading on occasion to her left arm, face, and leg.' But she was only at Leftfield for six weeks. So she was experiencing seizure symptoms before, she just didn't know what it was, and maybe the tumor was already there?"

"So Jo-Anne had brain cancer, and your mom conveniently also had the exact same tumor in the exact same place, and she found out because of her experience inside Jo-Anne's body when she was in the MRI and because when Jo-Anne was in *her* body, she told Mina that she was sick. Does that sound right?"

"We can talk through it to death. Or I could...go back. Do it right this time, with a babysitter, like Mina did for my mom. Get real answers." Bridge pushes her bowl away. "Dom, I *need* to go back."

They don't like the raw urgency in her voice. "Hold up. That is at least eight steps ahead of where we are. We need more information from *Jo.* There are, like, a million more boxes of this stuff. We don't know if it's dangerous, what it does to you. I'd like to remind you of this little gem from Rabbit here about 'side effects.'"

"Um, don't mean to interrupt?" Walmart Adam Driver has appeared at the edge of their table. "I couldn't help but overhear."

"Rude," Dom says, beaming at him in the dangerous all-teeth way they reserve for dude bros who dare to interrupt. "Think you should move on."

But he's not talking to them; all his attention is focused on Bridge. "You're Professor Kittinger's daughter, right?"

Bridge narrows her eyes. "And you're the guy on the bicycle who was lurking outside the house. That's creepy as hell, dude."

"You been stalking us?" Dom demands.

The guy is flustered. "It's not like that. I've been trying to get hold of you, Bridget, but I didn't know how. I sent a bunch of e-mails, some messages on Lifebook. I was cycling past the house two days ago and I saw you with all the boxes—and that sweet ride." He flashes a smile at Dom as if they will be flattered that he noticed their car. "I rang the doorbell, but no one answered. I guess you were busy?"

"A little," Dom says. "Whole dead-mom thing."

He's uncomfortable with their animosity, which is exactly the point. He focuses on Bridge again. "I am so sorry for your loss. She talked about you all the time. She was an amazing woman. I was working with her, and—can I..." He gestures at the empty chair and, without waiting for a response, slides right in with his matcha and entitlement.

"One of her grad students?" Bridge is still tolerating him.

"Ha. I'm not smart enough to be a scientist. Sorry, I didn't introduce myself. I'm Caden, Caden Lyall. She came to me about a month, maybe a month and a half ago, to ask me to help her with an animation. I don't know if you've seen any of the videos?"

Fishing. "On her computer."

"Right. She asked me to convert zoetrope patterns into an animation loop and write songs for it, but she was really specific which instruments and what chords to use. I'm a musician too, but only in my spare time, unfortunately. I didn't really understand what she was trying to do, but then she showed me."

"That's surprising." Bridge is playing it cool, but her whole body is tensed forward.

"I had to understand so we could codify the doors. You know what I'm talking about?"

Bridge seems to sharpen, but Dom doesn't trust him. He's feeling them out, possibly bullshitting from on high based on a passing acquaintance with Jo and the eavesdropping du jour.

"If I can tell you how the file names work, would you believe me? You obviously found them on her computer. It's always two letters and two to three numbers. AJ-20-m, for example."

Dom glances at Bridge for confirmation.

Caden speaks again, lowering his voice so only Dom and Bridge can hear him over the clamor of the coffee machine. "The letters indicate the different realities we're dialing into, for lack of a better term, and not all of them work—some of them are incompatible with our universe. Hang on. I'm getting ahead of myself. The numbers are the duration of the switch. Twenty minutes is twenty m, for example. The longest stay we ever managed was four hours."

"And it's music-related?"

"Yeah, think about how vodou drums are used to induce altered states, or trance music—even without drugs," he adds quickly before Dom can interject. "But in this case, for the work your mother was doing, you have to use an instrument with microtonalities, as in overtones and rich harmonics. The sitar's perfect for this, because you can bend the notes, and the strings have sympathetic resonances and intermodulation, so it's like you can play notes between the notes."

"Wouldn't those just be more notes?" Dom is still disgruntled.

"Yes, of course, but they haven't been codified in the Western paradigm. So you could say it's not a G or a G-sharp but something in between, and we wouldn't give it a name or normally use it because maybe it sounds wrong to our ears or discordant, but it does exist expressed as a frequency."

"Notes between the notes," Bridge says. "To open the doors between the worlds."

"Or the chasm between bullshit and taking advantage," Dom cuts in. "Obviously you knew Jo enough to know how her file names worked and that's peachy—"

"I can show you," he interrupts. There's no way to make that sound not-creepy. "If you have it? You know what I mean."

"The dreamworm."

Damn it, Bridge.

"Did you find it?" Caden asks.

"Were you looking?" Dom challenges. "Know anything about a broken window?"

He squirms. "I do. Yes. I'm sorry. I didn't know what else to do. Jo was in the hospital, and they wouldn't let me see her. I was worried someone else would get their hands on it and not know what it was."

"Who? CIA? FBI? FSB?" They're thinking about Rabbit's paranoia, his fear of what the government might do with it.

He looks confused. "What? No. Someone who would throw it out. Waste it. Everything Jo fought for. Her whole life's work. It's irreplaceable."

Bridge looks terribly uncertain, terribly vulnerable.

"I can show you how to do it safely," he pushes. "I've got a setup at my place."

"No chance in frozen hell," Dom says; this is directed at Bridge as much as Caden. Not under their watch are they going to follow some amateur stalker-burglar-*musician* guy back to his apartment where no one can hear them scream.

"I know, I'm a total stranger. I'll give you my socials, you can look me up. My mom will vouch for me. I can give you her number."

"Can you give me mine?" Bridge says.

Baffled boyish look. "If I had your number, I would have texted you instead of following you in here and making it weird."

"My mom's number, I mean," Bridge says. "As in give me the scoop on Jo Kittinger. The inside story. You spent all that time with her, she showed *you* how it worked." Dom is deeply regretting coming to this café and getting anywhere within reach of this Caden.

"I can tell you what she told me," he offers. "And I can show you at a location of your choice. I would just need to pick up my gear."

"What time?" she says.

"I could go grab it now? My place is eleven minutes away by bike. Thirty by car."

"How about this evening," Dom counters, because they would like to gather some more information first, please, even though Bridge is keyed up, ready to go, giving them her disappointed face. "And yes, you should give me your socials."

BRIDGE

The Experiment Must Continue

Dom is sitting on the floor in the center of several circles of books and papers interlaced into the scruffiest occult symbol ever. *They're doing this all wrong*, Bridge thinks. They're supposed to be banishing ghosts of her past, not summoning demons.

Both of them are grumpy. Dom is mad about Caden, who is coming over in a few hours with his mysterious "equipment." According to his website, he's a "content producer" whose usual fare is animated video intros for streamers and music for commercials. YouVid also has some grainy footage of a deeply mediocre live gig from 2016 with his rock band Five-Eyed Cat. Dom says they're no longer scared Caden's going to ax-murder them. Much worse—he's going to waste their time.

"Ojo al pillo, ese tipo es un traquetero," they mutter.

"I don't know what that means."

" 'Eye on the thief.' Just saying."

She found the e-mail he'd sent Jo, the Lifebook messages. She hasn't mentioned them to Dom, because he does come off as very intense. Also there's the whole breaking into the house thing. *Wouldn't you, though?* she thinks. *If you'd found a way to connect to other worlds?* She feels pretty damn intense herself right now. But the sense of betrayal is a freshly scraped-off scab, bleeding over all reason. Why would Jo tell Caden and not her? Why would she show him? Maybe those answers are in the diary entries.

Some of them are like knives. Take this one:

February 20, 2015

I'm due for another MRI next week. It really is the bleakest month. There's another anomaly, which could be a shadow on the brain (good news) or maybe another tumor (bad news). Each one a warning, stepping stones on the way to the inevitable, although my surgeon tells me not to think like that. Save the morbidity for when you're dead.

It's a lifelong war. The scars under my hair look like worm trails. Like the ones Bridge cuts crisscross into her thighs with a craft knife and thinks no one notices, even though she's been wearing stockings under her shorts and locking the bathroom door so I can't catch her naked. She did a DIY nose-piercing with a safety pin, and the wound is inflamed and it's going to leave a scar. I left Neosporin on the counter because she won't talk to me about it.

As if her rage were unique, as if you could bleed it out like a poison. I want to grab her and shout at her: Don't bleed unless you have to. Don't give them anything unless you have to. Depression is anger turned inward. She should let it out, blaze rather than bleed. Light fucking bonfires with righteous fury.

But we don't talk. She skulks around the apartment, glued to her phone. I grade papers. The closest our orbits come are when we watch that sketchy lawyer show she loves on Thursdays, and then she's gone again, to her dad's house, and I'm sure they don't talk either.

* * *

The truth: She had been dying for her mom to talk to her. If only she'd said any of that out loud. She would have done *anything* for her to say any of that out loud. Why didn't Jo tell her she knew she was hurting herself? Bridge smarts with the humiliation. And fury, outward-bound: *Thanks, Mom, for the posthumous advice.*

"Hey, check out this article about a Haitian artist." Dom shows her a page printed from a website. "Doesn't this look like our dreamworm?"

It's from Diaspora Connections, a snippet on the Atis Rezistans in Port-au-Prince. The photograph shows a slim Black man with a shaved head in a T-shirt and jeans, standing in defiant mischief in front of a huge painting against a peeling wall in a kind of outdoor artists' alley full of wood carvings and scrap-metal sculptures.

The painting is a self-portrait that resembles religious iconography, but in it, the saint figure is caught in motion. Faces overlaid on faces, like a study in animation against a background of muted grays and greens threaded through with gold, unraveling from what is absolutely the dreamworm spindle, hovering like a halo above his head. The gold threads twine around his outstretched arms, holding him aloft. In places it looks like they're penetrating his skin. A crucifixion or a martyr shot through with arrows.

"Who is this guy?" Bridge takes the article from Dom.

The Artists' Dreaming

In his dreams, Olivier St. Juste lives in a loft apartment in Brooklyn, New York, and his paintings sell for tens of thousands of dollars. He wears expensive suits and goes to good restaurants. In reality, he is one of the hopeful "resistance artists" in Port-au-Prince. He used to be a schoolteacher but now spends all his time painting. He says he is inspired by his dreams and the possibilities of the other lives he knows are within his reach, if he stretches out to grab them. "The paintings come to me from the other world. I've seen them, already complete, so I know what I am trying to achieve when I pick up my paintbrush. The dreams show me."

"Didn't your mom go to Haiti?"

"Yeah, and there's a creepy wooden statue in her living room that could be from this market. Do you think she went to talk to him?"

"Definitely. And as much as I hate to give this to you, this does put another check in the 'Hey, maybe this *is* real' column."

Bridge flips the page over, but there's nothing printed on the back. A tantalizing snippet. "Please tell me this fell out of a diary where she writes about her trip to Haiti in exquisite detail?"

"Afraid not." Dom flicks through. "This one seems to be mainly shopping lists and notes from a neuroparasitology conference. '*Taenia solium* larvae in the brain and neurocysticercosis.' Also '*Varroa destructor* and honeybee populations.' That's a hundred percent going to be my band name."

"*Mainly Shopping Lists*?" Bridge teases, and Dom pulls a face. They're both garbage at staying mad at each other.

"Why did your mom not believe in filing?" Dom sighs, confirming their truce.

"Brain tumor." Bridge shrugs.

"The catch-all excuse, good for every occasion." Dom marks the printout with a neon-pink label. "You find anything useful? New Orleans? Argentina?"

"Personal stuff."

"How about Caden's e-mails? I have a lot of questions there—" The doorbell bleats its sickly chime, and Dom sighs again. "Speak of the nebuloso. I'll get it. Search him for weapons."

* * *

They're gathered around the kitchen table, Caden staring down at the dreamworm, nested in a clean Pyrex dish, with Holy Grail reverence. Bridge feels like there should be more ceremony involved. Should they set it on a gold tray, light candles?

"Where did you find it?" he says at last.

"Somewhere you obviously didn't look." Dom's still doing their best mongoose, ready to go Rikki-Tikki-Tavi on a bitch.

He has the good grace to flinch. "I'm really sorry about that."

"I'll send you the bill for the window repair."

"You let me know how much and—"

"Can we not?" Bridge interrupts. She's eager. A tug of excitement. Of need. "I don't care about the window. Do you know what this is? What Jo was trying to do with it?"

"Well, like you said." Caden launches forth: "It's a conduit for consciousness between realities. Simplest terms: The dreamworm is the key and the videos are the doors. But everything has to be calibrated exactly. Subtle alterations—say, a different pulse of light or a change in tone or rhythm—these change the reality, or world, you have access to. We've managed to code a few hundred realities, me and Jo, but there must be others we have no idea how to reach yet."

"So she was mapping—" Bridge starts, but Dom interrupts.

"Where did Jo get it? How come she trusted you?"

"I don't know if I'd say she trusted me. She tracked me down, and I listened and had the technical skills to do what she asked. She said she didn't have a lot of time, but neither of us realized she would go that quick. She talked about you constantly, Bridget. She was afraid of leaving you behind. I think she was very scared of dying."

"Why didn't she call me?" She hates the pain in her voice. "Or tell me any of this? I could have helped her."

"Honestly?" Caden says. "She thought you'd try to stop her."

It's true. She hates it, but it is true.

She can't help asking: "Did she leave anything for me?"

He shakes his head, maybe a little too quickly. "I have her old zoetrope if you want it back. She didn't want to tell me what she was doing. She'd ask me to tweak the notes or the pace of the visuals, then she'd go into the other room and lock the door and tell me not to let her out no matter what."

"In case she started acting as if she weren't herself and maybe tried to club you with a lamp?"

"Oddly specific," Caden says. "But yes."

She has a sharp memory of her mom's bedroom door closing in front of her. *Let me in, Mommy, I also want to go. Are you mad at me?* Sitting outside and sobbing into Bear's fur until the lock clicked and Jo emerged, looking tired, but she'd scoop her up and cover her in kisses and get out a treat.

"I feel like I may need alcohol for the rest of this conversation." Dom goes to open the refrigerator, which has been scrubbed clean with baking soda and vinegar and stocked with beer and grocery essentials.

"Not for me," Caden says. "You shouldn't either if you want to do the switch. You don't want to be impaired. Or sedated, even though that's the obvious solution to prevent any accidents. It makes the relocation harder."

"When I was a kid—" Bridge cuts herself off. Due caution is not the worst idea. Another memory, from when her mom would still let her go too, before she started locking herself away. Bridge remembers feeling dazed after she came back, and Mom was stroking her hair. *How was that, Bridge? Did you have a lovely adventure? Tell me all about it. What was it like? Was it a good one?* But she couldn't concentrate on her mom's words. Like she hadn't plugged back in yet, and there was noise on the line. "Sorry. I interrupted you."

"Long story short, Jo showed me how to do my own switches. It was the only way to grasp the mechanics and the nuance of the keys."

Dom jumps in. "Does the other consciousness know what's happening to them?"

"Not the first time, no." Caden looks shifty. "That's why we're so careful. We monitor your body in its present space, try to make the switch feel safe and comfortable. I came up with a low-tech solution—works pretty well, if I say so myself."

"So, more of a hijacking than an equal transfer, then?" Dom says. "Because that raises interesting issues around meaningful informed consent, don'tcha think?"

"There's no way to ask them until it's happening. Of course, Jo wouldn't go back if the other consciousness objected. She wasn't a monster! This is all semantics. Could I please show you?"

The equipment he's brought along turns out to be VR headsets. There's also a clipboard, a pen, a white lab coat. Bridge struggles with her headset and Caden comes to help her.

"It's part of the immersion experience to keep your switch safe and calm. It was my idea. Once Jo trusted me enough to let me into the room with her, I worked it up, along with the music and the visuals for the videos."

Looking through the visor at last, she can see the room in black and white like through a bad Photoco filter, but there is a pink grid overlay that maps obstacles, like the dining table and Dom standing as immovable and unimpressed as furniture, putting on their own headset. Caden presses a handle into each of her palms.

"Your mother was a genius," he says, soft enough that

only she can hear. "She wanted you to do this." Then louder, for both of them: "Look for the drop-down menu, top right corner. Now click on MirrorLab."

Bridge raises the handle and clicks as instructed and finds herself in a different kind of otherworld. *Oh,* she thinks. Horrified. Mortified. *Is this it? Is this what he meant?* She is sitting on a big cartoon armchair opposite an anthropomorphized deer in a black blazer who is holding a clipboard and a pen poised above it, head cocked to listen. One spotted ear twitches. There is a digital clock on her desk and a window overlooking trees that sway in a repetitive loop. Bridge looks down and finds she has big blue paws where her hands are supposed to be.

"This animation is awful." Dom's voice from somewhere across the room.

"It's open code, a freebie I found online." Caden is defensive. "It's supposed to be a model for virtual therapy."

"I bet people use it for sex," Bridge says.

"Of course they use it for sex," Dom retorts.

"I think there are better simulations for that," Caden mumbles, embarrassed, and she feels sorry for him.

The deer is talking to her, as gentle and reassuring as a sleep-meditation app. "Thank you for agreeing to take part in our VR neuropsychology study. Everything is going well and you are safe. Make sure you are sitting comfortably and breathing normally. Today we will be exploring how calming breathing techniques affect brain waves. Your participation is invaluable and will help other people. You'll be doing some simple exercises and telling me how you feel."

"Whose voice is that?" Bridge says, pulling off the headset. She hates being a fuzzy blue critter, hates the B-movie sci-fi of this. Is this what he meant about entering other worlds—fucking video-game pretend?

"It's an actor. I paid her two hundred dollars. Don't worry, she doesn't know anything about it."

"You may feel dislocated," the voice says through the headset speaker, "especially if you've never used VR before. This is part of the process to help you get outside yourself, to still your mind. Thank you once again for participating. Your experience will last only as long as the timer..."

"The clock syncs to the file, so if it's a twenty-minute flip, it counts down twenty minutes on the clock behind Dr. Fawn's head," Caden explains.

"And what if they pull the headset off?"

"We, me and Jo—your mom, I mean—we'd do it one at a time and the other person would monitor them, talk them down if they got upset, get them to wait it out."

"Does it ever go wrong?" Dom asks. "Get violent?"

"No. I'm sorry you had that experience with Bridget—the alternate—but she was dumped in with no safety measures, all of you completely unaware. We take deliberate steps, try to do this as ethically as possible."

"By which you mean you trick people into believing they're in a game so they don't freak out."

"I'm eager to hear your alternatives," he snipes back and Bridge is sick of it and sick with the fear that *this* is all there is. A simulation. A joke, a cartoon.

Dom removes the headset, unhooking one pineapple earring caught on the straps. "Count me out, friends. I'm not eating that disgusting thing, I'm not going to play in VR-trip-land. But I will babysit you. I'm guessing that's what this lab coat and clipboard are for?"

"That would be terrific," Caden says, a little too grateful, as if he was hoping for this exact outcome. "I can guide Bridget inside, then. But if they take off the headsets, you have to keep them occupied until the time runs out. Placate them, be reassuring, say the experience will be over soon. Do *not* tell them anything about our world or the dreamworm or what we're really doing."

"In case they invade?" Dom snickers.

"I'm serious."

"As brain cancer. I get it, I get it." Pointed glare at Bridge.

"Will we be in the same place?" Bridge asks Caden, dodging Dom's look. She wants to do it already. She feels like the dreamworm is waiting for her. A pang. A thrill.

"It's incredibly unlikely that our alternative selves are in the same room or city or even know each other. A compatible universe isn't necessarily identical."

"Only close enough," Bridge says, which is not an original thought. It's something her mom would say when she was a kid and asked what they were looking for. *Close enough, Bridge, but even better than here. We'll keep looking.*

"How many have you done?" she asks Caden as he lifts the dreamworm out of the Tupperware like it's the baby Jesus.

"A few. Eight, ten maybe." He sounds unhappy. "Jo did a lot more. She had certain compatibles she kept returning to." He has a scalpel, and he's teasing one of the strands loose with practiced ease. He offers it to her on the tip of the blade. It looks gold in this light.

"*Compatible* as in what?" She takes the limp curl and puts it under her tongue like it's acid. It still tastes like earth, with the consistency of raw tofu, but there's a sparking too—or maybe that's her nerves.

"Can we agree that your consciousness—who you are—is a pattern of firing neurons?"

"Little loose on the neuroscience, but, I mean, sure."

"Okay, a song, then. It doesn't matter whether the tune is held by the structure of the brain or comes from the mind-body connection or a soul. It's complicated and ever-changing, but it *is* a song, a recognizable pattern of notes, so you can replicate it in multidimensional space, connect to another iteration if enough of the notes are the same."

"Wooo, quantum physics, spooky action." Dom waves their hands.

"Actually, it's more about the fundamental mathematical structure of the univers—"

"Does it matter?" Bridge interrupts. "I get it. You have to match the pattern to the person and to the universe."

She picks up the headset again. It does feel like some kind of bargain-basement interstellar mission. It's not going to work, she knows it, and she will never hear the end of it from Dom.

But, oh, that's not true. She also knows that's not true, and she feels giddy with it.

"And match to some version of you that exists in the alternate timeline." He slices another sliver (*Slither,* she thinks) of the dreamworm and licks it right off the blade.

"What happens if there isn't a version of you on the other side?"

"You don't go anywhere; you get a splitting migraine that takes you down for a week. At least, that's what happened to Jo."

But there's something nagging at Bridge. She's thinking about her dog Bear, back when she was a kid, the one who had a stroke and had to be put down.

"Do you know which ones she kept going back to?"

"She was very cagey about that. Which one did you go to last time?"

"ZC. It was the first file name listed, so I clicked on it."

"That's a boring one. Let's go somewhere else. SG. I think you'll like this one."

"Can I be a rock star?" The fizzing behind her teeth has become a deep cicada buzz in her jaw, her neck.

He twitches. "I don't know who you're going to be. Consider it a surprise."

"Or a weeklong migraine," Dom says, looking very poised in the lab coat. They've even removed their pineapple earrings to look more lab-researcher-y. "Don't worry. I'll be right here, watching over you crazy kids. And I got more generic aspirin where the last batch came from."

"You have to do what I said," Caden lectures. "Keep them calm. Don't let them leave the room. Assure them it's a simulation."

"I'll be the best damn pseudoscientist you ever met."

"Okay." Bridge settles the VR headset back over her hair.

Dr. Fawn is blinking at her from under those huge lashes. Her deer ear twitches, another cheap animation loop. "We're going to play a video for you now," she says.

"Okay," Bridge says stupidly, as if the cartoon can hear her. The anticipation is like the low-grade clutch of electricity through the ungrounded pipe in the bathroom of her shitty shared apartment. And maybe her housemates have rented out her room even though they said they wouldn't, maybe the managers have given away her shifts at Wyvern Books. But none of that matters anymore, all her non-plans. It feels like her whole life has been leading up to this moment. She has been preparing to become.

Something touches her in the real world, not the VR version of the living room. Caden is taking her hand, sitting beside her on the couch. She clasps his hand tight, as if they are on the clunking ascent of a roller coaster, too late to get off, climbing higher and higher, and ahead, the inevitable drop.

BRIDGE

Adrift

The smell reaches you first, a mix of brine and mechanics, and then the ground shifts under you, a treacherous thing. You grab at the nearest point of stability in this abruptly narrow space, which happens to be a wide and beardy man. Clutching at his green shirt, you accidentally slam your head into his chin, snapping his head back with the nasty crack of skull hitting jaw.

"Fuck!" He reels back. "Ow. Shit."

"Oh my god, I'm so sorry!" You reach for him automatically, and your arm is not your arm but someone else's: toned and tanned and covered with tattoos of curling snakes and flowers in luminous colors. You pull back and cradle this stranger's arm against your chest as if to undo this spell.

"Yow." He stretches his neck and rubs his jaw. "That's a vicious headbutt you've got there, love," he says in a foreign accent—Australian or Kiwi, maybe; you can't tell the difference—and the ground is still shifting, capricious. You're on a boat, you realize, the walls of the cabin curving in, small portholes showing snatches of sky, an ocean below, or maybe a lake, reaching deep and dark beneath your feet. Vertiginous. "Nearly bit my tongue off."

You laugh, you can't help it, an anxious apologetic noise. "I'm so sorry. I tripped." Another nervous laugh, because that's no lie. Tripped through time and space to be here, somehow, inside a tattooed girl on a motherfucking boat. Which was supposed to happen, was the intended plan, but it's still a shock to the system.

"It's all right, no worries. Pretty sure it's still intact." He sticks his tongue out, pink against his dark beard, and pokes at it, testing. "Am I bleeding?"

You lean in to look, fascinated, because apparently they are this familiar, the tattooed girl and beardy man with his wicked eyebrows and that trouble-charmer glint in his eyes. Eyes that in your own life would probably glide right over you, looking for someone hotter, more interesting.

"Uh, no. No, I don't think so." You examine his tongue. The ocean swells beneath the hull, and the bright square of sky through the open hatch is distracting—fiery red and scuffed with cirrus clouds.

"Known you were a streetfighter, would have set you loose on those pickpockets in Alghero," he grumbles.

The open hatch is a lure that tugs at you, but you need to check, to see for yourself. "Where's the bathroom?"

"What?" He looks so genuinely Labrador-dog-confused, you have to stifle another laugh. *Keep it together*, you tell yourself. This is real, not a simulation. You're really here. The Somewhere Else. The Not-Real. Like when you were a kid. And of course, you've just asked an absurd question. The head is in the head, of course, and there's only so much room on this boat. You spot the little wooden door on a latch past the kitchenette table, squeezed in front of the crawl space for the double bed. Could have landed on a luxury catamaran, cocktail in hand—just saying.

You duck your head beneath the too-low doorway. The smell is stronger back here, salt mustiness, the peculiarity of fiberglass, the chemical tang of the toilet. The bathroom is a squeeze, a showerhead tucked up above the commode, a plastic sluice beneath your feet, which are bare—and also tattooed. A faded blue rose on your left instep.

Two electric toothbrushes in a cup clipped to the faucet, natural eucalyptus deodorant, a hairbrush snarled with his-'n'-hers brown and black hair, toothpaste smears in the sink for that real feel, and you wonder how the girl who should be here feels inside *your* body back in Portland, and how she feels about Dr. Fawn. Above the sink is a small mirror. And the woman in the reflection is not Bridget Kittinger-Harris, not by a long shot.

You knew this for sure already from the tattoos, from the nimbleness in your body, the casual strength, even when you were losing your footing and headbutting a total stranger. But there is no arguing with a mirror.

You try to imagine your own features in the reflection. Puff out your cheeks to summon your rounder, paler ghost. This face has spat out the marshmallow padding you apparently carry under your own skin. Lean and mean, to match the physique. You can feel how taut your stomach is, the definition in your arms beneath the full-sleeve tattoo.

Same nose, same chin, only *her* eyes are hazel, more like Jo's, skin deeply tanned, freckles and laugh lines, her hair a sun-bleached brown and in braids tucked behind each ear, like a pirate girl from a childhood storybook or someone you might see at a trance party juggling flaming sticks. You have never been any of those people: pirate or poi dancer or Able-Bodied Seawoman.

There are flaws too. The mirror woman has one chipped incisor on top, a crescent missing, which together with the pigtails makes her look girlish. She stinks of sweat. *Thanks a lot, natural deodorant.* Not quite identical, but fraternal twins. What was the word Caden used? *Compatible.* You lean in closer, staring into the hazel eyes, searching for the spirit that animates the body, looking for some indication of *you* inside looking out. You breathe on the mirror, write *Hi*... in the condensation, each period a jab at the glass.

"You all right in here?" Beardy guy pokes his head around the door. *Are you?* No one ever talks about what it's like for the possessor driving the possessed, an unfamiliar rental car with the turn signals on the wrong side. And what if you never make it back, what if this is it, now, stuck in this body, this life, on a yacht in the middle of the ocean? And if you hadn't been here or somewhere like it long ago, you might be freaking out a whole lot right now.

"Fine. Sorry." If you keep apologizing, maybe that'll get you through. Old memories are rising like a diver's bubbles in murky water. You remember feeling out of place, faking it, having to play detective like this—even more than the normal awkwardness of being a kid at a loss in the incomprehensible world of adults.

"You taken a spell, love?" He touches your forehead with the back of his hand and you bear it until he gives his assessment. "You're not hot."

"Need some air," you say, pulling your lips into a smile, hoping this is the way you smile here, with that chipped tooth. Squeeze past him, making for the hatch and the steep ladder. The ground lurches and you stumble again, and it's infuriating that you don't have her sea legs. You'd expect the body to have sense memory, some level of physical competence. Are you so certain it's a full switcheroo and that *the other* is not here with you, riding shotgun? You feel a bit sick, actually, a weird tightness, and maybe that's a side effect of the transfer. Or is it the other you trying to fight her way back up? But surely you'd have memories, then—this man's name, for one—or some idea of how to balance on a heaving boat. There's a tight pain across your taut pecs, which could be from overuse, all the keelhauling and petard-hoisting Not-You has been up to. Or it could be a heart attack. Or a panic attack. Probably a panic attack. You need to get some air, calm the fuck down. This is what you were expecting. This is what you wanted. But there is a fist in your chest, and in your stomach too.

You scramble out onto the deck and barely make it to the railing before your guts contract and the bile rises, hot and sour, and you're chumming the ocean below. You retch and spit until it feels like it's all out of you, and Beardy is behind you, wrapping his arms around you, and you have to admit, it feels good to lean back against him.

"Yikes," he says.

"Urgh," you manage in agreement. The wind is rucking the sails, snagging the fine loose hairs that have escaped your practical braids. The horizon rises and falls like breath, but it's not making your stomach do the same anymore.

"I'm fine, it's fine, just..." You realize you can't say *seasick* because Not-You wouldn't be. "Had a turn." *A trip. A worm. A dream.*

He checks you over. "We can go back. See a doctor in Sardinia, rest up."

You extricate yourself from his arms gently. "I'll be fine. Wouldn't want to"—mad-libbing here—"affect our schedule." More than a detective, you are an archaeologist-anthropologist, working through the artifacts and rituals of an unknown life, trying to observe and not disrupt.

"It's no worries, love."

"Where are we now?" This seems reasonable to ask.

"Exact GPS? I'd have to look, but halfway to Tunis."

"Can I get some water?"

"Of course." He moves to kiss you, and you cover your mouth.

"You really don't want to do that right now."

"Right. Yes. I'll bring the toothpaste too."

"Hey..." You don't know what to call him so you leave it trailing.

He turns at the top of the stairs, ladder, whatever it is.

"Is my mother here?" And it's only now that you've said it out loud that you feel the yawning chasm of it, a Mariana Trench of loss, and you're sitting at the bottom with the entire weight of the ocean pressing down on you. And the words she said in the hospital: *You're not my daughter.* Because what if you weren't? Not there. And maybe that means... you're not ready to think it.

He looks at you, incredulous, worried. He starts to say something, but it's too late, and it's too soon, you don't want to go—

Jo's Diary

April 13, 2006

Highway amnesia: When you glance in the rearview mirror and see the distance falling away behind you, and you don't know how you got here. A slow process of things slipping from the way they were supposed to be, the way you thought they were. When you're inside your own life, you can't see it. Which is why I came here, dragging Bridge along on a pretend vacation. I needed to know it was real. If what's growing in my head is what's causing ghost symptoms, according to the experts: somatization, current stressors, as they suggest, very kindly, that I consider antianxiety medication. As if it's my emotional state that is making my left arm feel like it's telescoping, an invisible giant club attached to my shoulder, and causing the tingling, the dropping things, the occasional loss of consciousness. The tumor is back, I know it, I can *feel* it, and to hell with what the doctors say.

Dave took this as a diagnosis that I was crying for attention, and the whole incident at the lab—"Endangering our child!"—proved that I am not ready for responsibility. "You're fragile, my love. You need to take it easy." He is away again. All the time, in fact.

New Orleans is wracked, a whole other city post-Katrina. We walked through its ghosts today, the St. Louis Cemetery with its marble, but also the stricken houses, the broken streets still strewn with detritus, more people begging than I remember.

I needed to know if it was real. Not just the darkness growing where the experts can't find it, but what happened before. Leftfield. The dreamworm, the other Jo. Jo-Anne. Did she give the tumor to me or was it always there, lying in wait? All the strings lead back here, the Fates tugging on them, on me, the marionette.

I couldn't find it at first. So much has changed, in good ways and bad. We stopped to ask a woman under the bridge for directions, ask if she remembered a house called Leftfield or the old flour factory up this way? It was all hardwired into me back then, neurological pathways through dingy backstreets that I walked bundled up in an oversize coat from Goodwill and a knit hat pulled down so people couldn't see I was a girl. It felt rougher than I remembered, more forlorn. That vacancy was the space where anything could happen.

I felt naked being back here without that armor and with Bridge clutching my hand, wide-eyed with alarm, so very clearly a target. The old me, that spiky, nervy fourteen-year-old nicknamed Tic Tac, swaggering under her bulky coat, would have homed in on us, the lost tourists, right away. She would have headed for the kid, pulled a coin out of her pocket to dazzle and beguile, offered to help these poor misplaced people back to the main drag. I always faked compassion; easier to score a dollar or two if you seemed helpful, and people getting mugged brought down the whole vibe, brought in the polis. I would have said it like that too: poe-lees. White girl trying too hard.

Sometimes I think I see glimpses of that kid in Bridge, or the potential to grow into her when puberty hits, but her face is softer, rounder. She's more her father than me, with Dave's olive complexion, his long nose, his fine dark hair.

Maybe a bit of my brother Kev too, the freckles, the naked curiosity in those big eyes.

Bridge was goggling at the homeless woman, who had her belongings piled in a broken shopping cart that probably doubled as a shelter, tarpaulin stretched over the top; a radio was hanging from the handle playing snatches of music through static hum beneath a propped-up green frog umbrella with a big smile and pop-up eyes, although one was drooping. It looked like the frog was suffering from Bell's palsy, which Dave got after that bad ear infection, leaving the left side of his face sagging off his cheekbone. It was temporary—it lasted barely three weeks—but he refused to go to work or walk Bridge to the bus stop. The half-melted man, eye weeping, constantly dabbing at his mouth with a handkerchief like a Victorian dandy.

I thought maybe he would be able to relate, finally, to my fear of the cancer coming back. But the difference, Dave explained, so very patiently, was that his Bell's palsy was real, writ large across his damn face, while my tumors were all in my head, metaphorically speaking. Of course, the epilepsy was real. But that didn't mean the cancer was going to return. He said he wouldn't pay for one more test to satisfy my obsessive paranoia, and obviously my therapist was useless, so he wasn't going to pay for any further sessions either.

"Grow up, Jo," he said, "your child needs you."

I say it to myself on repeat. A motivational mantra: *Your child needs you.*

She needs me to live. And I can't, not with him.

My siblings and I grew up skulking in the shadow of my father's undiagnosed depression, which made him unpredictable. We were always tiptoeing across a glass floor. I thought I'd married the opposite of that: a man who'd literally caught me when I fell, mid–grand mal seizure, in the kitchen at that house party. But self-loathing has other ways of expressing itself. It would be easier if he'd ever raised a fist to me. Violence is a reason for leaving. So is infidelity, although for all I know, he has been cheating on me, all those long trips away. Why wouldn't you fall into easy dalliances with exciting strangers, especially when your own wife is so fragile, so unreasonable in her expectations? The emptiness of reassurances. *You'll be able to go back to your studies eventually. Right now, you need to look after yourself. Your child needs you.*

Cotton wool can be a prison too.

The woman with the frog umbrella pointed in the direction of the river. "Huh. Uh-huh. Bread factory was up on Eleventh. That what you mean, honey? Hey. You shouldn't be walking around here, you and your child. Going to get mugged. You head back now. You get."

I tried to offer her a dollar. I was down to $178—I'd counted this morning—but she only scowled at it and told me I had a bad heart. I called after her as she rattled away over the cobblestones: "It's a bad brain, actually."

"God hates you for your bad heart," the woman shouted back. The droop-eyed frog watched us balefully, rocking in the cart.

Bridge was upset. "Why did she say that?" She tugged at me.

"Some people are hurting."

"That was mean. She was mean."

I didn't know how to explain to her that I had screamed much worse things at people I'd thought stiffed me when I was a stupid kid here. Screamed, "Is that fucking it, you fucking cheapskates, fuck your mother in the asshole," and ran, laughing at my bravado, high on adrenaline, trying to impress Mina or Rabbit. Told myself I didn't feel bad about it afterward. They had it coming.

Maybe this part was more familiar. The old railway tracks buried in the tarmac. I remembered walking along them like a balance beam until they submerged completely into the street. There are buried things everywhere you go.

We walk through the world as if we are not, always, standing on the edge of calamity or dreadful cliché. It's easier not to look. I spent so much of my life not looking. Sometimes I specifically averted my gaze. I should have seen it coming. I fucking *did* see it coming. On the edge of calamity, or dreadful cliché. *To have and to hold.* To *have.* To control. I feel so stupid. Did he know my therapist had been urging me to leave him? Wouldn't want to be out of pocket for that advice, huh, Dave?

Writing for myself, for Bridge maybe one day in the future, to help her understand. To try and interrogate myself. The detective behind the desk and the unreliable witness. Running away didn't help when I was fourteen, and the interrogator in me says it won't help now. But sometimes you're not running away, you're running toward.

When I was dragged home back in 1987, it was to the same shitty family dynamics: Dad sad and mad and drinking too much, Mom trying to hold it together with three teenagers, working shifts at the Piggly Wiggly, except now I was the gold-star troublemaker, even ahead of Kev with his weed-smoking and wild friends. I was the one who had given them all so much worry, and *Goddamn it, girl, thank your lucky stars you didn't come home pregnant.*

But I had a tumor. Like Jo-Anne, who had the same malignant dark matter growing inside her skull. We caught mine early because I insisted, even though everyone said I was hysterical. The doctors said I was so calm inside the MRI, and I couldn't tell them I'd been in one before, inside Jo-Anne. I realize I didn't catch it from her. I already had epilepsy, but it had gone undiagnosed, like so many things in our family. The tumor was also blooming. Maybe it does in every version of me.

We made our way between the warehouses, ugly and empty, with broken glass and boarded-up doors and windows, the rush of traffic on a swoop of highway above. A roller door had been kicked in, all dents and scrawled tags. I heard a trace of music from somewhere, a clutch of mournful trumpet notes. It could have been a car horn in the distance. And there. The burned-out facade of what used to be Leftfield. Bridge was scared, clinging to me with all the uncertainty of a toddler. I had to know if it was real, though. That I didn't make this up. I helped her under the fence, the wire sagging on its posts. The front yard was a snarl of overgrown brush, kudzu and ivy and clutching brambles. Some wit had scrawled a message, descending down the face of the front steps, reading top to bottom:

FUCK ALL YOU
GENTRIFYING BITCH ASS
MOTHERLESS SONS

There was a rustle in the greenery, and Bridge gasped, and I wished I'd brought pepper spray, but it wasn't a mugger, it was a rabbit, poised on the top step among errant dandelions. We all froze, and then one ear twitched decisively, and it was gone into the long grass. If I believed in fate and those tugging strings, it could have been read as a sign.

Bridge wanted to go chasing after it, but I needed to go in, to see. The front door was boarded up, but someone had pried open a window, propped it up with a plank and bricks, and we climbed through carefully into the still interior.

Sunlight streaked through the broken roof, across the

floorboards of the entrance hall, where we used to have house meetings and MC would assign the chores. There were holes knocked in the walls, more scrawled tags, full of hope and hurt: *I was here, this is my mark, I exist, I am legend.* But I could still figure out the lay of the land. The past is an imaginary country.

When I was fourteen, I thought I'd come back. But a million little things got in the way. Kev's accident, which my dad never recovered from. School. Life. Working three jobs to take classes part-time, waitressing, doing phone-sex work, which I was surprisingly good at, given I didn't lose my virginity until twenty-two. A late bloomer (cancer joke). Fucking around, a year of community college. A "mature" student at the ripe old age of twenty-four, because it took me so long to save up. I got into a college with a good biochem program because of my killer essay—who can resist someone who wants to be a neuroscientist because she's had first-hand experience? Begging the physiology professor to let me join his class even though it was full. Playing the tumor card. Working two jobs, no longer phone sex, in case some gomer recognized my voice because it was a small university town. And then scooped off my feet by Dave, the law student, three years ahead of me.

Getting pregnant, too young, only twenty-six, and Dave talking me out of the abortion.

That's not fair. I talked myself out of it too.

My teen brush with brain cancer wasn't genetic, the doctors said. I couldn't pass it on, but I might get it again one day—unlikely, but possible—so if I wanted to have children, this was the time. I believed them. I wanted the chance to be a mother, but I wanted other things too, and I didn't realize that so many doors would close. Or that Dave would hold them shut.

Bridge was so determined to make it out into the world, so hungry for it, she tried to come too soon, and I had to spend three months lying on my back while Dave assured me that neuroscience would be there when I got up. She still arrived seven weeks early, and the doctors said she wouldn't live, was too weak, too small, a tiny yellow thing who wasn't strong enough to latch, so I locked myself in the bedroom with her and fed her with a dropper like Kev and I did with the baby racoons we found, blind and pink and snuffling, after Dad shot the mama, years before.

We couldn't afford a nanny and Dave wanted to move to Florida to be near his parents, but then I'd have to give up on the dream of picking up my studies.

He was always away, his job took him away, so it was just me and Bridge, and I never realized how selfish I was until I had her, and she demanded everything. Everything. A small and terrible god. Love and destruction. Meanwhile, the seizures got worse. Stress, the doctors said. You definitely shouldn't return to work or studying. Not yet.

But when Bridge was old enough, at preschool, I begged Professor Watson to let me come back to school part-time, at least to help out in the lab, maybe start doing prep work for my PhD. Dave had promised I could start as soon as I was well enough. But I didn't tell him I was going in to the lab.

During school vacation, I had to bring Bridge in with me some days, but mostly she sat quietly in the corner. Mostly. Dave didn't know. Until he did. The furor over an attempted rodent jailbreak. The rat didn't even escape. You'd think it was the end of the world.

I had defied the protocols of a professional lab, but, much worse, of being a mother. *What kind of mother was I?* It didn't help that the headaches were getting worse. The aura came swimming up to swallow me, my own personal halo.

Everything I am, I was, all fading away, a reverse Polaroid.

Being back here was a reclamation. A way of leaving.

This was the room we cleared out for Travis, Mama Capitane's friend who was dying of AIDS. We were so naive back then; we didn't know if we could catch it from going into his room, breathing the same air. But MC wasn't worried, so I wasn't either.

I am not convinced I am dying. Not yet. But I will, I can feel it—the seizures have been getting worse. And there must be someone smarter than me, a better me, who has figured it out. A cure. A life I want. If I can find it.

Bridge pulled on my arm like a bell. "Can we go now? There are no bunnies. I don't like it."

There was no life left here, no clues written on the walls, no guest register listing Rabbit's phone number, his real name. Only a piece of card and plastic film on the ground, and I stooped to pick it up, thinking it was part of the zoetrope. But it was discarded packaging for a microwave mac-and-cheese.

April 15, 2006

Sitting in Mina Remington's studio felt like coming home to my younger self, that complicated kid: so angry, so scared. As if the people from your past hold strings outside the labyrinth to lead you back to the person *they* knew.

She handed me a glass of homemade grappa poured from one of her many bottles in assorted shapes and sizes, all steeping mysterious herbs, and said my hair looked better now.

I told her I'd been thinking of cutting it. Dave liked it long, said it was more feminine. But, yes, it couldn't be worse than the gentian-violet hack job I had the last time I saw her. Mina looked amazing; there was a precision to her that was very birdlike, a falcon, maybe, or a crow, with her penchant for collecting treasures.

Her building was an old art deco cinema converted into artist spaces, with a forge on the ground floor and a salsa studio on the top. There was a painter in the projector room doing a life-drawing class, a naked young man posed on a plinth, and Bridge, my tiny prude, gasped and slapped her hands over her eyes.

Mina was in what used to be the air-conditioning room, which had huge fans to push air through the cinema's hidden passageways and, especially, into the projector room, because film stock is extremely flammable. She pointed out the places where the building had burned twice before, the black patina on the wall like mold.

Now it was part photographic studio, part forest witch's den, with dried greenery and fossils and husks of sea creatures. I didn't know "food artist" was an actual profession.

We had already been through the tearful reunion, the reminiscing about Leftfield, both of us veering away from any mention of the dreamworm. A black hole neither of us was ready to talk about yet.

I told her about getting brain cancer and Kev dying and getting pregnant and getting married and stories about Bridge. She was still awake when I was talking about when we got locked in the zoo because we were so entranced by the sloths that we missed closing time and we had to walk around until we found a security guard to let us out, and she said I wasn't allowed to tell that: "It's private."

"You wait till you're a teenager, kiddo," Mina said, her voice Eartha Kitt–esque from cigarettes or too much of her own grappa. The sun was still out, late-afternoon light pouring through the windows. "Then your mom will really embarrass the hell out of you."

She showed Bridge some of her collection: the twisted bulbs of kelp and spokes of seaweed, an albino python skin, necklaces used for trading in West Africa, a chip of meteorite, a baboon's skull with one broken tooth. Then she brought out her favorite — an artichoke flower, brown spiky petals around a tawny-gold head. She rubbed her thumb gently over the feathered center and showed us the fine silvered threads that came away, all clamped together.

"But look what happens when we bring it into the sunlight." Bridge dutifully followed her over to the window, where a still life was set up on her infinity curve table, flowers and gold leaf and polka-dotted anemone shells. Mina held it up in the rich afternoon light and brushed over it again, and Bridge gasped as this time the seeds opened up into fine feathered spokes, like dandelion tufts.

"It's like stars!"

"I love stars." Mina pulled down her top to show the stars tattooed on her collarbone. "And sunlight. You find the people that are like sunlight for you, kiddo, who make you bloom."

"I'm hungry," Bridge said, and we both laughed. Mina said it was lucky she had a full kitchen, but her food artistry was wasted on Bridge, who ended up eating toast and sitting on the couch with Mina's art books while we talked.

I got the recap of Mina's life too. We were half a bottle down by then. She stayed at Leftfield for another two years, until Travis passed and MC let the cops shut them down. "I think it broke her. She held him for all that time, love and stubbornness."

Mina fell in with a bunch of assholes, went in and out of rehab. "I'm clean now. Two years in January. I got married.

Divorced. We got remarried. Tempestuous. Love is, don't you think? Maybe that's the wrong kind of love. It's powerful, though. I think we're going to get divorced again. I think that's okay. At least there aren't any kids. I wanted them, but"—she circled her hand around her stomach—"my ovaries are twisted. Dead. Maybe..."

I suggested she could adopt. Bridge was asleep on the battered leather couch by this time, a throw fur tucked over her that Mina must have put there when I went to the bathroom. The other studios were quiet by then, the sky outside the windows shading to darkest blue, like deep oceans.

"Maybe in another world, you know." Wistful, dangling. She got up, took my glass, and weaved, ever so slightly, to the array of bottles and poured out another shot. A full glass, really. "Try this one, it's aniseed."

Here, I thought. *Now.* "It was real, wasn't it?"

"Was it?" She had arranged herself on a woven rattan throne, the kind for African royalty or Black Panthers, legs kicked over the edge, feet in her unlaced army boots. "I've taken a lot of drugs. Methadone too." She scratched casually at old track marks trailing down the inside of her wrist.

"But not like that."

"No," she admitted. "Not like that."

"Do you know where Rabbit is?"

"He died." She didn't look at me. "Murdered, probably, house set on fire to cover it up."

"I didn't know."

"How could you? You weren't here. They didn't find who did it. But that's New Orleans."

The silence between us stretched out, moving from comfortable to something heavier and denser. I thought of the dry ice I used to bring home from the lab for Bridge, the viscosity of the furling clouds.

Finally I said: "I need it, Mina."

She laughed. "I know that song. Sung it myself about dope. You don't want to get addicted."

"The cancer is back. No one believes me, but it is. And I know, I *know,* if I can get back there, one of the others will be able to help me."

"And maybe I have babies. Maybe I'm married to someone else. Maybe. Maybe. Maybe." Each word like a kick.

"Do you have it?"

"Maybe it's dangerous. Maybe that's why Rabbit was killed. He said there was someone following him. He was always paranoid. Remember when he was convinced poor Travis was an undercover cop? But maybe this time he was right. Aren't a lot of Leftfielders left. Gobi died too—mugging or a gang fight. I don't know the details."

"I can pay you."

She got up, prowled over to the refrigerator. "I'm not a junkie. I don't need you to pay me. I have a job." She came back with the remains of a pizza. "Hmm. This barely qualifies as food. I'd cook for you, but it's late and I'm drunk."

"I'm lost," I said. "I'm dying."

"Aren't we all, Tic Tac?" She leaned forward to take my hair between her fingers. "You shouldn't cut it. It's beautiful. Look at these waves." She glanced over at Bridge, asleep on the couch, a little bundle of girl, all scrunched up under the blanket like a balled-up pair of socks. "What if you're wrong?" she asked. "If there's no answer for you on the other side?"

"Then I'll have tried. It's all we can do: try." I was drunk. "We're all we are and this is all there is and she's all I have."

"Yeah, yeah, all right. We both know that's not true." She stood up again, wobblier than before, and made her way very precisely to a glass medicine cabinet full of growing things, drooping ferns and philodendrons and other plants

I didn't know the names of. She opened the doors, reached behind the baboon skull and a bowlful of shells, and pulled out a roll of cheesecloth, the contents swaddled. She brought it over to me, her mouth twisted in the slightest sneer. I felt the air closing in, the aura of a seizure sun-haloing around my peripheral vision. *Not now*, I thought. *Not now*. Deep breaths. *Fight it off. Come back to yourself.*

She placed it in my hands and I unfurled the cloth. The cocoon had dwindled since I had last seen it. I remembered it being the size of a fat cucumber; now it was a spindly carrot.

"Where did you get it?" I asked, and she looked at me, bemused.

"You really don't know?"

"From Rabbit? Did he leave it with you?" I was confused.

That disbelieving smirk, a tinge of disgust. She shook her head. "He made it. He never showed you?"

"Does he grow it? Cook it?"

"Jo, forget it. Just take it, okay? I don't want it here. I don't want to be involved. That's behind me now. I don't want to know."

"Okay. Thank you. I can't. Not enough." I was crying. I could feel the cocoon's heat through the leather, like the heat of Bridge's head when she curled up in bed next to me, the furnace of her brain building synapses, sending signals for tissues and muscles and sinews to grow. She was stirring on the couch, sitting up.

"Mom?"

"Shhh," Mina said to me. "You're going to frighten your kid. Be careful with it. You be careful with you."

"I will," I said. "Thank you."

"I hope you know what you're doing."

"I don't. I really don't. But what choice do I have? I don't have a choice."

DOM

Good Hosts

They thought they were ready to believe, especially after the journals and the Haitian painting, but this feels like a cheap charade. They spend the first few minutes watching closely for this "magical transfer of consciousness," but Caden and Bridge are both sitting there on the couch, looking around at a reality only they can see, occasionally moving the controllers. Dom is going to feel very stupid if they have been suckered into a whole new conspiracy.

At least they found another diary: New Orleans, Part 2! Bridge is going to be pleased when she emerges from VR-land or, alternatively, an entirely different universe—the jury is still out-ish. They felt a twinge of guilt reading it without her, but there's so much to get through, especially with Jo's nearly illegible handwriting. It's prescreening, really. They've already marked up the notebook, added stickies to the important bits, like this guy Rabbit being murdered. That feels like a potentially bad thing.

They glance over at the test subjects, and they seem to be doing fine, so they settle down with a beer at the dining-room table and get out their iPad to do some extracurricular research. First up, Mr. Olivier St. Juste. But there's nothing under that name. No follow-up articles. No New York art scene info. Guess he didn't make it big after all. *Weird art* and *Haiti* brings up more on Atis Rezistans, which is completely fascinating, and they could spend hours perusing the pictures of giant rusted snakes twisting across the ground, scales made from ripped-up soda cans or plastic bottle caps. Welded abstracts of old plumbing and rubber, intensely creepy works incorporating plastic toys, like baby dolls and ponies, and one that is going to live in their nightmares—a grinning human skull emerging from black petals cut from a tire, screwed onto a bicycle seat with tufts of horsehair. But St. Juste's painting comes up again only once, like eight search pages in, and it links back to the original article. They'll have to keep digging.

A darker hole: Clicking through to the forums, both the obvious ones and the deeper, nastier hell pits. And there are Just. So. Many. Conspiracies about alternate universes and how to get there, people who feel displaced, along with more innocuous Hypefeed quizzes about *How do you know if you slipped into another reality?* Is it Berenstein Bears or Berenstain Bears, YouTube or YouVid? "Do you remember Nelson Mandela dying in prison?" Throw in a ton of quantum-mechanics explainer videos (on YouVid, thanks very much) and multiple-universe theories, deep dives into popular culture, Rick and Morty memes, superhero movies, and, surprisingly, way too many stories of transdimensional erotica, including a piece about twin-cest with your alternate-universe self.

There are documentaries and books on squatter culture in New York and London but almost nothing on New Orleans in the 1980s. Leftfield does not have a memorial page, and the only results on Checkit refer to soccer, grammar, and a techno band. Searching *Rabbit,* unsurprisingly, does not get them anywhere. They're just starting in on *Mina Remington* when someone taps them on the shoulder with bony deliberation.

"Holy crap! You scared the shit out of me. Don't do that!" they yelp at Bridge, who is holding the VR helmet dangling from one hand. But there's something different about her. The way she holds herself is straighter, stronger.

"Hello," she says in a voice subtly different, more certain. "I don't remember signing up for this. Can you end the experiment? I'd like to go back to the boat, please."

AMBER

Death Ripples

The wind is rustling in the reeds of the inlet, the water slap-slapping against the edge of the deck where Amber has pulled out the old rattan bench she picked up from the side of the road and scrubbed clean and left out in the sun and scrubbed again, because she knows the kind of things people get up to. She's wearing baggy shorts, a sleeveless T-shirt, the sun warm against her thinning hair.

Mr. Floof II is asleep in her lap, a small hot lump, paws twitching as he dreams. She's got a Bluetooth speaker on the deck beside her playing a podcast about the cult of Amway: how the founders made all that coin and then got involved in politicking. She doesn't like listening to music. It leaves her cold because of her work, reminds her too much of the Frequency Machine and all the effects it can have.

The podcast is called "The Dream," and that would be a nice dream, Amber thinks, to operate out in the open, recruit the people who need to be recruited. Like Amway, you got to buy in. But multilevel marketing ruins lives, and she saves them. Saves the whole damn world.

We all do. The voices in her head chime in, reproachful. Louder than usual with the fresh dose harvested from the boy's arms. Trees can talk to one another, Amber recently found out from another podcast, via chemical signals exchanged through the tangle of roots and mycelium in the soil. Probably there have been others like her (*us*) over the centuries. The worm must be ancient and terrible. But if there is a secret society, a reality-spanning agency of worm-killing Pinkertons, they haven't seen fit to bring her in to the program.

She's on her own. Except for all her others—the other Ambers across all the realities she can reach, a galaxy of voices. The Ourmind. All inextricably linked since what happened to Chris.

How many have they been through since then? The Dictator, of course, who stole Chris's life. The Disciple—the man who helped him do it and built the box. The artist in New York, who had friends he'd been sharing his precious gift with, all of whom needed to be taken care of, and, boy, was that a mess. The noodly British man who worked at the phone shop.

Some maybes she'd looked into, but they didn't go anywhere and she left them alone. "Don't go chasing anything into the swamp unless you really have to," Amber says to Mr. Floof II. Just because you get used to killing doesn't mean you have the appetite for it. She's not some kind of serial killer. Or only when she has to be. *When we all do.*

We are already hunting down the other iterations of Aiden, the others are telling her. *We have a name, his driver's license, date of birth.* That always makes it easier. Sometimes they'll be living in the same city, doing a similar job. *We will have to hunt them down, one by one, and exterminate them.* She gets no pleasure from this. It's an ugly job and a necessary one, and *We've seen what happens if we don't do it properly.*

In the reeds, a belted kingfisher is clutching sidesaddle to a stem that dips and sways. Its head doesn't move, intent on a fish in the water. Amber is intent too—watching the police car turn down the dirt road that leads to her house. There is a flutter of unease among the voices in her head. *What do they want? Why are they here? We've made a mistake.*

Relax, she thinks back into the Ourmind. It's unfortunate but not unexpected, and she knows how to put on an innocent act, like a certain little dog who has absolutely no knowledge of that chewed-up slipper she found under the couch.

"We've got visitors, my boy." She gently pushes him off her lap. The kingfisher left while she wasn't paying attention. Flew off with prey in its beak, leaving only death ripples. Pity—she always likes to see the bird in action.

She's holding Mr. Floof II in her arms when she opens the door to the officers. He snarls, and she tells them not to mind him, he only thinks he's a big dog, and don't they want to come inside? She doesn't get a lot of folks willing to drive all the way out here.

"That won't be necessary," the male officer says. He has acne scars over his ruddy cheeks and he compensates by puffing out his chest like a rooster. His partner is a petite dark-haired woman who lets him talk. She's the one to watch; not a lot to say, but *looking* with intent.

Amber is relieved she doesn't know either of them. She's been careful not to let anyone in this small community know she's a former cop, former vet. Retired from the force five years ago, and a whole state over, never one for staying in touch, all that social media guff, she claims. The truth is she only uses it for hunting.

"Is it a speeding ticket?" As if she would be that stupid. "I don't drive much now, but I used to be a speed racer back in my day. Had a cute set of wheels, an old Mini Cooper." Just a lonely lady rambling. Move along, Officers.

"It's a possible homicide," he says. "We're making inquiries door to door. Checking if anyone's seen anything."

"Oh no. That's bad news—was it someone local?"

"You know, I *could* do with a glass of water," the woman says, glancing past her into the house.

"Of course," Amber says. "Come in, sit, make yourselves comfy."

Lady cop is taking it all in—not that there's much to see. Amber is careful. There's no indication of what she gets up to here. It's neat and anonymous, like her van, which is out of sight in the garage, thank you. The plastic-wrapped couch is spotless, the Frequency Machine and the instruments of Extraction have all been put away, as have the pull-up backdrop for filming her videos, the wig, her goofy sweaters. She is particular about keeping her online identity separate from her real one.

The woman fingers the petals of one of the silk flowers in a vase on the dining-room table.

"Pottery Barn," Amber offers, pouring two glasses from the filter jug in the refrigerator. "Outlet. It's so much cheaper. I also picked up the baskets there." She nods at the trio of woven baskets on the mantel above the fireplace. They remind her of birds' nests.

"Looks so real," says the cop, taking the glass and sitting down beside her partner on the couch where not even twenty-four hours ago Aiden was screaming, with golden threads worming their way out from under his skin to the tune of the Frequency Machine. She raises the glass. "Thank you."

Amber takes a seat on the stuffed chair opposite, nests Mr. Floof II in her lap. He grumbles and settles, and she folds his ears between her fingers, the velvet pink. He's already dozing off, poor thing. He's getting old. She doesn't like to think about it.

Rooster cop is all business. "Like I said, we're looking into a possible homicide." He pauses for dramatic effect. "A hand has washed up."

"A hand? A human hand?" Amber leans forward, flares her nostrils, playing the nosy neighbor, eager for a little juicy gossip, especially if it's gory. "Oh no. That's terrible. That's downright gruesome. I don't want to ask about the details..." Leaving a dangling pause for them to offer them up like appetizers. But they don't take the bait, too professional. "No, don't tell me. I don't want to imagine." Said with Puritan relish. "The crabs." She shudders. "Do you know who it was?"

"We're still trying to get an ID, looking into missing-persons reports, new indigents in the area." He says something else, but she doesn't hear it, because something has happened. Beyond this room and this house, out past Florence and the state. *Out there.*

Mr. Floof II's paws are twitching. His lip curls back and he utters a series of high-pitched yips, as if he feels it too. Or maybe he's reacting to her, the way she's suddenly sitting upright, like a rebar has been stuck down her spine, her muscles all tensed, and the skin crawling on her forearms. She rubs at them to cover the thin veins writhing beneath the surface. Like calls to like, especially after her fresh dose, the dead boy's harvest.

Someone's here. Where they shouldn't be. Starbursts across reality. Death ripples.

Where is this coming from?

Consternation.

Another one.

Already?

And then it's gone. She keeps rubbing her arms. Hopes the cops haven't noticed. But why would they care?

"Gives me the shivers thinking about it," she says,

glancing down at her sunbeaten skin, the wrinkles on her hands, dusted with age spots and freckles she needs to get a dermatologist to check out—but her body is her own again. Nothing stirs beneath her skin. She could disregard it as an aberration. An anomaly. If she hadn't spent half her damn life, *every life*, watching for it.

"You all right there?" Lady cop says.

Careful, now.

I know! She snaps back. *She* is the one who has to get involved, help out the others when mistakes are inevitably made or the work is too overwhelming. *Don't try and tell me.*

"I'm thinking what a waste. What a terrible waste of a human being. I saw a lot of that in Desert Storm, you know."

The guy cop raises his eyebrows, a twitch of disrespect. She has to lean in to it. Sloppy to have said anything, she berates herself. Out of practice.

"Only in the canteen," Amber says, as in behind the lines, serving up slop to the *real soldiers*. "But we still saw those body bags piling up, day after day. And I know, I know, they were fighting for freedom. It's still a waste. A tragedy. You never get used to it, do you?"

"Well, ma'am..." Acne in Chief says.

"Maybe *you* do, Officers. I don't envy you your line of work. Not one bit. And you know"—she lowers her voice, tutting—"now *drug traffickers* are using these waterways. Up and down the Pee Dee. Used to be the only problems around here was someone's pet python got out or a gator grabbed someone's dog. Don't worry, I keep a close eye on my baby here." She pats Mr. Floof II. "Is it drugs? Fentanyl is such a problem now. I thought heroin was bad. But fentanyl!"

"We really couldn't say. Have you seen anything like that? Strangers? Suspicious activity? Maybe you heard boats running at night?"

"I sleep pretty heavy." She mimes glugging from a bottle. "But I'll keep an eye out. It's drug runners, isn't it? They do that, I heard a podcast about it. I like the true-crime ones. They said the cartels cut off body parts to teach their rivals a lesson. Do you think it's the cartels all the way out here?"

"I don't think you have to worry about the cartels, ma'am. Probably someone got drunk, fell overboard," the woman says.

"Well, that wouldn't surprise me neither. People get to be so reckless with their lives. Is it . . . only the hand?"

"All that's washed up so far, ma'am." They're getting up to leave.

"Are you sure I can't fix you some iced tea?"

"We're all right," he says. "You call down at the station if you think of anything." He goes to shake her hand. "And thank you for your service."

She's willing them out, but lady cop has spotted the photo on the refrigerator. "This from your time in the army?" With luck she doesn't know enough to tell a grunt's uniform from a Marine's.

"My buddy Chris and me," Amber says. It was stupid to leave it up, but she doesn't have visitors—or only ones who won't have anything to say about it once she's through with them. "We served together, but he died. Afterward. Not on active duty."

Don't talk too much. That's how you get caught.

"And what happened to your leg?"

She's wearing shorts. Should have pulled on sweatpants. "Car accident," Amber says. She's already flown too close to the truth. An alligator bite makes her more memorable. She shouldn't have said anything about being in the army. "Rolled my Mini. Damn fool thing to do."

The lady cop echoes the glug-glug-glug gesture Amber made earlier.

"No, oh no. I don't drink and drive. Other guy went too fast around a blind corner."

"Lucky," the cop says. "You being a speed racer and all."

"God was looking out for me that day. And every day." Pulling out the big guns. She hasn't believed in a Father up above since she first encountered the worm and all its atrocities. "You want, I can pray for you and that poor dead man in the swamp."

"Appreciate that, ma'am," lady cop says. And that's the end of that.

But while she's watching them driving away, the Ourmind is in uproar. It's a fever ripping through them. Another childhood memory, lying in the dark, burning up, the pressure in her head that turned out to be encephalitis. They had survived all that. They would survive this too.

They didn't see, she assures them. *And even if they did, who would believe this? Besides, we have business to get to. This new arrival. So close behind the other one. It's likely that they know each other.*

A Nest.

An Infestation.

BRIDGE

No Place Like

Back. In her own body, soft and pinchable. The buzzing resolves into the crackle of cicadas in the trees. The faint scent of jasmine, the distant sound of a motorcycle, a familiar voice, although she can't make out the words just yet. She's not on a boat. But also not on the couch where she left herself. She's in the backyard on a peeling wooden bench. Caden is beside her, holding a beer. She has a glass of water in her hand. Slo-mo surfacing attention, like coming up from sleeping pills. Dom is midsentence, jittery, talking too fast.

"Vaccine mandates, everyone masked the hell up, President Harris took it really seriously. The whole pandemic was over and done with in six months."

Caden jerks to his feet, slopping pale ale. "Why are we outside?"

"Oh, thank God." Dom sags with relief. "You're back."

Caden sits down and leans forward, intense. "You were supposed to keep them in the room. I was specific! You said you were going to take this seriously."

"They didn't like it," Dom says. "I wasn't going to keep them prisoner. We came out here, had a beer and a chat. It was revealing."

"What did you tell them?" Caden demands.

"Well, *Aiden*—which I guess is close enough to Caden—thought it was a dream and that he'd been here before. Carpenter, makes furniture, although he used to play in a band. He wanted to hear your music. He was pretty chill, but Bridget Two, Bridgette, was more freaked, because she was last on her boat, sailing around the world with her boyfriend. Ben? Brett? They're filming it for YouTube, which is like YouVid, but with no moderating or fact-checking. Total free-for-all."

"You *told* them they were in another reality?"

"Showed them the dreamworm, tried to cover all the stuff you'd said about consciousness patterns lining up, like turning over cards to find matching pairs. Is that a good analogy? Because it felt right when I said it. Do you know they have a new cold war going on, along with multiple pandemics? For years now. They're on their sixth booster shots, flare-ups every few months and everyone having to mask up again. But we have a lot in common too: Britney, Lin-Manuel Miranda, electric cars. All the good things."

"You showed it to them. Shit." Caden stands up to pace the garden. "Shit. *Shit.* How could you do that? No one is supposed to know." There is the faintest crack—a snail shell breaking under the weight of his shoe, its whole world collapsed, just like that, leaving a smear of gray sludge behind on the grass. He doesn't even notice. "You asshole," he snarls.

"Hey!" Bridge shouts. "Don't talk to them like that."

"You asshole." He gets right up in Dom's face. "You don't know what you've done."

"Cabrón, your invitation to be on this property has just been revoked." Dom stands and reaches for the back of his neck to scruff-march him out, but Caden ducks away.

"I'm sorry, but—"

"Get the hell out of here. Vámonos."

"Bridget," he says, and he seems abruptly shabby in his self-righteousness. "You don't know how serious this is. If your mom were here—"

"But she's not," she says, icy as that shower a whole lifetime and two out-of-bodies ago.

A complicated look crosses his face that she can't figure out; it shifts into contrition. "I'm sorry." He shakes his head. "Let's all take some time to calm down."

"Only one yelling and swearing here is you," Dom says, sitting.

"You're right. I apologize. Unreservedly. I'll go. But can we talk later? Please? There are things I need to tell you, things that your mom wanted you to know."

"Oh, now he wants to tell us," Dom sneers.

"Everyone is taking a time-out," Bridge says like they are little kids, just as badly behaved—and yeah, she twigs that Caden's being manipulative, and she doesn't like it either. She puts her glass down on the bench. "We will reconvene later."

"All I ask." He gives a regretful half-smile as Dom stands up, ready to follow him inside. "Don't worry. I'll let myself out."

Dom takes up a guard-dog position, leaning against the kitchen door so they can see all the way through the house to the front door. Bridge feels clumsy, not yet fully in her body, and she accidentally knocks the water glass over. It shatters on the ground.

"Let me." Dom comes to help her.

"No, it's okay. I'm used to picking up the pieces. This is my life now."

It's not, though. Not anymore. She has other lives. She's been inside them. She is *this* girl—with her friend remonstrating with her not to cut herself—and somewhere else, she is a woman with two small children in a mountain town, and also a sailor babe with tattoos on a yacht, and who knows how many others. Is it infinite? All the possibilities, all the other directions, the choices, a million-million choices open and waiting for her.

Until now, decisions have always felt like a trap.

This path branches only this way, and halfway along you realize it's not the direction you wanted to go, so you have to double back, and double back again, but each time you return to the crossroads, you've added new failures, so when you set off again, you're trailing all the baggage of your previous aborted choices, like a just-married car festooned with tin cans and junk. It bogs you down, gets tangled in the tires. And what's the point of a business degree when capitalism is the worst? How do you know when you should break up with someone? Why does it feel like everyone else seems to know where to go, what to do, who to be with? Certainty has always been a foreign language to her. Habla "lost and afraid"?

Dom is back with an empty shoebox to put the broken glass in and a handheld mini-vac they have found somewhere.

"Thank you."

"Cabrón left his beer. You want it?"

"No. I feel like there's too much whirl in my head already." She pours it onto the grass. Maybe also in tribute to the dead snail. She tries to sense if there are ghost thoughts lurking, traces of another mind inhabiting her. "Thanks for looking after us."

"No sweat," Dom says. "The transfer students were very nice. That's what I'm calling them."

"The otherselves."

"Better. They were also very confused, the otherselves— and very convincing."

"Not like Couch God, then?"

"Not even a little bit. I did appreciate that neither of them tried to attack me."

"Was Bridgette—my otherself—okay? Not scared or upset?"

"Yeah, she was fine, she treated it like a confusing dream. She seemed very practical."

"Do you think... she liked me? My life?"

"We didn't get into it. Did you like her?"

"It was amazing, Dom. I can't describe it. You have to do it."

"No. One hundred percent absolutely not. It's wild and dangerous and we don't understand it."

"Isn't that a reason to try, for science?"

"I think you were incredibly lucky. And I don't think you should do it again. For science or any other reason."

"Yeah, lucky I didn't have to do any actual sailing. I might have broken the boat."

"No, lucky that you transferred into Bridget Two on a yacht in the Med and not into the migrant version of you fleeing a war zone on a sinking dinghy without enough life vests. How do you know who you're going to trade places with? How do you know you're not going to die in there?"

"You're being dramatic," Bridge says. "It's only twenty minutes."

"All it takes is a second. Wrong place, wrong time. You don't know what's on the other side."

"I need to know where Jo went, what she was looking for. Caden is a dumbass, but he might actually know."

"It sounds like your mom went all over the place before she died. How is that going to help you? Going to all the universes Caden said they coded? For what?"

Caden's words. *She was afraid of leaving you behind.* He'd said she was afraid of dying, but what if it meant something else?

All those trips when she was a kid, Jo had promised her they'd be together.

"Maybe she's alive," Bridge says. It comes out in a rush, the suspicion she's been carrying inside her for two days now. "In one of them."

Dom is exasperated. "But that's not your mom. It's the other Bridge's. I know you want closure, but hijacking someone's life to talk to not-your-Jo is not going to be the catharsis you want. What if she's a better parent? Or a worse one? How is that going to make you feel? That painting by the Haitian artist all tangled up in the dreamworm, the blur of his head... do you want that to happen to you? Metaphorically, obviously. Although, heck, we don't know what this thing is, how it works; it might be literal too. Your head spins off, I'm gonna be so mad."

"She didn't know me at the end. What if she was someone else? Caught in the mind-swap." *You're not my daughter.*

"That is a horrifying idea. That's the worst thing I've ever heard. That you can get stuck? You should burn that thing. Now you know it's real. You're not crazy. I know you're not crazy. So this is when we should walk away."

"This could change the world."

"Or bring it all crashing down. It's like you've never read a comic book or watched a movie." A tut of impatience and then they soften. "Mainly, I don't want you to get hurt. In principle, this is all so damn cool, big mystery, other dimensions, a hidden reality that lies beneath and folded all around ours. But... your mom died, baby girl. None of this changes that."

They wrap her in their arms and she leans in to them.

"Maybe you're right."

"I'm always right. By the way, I did some digging around the internet and I have more reading material for you. And I found Jo's diary about your trip to New Orleans, put it aside for you. Rabbit's dead. They found his body cut into pieces. Happened years ago, but still, I want it noted for the record. I also want to try and track down Jo's friend Mina Remington, and I'm going to go through the New Orleans murder reports and cold-case forums to find out exactly what happened to Rabbit."

"I just don't think this is relevant." Irritated. Bridge knows this isn't where the answers lie. The way Jo turned to face the wall.

I don't know you.

And yes, it's too awful to contemplate that maybe an otherself Jo might have been the one accidentally dying in that hospital bed. But isn't it worse that her mom might be trapped somewhere out there? Lost. Alone. Unable to find her way back because there's nowhere to come back to.

Why did she leave the dreamworm for Bridge to find? And where the fuck are those instructions?

Grief is a process of letting go, but what if you don't have to? What if you shouldn't? She needs to go back. Now, or as soon as possible. She doesn't know how to explain the urgency to Dom, the *need.*

"The point is we don't know," Dom says, still trying to make their case, not privy to the turmoil in her head. "Can you...wait? A moment. Hold off on the consciousness flips until we know more. Do more detective work, not fieldwork. Please?"

They look so worried. She doesn't want to lie to them.

"For now," Bridge says soothingly. Already planning to phone Caden and arrange the next trip and the next and the next. However many it takes to find Jo. If she's out there. Big fucking *if.* But if there's any possibility, any at all, how can she not try?

Jo's Diary

June 20, 2022

Stasia said it's not my fault, but she was shaking with anger and desperation and exhaustion, and I remember someone saying that to me before and not meaning it then, either. Because I *am* crazy.

"But I had to try. I had to. I don't want to die. I don't have to die."

"You don't want to *live*," Stasia said. "Not here, not now, not with me." She was sobbing, and I wanted to put my arms around her, but she turned and walked away. The gray coming through her auburn hair, like a fox's fur, makes her more beautiful than she's ever been to me, even angry, even disappointed.

"I do," I said, "I do. You know I do. We're glorious together. I love you." I teared up, "I didn't know I could feel like this. How many times have I told you that?" A terrible cliché, the middle-aged woman stumbling into her bisexuality, but the past three years with Stasia... I tried to take her hands, make her look at me. But my arms won't do what I need them to do these days, the telescoping is back on the one side, the seizures, the halo around my vision. My own personal aurora borealis. Three months, the doctors say, if I'm lucky. "I only want you, doofus. The life we've built together."

"And you blew it up overnight." Stasia starbursts her

hands. "Boom." Every word she said burned into my brain, poor wrecked thing that it is. "I know it's not you. I know it's the tumor. But how could you do this to me? To us?"

"I didn't know it was a scam! I was robbed. It's not my fault." But whose was it, then? Enough of the important bits are still working for me to know that I was so desperate I sent the man in Ushuaia a photograph of the painting from Haiti. And he sent me back a doctored image, close enough to be convincing. I should have gone back to Port-au-Prince, where I'd found it before, rather than chasing shadows in Argentina.

"Eighty thousand dollars, Jo." As if I didn't know the number I'd withdrawn from our joint account, the teller at the bank asking, "Are you *sure* you want that in cash?" I also knew it wasn't the money. Not really.

A lot of it *was* the money. It was a lot of money. "I know. I know, it is my fault and I'm sorry, but if I can find it, if I can just find it, everything will be different."

Stasia was pacing the kitchen, opening drawers. She turned, holding a spatula, and waved it at me. "I don't want to fucking hear it, Jo. It doesn't exist. It never did." She realized she was wielding a plastic instrument and put it back, slammed the drawer.

"What are you looking for?" I said, but she ignored me, walking back down the corridor, past the shelves lined with our books, the paper proof of our entanglement, of our minds, the beloved texts that lived inside us. We had a ritual where she read me poetry on the porch at night with gin and tonics with mint from our garden: Anne Carson and Koleka Putuma, because I was a heathen, knew only the ones I'd studied in high school.

She started taking books down, filling her arms. I thought she might throw them at me.

"What are you doing?"

"You've told yourself this ridiculous story your whole life, Jo, and I treated it like it was an adorable eccentricity, your delusions, your mad adventures."

We were supposed to go on more adventures together. We'd gone to Copenhagen and Reykjavik two years ago. We were talking about going to Cape Town next October to visit Will Cunningham, a colleague I'd met at the conference in Hydra; he'd offered us a guest room in his house at the beach. Then came the diagnosis.

I could have sold her on Argentina: one last trip, salsa dancing, tapas, paying homage to Borges and walking the labyrinthine dream streets of his Buenos Aires. I could have spared her the details, waited until I got there to confirm it was the real deal. But even if I had, she would have balked at the critical moment, handing over eighty thousand dollars for the dreamworm.

So I went in the middle of the day, when I was supposed to be teaching my class, even though the university had offered compassionate leave, reduced my hours. Went straight to the bank, then on to the airport before she could notice the money was gone.

Portland to LA to Buenos Aires, wearing sunglasses on the plane as if I were on the run, but it was because of the light, which was making my headaches worse, the halo always with me. I stayed overnight in Buenos Aires in a tiny hotel with a balcony looking out over Recoleta Cemetery, tombs and crypts and statues, which reminded me of walking through another city of the dead in New Orleans with Bridge, and wasn't this a sign that I was on the right track? The parallels in my story—parallel experiences, parallel lives. Boarding a tiny plane to Ushuaia, southernmost city in the world, gateway to the Tierra del Fuego, to Antarctica—and an ex-CIA operative, he claimed, who said he had the dreamworm.

I took a taxi through the town, ramshackle and cheerful with backpackers' lodges and cold-weather-gear shops catering to the skiers and snowboarders and Antarctic tourists. The tallest building in the town was a giant cruise ship, bright white as an iceberg against the ocean. Performers juggled machetes at the traffic lights, which creeped me out. I found my way to the hotel the seller had recommended, a brutalist structure high on a hill overlooking the ocean, surrounded by snow-draped forests. I felt sick as I handed over a fortune in pesos for the night, in cash, so there wouldn't be a record. Still trying to hide it from Stasia. I didn't want her to find me, to phone me, to try to talk me out of it. Rash decisions and rushed ones. I hadn't even looked at the prices, hadn't realized it was a five-star outfit. Idiot.

Bertie Delinois was sitting by the fireplace in a large leather chair in front of the huge windows overlooking a snowy forest. He stood up to meet me—wrestler physique with a squat face beneath a blue Yankees cap.

"Julia?" I'd given him a fake name. More subterfuge. As if this were a ward against him lying to me in return. "Good to meetcha." He pumped my hand, squeezing too hard. "Thought you'd be hungry, so I ordered a little something."

A plate of tapas, bread and sausage and empanadas. Two glasses of wine. I shuddered to think how much that was going to cost me. The gambler's dilemma: too invested to leave now. He'd told me something had "gone bad" on an operation, and he could never go back to the U.S.; too dangerous for him and his wife and his two kids, but he still had some old contacts, there were still people who needed his services. He'd evacuated a lot of people from dangerous situations along with their valuables, and it turned out he had an eye for hard-to-get antiquities and collector's items.

Bertie said he'd gotten the caterpillar from a Dutch guide,

Noor de Jong, who was working the tourist boats—the smaller ones, not the giant cruise liners. She took the guests on excursions onto the ice for hiking or into the bay to see the whales. It came up out of the ice, in the thaw, and that's how she found it. She could have given it to any number of scientists, but she knew there were private collectors who would pay for artifacts, peculiar lichens, interesting fossils. I should have known that was bullshit, but it was just credible enough. The world is strange and full of secrets. And I wanted to believe. It *could* have come up in the thaw. An old infection from someone who worked in Antarctica, maybe on one of the original sealing vessels, or maybe the dreamworm has been around for millions of years, some ancient fruit from the swampy jungle that made up Antarctica or the giant mushroom forests that came before. Maybe that's what Mina meant when she said Rabbit made it. Grew it from millennia-old seeds.

Bertie was supposed to bring it with him, but he hadn't. He said Noor wanted to meet me, half of it was going to her, after all, and he wanted to show me it was legitimate, that he wasn't trying to screw anyone over. He'd arranged for a taxi back to his house for us; we could have wine, share stories, his wife would cook dinner.

I protested. I really wasn't interested. He got Noor on a video call to talk to me, to reassure me. She was jaunty and cheerful, holding up the specimens for me to see. "I can't wait to meet you," she said. I was overwhelmed. I wasn't thinking. The light was too bright through those huge windows. The tingles were running up my arm, fizzing in every nerve ending. I got in the taxi with my bag. With all the money. Like a fucking idiot.

They threw me out on the side of the road, Bertie and the taxi driver, in the cold, three miles from town. There was no license plate. All I had was e-mails, a grainy photograph of a specimen supposedly dragged from the ice, and the names Bertie and Noor.

The van full of snowboarders passing by stopped to pick me up, and when they took me to the police station, the cops shrugged. The security footage from the hotel showed only a big man wearing a baseball cap. The taxi didn't have a license plate, wasn't a taxi at all, in fact. None of the ships in town had a Noor on their crew list.

I couldn't bear to phone Stasia or Bridge. How shameful. How stupid. How typical. In desperation, I e-mailed one of the neuro grad students, Tendayi Kandera. I'd assisted with her application for a study visa, which involved whole mountain ranges of paperwork because she was from Zimbabwe via the University of Cape Town—a favor for my old pal, Will Cunningham, who had been supervising her research. So it felt like I could ask for a weird favor.

She thought it was a scam at first, one of those Lifebook hacks where people claim to have been robbed and *Help, please wire money.* But I didn't need cash. I needed someone adept at searches to find Noor for me.

That only made it worse. Because Noor was a real young woman in Coevorden in the Netherlands who makes videos on a website called TenTen: *Let our experts produce original custom content for ten dollars!* An American man paid her fifty dollars in Ethereum (Tendayi had to explain that this was one of the cryptocurrencies) for that phone call and to hold up a glass slide with dead earthworms and a yellow filter. She'd never been to Argentina or Antarctica, although she rode a barge once. It was far from the weirdest request she'd ever had—"Usually it's sex stuff." She charged me ten dollars to take my video call, then cut me off when I started yelling about reporting her to the police for being complicit in a robbery.

"You sound like a very stupid woman, you know?" Noor said, bored, before she hung up. "I think you deserve this."

All of that Stasia would have forgiven, I think—the squandered money, what that meant for our future (considering I didn't even have one, not without the dreamworm)—if I hadn't lied to her, hadn't disappeared without telling her. The unbearable cruelty of letting her worry. Of having to hear that I'd been punched in the side of the head, thrown out of a car, robbed on a foreign continent only after the Ushuaia cops arranged for me to call her from the station.

I was trying to make it right; if she'd only listen. But she dumped the books on the bed, started pulling clothes out of the wardrobe.

"I know, I know, please. Don't go. I can find it, I've got other leads to follow—"

Stasia screamed then, in frustration and fury. A long howl of agony. I was so shocked, I sat down on the floor. Sparkles all down my arm, little tics.

"No!" She noticed I was about to have a seizure. "Don't you dare. Not now. Don't make me feel sorry for you."

"I can't help it. Emotional upset..." I was breathing deep, trying to get it under control.

She sat down next to me, held me. "I can't do this. It's bad enough being here while you...die." She could barely say the word. "But I can't watch you destroy yourself."

I wrapped my arms around her, feeling my bones against her soft abundance of health. She was crying again, and I clung to her and kissed her hair. The sparkles were fading. A reprieve. Love conquered all, even seizures. Not for long, though; love was a salve, not a cure. And there was a cure...

I knew I shouldn't have said it. I knew what she wanted me to say, my love sobbing against my chest: *Okay, you're right. I'll let it go. I'll die quietly and politely, like a good girl.* But instead: "I don't have to die, if you'd listen, there's this man in Sacramento—"

She pulled away, face twisted with hurt, and then a coldness set in, an Antarctic chill, if you will, that I'd never seen before. Not even in our worst arguments.

"You're lost in this thing, Jo. Maybe you always have been."

DOM

Big Bird

The buildings down this side of Martin Luther King Boulevard are all brand-new constructions designed for the creative-class up-and-comers to live and work and play, uniform glass and steel with bold pops of color. One standout has a mural of abstract florals across the entire facade. There are ground-floor coffee shops bursting with plants, and outdoor hangout areas with twisty benches and bike racks and a dog park. Of course Caden would live here. Hipster terrariums. This thought was followed immediately by the grudging admission *It does look kinda nice. A way for young people to have a community when village life is dead.* Followed by the counterpoint: *If you have money.*

Which brings them right back around to the tent cities, which are the egalitarian version, if only they had proper facilities like, oh, say, a sewer system and running water. These would be good observations to make in their internship interview with the architect next week, assuming they don't get worm-napped.

A slow start today, it's already lunch time and they've made sandwiches to go. Bridge is rereading the last journal entry—the one in which Jo went to the man to find the worm to open the doors and betrayed her girlfriend and lost her cash and came back empty-handed. Worst nursery rhyme ever.

"Another reference to Haiti," Bridge notes. "'Gone back to Port-au-Prince where I'd found it before.' Definitely the important section we're missing." She is writing bullet points in Dom's notebook, and they're trying not to wince at her untidy scrawl as they focus on looking for parking.

"Who is the man in Sacramento?" Bridge underlines it in the notebook. Too hard.

"She didn't mention him?" Dom puts the Grand Am in reverse and steers it backward into the tightest parking bay of all time in a delicate eight-point maneuver.

"Not to me. Maybe to Stasia. Or this grad student, Tendayi. Jo seems to have been a big fan of hers." Jealousy spikes her tone. Jo's students got only the good parts of her.

"Or to Caden," Dom says. "I suspect there's a whole bunch of intel he's not sharing, and I hate that he's the one with the music and video codes."

"The doors," Bridge corrects. "We haven't told him everything we know either."

"He's not the bereaved daughter who deserves answers," Dom says. Although they're worried that maybe Bridge doesn't. Not at this cost, stealing moments from people's lives, borrowing their bodies without permission.

Dom gets out and looks up at Caden's building, which is especially soulless. To call it *spartan* would be a disservice to that ancient warrior people, because surely even those proto–Marie Kondos had *some* sense of aesthetic. Blond concrete with black aluminum-frame windows, all alike, but you *know* it's cool because the right corner of the building is marked with a fade of red stripes and interlocking yellow triangles, like a skater T-shirt design from the early nineties.

They have to sign in with security, a woman with fantastically impractical long spangled nails and enviable ennui. She points a webcam at them and awards them with visitor stickers.

"We look like the first characters to die in a webcam horror movie," Dom jokes, admiring the jaggedy printouts of their faces stuck to their T-shirts.

"Yeah," Bridge says, distracted. They tried to convince her to come along to talk to the grad student, Tendayi, which is their next stop. A small delay, sure, but more information-gathering. But Bridge refused, focused on going back. An intensity has descended over her, and that last line of the Argentina diary entry is worrying Dom: *You're lost in this thing.*

The elevator doors close, revealing that they're mirrored, a thousand Doms and Bridges looking back at them with some garbage motivational words laser-etched into the glass: *Being is presence.* Pretentious and impenetrable. Fuck, they hate these kinds of places.

Caden is waiting for them, looking hangdog. He's wearing a knit hat low over his eyebrows, tufts of hair sticking out. His eyes are Buscemi-esque today, pouchy and forlorn. "Thanks for this," he says.

"Thank you for agreeing to babysit me," Bridge says.

Coño, they wish there were a better plan. But divide and conquer. If he lets anything happen to her…

His apartment is a geek den of musical instruments, from a keytar to violins and a sitar, which they know well by now (*Thanks, Jo*), and others they don't know the names for, all fighting for real estate with laptops and monitors and a death trap of black cables coiling across the floor. An echo of the red and yellow motif is painted above the couch, mostly hidden by DIY foam soundproofing and the huge speakers triangulated to face the desk. The white roller blinds are pulled all the way down, gray nothingness over the windows.

"Is that my mom's?" Bridge points to a zoetrope perched on a bookshelf cobbled together from yellow plastic crates and bare wooden boards stacked on cardboard boxes frothing with more cables.

"One of hers," Caden says. "We were using it as a base model to calculate the patterning to simulate the particular brain waves—gamma, I think."

Dom spots a narrow wooden box polished to a satin sheen and sprouting two antennas like a Cold War–era radio. They can't help themselves and dainty-step between the snarls of cables to reach it. "You have a theremin!"

"Do you play?" Caden leans over and turns the wooden knob with a satisfying click.

"Always wanted to." They swerve their hand over the instrument, summoning an electronic ghost orchestra from thin air.

Caden blinks, pleased, throws them a bone. "I reacted badly yesterday and I want to apologize."

"No, it's cool. I broke the rules." Dom conducts their hand over the theremin, and the lament of spectral violins moves in sway. "But it made me wonder if anyone else knows about this, could be looking for it?" Watching Caden for a twitch of anxiety, realization, but he's shaking his head.

"Me and Jo, obviously, and now you and the alters you told yesterday."

"Otherselves," Bridge says, and they can all hear the weight of the rightness. "Hey, can we skip the VR this time? I think it's more ethical if we tell them what's going on. Now that we've already broken the seal of discretion."

"That's not how Jo did it," he says unhappily, "but I'm happy to go with whatever makes you feel comfortable."

"You said there were things that she wanted me to know?"

"It was about what she was doing. All those trips. She said she was trying to find the—"

"Cure."

"Solution, I was going to say. She said she was doing it for you."

"*Solution* sounds very final." The theremin wails, accusatory. "Did Jo ever mention her friend Rabbit?" Dom asks. "Murdered in New Orleans."

Caden leans down and flips the switch, and the theremin dies mid-warble. "Never heard of him. She only ever talked about her daughter. And her girlfriend, once or twice, saying that maybe they'd been able to make it work in some other universe. Who's this Rabbit guy?"

Bridge ignores Dom's warning glare. "It's the man who introduced her to the dreamworm back in the eighties. We found her journals."

"Does she say where he got it from?"

"Haven't gotten to that chapter yet."

"If you need help reading..." he offers.

Dom cuts that off at the knees. "I already portioned out doses for you. We have only so much, so here's enough threads to get you through the day. You sure you're okay to babysit Bridge? You're not going to abandon her to go on your own missions?"

"That was the deal. Again, I'm really sorry..."

Dom waves it away as if they've already forgotten about it. They have not. They despise him, and this trendy zero-personality apartment, and how he's snaking his way into the middle of this; he's holding things back, they're sure of it. But what can you do? Bridge is determined. They reach into their backpack and hand over a small Ziplock bag taken from Jo's kitchen. Ten strands, already cut to length. The main spindle is in the Tupperware in their bag. "I wasn't sure if you needed a fresh dose for every switch?"

"One dose lasts two, three hours," he says. "So it depends on how hard you're pushing."

"Not too hard, Bridge. Comprende? I'll be back in a couple of hours and I'll take over babysitting. Have fun with the parallel-universe-jumping, kids. Don't get murdered."

BRIDGE

Falling Off a Horse

You find yourself standing outside a school. You can tell by the shrieks of kids from the playground and also the sign on the gate that reads CHANNINGSWORTH ELEMENTARY and the banner beneath which reads SUMMER DAY CAMP. Which means you're a parent, and these others, waiting here with you, all standing slightly apart, are probably parents too. They are mostly older, and they have better shoes than your scuffed-up Doc Martens and are dressed like proper grown-ups.

The high pitch of the bell blasts across the intercom, and moments later the doors swing wide, and a woman stands aside for the spill of children, and, oh, shit, how are you supposed to identify which ones are yours?

It's a moot question because someone barrels into you, clings to your legs. "Upya, upya," the girl says, dark hair and your eyes, and initially it sounds like a foreign language, but her grasping hands and outstretched arms make it clear that you're supposed to pick her up. So you do, and, hoping you're doing the right thing, you swing her around. She is heavier than you'd expect, and the heat of her as she nuzzles into your neck is deeply shocking. Or it's the humanness of her, the deep DNA chime of *mine*, even though you've never met her before. Not counting that time outside the supermarket. The first world you went to, the first file on Jo's computer.

"Oof," you declare, to have something to say. "You're getting so heavy." She giggles and squirms and flops loose against you. You notice a long thin scar along your arm as you set her down. A break from a long time ago, and this feels familiar.

"Like Mixy," she says. "The heaviest cat in the worrrrrld."

"Where's your brother?" That's right, isn't it? A little boy, you remember from the last time. And what are you supposed to do with them, where are you supposed to go? It wasn't this complicated when you were a kid.

"I miss Mixy!" says the girl. "Why can't we go back and get her?"

"You know why," you try, fishing.

"Because she's sick." The little girl pouts. "And Daddy had to stay behind to look after her."

"Where's your brother?"

"I'm a cat like Mixy Minxy Manx. I only speak cat. Meow."

"Okay, meow," you say, exasperated, lost, the little girl weighing heavy in your arms, and you wish you had the biceps of Sailor Bridgette right now. "But do we need to wait for him?"

"Meow, meow, meow, meow," she chants happily and thuds her head into you, like a nuzzling cat, only she does it too enthusiastically, and her skull is astoundingly hard when it cracks against your cheekbone.

"Ow."

"Me-*ow*," she says back and goes for another thudding nuzzle. You try to lower her gently, but she is meowing and shaking her head and it's impossible.

"Hi, Mom!" Someone takes your fingers and gives them a little pull, and you look down to see the boy. Your boy? Yes, almost certainly, the same eyes, your fat cheeks like in the photos from when you were a kid. Still clutching that worn-out blue octopus, and you think it's familiar. Maybe you had one when you were a kid, in your world. And this one? You could have arranged this better. You don't have time to look after someone else's kids.

The woman standing with your boy (a teacher?) looks amused. "We thought we'd come find you. Marlon was getting worried."

"Yes, sorry," you say. "I had my hands full of cat."

"Hi, Jess!" The woman waves at the girl. And now you have both their names. This is a cinch.

"Meow," says Jess, and pretends to lick her paw, rubs it over her face.

"Thank you." You smile, hoping the exchange is at an end.

"No problem," she says, but she's hovering, waiting for something. What, a tip? Do we tip here for child delivery?

"Hi," you say to prompt her.

"Mrs. Henries would love a chance to sit down with you, when you have a moment, to talk about Marlon's behavior."

"Now?"

"I've put a meeting request in the parent portal. Choose a time slot that works for you."

"Can you tell me what this is about?"

The small solemn boy replies, "Lara wouldn't let me have a turn on the monkey bars, so I told her she was a stupid fuckhead."

You laugh—you can't help it. Even though it's clearly the wrong thing to do.

"Now, Marlon," teacher lady says, half kneeling in front of him, brow furrowed in disapproval—at you, not him. "What did we say about bad words? Do you remember? Words can hurt people's feelings as much as a punch or a kick."

"And we don't hurt people," he finishes with a grave little-boy sincerity.

"I am so sorry," you say, apologizing for both his behavior and your barely restrained amusement.

"Have a look on the parent portal. I know it's hard being a single mom, but we do need to discuss this."

"I will, thank you!" You nod frantically and turn away, lugging the girl, the boy's sticky grasp on your fingertips. This is not what you need. There are things you have to do here in the time you have available, and you cast your eyes around as if someone among the parents might offer a playdate out of the blue—that's something parents do, right? But people are dispersing to cars or toward the bus stop. You have to look inside your yellow purse to see if you have car keys somewhere, buried beneath the wet wipes and disposable diapers. (Ugh, you've never changed a diaper in your life, and how old is Jess that she still needs them?) You give her a sideways glance, as if you have a barometer of children's ages installed in your head that will magically provide the answer. Three? Marlon must be five or six. Too young to use the word *fuckhead*. Did he get that from her? Or from their dad? Where is the father? Another puzzle.

"Jess, can you walk by yourself, please?" You try to set her down, but she grips on to you like a koala.

"You're different," Marlon says.

"I'm tired. That's all." This is something parents say all the time. *People* say it all the time. You don't care what universe you're in, this is a universal truth: everyone is tired, all the time.

You haven't found any car keys, and you can't ditch the kids, and you don't know where to go, but you can see a little park down the road, and even though the wind is sharp, you can go and sit there for a while until the other you comes back. She will know what to do with the children.

So you take them to the coffee kiosk and buy them hot

chocolate with marshmallows and whipped cream, but there isn't enough money in your purse to buy a coffee for yourself, and you still don't know the PIN to your bank card.

Your driver's license says Bridget Ainsley, and the girl in the photo looks small and nervous and criminal, even by driver's-license-photo standards. Why the new name? Did something happen? Is that why you/she tried to attack Dom with the lamp? Where *is* the father?

You head to the park, and Marlon runs to the edge of the grass and starts picking up stones and arranging them along the length of the seesaw, singing to himself. Jess insists on sitting on your lap, purring and nuzzling, which makes it hard to look at your phone. You are grateful for face recognition, because you don't know the pass code.

"I want to play a game!" she says, grabbing for the phone.

"In a minute," you say. And then, inspired: "Cats don't play games on phones."

"What do they do?"

"They stalk! And they pounce! And they chase their tails."

"Okay!" She hops off your lap and you can check the phone at last. You search for Dr. Jo Kittinger and Joanna Kittinger and Joanne Harris. You log into something called Facebook, which is mostly the same as Lifebook, thank you, compatible universes. You're not sure if it's reassuring or depressing that Big Tech has its claws sunk across realities in the same ways.

You click through to friends and family, but your profile is under a different name—Amy Belle, not even Bridget Ainsley—and the photo is of a woman's butt on the beach, an anonymous butt in a striped sarong that could be anybutt, which is weird. And, weirder, you don't have any friends. You scratch absent-mindedly at your wrist, find a pimpled rash down the length of your arm, alongside your scar. Maybe you are in witness protection? Enigmas wrapped in mysteries when you already have one to solve: the Case of the Missing Mother.

"Leave me alooooone," Marlon says.

"Meow."

You need to leave this otherself a message. There's a coloring book in the bag, with a stubby little snowman and a princess with frosted hair on the cover, and crayons, and you write a note in a speech bubble above the snowman's cheerful face—*Look in voice memos* and your new mantra: *Sorry.*

You record something for her, urgent and whispered so the children don't hear, Bridget to Bridget. *Hey, you, it's me, who is also you, and I hope we can work together. I don't want to hijack your life, your kids are lovely, but I don't know the first thing about parenting and you're probably a lot better at this than I am.* You're rambling, but where do you even start? *I need to get hold of Jo, my mom. Something happened to her in my world, and now she's lost and I need your help. Please. Please help me find her. I need to talk to her—*

The phone rings in your hand and you nearly drop it in surprise. An unknown number. "Hello?" you say, and you hope this is how *you* sound on the phone. There is silence. Someone breathing.

"I'm sorry"—there you go again—"I'm not interested," because there will be irritating sales calls here too. It's probably a constant across all known existences.

"You bitch," a man says in such a tone of warm delight that you think it must be a joke, the same way you and Dom fool around calling each other disgusting slurs out of deepest love and affection. But the voice turns ugly, cold. "You fucking bitch, you thought—"

You jab the red button hastily to end the call. The phone rings again, and you fumble to turn it off. It's an older model, and it takes you a minute. Jess comes trotting back to you as you drop it into the yellow purse, and you turn to give her your attention. She puts her arms around your neck and says, "I love you, Mommy," pressing her nose to yours. It's too much. You can't. You want to push her away from you. You're a good mom. Even though you're not a mom at all. And that shakes you. But you hold on to her tight instead until it ends.

A rush of color, of light, of sound, and you come back crying a little to find yourself in Dr. Fawn's office. You rip off the VR headset and Caden is sitting beside you, scrolling through his phone.

"I thought we said no VR?" You want to be mad, but you're tired, shaken by the phone call.

Caden looks irritated. "I thought that was to humor Dom? It's obviously the best way to do it. How was it?"

"Bad timing," you say, sitting up straighter. You don't mention the furious man on the phone. It's not a good universe, you think. It's complicated, the situation with the kids, the fake profile. It's the same otherself who tried to club Dom with the lamp. It gives you bad vibes and there are a million other universes to explore.

He hands you a glass of water. "Want to take a break? We could take turns. I do the next one, then you? You don't want to burn out."

You don't trust him. The Ziploc baggie is in your pocket.

"No, I have to keep going. I have to find my mom. No VR this time. I need a favor. I need you to talk to the otherselves when they're here, ask them about their moms. Take notes. Please? Until Dom gets back?"

"Yeah, sure." But he looks grumpy about it. And you don't care, because you have to get back on the horse.

AMBER

Infestation

More ripples. Shivering out across the Ourmind, all the danger signs they will have to follow up on.

What do we do?

Cut it out. The same as always. Hunt it down. Her own thought but also simultaneous consensus. Every version, every contamination. *Burn it with fire.* But that twang of unease.

Where is this coming from?

How could this happen again?

So soon.

I can't. A flash of memory, linked minds: the metallic *shunk* of an automatic lock on a prison-cell door, the reek of an open metal toilet. They don't always get away with it. *Please don't make me.*

I thought it was over.

Quiet down! she thinks into the clamor.

Friends. He has friends.

Disciples, maybe. A cult. They're taking it as their communion. One of the Ambers is obsessed with cults, another with therapy. They all have their coping mechanisms for what they've had to do, but they can never lose sight of the real monster, the one that gets under your skin, into your brain, that tears through reality, unravels you from the inside.

An army. Spreading.

We have to cut it out. Stop it. Shut up! Amber tries again to be heard through the chatter. She is packing up her tools. Black tarp, a hammer for caving in the skull, pliers for teeth, the medications she needs for immobilizing. Her HK45 as a last resort, a box of jacketed hollow-points. They still have to find whoever is causing these ripples. The multiples of them.

The others are making their own plans. One of the Reluctants, Amberlynn, is whining again. *I don't want to, please don't make me, you know I'm not good at this.*

We need to take drastic measures. Her opposite, someone overzealous. The fleeting image of an AR-15, the heft and the dull tug in their hands as it discharges. As if they would be able to cover *that* up, as if it wouldn't leave a terrible mess, ruin any chance of harvesting. Although it happens; they had to burn the artist in the loft where he lived—and died—in Brooklyn.

SHUT UP!

The others quiet.

I can't get arrested. I can't go to jail. Please. Who'll look after Mr. Toe Beans?

Amber ignores Amberlynn—trust her to start whining about her cat. She is resolute. A few of the others take some persuading. But she has rank here, the most experience. The first. It will still take time to set all the tumblers clicking.

Find Aiden Lyleveld. Find his friends, his family, his associates, his coconspirators. Interrogate him, them. But don't kill. Not yet. Not until we know we have the others.

If they're even connected.

They are. She feels this in her gut. And she remembers one of her maybes, a little girl at a party years and years ago. It stopped abruptly, so she never followed up. She should have.

Watch for signs. Don't act. Not yet.

DOM

Science Is Hot

Driving to Everard University, Dom has to admit that they are, deep down, a city kid. These lush trees with their thousand verdant shades, all of them intense, makes them feel uneasy. Anything could be out in those woods—monsters or meth cooks—and they don't even have their label printer to jam in their pocket and make like it's a gun. Which is all ridiculous, they know. The real dangers in Portland are police brutality and the anti-vaxxers who could have derailed the pandemic effort, dragged it out for years, like in Bridgette's reality. Also, it seems, dreamworms and how you can become obsessed with them.

In the waiting area, they prowl past the historic photos from the college's "storied history"—as if the past doesn't contain entanglements of perspective. For example, among all these eager white faces in the sepia photographs, there is no indication of the Multnomah people who came before or even the BLM protests and antifa activism of the past five years. But then, the brochures for various university societies include ones supporting trans rights and investigating Black history. The world does change, slowly, and painfully, with a lot of resistance. Wouldn't it be great if we could help it along?

That must be a thing: Divergent histories in the other realities Bridge and Caden are visiting. It opens up a whole binder of brain-hurting what-ifs. It's not time travel, Caden said, but what if you could study a different parallel reality where things were better than here?

Yes, all right, they'll admit they are tempted, sorely, by the dreamworm. The spindle is safely tucked in their backpack. They could do it right now. But they are also terrified of who they might be on the other side. They've fought so hard for *this* life, to be exactly who they are.

The elevator pings, and a young Black woman in very good stripey-linen tie pants and natural hair strides out to meet them, smiling to reveal the slightest gap between her front teeth. Not at all the serious academic Dom was expecting. Gawky and cool and enthusiastic all at once.

"You must be Dom?" she says in what's probably a Zimbabwean accent, based on Jo's diary and the woman's profile on the science department website. "So lovely to meet you." Her handshake is cool and dry, long elegant fingers made for playing the piano or scalpeling through delicate cerebral tissue. "Anything for Professor Kittinger. It's so awful what happened.

"So, I was about to do a fresh harvest." She grins, full of mischief.

"Of... brains?" Dom scrambles to keep up with her as she leads the way through a set of double doors and up a staircase, speckled cream with grooved edges, which feels very seventies, like Dom's lita's apartment in Arecibo with its yellow lights and crenellated balconies.

She laughs. "Tapeworm larvae. It's the leading cause of epilepsy in Africa, and we're beginning to think India and some parts of South America too. Jo was really interested. I don't know if you knew about her condition?"

"Epilepsy since she was fourteen. But it was a straightforward brain cancer that killed her, from what I understand, nothing to do with worms." Loading the emphasis there.

"Oh no, definitely not. She hadn't shown any sign of lesions and she had multiple scans. Perks of the job. But no brain cancer is straightforward, per se. The brain is an infinitely strange and complex organ, and we barely understand it."

"That's encouraging." Dom has been puzzling over the stained-glass window on the landing, which depicts a sea-cucumber-ish thing, vaguely star-shaped with branching tendrils and a fat sectioned tail connecting to another tendrilled star. It takes them too long to haul out their memories of high-school biology and identify it as a neuron. Of course.

"If you don't know your own mind, it's because we literally don't know our own minds," Tendayi says.

"I'm going to quote you next time I'm being indecisive."

"Please do." She smiles back. "I didn't work with her directly, just so you know, so I'm not sure how helpful I can be."

They've come out on a corridor painted hospital blue, a row of wooden doors with opaque glass windows and brass name plates, exactly how Dom imagined—a little Raymond Chandler, a little Lovecraft. And oh, look, a sign for the Museum of Surgical History. Tendayi unlocks the door marked 609 NEUROPARASITOLOGY, which opens onto parquet floors scuffed by decades of wheelie chairs. The windows are dingy, propped half open; a Swiss cheese plant is spilling out of its pot, intent on taking over the room. Textbooks and computers, a great hulking machine with something that looks like a Faraday cage.

"Our patch-clamp rig. It's where we do the electrophysiological recordings. How much do you know about tapeworms?"

"I know they're disgusting. Some idiots have tried to use

them as diet pills. They can grow as long as a school bus inside your intestines. Did I mention disgusting already? How does the epilepsy work?"

"So, adult tapeworms in your intestines is not the problem. You get that from undercooked pork, for example. Pigs eat the tapeworm eggs, which hatch, burrow through the pig's intestinal wall and into the muscle, and turn into cysts, which humans ingest when they eat the meat."

"Oh my God, vegan for life."

"The cysts grow into adult tapeworms in your intestines and can cause some gastric symptoms, but mainly they're just hanging out, and they want you to live so they can live and lay their eggs, which come out your butt in your feces."

"But that's *not* the problem?"

"No. It's when the life cycle gets interrupted. It's when humans eat something—usually unwashed veggies—contaminated by the feces of an animal or person infected with the adult tapeworms. That means they're ingesting the tapeworm *eggs*, not the cysts. Those eggs develop into larvae that burrow their way through the gut, enter the bloodstream, migrate to various organs, including the brain, and *become* cysts. But, get this: For reasons we don't understand yet, five to ten years later, the patient develops epilepsy. We think it's because there's some kind of protein inside the tapeworms' bodies that reacts with human brain chemistry, but we're not sure. And that's basically what I do here. Try to figure that out."

"Por dios. I am scrubbing the shit out of all my vegetables from now on."

"Well, exactly!" Tendayi grins. Are the two of them flirting? Dom thinks they might be flirting. "Do you want to see what I do here?"

"Uh, yes. All the sciencing, please."

"Right." She removes a flask containing a goopy white liquid from the bar refrigerator beneath the counter. "So here are all my little larvae buddies, and I put them through the homogenizer, turn them into mush. I'm not boring you?" She looks at them, self-conscious about her enthusiasm.

"No, qué foquin cool. Science is hot."

Tendayi smiles. "I'll try to keep it simple. We have a protease inhibitor to stop the important proteins breaking down, and we spin the larvae at four thousand revolutions per minute in a centrifuge machine to separate the cellular membranes, the liquid proteins, and the fat. Like a three-layer cocktail." She holds it up to show them. "Then you load it into the headstage." She carefully fills a glass pipette with the mush and attaches it to the back of something resembling a glue gun. "Another headstage with an electrode lets us patch the cell and measure the electrical activity. To do that, you need to suction onto the membrane of the cell and burst through it"—she makes a goofy slurping sound. "That gives us full electrical access. You still with me?"

"Mostly. There's no test at the end, right?" On the screen is what looks like a very boring ultrasound.

"Okay, so if you look at the screen, that thin gray line is the cell's electrical current, and then on the screen over here, that sharp needle is the micropipette containing the electrode. And then we bring in the micropipette full of tapeworm mush and we're going to puff it onto the patched cell—rat brain, not human, don't worry—and record the response."

"Poor rats," Dom says, thinking about Bridge trying to set her mom's lab rodents free all those years ago.

"I know, also a vegan over here. I struggle with it a lot, but if you saw what parasite infections do to people who don't have access to clean water or medical care, especially kids and the immunocompromised—and then there's the stigma. People with epilepsy in rural communities are accused of being cursed or possessed or doing witchcraft; sometimes they're forced to flee their homes. Or worse. If I can help them…" She trails off. "We all have to make our own moral compromises. I believe this is the best methodology we have right now."

Bridge's argument right there, Dom thinks. "So I wanted to ask you about something in particular," they say, unshouldering their backpack. They take out the Tupperware, pop it open to reveal the spindle.

"Oh." Tendayi is clearly dismayed. "Is that the dreamworm?"

"If I say yes, are you going to throw me out?"

"I wasn't involved. It was a misuse of university equipment. Jo was up here at strange hours before she lost her access. It's so sad what happened. To throw everything away like that. Her reputation. Her funding."

"Did she tell you about it?"

"Ugh." Tendayi is flustered, furious. "Listen, I can't be linked to Jo's 'meltdown scandal.'" She air-quotes too hard, jabby. "It would follow me around for my entire career, especially as a woman, especially as a woman of color, and especially one from Zimbabwe. Visas are still really hard to get even with the Africa Rising policies. Jo did real damage to the university's reputation. The psychedelic-studies people were pissed, too, because their critics were claiming this was what happened when you allowed people access to psilocybin. I think everyone was relieved when it turned out to be a tumor pressing on her anterior prefrontal cortex."

"But you don't think that."

"I don't have enough information." She is cagey.

"If it works the way it's supposed to, this is a big deal, no? Taking the dreamworm, using music and images to transfer consciousness?"

"If." She winces. "Have you tried it?"

"I did babysitting duty while Jo's daughter took a trip. I really, *really* hate to say it, but I think it's real. And you're the only other rational person I can talk to about this. Jo's notes mentioned side effects, but she didn't say what they were. And she said that the guy who originally gave it to her made it. I'm trying to figure out if that's like Albert Hofmann cooking up LSD in his lab or maybe—"

"It's a parasite?"

"It's in the name. Dream*worm*."

Tendayi throws herself down into a wheelie chair, annoyed but also ready to get into this. "Purely theoretically?"

"Pure as glacier melt."

"*If* it was a parasite—and I'm not saying it is—you'd have to look at the life cycle. Is there an intermediary host? Is it changing that host's behavior to help it infect the next host for the next phase? For example, toxoplasmosis makes rats fearless, so they run toward cat urine instead of away from it. There's a Czech biologist who has data suggesting it also makes men more reckless, impulsive, thrill-seeking. He says you can track *Toxoplasma gondii* infection rates in humans by the increase in car accidents." Her earlier irritation is gone, drowned in geeky enthusiasm. "It might even be a factor in schizophrenia—there was a sudden spike of diagnoses in the 1700s in London and Paris that coincided with 'the cat craze,' when humans, especially boho poets and artists, started keeping cats as pets for the first time since the ancient Egyptians."

"What I'm hearing is you're a dog person," Dom says, but they are loving the gruesome parasite arcana. Unless you extrapolate it to their current context, that is.

"There are at least fourteen hundred parasites on you right now. And yes, some of them, right down to the bacteria in your gut biome, are trying to influence your mind."

"So another example would be the cicada thing, where they get a fungus like meth that makes them party till their butts drop off?"

"Yes! Exactly. It's the same with rabies—initially, it makes you hypersexual and it makes you bite, which probably accounts for a lot of the mythology around werewolves and vampires."

Dom is here for this. "Or *Cordyceps*—the mind-control fungus that turns ants into zombies, makes them clamp onto tall grass so birds will eat them. It's in that book."

"The one by Merlin Sheldrake?"

"No, the horror one, *The Girl with All the Gifts*."

"I'll have to check it out." Definitely flirting. "Interesting thing about the zombie ants, it's not like a switch that gets flicked. *Cordyceps* doesn't give ants lockjaw and that's it, they're done. They cling to the top of the grass stalk, but if they don't get eaten, they come back down and continue to socialize with other ants, possibly infecting them too. Then at sunrise, they'll climb back up and wait. It's a *consistent* behavioral change, and that's what makes it so potentially dangerous. Okay, okay, but also *Polysphincta gutfreundi*, the wasp that lays its egg inside a spider's abdomen and as the larvae develop inside the spider, they release chemicals that interfere with the spider's nervous system, forcing it to spin wild three-D designs that are unlike any kind of web they would ever think of spinning."

"As much as we can infer spider consciousness and aesthetic choices," Dom mock-protests, wanting to get back on track, even though they want to ask her if she's seen the photos of webs made by spiders that were on caffeine and cocaine and acid. "So, I'm thinking, or hoping, that the dreamworm is like a really powerful hallucinogen, like DMT or ayahuasca. But instead of making you hallucinate, it jolts your consciousness across time and space, and... shit, yeah, I know it's absurd."

"It's not an animal, I can tell you that much." She leans forward, her hands on her knees, conspiratorial. "Please don't tell anyone, but after she was banned from the lab, Jo brought that thing in and asked me to analyze it."

"Through all the mushing and the spinning and protease inhibitors and puffing with the headstage." *See, paying attention.*

"Yes, and I ran a gel matrix to separate out the proteins, but there weren't any. In layperson-speak, that means it's not biological. Or the sample was so hopelessly degraded—as in very much super-dead—that it wouldn't show. Jo wanted me to stain it with fluorescent markers, get it under the confocal microscope, but it was enough, you know. Jo was... sick. I thought if I indulged her any more, I'd be hurting her. Playing into her delusion. Sometimes you don't want the answers, even if you're a scientist. Jo didn't want to believe her experiences were caused by the brain tumor. And I can't tell you what to do..."

"Because you're not *Toxoplasma gondii*."

She gives the faintest whiff of a smile. "No. But if it were me, I'd destroy that thing."

"Or... can I ask you a favor?"

"You want a tour of the Museum of Surgical History?" Trying to divert. "It's wonderful. Even more disgusting than parasites."

"I would on any other day. But if I could ask you to look at—"

"I knew this was coming."

"Bridge is my friend and she's a fucking moron, but I love her and as far as I can tell, this is a real deal. I need to know. If we can get any closer to understanding—"

"Give it to me." Tendayi holds out her hand.

"Let me cut off a piece," Dom says. They're not trusting the spindle with anyone, even a scientist with a slight, extremely cute gap between her teeth.

"I'll do it, actual lab equipment here." She gets a scalpel, a glass slide. "I'll use the confocal microscope this time." She looks tired. "I'll let you know what I find—if anything."

"And... another favor." Dom squirms.

"Uh-huh?"

"It seems to be related very strongly to music, so maybe if I sent you some files, you can examine it while the songs are playing."

"I will have you know this is a reputable science laboratory and not a nightclub!" Tendayi puts on a very British accent, hands on her hips, playing it up. "As in yes, that sounds intriguing, actually."

"And maybe I could take the scientist-slash-DJ for a drink sometime to say thank you?"

Tendayi smirks, playful. "You should know I only go to those hipster bars where they serve cocktails out of test tubes and beakers. I like to be in *my element*."

Dom groans at the pun. "It's a date, then... if you want it to be a date."

"Let's see how it goes." The mischief in her smile is encouraging.

AMBER

Jackpot

One of the Ourmind has found a lead entirely unrelated to Aiden Lyleveld and his iterations, three of whom are unfortunately already dead, taken care of by vigilant Ambers who'd moved before they decided on their new strategy: to root out the source of the rot.

One is under a fresh layer of new concrete at a construction site in Los Angeles, his body riddled with threads. Another is half-buried under cardboard in a meth house in Albuquerque, burned beyond recognition. Only a slim harvest there. Not someone the original source returned to; who would want to revisit a junkie? The third shot in the head, blood splattered over the windshield of his Mercedes, in what would hopefully look like an attempted carjacking outside Portland. No signs of infection, but his zealous slayer felt it was better to be safe than sorry. And of course, Amber has already killed the one in her universe, fed him to the gators. Minus a hand washed ashore.

Luckily, the others are finding ways to interrogate the remaining Aidens. Many of the Ambers are cops or former cops. You can talk your way right in the door most times. *Excuse me, sir, we're canvassing the neighborhood to ask if anyone saw something on Saturday night. An attempted murder.* You can get a long way on other people's curiosity. If she were a man, people would be more mistrustful; they might phone the station to check on her. But she is five foot five and middle-aged and charming, and most people reckon they could take her. They're wrong, but she's not going to correct them. Not until she has to.

Sometimes you can follow them, learn their routines or engage them where they are. There are a number of musicians among the Aidens, and in those instances, it is easy for the Ambers to reach out to them about playing a corporate gig, writing a jingle for a grandkid's video channel.

They do their research. Amber has always been a reader. She likes books that tell her about the ways the world works, who people are, history and sociology and criminology, how gangs and the military and failed utopian lesbian communes and Japanese feudal structures are all prone to weakness, mean-spiritedness, the fear and goddamn incompetence that unravels them. The Ourmind will never let that happen. They are united in their purpose.

She has firsthand experience of the bungling, the supply-chain snafus, the bullies and the idiots in the military.

She remembers that shit-heel Parker in her battalion, the guy who'd tried to climb on top of her in the middle of a nighttime mortar attack. Hellfire raining down on them in their tents. She'd punched him in the throat to get him off her. Later, she and Chris ambushed him as he came out of the showers. Chris hit him in the gut to drop him low enough so she could clap her hands over his ears and burst his eardrums.

The medic attributed it to the mortar fire because Parker was too ashamed to admit he'd been taken down by the "unrape-able" cunt and the skinny faggot. She was twenty-seven, Chris was only nineteen, a little brother to her, and they already knew they were the only people they could count on. Lucky to have each other's backs through two tours. She was supposed to look out for him. Protect him.

But later the doctors said it was PTSD that was causing Chris's out-of-body experiences, his personality changes, the dislocation. Maybe a brain injury. He tried to show them the yellow threads he'd pulled out of his arms, but they dismissed him or shrugged and said it might be a parasite he'd picked up in one of the hellholes he'd served in.

But it wasn't. She knows that now. The worm came from much farther away and much closer.

Occasionally, she wonders if she's in fact mad. The chaos of voices. The horror she's witnessed, personally, up close. The horror she's inflicted. But then she remembers how it was at the end with Chris.

Spasming on the floor of his house, gold threads corkscrewing their way out of his insides, piercing through his skin, twisting in the air like plants trying to find the sun. The way they spilled from his mouth, ripped through his eye sockets. Shining gold death through the blood and gasoline. And the sound they made. A terrible music all mixed up with his screaming, and she should have lit the match sooner. Should have spared him that. Even in those last horrific moments, she was desperate to save him. But he was so far gone, not even the Frequency Machine could save him.

What had been done to her friend, her kid brother in all but the paperwork, was deliberate. It was the Dictator, coming back again and again, trying on his life. Auditioning.

She doesn't know why the threads haven't affected her—any of the Ambers—the same way. Why she can use it to go searching. She was the first among them, the Source.

She'd taken it trying to understand what was afflicting Chris. And by rights, she should have infected all the others, the way Chris was infected and reinfected every time the Dictator came back, traded places with him.

The Ambers are different, somehow. Chosen by God, or, more likely, by the devil to do the devil's work. There are bacteria that can destroy viruses, viruses that can explode cancers.

But she's seen how it works in others. The Source infects every mind they touch—what she calls the Nests—worse every return trip. A compounding effect, until they start extruding. That's when she can feel them. Sniff them out if they're close enough, like a truffle pig.

This was how it played out for Chris and for the Haitian artist Olivier St. Juste, whom she burned to death in his loft apartment in her world, and for the unhappy line cook Wilhelmina Remington in New Orleans and for Aiden Lyleveld. And now, for this new girl.

Bridgette Harris. Not her reality. Another.

The find has been made by one of the Ambers who works private security, levelheaded, a good soldier, even though she goes to therapy. (Amber 5, Amber calls her privately, holding the thought tight. The Ourmind doesn't have to hear *everything* you think.) The video was forwarded to her by someone in her Tomesians support group, and it is not, shall we say, subtle. What a relief, Amber thinks, to be living in this age when everyone's the star of their own personal documentary. But this is also dangerous. Stories are their own kind of contagion. She can't have word getting out. Especially not by some *influencer*.

Bridgette's latest video already has forty thousand views and a handful of reaction videos, and the comments are circling wider, mostly mocking but with some sympathy for the poor girl who's lost her mind. Armchair psychologists and trolls and people accusing her of faking it for attention and the handful of true believers who feel they've always known this. But this girl already had followers on her channel. She had a reputation as someone down-to-earth and practical—a no-nonsense adventure girl sailing the world with her boyfriend. Not the kind to make things up. This makes her more credible, more dangerous, and it means Amber needs to take care of it herself, despite Amber 5's protestations that she handle it.

Amber prepares her space, locks the doors and windows, draws the curtains in case those snooping cops come back to tell her about more body parts washed up. She turns off her phone and gives Mr. Floof II extra treats. She has already pureed one of the fresh threads she took from Aiden into an almond-milk smoothie. It's more palatable, but even though she washed them thoroughly, drinking the smoothie, she imagines she can pick up the iron aftertaste of blood.

Enough of a dose to allow her to stay there for a while, bind her mind to the other's.

She has control of them—the worms—with the Frequency Machine. It makes them dance to her tune, unraveling through flesh so she can harvest them. But if you play a different song, you don't have to switch consciousness. You can commune.

This works only for the Ambers, though; she knows this because she has experimented with some of the Nests to see if the machine would work for them, create their own Ourmind. But it only works for her. A fluke of genetics, a quirk of brain chemistry. It's possible she could do more with the Frequency Machine, but she hasn't unlocked all its secrets. The Dictator could have told her, but he is dead, along with Chris.

"Mommy is going to take one of her special naps, okay, buddy?" She lies on her bed, raises the kaleidoscope to one eye, puts on the music box. Mr. Floof II jumps up and curls against her hip, soft and dense.

The ceiling fan whirs the humidity around and she closes her eyes, lets herself get caught in that same spin, reaching out across spiraling fractals that condense and rearrange, pulling on the threads that connect them.

Consciousness is a kind of gravity, and like gravity, you can break free of your own earth. She sinks through the impossible golden geometries blazing on the insides of her eyelids, past the snags and hooks of minds and thoughts trying to catch her, all her other incarnations. Until she finds her, Amber 5, sitting at the boarding gate of the next flight to Tunis, and latches on, Riding Shotgun with her mind.

A Reliable, but also a Reluctant, a Resentful, because she does not like the mess of it. She presents it to her psychologist as violent fantasies, and he is amused rather than concerned. They are of an age, the Ambers, where they slip through the cracks—overlooked, unseen—and when you are practically invisible, in middle age, you are apparently *allowed* to be angry, entertain murderous thoughts.

Amber 5 has downloaded Bridgette's sailing videos to her iPad, and she clicks through them grudgingly, so Amber can see with her own eyes What They Are Dealing With. She is dimly aware of her own body waiting at home. A vacant room, and she is only popping out here, to the hard plastic seats of the waiting area, and the flight attendant has just made the call for business class and priority to board, so she still has a while before she is loaded on with the rest of the cattle. They are none of them rich, the Ambers, unfortunately. They spend everything they have on the Calling.

Bridgette H. and Ben D.'s channel is called SolSailes. From episode 119: The girl, Bridgette, and her boyfriend, Ben, together known affectionately to their fan base as BB, are walking away from their boat, the *Golden*. They traverse the wooden dock that moves with the water, going between yachts, through the yacht club. Quick cuts: They walk the Sardinian streets, the fish market, a glossy dorado on a plate at a restaurant with plastic tablecloths, do cute-couple things, make witty observations that are utterly banal. They do not have quite the necessary charisma or the looks, the hairy young man and the tattooed girl, although they are trying. They have studied the format, but it comes off as formula, Amber thinks—and she has never even watched a sailing channel before.

Older episodes had three thousand views at best, the time they swam with a sunfish. Average of six hundred to eight hundred. This one has thirty-nine thousand. It cuts to them sitting at the little table inside the cabin. The woman is clutching a cup of tea and shaking her head. "It felt so real."

"It must have been something you ate. You threw up over the side, babe."

"I was in my body, but it wasn't mine, no tattoos, sitting in the garden with this Adrian guy, who was really calm, I think he'd done it before, and our guide, Dom, who explained everything about this yellow slug in a plastic box that let us swap places and we started talking about all the differences. They never really had COVID, but they also don't have Lizzo. And there were different names for social media. Lifebook, Checkit."

"It sounds like a very intense dream or hallucination and we should get you to a doctor. Could be a brain tumor, like your mom had."

"It wasn't a dream, it was real. I don't know how to explain it. And you said I was acting weird. Like I wasn't *myself*."

"Well, I'm glad you're back now." He moves to kiss her, but she ducks away, the glassy sparkle of tears coming.

"I'm being serious, Ben!"

"Straight to the doctor in Tunis. In the meantime, any of our viewers got any insights? Hit us up in the comments and don't forget to subscribe."

Amber skips through the next episode, which is uneventful. No further Incursions. Orcas keeping pace beside the boat. Bridgette seems subdued. And then episode 121. The couple walking the streets of Tunis. No mention of the doctor. Drinking bright cocktails at a cheap bar. They are clearly not sponsored. Ben has just set up the camera to face the table when Bridgette jolts in her seat.

"Hi, it's me," she says in a different tone. "The other Bridget."

"Not funny, babe." Ben's brow is furrowed.

She grips his hands across the table. "No, really. You have to believe me. I don't have muscles like this, or tattoos. I don't even know what your last name is. I'm from another reality. We swapped before—I got seasick, remember?—and she'll be back with you in a few minutes, I promise, you can ask her about it. I'm trying to find my mother."

"This isn't funny, babe. Cut it out. You're not making any sense. You need to calm down." His palm reaches to obscure the lens of the camera.

She clicks episode 122.

A tearful confession, filmed in close-up. "I know Ben doesn't believe me."

"I believe you felt it was real..." From off camera.

"We might break up over this."

"For God's sake." Off camera again. He moves forward and tries to take the camera from her. "Turn that off."

"No, I'm live-streaming this."

"Seriously?"

"You won't listen." She props the phone up on a shelf so the lens can take in the room, both of them. He looks tired.

"All right, have it your way. But what do you want me to do? If it's real."

"It was real."

"Then what do we do? I know you're grieving, it's awful that your ma died. But do you know how ridiculous you sound?"

The phone slaps facedown, so the rest of the podcast is audio only, although you can still see the flow of comments, emojis: Angry face emoji, cry-laughing, mind-blown.

> *Hey, could be a brain injury, remember when B. got whacked by the boom two weeks ago?*
>
> *Man, if I could get to another universe, it would be to leave my mother behind!*
>
> *Couldn't get enough views, turning into a dramedy? The sci-fi element is boring.*
>
> *No, it happened to me. Woke up in a whole other town in a girl's bed.*
>
> *You wish, weeb.*
>
> *I hope she gets the help she needs.*
>
> *Don't break up you guys! Believe women!*
>
> *They're both being childish af*
>
> *Can someone pick up the phone. I can't see shit.*

She clicks on the next video.

The two of them sitting on the railing of their yacht, someone else holding the camera.

"Hey, thanks so much for all your good thoughts and wishes," Bridgette says, "and your concerns. We're not faking any of this or trying to turn this into a sci-fi drama thing.

I did go to the doctor, and he said it's not schizophrenia or anything like that. But maybe a lingering concussion, like some of you guys said. And we're totally okay." Ben squeezes her hand and they smile at each other, although it does not seem entirely genuine. "We're going to stick around here for a bit so the doc can monitor my symptoms. So if you have any great recommendations for off-the-beaten-track secret spots in Tunis, hit us up in the comments. Look after your heads, friends. We'll keep you posted!" She waves and the camera cuts out.

Yesterday. Amber 5 points to the upload date. This one has forty-three thousand views.

Still time, then. But this is very bad. They can't have more publicity. She can find them in Tunis, track down the boat, befriend them at the yacht club, or go visit them in the hospital bearing gifts, a sweet older woman with a kindly disposition who has heard their story and come to offer advice and maybe some money to help them out. Ask them if they have heard of Tomesians—any evidence of yellow threads? It hasn't come up in the videos yet.

Use them to lure the others, another one says—Ambyr, one of the Devout. Overzealousness can be its own problem.

Only two Incursions, Amber 5 says. *Foreign country. Do we really want to make a mess?* As if that were a real question.

Amberlynn pipes up: *I nearly went to jail. I just want to remind you.*

They're streamers, they have a following.

Shut up, Amber thinks into the commotion. Shared consciousness doesn't mean they agree. *We find them, talk to them, learn who the Source is, then do what is necessary. Like always.*

Again that chime of memory, the garden party in Florida. She'd felt the child, that itch at the edge of her mind. The threads always seeking out others. She'd been in the vicinity, sixty miles away, and had turned her car around and driven down, following the signal like those old cartoons where the character is levitated and carried along by the scent of apple pie. She'd pulled up outside a house with balloons, wandered into the garden party, and found *her.* She regrets not following up. The mother was there, she remembers, but she got no sense of infection from her. Or from the father. What was the child's name? She'd decided back then it was an accident, because it stopped, abruptly.

But now, she thinks it might be possible that the child's name was Bridgette.

We'll find her, Amber 5 says.

And the other people who were there, Aiden. Who could be an Adrian. Sometimes the names change. Sometimes that makes them harder to find. Marriage, for example, is a real bitch.

And the friend, Dom, who knows, who tells. And they Really Can't Have That.

Jo's Diary

March 2, 2017

History sits heavy here, even if you're holding a stiff gin and tonic on the balcony of the Hotel Oloffson with white ironwork in what they call gingerbread-style overlooking the tropical gardens and a pool that has gone a toxic shade of green and, on the double staircase below, a statue of Baron Samedi tucked in an alcove. The hotel appears, thinly veiled, in Graham Greene's *The Comedians,* which I haven't read, although I meant to, on the plane on the way over. In the book, it's the place where CIA spooks and ambassadors and dignitaries are rumored to meet, where deals are made about payoffs and who the next president is going to be. A clatter of American students trailed in, bright twenty-year-olds on a sociology excursion with their professor, who seemed out of his depth. He tried to chat with me at the bar, told me this was the place where the first HIV tests in the world were performed, on the head chef and the bartender, both of whom were positive, both banished immediately, because no one knew how it spread. It made me think of Travis and how Gobi wouldn't go into his room at Leftfield. How frightened we are of the things we don't understand.

I am trying to understand.

I'd come here on an expensive whim and the breath of

possibility. A snippet of an article on the artist Olivier St. Juste, posing with his painting. There's a big Haitian population in New Orleans, which might explain where Rabbit got it in the first place.

I'd hired a guide, a local photojournalist, Jacques Philogene, recommended by a friend of a friend who had done documentary work here. It's something Bridge has talked about—making documentaries—but not to me. I only overhear her with her friends. I can't believe she's eighteen already. Heading off to college, a whole new life, a chance to discover who she is. But Texas? I know Austin is supposed to be wonderful for artists and creatives, but it feels so very far away, adding to the distances between us.

A waiter ushered Jacques, a young Black Marlon Brando with a potbelly and dreads, over to my balcony seat. He was carrying a spare motorcycle helmet over his wrist like a bracelet because taking a car is madness in Port-au-Prince, and he already had two mototaxis waiting for us. I climbed onto a battered Suzuki 800 behind a young man who was probably barely eighteen himself.

The bikes edged through the cars that were going nowhere, cunning, like little fish, through the congested city. For a while, we were stuck behind a vibrantly painted bus with the legend IN GOD WE TRUST and a portrait of Rihanna like a saint.

Port-au-Prince is two different cities, one on top of the other. Dirt streets and chickens and corrugated-iron shacks in bright colors. The brush is tangled with plastic waste, the highways clogged like heart disease, three lanes forced into four, no, five, as a convoy of black Mercedes flashing blue lights barges in on their way up to the mansions in the hills of Pétion-Ville, where the fancy restaurants and rooftop bars are guarded by men with machine guns.

There were signs of construction everywhere, some sites half-abandoned, huge metal gates and electric fencing, and tumbledown houses and apartments, bright pennants strung across the street.

The earthquake had reduced downtown to something resembling a war zone, buildings severed down the middle, still leaking electrical wires, iron girders jutting, while people carry on. The furniture, the art and bric-a-brac, toys, crockery, vases, all the things that made houses homes were long gone. Just these riven buildings, gaping memorials. How could they bear to leave their homes like that, open wounds? Because they don't have the resources to patch things up. They don't know where to start.

Like trying to talk to Bridge about her life, and mine. I want to explain so much, but it feels like we're the wrong polarities, or the same ones—magnets repelling each other.

We ended up at the bus stop, dozens of minibuses, touts shouting out destinations, gesturing for new passengers, women cooking corn and plantain for travelers. I had to peel myself off the back of my driver, my hair plastered to my skull from the helmet, a slick of sweat in all the crevices of me. I was the only blan. Bridge would call this "problematic," the white American adventurer parachuting in, and I get her point. Like, for example, how I hadn't expected vodou to be so intrinsic to the culture. I thought it was overhyped by Hollywood with all the zombie stuff. How very American of me not to understand it's the national religion. How fucking disrespectful, Jo.

I was trying to be brave, trying to summon up the ice-cold kid who swaggered through New Orleans, the mother who stole her kid, who left her husband, who finished her damn PhD at thirty-nine. The truth is, I managed each of those only because other Jos had. Because I saw it was possible.

Consciousness is experience. Experiences are doors of their own—to other possibilities.

It was hours to Jacmel, the rickety minibus sweeping along the road that curved around and over lush green hills, past fields of sugarcane and tangles of forest and little villages. Sometimes people would come out to stand and watch.

By the time we reached the resort town, it was early evening, magic hour lighting up the Victorian buildings in vivid pinks and blues and yellows, the same gingerbread ironwork detail. We walked along the promenade over tiles patterned like waves, young men sitting chatting on the wall, kids playing on the beach.

At Hotel Florita, we sat and had a drink, talked about children, Bridge's mercurial indecision and the difficulty of stubborn teenagers, and how that was not so different from the immovable force of four-year-olds. He showed me a picture, his son, Sadrel. He had Jacques's cheeks, his smile. Jacques and the child's mother weren't together anymore, but he had been at her house when the earthquake hit. It was still raw, even seven years later. Jacques said he felt the trembling start, like the earth was trying to shake them off, and he and his girlfriend ran out of the house in time to see the two-story apartment building next door crack in half and slide to the ground, throwing up a choking dust like fog. People were screaming, but he couldn't scream. He couldn't find his voice. They ran to his parents' house, but it was gone, broken bricks and rubble, and he dug with his hands until they bled and he found his voice, but everyone else was also screaming and digging. His parents died, along with his little brother. He couldn't reach them. So many people's families died. He stopped talking then, and I ordered another round and changed the subject to his ambitions.

He said he wanted to be recognized for his work on his

own terms, not only for helping foreign journalists as a fixer and photographer.

"They treat me like I'm a door," he said. "And I do not get the byline." He downed his drink and told me, to my surprise, that we had to go. Another mototaxi, still farther to go to meet Olivier, and then only tomorrow morning. The bikes were gathered on the promenade waiting for passengers. Behind them, the beach was silvered under a three-quarters moon; the waves were a dark weave tipped with filigreed lace, like the balconies.

I clung tight to the driver of my mototaxi, feeling his sweat through his thin blue T-shirt. I'm sure he could feel mine. The night was thick and black, only the narrow beams of the headlights on the smudge of road through the brush and the cane fields and the roar of wind and the whining engines. I was a little drunk, hanging on. I thought again about dying here and how stupid that would be after surviving brain cancer twice. Or maybe nearly dying justified everything else. Knowing that you are going to die makes it even more essential to live.

And then out of that tarry night rose the sounds of human voices singing, chanting, a drumbeat that made the dark thicker and more resonant. Ahead the prick of brake lights resolved into other cars and bikes at a standstill and men and women coming out of the darkness, dancing, singing, streaming around us, smiling ferociously. Car horns joined the chorus—in celebration or protest, I couldn't tell.

"What is it? What's happening?" I asked.

"Carnival. Like Mardi Gras," Jacques shouted over to me. "It's a festival coming up, you should stay."

I could, I thought. *I could fall into this life. Stay here, work in the local hospitals. They must need neuroscientists. But it's not enough. It's not what I'm looking for.*

Finally the crowd thinned, released us, danced away down the empty road into the darkness. The mototaxis started up again, wind rushing past, the *brup-brup-brup* of the engines, and I lost all sense of time in the dark, all sense of myself. My driver never said a word to me.

We went through two more processions like that, two more parades of swollen drums and voices emerging from the darkness, before we arrived at our destination, a house on the hill belonging to an architect friend of Jacques's that we had to hike up to using our cell phones as flashlights. I took the bed, too tired to absorb the details, and he slept on the couch.

I woke late. The doors were flung open onto the deck to reveal a lapis lazuli ocean beyond the trees. Jacques was sitting on the deck on one of the ironwork chairs, another man with him. Small and thin, smoking a clove cigarette, one bony arm folded around himself. A white T-shirt, faded denim jacket. He looked at me with cool assessment. I recognized him from the article. Jacques excused himself to make coffee.

"Mwen kontan rankontre ou," I said—one of the very few Creole phrases I'd managed to learn in my two days here—mangling the pronunciation. I reached to shake his hand, but he ignored it. "I'm Jo. And you are the artist Olivier St. Juste?"

He nodded, drew on his cigarette. "You are the doctor? Désolé. My English…"

"Mon français," I apologized back. "I think we must wait for Jacques? Attendez?"

He nodded and we sat in brittle quiet while he smoked until finally Jacques returned, bearing coffee thick as treacle and some bread with jam that he had rustled up from somewhere.

I turned to him. "Will you explain I'm not a medical doctor?"

"Yes, you are the useless kind with the letters but not the stethoscope," he teased.

"I saw your painting."

"You are too late." Olivier St. Juste taps the ash off the end of his cigarette onto the tiles and talks some more, and Jacques interprets.

"He says he sold it to an American woman who also saw it in the magazine. Blan like you, older, blonde hair. She is coming back again next month, she wants to buy all his work and make him famous. He wants to know, forgive me, what you will do for him."

"I'm afraid I'm not in the art world. But I'm very interested in the imagery in the painting and I was hoping to ask him about that. I can pay," I said, unfolding a handful of gourdes from my travel wallet, the paper notes too small, too colorful to feel like real money. He looked at them, then plucked them up and folded them away into his jacket.

I took out the article, point at the worm halo in the painting, the multiplicity of faces, stumbling over my words. "I've seen this, what he painted. I call it the dreamworm. Can you ask him about his experience, what he said in the interview about being someone else and seeing the paintings? Is he awake when it happens? Ask him if it sounds like you're in a plane, very loud wind, and that you're falling through colors, and then suddenly you are someone else, you, but not. Tell him it has happened to me too. That's why I know about this. This is why I came all this way to find him."

Jacques raises one eyebrow above his Ray-Bans. "Relax, I will facilitate. Not all at once, all right?" He turned and started talking to the artist in Creole, and Olivier jumped up and slapped his hand on the table.

"Oui," he said, "oui," which I understood, and then a long stream of Creole I didn't.

They talked for ages and I sipped the treacle coffee, spread orange jam, sharp and bitter, on the toast, wishing Jacques would interpret as he spoke.

"All right," Jacques said at last. "He says for him it is the same. Although I think maybe you have given him the words you want him to say. It happens when he is awake, not at his choosing. He feels like there is another Olivier who is in control, and he wears his body like a coat. Sometimes it is very inconvenient. He has slept with his wife using his penis." Jacques shakes his head at the absurdity. "He would kill him if he could for that. He is a very talented artist, the dreamwalker, but Olivier thinks he steals from him. He steals his art, his ideas, and he thinks he walks through other people's dreams as well because he's seen his paintings, and they are of many different faces like brothers. The dreamwalker paints his life, and now Olivier has decided in retaliation he is going to copy his work. He is not as good yet, but he will keep practicing. But he would prefer it to stop. He doesn't like the other man, or his friends. He wants to know if you can make it stop. He has his own art that he would like to make, and maybe this other man is too much of a problem in his life if he keeps returning."

"Has he seen the dreamworm? The thing in his painting?"

Jacques relayed this, and Olivier took a tobacco tin out of his pocket and put it on the table between us. He kept his hand cupped over it, protective.

"Is that it?"

"He can show you. Maybe even give you some. If you have dollars. I'm sorry. I'm only relaying what he says."

"It's fine. That's fair. I have dollars. May I see?" I leaned forward, and Olivier nodded, lifting his hand away. My hands were shaking. I twisted the lid and opened it, sick with anticipation. There. The dreamworm. Only a twist of it, maybe four yellow strands, shining gold, knotted together.

He rubbed his hands all the way down his arms and up again as if he were cold and moved to take back the tobacco case. It was my turn to cup my hand over it.

"Please ask him." I nudged Jacques.

"You come again, I will tell you," Olivier said in English and then switched back into Creole. I waited impatiently for Jacques to interpret.

"He says . . . I'm sorry, I don't understand this." He checked with Olivier. "He says, 'I will *make* it for you.'" The same thing Mina said about Rabbit. "If you come back, you can buy more. He will sell his art and his dreamworms."

"I don't know what that means. Is it something that grows here? An insect that's endemic?"

"I wish I could tell you," Jacques said. "That's all he has told me."

"Tell him I'll buy everything he has now. All the dreamworms." Searching my wallet. Too desperate, I knew. Making it obvious I would pay any amount. I took out a hundred dollars. Surely that would be enough? But Olivier shook his head, reached for the tobacco tin. I couldn't let him take it.

I emptied my wallet onto the table. I don't even know how much was in there. Six hundred? Seven hundred? I try to remember how much I withdrew at the airport.

He made the notes disappear into his jacket and stood up, gesturing for me to take the tin. He was ready to leave, one hand resting on his chest. "Merci, et pour le déjeuner."

"Wait. Attendez. S'il vous plaît, attendez." Following after him. "Please. Where did you get it? I have to know."

He gave a little wave, a little dip of his head. "Next time I see you. You come back. Bon vwayaj."

Jacques was brooding, pissed off, on the ride back to Jacmel and from there back on a minibus to Port-au-Prince. I was squeezed between my guide and a young man with a battered suitcase on his lap, the road winding through banana-leaf valleys and green hills covered with brush puckered and ruffled like broccoli (or brains, I thought, my hand dipping into my purse again to feel the tobacco tin).

"You paid him too much," Jacques said eventually. "You're going to cause trouble. Does this worm really do what you say?"

"Yes. If it's the same thing."

"Then I take it back. You should have paid him more." He smirked. "Me too. We should make another stop. I want you to see a houngan. A vodou priest. It sounds like you are messing with the spirit world already; perhaps you need some perspective."

Another motorcycle ride, the bike threading the traffic, to a town house in the suburbs of Port-au-Prince that's undergoing renovation, flaps of tarp on the roof. Joseph Felix met us at the security gate, a shiny-headed bald man in his late fifties with a lopsided smile and a black T-shirt who looked nothing like my idea of a vodou priest.

He led us down the alleyway into a darkened room with a dirt floor that was clearly used for rituals. A pillar was strung with ribbons; there were traces of colored powder mixed up in the dirt. A young man watched a young woman draw strange symbols on the wall with chalk, occasionally correcting her. They didn't acknowledge us.

Joseph led us upstairs, past the family room, where some

kids were watching a soccer match on TV, up to the top floor, a rooftop deck still being built. He gestured for us to sit on a battered floral couch and the two men spoke for a long time, with Jacques interpreting, skimming the details, summarizing. He explained that vodou was sacred here in Haiti; the lwa were a mix of Catholic and African spirits, the little gods, the mystères or anges, who were between us and Bondyé, the creator, who made us from clay and water and who did not involve himself in our messes and complications. But les invisibles were mischievous; they liked to interfere. The lwa could ride you like a horse.

Joseph stood up and beckoned for us to follow.

"He wants to show you his consultation room," Jacques said, and we traipsed back downstairs through the basement with its earthen floor and the young woman still making markings on the wall and the young man studiously correcting her.

Joseph drew aside a curtain to reveal a small room filled with wonders. On the little table was a bottle of rum, a nested tangle of nails and bells on a saucer, a pair of open-jawed scissors. A huge round mirror hung beneath a curved sword was "the mirror of the universe," a little mermaid doll stood in for La Siréne, the lwa of the ocean, and she was leaning against a Mother Mary figurine in her signature blue—Erzulie, the lwa of love. In an alcove in the corner was a shrine of sorts, with a photograph of a man, his face struck through in ballpoint pen with diagonal arrows tipped at both ends, blue and red playing cards, facedown, and bottles carefully arranged around a human skull, mummified almost, with teeth bared. Through Jacques, Joseph explained it was his teacher, the mambo who'd taught him vodou.

"What is going to happen to *your* skull one day? Will your student display it like this?"

"No." He looked embarrassed. "My kids would not be okay with it." He showed me a photocopied book full of hand-drawn illustrations, and Jacques explained, "These are the vèvè, which you use to summon the lwa so you can ask them questions, if they will entertain them. Different symbols for different lwa."

"Can you ask him about the worm?"

Jacques repeated the question, then listened intently before turning back to me. "In vodou, there *is* a door between the worlds, a crossroads. It's guarded by Papa Legba, who decides your destiny, and he is an old man, wearing rags. He says to tell you that vodou says that every human has a soul or espri that is divided into two parts."

"Like the hemispheres of the brain."

Jacques interpreted and Joseph grinned. "He likes that, but he says that is your kind of magic, not his. So, he says, these two parts: there is the little good angel—"

"And the bad angel, the devil on your shoulder."

"No, no, no." Joseph shook his head, understanding this much. "No devils." He started speaking rapidly.

"No," Jacques interpreted. "There is no devil or Satan in vodou tradition. You have the little good angel, which is your conscience, and the other is gwo bònanj, the big good angel. This is your mind, your intellect, who you are as a person, what defines you."

"Ego and superego."

"Maybe, in your Western thinking. He says you must not try to understand it from this perspective, you must listen. Maybe these things are not compatible. Both these parts, the little good angel and the big good angel, live inside your head and are governed by your lwa, who is linked to your spirit. Everyone is different, everyone has a different lwa.

But when it comes to dreams—in vodou, it is understood that the gwo bònanj can leave your head at night while you are asleep and travel."

"Astral projection? Sorry. I'm going to leave my Western preconceptions at the door. Do they travel here or to other worlds?"

"Only in this world. They can go visiting, see things, have experiences while people are sleeping. But not while they're awake. And he doesn't know about any worm, so he thinks this has nothing to do with vodou."

"Can I show him?" I opened up the tobacco tin and showed him the dreamworm with the same reverence with which he had poured out rum for the lwa. But Joseph sneered, pushed it away, and said something to Jacques.

Jacques interpreted. "He says it looks like rotten noodles. Like it will make you sick. He thinks you should not eat that."

I couldn't help it—I laughed. I pulled out a fold of gourdes, payment as agreed, and tried not to think about how much I'd already spent on this trip.

"Mèsi." Joseph smiled and tucked it away, walked us back out through the basement and the woman still drawing weird symbols on the board. The young man was gone.

As we stepped outside into the late-afternoon light with the mototaxis waiting for us, I turned and asked him, "Was that vèvè? The symbols she was drawing. Is she studying to be a mambo? Learning vodou?"

"Mwen pa komprann?" He looked askance at Jacques, who shrugged. Jacques repeated it in Creole, and Joseph looked confused and then gave a big bark of a laugh, and Jacques joined him, doubled over, crying in delight.

"What? What did I say?"

"That wasn't vodou—those symbols were math. She was doing her physics homework."

Four hours before my flight, I asked Jacques to take me shopping for curios, presents for my friends and my daughter.

"Things to hide a tobacco tin between?" He grinned.

"You're too astute for me, Jacques. And I'm only an amateur smuggler."

"You forget I know Americans. I know just the place." It was the artists' alley featured in the article. A rusted sign with a skull and crossbones announced REZISTANS ART: ATIS REZISTANS at the edge of a parking lot that led into a series of makeshift studios in tin shacks and containers and small rooms, their contents spilling into the shared space, artwork made from recycled objects, rusted cans, old toys, rubber and pipes and bicycle parts, and, glaringly, a couple of human skulls in the mix. *Outsider art,* I thought, but then immediately: *I'm* the outsider here. I asked Jacques where the skulls came from. He said they were from the earthquake; there were so many bodies, so many unclaimed, because their families were dead too. He shrugged as if this was to be expected.

I picked out a wooden statuette, a carving of an impish sorcerer, with horns and one marble eye, his tongue sticking out, holding a giant phallic snake stuck with nails ahead of him like a staff.

Jacques took a photograph of me holding the tin and the curios. "If you change the world, don't forget to credit me," he said.

I boarded the plane with a suitcase full of decoy souvenirs and seven strands of dreamworm tucked inside a tampon box in my handbag. Old tricks from Leftfield.

But I didn't count on the stress and my epilepsy. The tingling came on strongly down my arm while I was waiting in line at Miami International. *Not now,* I thought. *Please not now.* The aura rose up, and I felt myself dropping, just like the day Dave caught me at the party.

But this time it was a security guard who caught me, and in the mess, the absolute mess that ensued, Customs decided to go through all my bags, and they found my precious strands and confiscated them, and the more I pleaded, the more I begged and wept and asked them to check my university credentials, the more they hardened.

"It's illegal to transport biological material. It will have to be destroyed."

I sat in the airport clinic and wept and wept and wept.

AMBER

Guile and Conspiracy

Amber is in the driver's seat, not shotgun, speaking through Amber 5's mouth, inhabiting her. This is too important to trust to her alone. The streamers have come to meet Amber 5 at the bar of a luxury hotel, where she is *not* staying, but appearances matter. Bridgette and Ben are far from the yacht club and their mooring and anyone who might recognize them from their channel. Another advantage of being here. The rich are too self-absorbed. There's a glass piano in the atrium, a hanging garden of plants draped from the balconies overlooking the deck. The breeze carries the scent of the ocean and sandalwood spices (although Amber suspects it is a signature scent piped through the hotel ventilation). Unfortunately, it's mixed with the faint reek of yesterday's fish from the restaurant's garbage bins.

She's told them, through the other Amber's mouth, that she's CIA. No, she doesn't have a badge. That's only in movies, but she tells them things she has learned about them, a little data-mining she did en route, and that's enough to convince them. As if everyone were not an open book these days, shedding the detritus of themselves all over the internet. And of course, she knows about the other things, and here they are, desperate for an explanation, and here she is—and she has one.

She has brought them bottled water. "You shouldn't drink anything anyone gives you," she says and looks around meaningfully. This is because she cannot afford the cocktails here, but they don't need to know that. "Only food you've cooked yourself, bottled water, beers the bartender opens in front of you."

"Is that how this happened? They drugged my food?" Bridgette is leaning forward, eyes shining. Excited.

"Not your food," Amber says. "Have you noticed any unusual marks on your skin?"

"Who are we talking about?" Ben says, defensive. *Sweet boy,* she thinks, *he'll fall harder than she will.* All that resistance waiting to be molded. If you poked it in the right place, he'd become the most ardent disciple. A pity he won't live long enough to spread the word. "Who is 'they'?"

"A Russian splinter group," Amber says darkly.

"Oh my God," Bridgette says, showing Amber her bare arm. "Here. It's been red and itchy." She frowns. "Oozing. Something like pus."

"They injected you." Amber examines the wound, grateful she is wearing long sleeves that hide the spasm through her own arms. "Have you heard of devil's breath? It's one of the most dangerous drugs in the world. Colombian gangsters use it to rob people. It makes you highly suggestible, like a zombie. You hallucinate, think you're somewhere else—"

"*I* wasn't hallucinating," Ben cuts in. "I saw her. It wasn't Bridgette. Not at all. But she wasn't high, tripping out."

"It's synthetic. Russian-manufactured, like krokodil." This from a documentary she watched. A little chuckle. "You're lucky it wasn't polonium. You'd be dead by now."

"We haven't met any Russians. And what would they want with us?" Ben protests. "We haven't done anything."

"You're influencers." This is giving them far too much

credit, but she knows they'll like hearing it. "The culture war is playing out on many levels, undermining democracy. It'll get worse. You'll get sicker, say more outrageous things. It affects your mind. You've already seen that."

"I'm sorry," Ben says, "this doesn't make any sense. You say Russian agents—"

"Quieter, please." Amber shushes him.

"—poisoned Bridgette with a synthetic drug because they want her to...post anti-American propaganda? Is this a prank? Are you pranking us? I didn't think you looked like the type, but if this is one of Dylan Stormy's setups..." He is standing, looking around for cameras. Another streamer, she imagines.

"I don't know this Dylan Stormy, but I can promise you he doesn't know anything about this, what it feels like when it happens, the falling away into someone else, the jet-plane sound that sucks you in..."

Bridgette is rubbing at her arm, the little wound where the threads would have emerged. Amber is amazed she hasn't seen them. Hasn't shown them to Ben.

Twice already. They'll be spinning themselves into her veins, her sinews, rooting themselves in her muscles, her flesh, until she isn't human anymore. And still, they will writhe from the husk of Bridgette's body, seeking out more. And if there are others here, in this world, they will twine around one another, forming golden bridges between the bodies, building their own structures, growing. She has seen a whole city brought down like this, where the other Amber—her name was Ember—didn't want to get involved, wanted to wait and see. Empty buildings and gold threads spanning the hollowed-out corpses, spreading and spreading and nothing to stop them.

Too late.

Ember died. Maybe that whole universe did.

She does it for Chris, for what happened to him, what was done to him, and because she won't let it tear reality apart. Amber will not let it spread. *We won't.*

"Ben," Bridgette says, tugging him down. "Please."

"I don't believe it. It's too out there. You can pay a troll farm to do that, you don't need to drug innocent people."

"All right," Amber says, placatory. "All right. I'm not coming completely clean with you." It's easier to believe a big lie than a small one, especially when it's weighted with truth. "It's worse. The personality change isn't from a drug and its side effects. It isn't brain damage."

"Well, that's a bloody relief," Ben says.

"It's real," Amber continues. "This other Bridget and you are swapping bodies and minds. It's more complicated than a drug, it's biochemistry and implants, technology from another world, another version of this one."

"Multiverse," Ben adds helpfully, finally taking the bait, awestruck.

A woman in a white evening gown, shockingly pale against her dark skin, has taken a seat at the glass piano and is playing a melodic cover of a pop song even Amber recognizes.

"I'm not CIA. Another agency. You wouldn't know it. No one does. Have you been in a hospital in recent months?"

"In Chicago, about a year ago. My mother died of a brain tumor. We tipped her ashes into the ocean in the Gulf of Mexico."

"I think I saw that video."

"Don't forget the doctor here in Tunis," Ben adds helpfully.

"Did you lose time there? Have the same out-of-body experience?"

"In Chicago? Uh, I'm not sure," Bridgette says.

"That's when they did it." Total certainty. "And she's going to keep coming back. You've seen it. You've experienced it. She intends to steal your life. You'll get sicker and sicker and lose yourself. What can you tell me about the second Incursion?"

"It was in some kind of bedroom music studio? There was the same guy there, Adrian—no, wait, it was a different name, but maybe it rhymed. He looked the same. I'm sorry, I was out of it, and it was so short. He kept telling me to stay calm and asking about my mother."

Amber takes notes, hiding her anger. Still far from tracking down every Aiden and Adrian Lyleveld in every iteration, but they will have to watch out for a new name. And if he's with the Source…

"Did this happen to him too? Is there an Adrian in my world? Did the Russians get to him?"

"I can't give you that information; I don't want to put him at risk." Trying to remember if they have already dealt with his iteration here. "He's in hiding, a safe place."

Or dead of a fentanyl overdose in his own bed. So tragic, Amber 5 reminds her.

Nice work, Amber says, commending her. If only all of them were so efficient. She could tell these two about his death, hype up the assassination angle, but she doesn't want them repeating it on their channel. "He's safe," she says again.

Ben looks worried. "What about us? Are we in danger?"

"I'm sorry, but you are."

"Can you help us? This agency you're with?"

"Of course. If you'll let us."

"What do you mean?"

"We're going to need your cooperation first. With the intruder, your hijacker."

BRIDGE

Again, Again, Again

You are the seeker. You have a quest. The chosen one by accident of birth—isn't that the way it always goes? You, Jo Kittinger's daughter, were bequeathed a legacy of all these other lives when your own pale life was already too much. There is an urgency inside your chest, like giant moths battering against your rib cage. You know you have to try all the doors. A methodology of detective work, if not science. You are quick off the mark. Your mother's daughter, after all.

Scouting trips, but you can't be leaving messages, like interdimensional mail, and waiting for the reply. Worse, you'd have to go back for answers, and you have realized there are easier ways to do this, recruiting Caden to ask questions.

Five- to ten-minute bursts in a row, quick-quick, enough time to switch and have Caden ask the otherself about Jo while you dig through her phone, her social media, try to make a connection on the other side. Not enough time, you hope, to get into trouble—like having to figure out what to do with children you didn't know you had. Like receiving a scary phone call you are *not* going to mention to Dom when they come back.

You have realized that was not your mother in that hospital bed. The Original Jo™ got stuck somewhere and that's why the woman in the bed didn't recognize you, and she is lost out there... that's why she left the dreamworm for you, the journals, because she *wants* you to find her.

So here we go. A new tactic, a bit of theater, morally dubious but for the greater good. You are lying in Caden's bed; the blinds are down so you can't see outside, and the lights are dim to try and hide his personal effects, although you've moved the musical instruments and general clutter into the living room. It does not by any means look like a hospital room or a psychiatric facility. But you are wearing a borrowed T-shirt and sleeping shorts, and one wrist is cable-tied to the bed frame as a precaution against you/the other panicking or fleeing or trying to attack him. This is not great ethically, but it's the best you can do in these extreme circumstances.

He is wearing the white lab coat, and you have developed a script for him that is more efficient, easier to pull off, than the elaborate faux-virtual-reality experiment. You have a different purpose.

He will hold up the laptop so you can watch the video, and when the change happens, another mind slipping into your body like it's a pair of shoes, he will see it in your eyes, and he will take your hand and say in a calm and firm tone: "Don't panic, you're not in trouble, you're not hurt. You had a concussion, and you're confused, and we want to help you as best we can. We need to call your mother. Can you tell us where your mother is?"

Caden has a spreadsheet of the keys and the file names, ready to make notes, but he is acting butt-hurt that he has to play babysitter, and there's a stiff coldness in the room that you hope the otherselves don't pick up on. Dom would be better at this, more tactful, more compassionate. But they're still busy doing their own kind of detective work.

It is best for you to focus on this part of the plan,

systematically working your way through the alternate-reality phone book, dipping in and out, because you don't know what comes next.

Okay. Let's go. Blitz.

You are sitting at a desk staring at a screen open to show some kind of layout software and the pages of a magazine. A man wearing a salmon-pink golf shirt is leaning over you, and you can smell his sweat under the cologne. He's shaved his head to hide his balding, but the fuzz has grown back to reveal the pattern anyway.

On the screen, you're looking at an advertorial (you know this because it's written there, very small, in the top corner) about winning an all-expenses-paid vacation to the Caribbean with Tropikale Rum, "the taste of sun and swagger."

The bald man is addressing you, disappointed. "You need to punch up the copy, babes. It's not rocket science. Give me that Bridget flair, okay?" He double-pats your shoulders in some kind of encouraging gesture and prowls over to a brunette who is scowling at printouts. "How are those proofs?"

You try to click away to Lifebook or whatever it is called here, that or your e-mail, but he spots you from across the room.

"Tick, tick, tick." He taps his life-tracker watch. "Company time!"

The older woman at the computer next to you leans over. All the people here are women. She is a graphic designer, you guess, given that she's dragging pictures around for an article titled "The Most Exotic Golf Courses in the World." "You know, my mother was a nurse and she hated doing catheter insertions so much, she would get it done as quickly and efficiently as possible, which meant she became the go-to person when they needed a catheter inserted. If you weren't so good at advertorials, Edwin wouldn't keep giving them to you."

You blink at her, trying to process this. "Have I told you about my mother?"

Her face creases in sorrow. "Yes. I'm so sorry."

Another. You are in an art gallery, sitting on a marble bench looking at a sculpture that is a tower of bizarre stuffed animals all piled on top of one another, like they have melted together. There are fish hooks and razor blades and fishbones jutting out of them. You don't like it, but you can't look away. You are distracted by your phone ringing, and you remember, *Oh, yes.* You go to decline the call, no need for a repeat of last time, but then you see that the phone is an older model, no facial recognition or fingerprint, and you do not know the code.

You are sitting in a restaurant by a window, writing in a notebook. You look down at the page. *Documentary ideas,* underlined. Then *Everything has been done.* Then *You have no POV* over and over across several pages, interspersed with the occasional *Fuuuuuuck* and *Fuck this* and *Why are you so useless, you useless fucking bitch?* And this is too familiar, too raw. When you dial MOM on your phone, the message tells you that this number is no longer in service. You notice that you have a Sam in your contacts, and your heart lurches because maybe here it worked out with you and him, but you are not here for that. There is no time.

You are in the ladies' room at the movies. In the mirror, you are too skinny and you have acne and your dress hangs too large on your frame. This is not a healthy you. You come out and you don't know which theater to go to. You haven't heard of any of the titles, so you go to the concessions stand and sit on the plastic-covered couches and scroll through your phone, going back three years to read all the condolence messages from people you don't know from when your mom died. Until a guy comes up to you, confused and annoyed, short and stocky with blond hair tied back in a low bun. "I thought you were going to the bathroom?" He puts his arm around you, and you wonder what you're doing with this bozo.

You are in a meeting with a lawyer and you know this room, even if it is a different lawyer than the one you dealt with before, and she is explaining the will to you, and this is not where you want to be, because you have lived through this before, and please—

You are masturbating in a dorm room. A woman is pounding on the door. "Oh my God, Bridget, open this door," she whines. "You better not be jerking off in there!" You hate her on principle—or maybe that is deep-baked into this body. *A plague on your house. Or dorm room, as the case may be.* You pull up your panties and go for your phone. The textbook beside the bed is *The Economics of Philanthropy*, bristling with pink and yellow sticky notes, which means this Bridge might actually pass her courses. Unless it's the roommate's copy. The phone battery is dead.

"Oh my God! Will you sto-op?" the irritating cow outside whines again.

"I have!" you shout back, casting around in vain for a charger.

You are in another bathroom. It is nicer than the last one, with one of those fancy diffuser things—you think that's what they're called. It smells of burned oranges and teak.

Your nails, tipped with gold and black, are dagger-like, and the woman in the mirror staring back at you with dark-lined eyes and a sharp undercut looks sophisticated-casual. Not you at all, although the face is the same under the war paint. You exit into an apartment. It has midcentury furniture in dark wood and a lot of plants, although some of them are (very good) fakes. There are photographs on the wall, large prints, glimpses of city lives, and somehow you know they are yours. You recognize your own eye, the things you are interested in, and you forget to do anything else. You look and look and look: at the man throwing a rock at a protest, his face contorted in rage and pain or ecstasy; the little girl with her hair in puffballs looking very small and very serious in the window of a barbershop; a naked man stumbling, wrapped in a flag, surrounded by pickup trucks and people with coolers and beers. Maybe this is what you were supposed to be doing all along. And maybe this is the gift of this. Maybe this is what your mother wanted you to find. And you could stay here, be this impossibly cool girl… and you have taken too long, captivated by ego, and you are already falling, pulled away from here.

You are spilling coffee down your front on a city street. New York, maybe? Philadelphia? You have never been to either city. A homeless man sitting outside the CVS, a dog in his lap, keeps apologizing—"Sorry, sorry"—as if it's his fault, and he offers you wet wipes from his backpack. His dog is small and sandy and well cared for, with a kerchief around her neck, and she wags her tail when you pat her.

"I don't have any change," you say, "I'm sorry." But maybe you do. You dig in your wallet and pull out a twenty. You hope it's not your last one, that it isn't rent money or a part payment to a loan shark, because who knows?

"Where is this?" you ask. "What city? I know that's a weird question."

"Cincinnati, last time I checked," the man says. That's where your mom grew up. But there is nowhere to go from here, and again you do not have time.

You are shitting in a public bathroom. There is not enough toilet paper. "Please do not leave your baggage unattended," a tinny announcement declares in, what is that, a British accent? "Unattended baggage will be removed and destroyed." Your guts are hot and twisted up, and you wish to be gone from here. Gone, gone. You can't even look at the phone. Never mind Jo—*you* might be dying.

You are asleep in bed, you are aware of the room, the edge of the mattress, someone here with you, but you cannot wake up. You try, struggling up through the dark and the dreams.

You are full of adrenaline and fury, running after someone, but you don't know who until you see the young man, scared and vicious, taunting and terrified, who has a woman's purse clutched against his chest and is dodging through the traffic. You don't want to get hit.

Another bathroom. Is this really how we spend our lives? A woman asks if you have a spare tampon. But you see, scrolling through your phone, that your mother's social media profile was last active two days ago. And maybe, maybe... you must remember this one.

Asleep again, unable to rouse.

Asleep, asleep, asleep.

* * *

In the bathroom. In the supermarket. Buying coffee. On a train to Cambridge, on a bus stuck in traffic that will not move on a four-lane highway. Driving through the suburbs and houses that all look alike, manicured lawns, and you don't know where you are supposed to be going. Driving again. More driving. Another bathroom, a bodega, a Starbucks, a bathroom, a bedroom, asleep, you manage to wake, reach for your phone, Jo is dead. Jo is gone. Jo died three years ago or yesterday or six months ago or when you were born. Brain cancer and brain cancer and brain cancer. But also comas. Two comas.

Another bathroom. Another bedroom. More television. An office job and an office job and an office job. This one is data entry, and here you're a photographer's assistant—and that seems closer—and here you are filling in time sheets for a film shoot in a production office, and a fish leaps inside your stomach, because this, isn't this what you want to do? Make something, film something? But it is *Rich Kids of Atlanta* season four and a woman with two cell phones is yelling at you.

A bookstore, trying to work out the cash register and the loyalty card for someone who is buying *The Secret*, and the cute boy at the other register is trying to get your attention so he can roll his eyes.

And somewhere between the new lives—again, again, again, back home in your world, yourself—Dom has taken over from Caden, is waiting for you when you emerge. They want you to take a break for the day, and they want to talk about fluorescents and science and tapeworms, but you have to go back, you *have* to, and there will be all the time in the world to discuss such things. They don't like it. But you are intent. You need this. You have to do this.

Back into the breach.

A restaurant with manga prints on the wall, and you are on roller skates carrying sushi. A bar where you are dressed in steampunk gear, with a leather apron and goggles on your head and too much makeup, which is even worse than being on roller skates. A vintage fashion store, where you are picking up clothes in the changing room, although it takes you a moment to realize you work there and you are supposed to be putting things away, not trying them on.

A lecture on the history of nuclear weapons. A study group whose members all look at you expectantly as if you have answers about deconstructing the colonial voice in African science fiction.

A philosophy exam where you are wholly unprepared, it looks like; blank pages and *I don't fucking know, I don't know* written in faintest pencil, as if you are going to erase it. So you don't feel guilty for getting out your phone to scroll through the names or when the moderator strides over and snatches the paper off your desk and ejects you from the room. You were going to fail anyway. But there is no Jo here, not alive.

Talking with your RA about changing your major (you have had this conversation in your own Original Life™ too many times). And you excuse yourself and go through your phone. Thank God for phones. You find a social media post in memories you made about your mother's coma. This year. The same time as Jo, your Jo, was hospitalized? Is that a coincidence?

* * *

You are making out, someone's mouth on yours, someone's fingers brushing your pussy. You panic, push the someone away. "Stop, sorry, stop, can we stop for a moment?"

The girl does, looking worried. "Are you all right, sweet? What is it?" She is beautiful, way out of your league, short purple hair and nipple piercings and a softness in her face that says she really cares about you. But you are not you. And it's not okay.

"I need a minute, sorry. It's not you." You find your eyes are pricking with tears and you curl up into yourself.

"It's okay," she says and she wraps her arms around you with intimate ferocity and you sag against her and feel your body shaking, sobs coming up from somewhere beyond your understanding or control.

"It's normal to miss her," she says and kisses your hair. "You don't have to get over it. She's your mom."

And this makes you cry harder because it feels so good being here, in her arms. But she doesn't love you and you excuse yourself and wait in the bathroom until you are gone.

Working and studying and masturbating and sleeping and eating and fucking and watching TV (a lot) and being on the toilet and in the shower, at the gym and reading a book and walking in the park and sitting in traffic and feeding a cat (but you are not sure if it is your cat), and swimming in a lake and holding a handful of pills in another bathroom, pills you flush away and hope to fuck they weren't methadone.

More TV. Curled up in bed, alone, with the blue glare of the laptop. You hope you are watching this ironically, a show about a blandly pretty angsty-boy police profiler who solves cases with a host of ghosts of former victims and his skeptical lesbian partner who is the by-the-rules good cop. But the show is also naggingly familiar. Is it possible you have seen it before in some other you? You are kind of a host of ghosts yourself. A whole haunted you-niverse.

And where the fuck is your international rock-star life? Why is all this so banal, so goddamn ordinary? Is this all you are capable of?

But Dom. Recurrent.

You are singing karaoke, drunk, at four in the afternoon, if that is the time here, wherever you are. Dom is here too, singing "Policy of Truth" with you, and you have never heard them sing and they are trying so hard, so full of bravado and so, so terribly off-key. You will have to remember this and tease them about it.

Riding bicycles along a wooden promenade by the sea, Dom dripping ice cream from the cone they're trying to hold in one hand, and swerving dangerously. You can hear screaming, but it's coming from the swinging ship in an amusement park. Is this Los Angeles? You always wanted to go. But Santa Monica Pier seems like a cheap thrill compared to Universal or Disneyland, and you wonder if you have already done all the murder-house tours Dom would have been obsessed with. You feel like you're missing out. Your mother is in a coma here too. But Dom gets weird when you ask them about the dates: "We're here to not think about that." This makes it sound recent. They are she/her here, and you want to tell her that there's another Dom, one who is different, and she could be as well, but it feels complicated and uncertain and you don't know if they, she, would want that here.

Dom lying on the grass next to you, staring up at a thicket of weavers' nests in the willow tree, both of you laughing. There is a waterfall somewhere nearby, or maybe the rushing is in your head, and when you look at them, their face is breathing, not like normal breathing, in through their nose and out of their mouth, but inflating and deflating, and you remember a children's book your mother used to read you about Moon-Face and Silky and a tree, far away, that could take you to other worlds on a swing or a balloon or something, and you remember to ask about your mother here, even though your drugged-up brain keeps wanting to swerve back to the weavers' chatter and the way they dart between the branches, flashes of black and gold, and build, always building, and maybe you need to do more of that too, building and tearing down and starting again but never giving up. But Jo is dead. Twenty years ago. And this is not the place for you...

And then: Sobbing, doubled over against a kitchen counter, someone rubbing your back, tentative, apologetic. "It's not you," he says. "Can I make you some tea?" Not Sam, thank God, you can't go through that again, but you have been through enough breakups in your life to know that tone of *You need to calm down, you're making me uncomfortable*, as if it's somehow terrible to feel things. And you don't want to stay here, you want out, away from this stranger's pity. But you still need to ask, through the Snot und Drang, your voice hoarse: "Can I call my mother?"

"Um, yeah," he says. "Of course. But don't you want something to drink first?"

You shake your head, chin trembling. It's hard to grasp that this isn't your emotion, because you're full of it, your whole body racked. You need to divorce yourself from this, focus on the wild hope of that "Um, yeah." *Jo is alive in this world.*

"Where's my phone?"

"Charging. By the bed." You stumble through the apartment with its cheap linoleum floors and walls painted a pastel blue, a tasteful cross on the wall. You're trying doors—the bathroom, a small study with an exercise bike, a desk with a laptop, a window overlooking hazy hills and an unfamiliar skyline.

And Jo, Jo is here. You have to remember *this* one. This key. Your phone is in the bedroom, on top of a book that reads *Love and Sex: A Godly Guide to Intimacy in Christ*, and you have to be kidding, right? This is the guy breaking up with you? But you have a small gold cross around your neck, and you remember the Bible camp you went to when you were twelve and trying to piss off your mother—and maybe here, that stuck.

But you are running out of time, and you lunge for the phone and scroll through to MOM and it rings and rings, and you try again and again, and the fourth time she answers.

Your *mother* answers the phone. You've found her!

"Bridget." Flat. Unwelcoming. "Is something wrong?"

And you try to get out the words, but you're sobbing again, your nerves already sandblasted by grief from whatever you/she was going through before you arrived, and you can't, you can't, and you are slipping away, the whooshing coming up to meet you, like falling out of a plane, back...

From: Jacques Philogene
To: Dom Serrano
Subject: Olivier St. Juste

My dear Dom,

It's good to hear from a friend of Jo Kittinger, although I am very sad to hear of her passing. Please extend my best wishes to her daughter and tell her that she (and you!) are welcome to come visit Port-au-Prince again.

Much has changed! I am not sure if you have been paying attention to our political progress these past few years.

President Nathalie Gurrier has introduced a crypto-based universal basic income system using some of the billions of dollars that France has agreed to refund from the reparations Haiti was forced to pay slave owners for their lost income after the revolution.

We have new hotels and restaurants for the tourists, the new Palais des Artes is an architectural marvel, and we are building (earthquake-proof) Cloud-storage facilities in a trade agreement with Brazil and Germany. The gangs are still a problem, unfortunately. Not everything is easily solved. We are working on it!

But of course that is not why you were writing to me.

To answer your inquiry, I am very sorry to say that Olivier St. Juste was murdered in his home with his wife a few weeks after Jo was here in 2017, and the house was set on fire with gasoline. Their bodies were burned very badly. It seems to have been a robbery. Perhaps the gang violence I mentioned. Olivier had bought a new television and fixed up his car, and maybe that attracted the wrong attention.

I did inform Jo of the sad news at the time, and of course there was the investigation, but perhaps she didn't tell you? Please give my most sincere condolences to her daughter.

Thank you for your kind offer to pay to assist with this inquiry. I don't feel it is necessary because this is information Jo had already. But here are my money-order details in case.

Bien cordialement,
Jacques

BRIDGE

A Million Little Pieces

Like she's swimming toward the surface, Bridge can hear Dom talking, but it's garbled, nonsense words—comforting in tone, though, drawing her up, up. She lies there staring at the ceiling letting the language sync, become real. There are downlights above her, turned on dim, but through her tears (why has she been crying?), they are all starred halos.

"We can get Eric here as well, of course we will..." Dom is assuring her. They sound weary.

Bridge sits up, wild, delirious. "I spoke to her. She's alive!"

"Safe word," they demand.

"Turtle," Bridge says. Their suggestion: "Like the tortoise in *Blade Runner* lying on its back with its feet in the air, and that's how you can tell if someone is a replicant." She feels like a film negative overlaid on top of another, on top of another, all the same photograph, but slightly different, now all blurred. It's hard to tell one from the other. It's hard to tell *her*. Physical things. Her neck is stiff, her wrist is sore, red marks are scored into her skin from struggling against the cable tie. Dom leans forward to cut her free so she can sit up.

"Dom, I spoke to her on the phone. She's there."

"I know, your otherself told me—although mainly she wanted me to call Eric, her boyfriend. She's Bridget Harris, dropped the Kittinger, if that's helpful. I marked everything down." They show her the spreadsheet, labeled with the universe key, duration, names, notes, and the critical column: Alive: Y/N?

"I have to go back. Where's Caden?" Rubbing at her wrist. "What's the time?"

"In his studio, recording. He wanted to go out too, but I said I couldn't handle two alt-reality body-snatchers simultaneously. And it's almost eight p.m. You've been at it for hours and hours and hours. I cannot see how this is good for you."

Bridge gives them that. "Yeah. Little woozy. I'm—"

"Not yourself?"

"Too much myselves. But that doesn't matter, I have to go back."

"Not tonight, baby. You need to rest, and we need to have a serious discussion. At home. And there are other possible realities that require further investigation. We can cross-reference against the ones your mom visited more than once. It's all here." Tapping the spreadsheet. "Sixty-seven total. Seventeen unclear, you didn't have enough time, worth checking up on. Nine are promising, but only two alive, unequivocal, confirmed, including this last one. Forty-six—"

"Dead." A fresh wave of grief, not just for her but for all the otherselves who have been through the same thing. But they don't have hope.

"Mostly due to brain cancer, anywhere from twenty years to a month ago. A lot of car accidents. Eleven. No, sorry, twelve. One heart attack. One rock-climbing fall."

She remembers the bouldering course Jo signed them up for when Bridge was, what, sixteen? How pissy she was, how lame it was to go climbing with her mom. Jo got into it, but Bridge had been a bitch, sulking on the mat. She can see now it was Jo trying to Velcro their relationship back together, but they were both the rough part—what's it called? The hook. And they couldn't stick. She realizes Dom is waiting for her.

"There was one other. One, uh, unnatural causes."

"What?"

"She was murdered," Dom says, meeting her eyes, giving it to her straight. "I'm sorry. Do you want the details?"

"No. No, I really don't." She swings her legs over the side of the bed. She still feels unsettled, as if she can see all those overlays, right through into other worlds. She glances at Dom over her shoulder. "Unless it was relevant? Like Rabbit?"

"I don't think so."

"Broad strokes?"

"Domestic violence. Not your dad, though," they're quick to assure her. "A man she was dating."

"That's something." Inevitable, she thinks, that among all the multiple times Jo had died, there would be something even more horrible than brain cancer out there. All the losses hammer at her, and she chokes. Dom pulls her close.

Bridge manages through the tears: "You know you're my best in the whole fucking world. In all the worlds. Most of them."

"The important ones. And the others, it's only because you haven't met me yet."

"Oh, hey." Caden pokes his head in, lurking with squeamish uncertainty. "Is she—"

"Herself? Yeah. She's been through a lot. We need a minute."

"I really think she should take a break." He fiddles with his shirt, plucking at the buttons, unhappy that they're still there.

"That's the plan, yes," Dom says. "Go home, get dinner, I don't know, sort through some more boxes."

"Sure, sure. So, I mean... you've been doing a lot. Which is fine, obviously. Important."

"You want your turn?" Dom cocks their head. Bridge stays tucked against them.

"I'm only wondering how much we have left. It's a finite resource."

"No kidding," Dom snarks.

"Can I—you know?"

"Yes, of course. Fuck, sorry." Bridge raises her head, wipes her nose on the back of her hand. "You've been great, Caden, really. Thank you. Of course you must take some."

"Okay." He smiles, relieved. "Thanks."

"Where do you go, Caden?" Dom asks.

"Everywhere I can," he says. "I want to live as much as I can, every life."

Bridge can kinda understand that, but even through her grief and exhaustion, his words don't sound entirely right. "Is there someone... in one of the otherworlds?" She's thinking about her mom and her tortured teenage love affair. Herself on a train to Cambridge—to see Sam, surely?

"No." He shakes his head, too emphatically. "It's, well, you know what it is—it's being on the frontier. Like surfing, when you go out past the break line and it's just you and the vastness of the sea, and you get a sense of your scale in the universe. It's deeply humbling, all these other... possibilities."

"Really?" Dom says. "Humbling."

Caden is unruffled. Or pretending to be. There's a neediness (one she now recognizes), a jonesing seeping through his nonchalance.

"If you tried it, Dom, maybe you would actually understand. I like seeing what I'm capable of in different circumstances. It's aspirational."

"You don't need to explain anything." Bridge waves him off, but Dom is already digging into the Tupperware, slightly turned away so he can't see how much there is left. They pinch off three strands, using a bit of tissue and hand them over.

"Oh," Caden says, that spike of hunger under the cool-don't-care. "Could I maybe get a few more? For the babysitting, using my place as your base."

Dom shrugs. "Sorry, man, all out. I'll have to get you some more tomorrow."

"Okay," he says, frowning down at the three strands in the tissue. "Yeah, cool. That's cool." Gives them a half-smile that says it's really not.

CADEN

Your Own Personal Star Maker

He can't wait for them to be gone. He watches them from the window, crossing the street toward the big ugly Grand Am Dom drives, which has managed to pick up a parking ticket. They swipe it off the windshield and he imagines he can hear them swearing. He waits, to be sure, until the car has driven around the corner and then he goes to look at the tissue on his desk beside his keyboard with its three strands, looking sad and limp. *Three?* Are they fucking kidding?

This could have turned out differently—if he'd found it before them. The irony is that he had looked in the freezer compartment when he broke into the house, while Jo was in the hospital and Bridge was sitting listless at her side, more interested in her phone than her dying mother. He'd caught a glimpse of them through the open door of the ward, got *that* close, before one of the nurses intercepted him.

Search *best places to hide your stash,* and the freezer is among the most common, along with in a sealed plastic bag in the toilet cistern, taped under the couch, behind the television, in the heating ducts, behind a painting, at the bottom of the cat litter (although Jo didn't have a cat). He had opened the freezer and hunted through it, but he expected it to be in its own container, not embedded in the damn ratatouille. Was he supposed to defrost all her frozen meals on the off chance it'd be there?

It's not enough. He has so much more to do. There are dozens like him that haven't quite made it, because music is hard, there are so many competing voices, it's so difficult to break through, so much luck and who you know. But there are a few successful Aidens too, a couple of Adrians, including a sound engineer doing forensic work with the cops, isolating a man's voice on a video where he's ordering a hit on his business partner and the distinctive sound of the air conditioner that proves it's not doctored footage.

One thing Caden's done better than all his otherselves is change his damn name. *Aiden Lyleveld* is a good moniker for a mild-mannered veterinarian or a junior logistics manager at an international shipping firm or a woodworker who makes custom furniture, and okay, yeah, some of them are musicians too, or producers—one in particular, in SG, is more successful than he could dream of being but also balding, fat.

But here, he changed his name to Caden Lyall as soon as he turned twenty, back when his band, Five-Eyed Cat, seemed to be getting traction. But by now, he's given up on his own rock-star dreams. The truth is he doesn't have the voice for the big time, but he knows he could produce the shit out of other people's music. Once he gets the track down, finds the voice to sing it, and it finally blows up, he's going to drop the last name. Become just Caden, plain and simple.

He settles the VR goggles over his eyes with the fake therapy app. He doesn't have a babysitter or care about explaining to his otherselves what's going on. Dr. Fawn thanks him for being part of the study. He cable-ties his left wrist to the radiator anyway; there's a pair of scissors tucked under his mattress, but Aiden from the SG world, who will be here momentarily, won't know that.

He hopes he has the timing right. From what he has been able to gather, SG Aiden normally wakes up late and starts recording around two p.m., working with musicians on the other side of the world in Yemen and Nairobi and Kyoto. Overachiever. But that's what makes him so good at what he does—and his songs are so very stealable.

Caden used to drug himself while he was swapping, but he found when he came back that he was groggy and couldn't remember all the notes. And he needs to remember. It's not technically stealing if they're songs he has written himself, albeit in other existences.

Besides, SG Aiden isn't a rock star. He's a producer with a $150,000 studio and a hit, a fluke he wrote for an up-and-coming rapper from Kenya, Sisterkilljoy, a dynamo with a shaved head who machine-guns her lyrics over a hostile bass line that's wound through a soaring melody he thought was Persian when he first heard it. But going through Aiden's hard drive, pulling up the files on his DAW and interpreting the confusing labels (it's reassuring to see his otherselves are as disorganized as he is, even if this one has made it work), Caden realizes it's something unique, that Aiden's brought in a lot of indigenous instruments, ouds and koras with extra strings that resonate to make the sound richer, deeper, very similar, in fact, to the kind of sounds he used to code the dreamworm doors, with all the complexities of the intermodulation. There's a Japanese shakuhachi flute in there, and ritualistic drumming with a triplet base, and he's pushed the A key, or maybe that's an effect from the instruments playing at 432 Hz instead of 440. But the best part is how Sisterkilljoy's rap segues into a dreamy chorus sung over a scratchy sample of recovered choral archives from missionaries in Zambia in the early 1900s. Talk about otherworldly.

He has no idea how SG Aiden found the track, but he's on the trail here. He plans to hunt down the rapper too. If he can find all the elements, he can reproduce the success. The song's so good, any musician would be elated to have it. Would pay real money. Career-changing money.

That's another thing he's trying to learn from his alter (what did Bridge call it—otherself? That's better, he has to admit): the schmooze and the moves. Aiden is still an introverted weirdo, but he's made the contacts, and Caden needs to memorize his e-mail address book and, more important, the tone of Aiden's correspondence. Caden doesn't have his confidence; not yet. At first he'd considered just stealing Aiden's life. If that was possible. It might be, he thinks, with the mysterious device Jo had him build.

That's something he hasn't told Bridge and Dom about. Well, there are a few somethings.

The note for Bridge, for example, on the kitchen table when he broke into Jo's house looking for the dreamworm. Of course he read it:

> *Bridge, I found the best one. Like when you were a kid and we'd go to the dreamworld. Come find me, I'm waiting for you. Like we always wanted. The instrument is the key. Rat-fooey and where I'd hide my sex tape. The very first one. Call this number when you arrive, and I'll come get you. I'm sorry to be so cryptic, but you'll see. I can't wait to show you. I love you. Everything is going to be okay. Better than okay.*

In-jokes and code. He realizes now that *rat-fooey* is ratatouille, the way a little kid might say it, getting big laughs around the family dinner table. He'd looked for a sex tape, figured it must be on her laptop, but he didn't have the password, and it was all useless without the dreamworm anyway. Frankly, he didn't care where Jo had gone, what she was doing, if she was still alive somewhere. She'd abandoned him, taking the worm and his hopes and dreams.

He has also not mentioned that he knows all about this Rabbit guy—who is not, in fact, dead. He's the one who gave Jo the plans for the device, a kind of radio transmitter. She wouldn't tell him what it was for, but Caden has his suspicions.

They'd built it together. She insisted that she needed to know exactly how to do it, but it turned out both their electronics skills were up to shit. There were a lot of YouVid tutorials involved. Jo burned herself on the soldering iron; he cut his fingers on the wiring. She'd taken the transmitter apart and built it all over again three times, without his help. And then she'd smashed it with a hammer and ripped up the plans and flushed them down the toilet. She said she had it memorized. But he hadn't been paying close enough attention, because how was he supposed to have any clue she was going to do that? He *didn't* have it fucking memorized.

Two days later, Jo was hospitalized. She hadn't left him any worm, and he couldn't get into the ward to see her. And a few days after that, she was dead and gone. Unreachable. In this world.

He doesn't owe Bridget anything. He's not her friend. Because as soon as she knows, as soon as she finds Jo, if she's out there, or realizes that she's gone for good, that's it. She'll cut him off, same as her psycho-bitch mother. And he needs the worm—for his career, for his whole life.

He noticed something else, just before he ran out of worm: doors were shutting for him, connection after connection coming up as only dead air. The kind you had to yank yourself back from, that would give you a whole-day migraine. Maybe it was Jo on the other side, blocking him with the device? If music is the key, could it also be the lock?

And something even more disturbing.

The last time he visited the woodworker, one of his favorite stopovers, hoping to pick up some skills (although it wasn't much good when it was *his* mind controlling his hands at the jigsaw or whatever it's called), he couldn't stop scratching his arm. And he's pretty sure he saw something *twitch* under his skin, which freaked him out so much he hasn't gone back to that world again.

And when Dom came back from seeing this scientist and was going on about parasites, Caden had to wonder: What if the dreamworm did lay eggs inside you?

But maybe it was just a trick of the light, or, heck, scabies, or a spasming vein. That woodworker dude was wiry from all that sawing and planing. And producer Aiden, in SG, has never shown the slightest sign of an itch.

He takes out one of the strands that Dom so very fucking generously *gave* him. It isn't fair. The worm's as much his as it was Jo's. He's earned it. He puts it on his tongue. It tastes like pennies and promises.

Jo's Diary

June 2006

Bluebeard's castle, locked in and I'm trying all the doors. I play the songs, spin the zoetrope, but my attempts to make my own patterns are pitiful, and Bridge complains that the slides of a running horse and a fat man who tumbles over and over—the ones Rabbit once used—are creepy and old-fashioned. She's only seven; I can't blame her. Apparently the ones I've tried to draw are even worse. I don't have the skills to do this. Math and music are related, the same parts of the brain, but I'm a scientist, not a mathematician, not a musicologist, and definitely not an artist. It's brutish stuff. But it worked before, with Rabbit, so I'm convinced it will work now that I have the key—if I try hard enough.

It was ugly when we got back from New Orleans.

I'd left without my cell phone, without telling anyone where I was going. I thought he wouldn't notice. He was in New Mexico that week, and I told him I'd dropped my phone in the toilet. *It was in my back pocket when I pulled down my jeans and then I peed on it,* I e-mailed him. *It's going to be in the repair shop for a couple of days, so we might be incommunicado.*

You're disgusting, he typed back. *Sorry, I meant* that's *disgusting. But don't worry, my insurance will cover it.*

He found out when the school phoned him. I'd e-mailed them to say Bridge was sick, but they called to find out how she was doing and when she'd be back, and I didn't have my phone, and he had to fly back two days early.

I was out of my mind with worry. What were you thinking? You better believe this is being documented as proof of how unstable you are. Lawyers, the threat of divorce and sole custody. He said he was tempted to open a kidnapping case. Child endangerment. *What were you doing, dragging her around New Orleans?*

But he won't do any of this. Because he loves me. He wants to make this work. No one else knows me like he does or understands how I can get—the paranoia, the terrors. Am I taking my medication? And do I honestly think anyone else would put up with this? Hasn't he seen me through years of seizures? He's had plenty of opportunities, so many women in his line of work, all the traveling, but he loves me, he loves our life, and he comes home to me. I need to trust him. He's looking out for me. He wants the best for me, but I make it hard sometimes. He hopes I got it all out of my system on this reckless jaunt of mine. He'll help me, and I'll get to finish my PhD in a year or two when I'm more stable. It's very stressful to be a doctoral student, he should know. But right now, I need to cut this nonsense out. Am I ready to face reality?

I agree with everything he says. I am duly chastised and shamefaced. I am put in my place. I have sex with him, because he expects me to, a kind of hostage negotiation. He still makes me come, devotional to my orgasm, the same way he places me high on a pedestal, bathed in the radiant glow of his love—as long as I do what he says.

He appreciates my "quirky" new hobbies—learning the sitar, the old-fashioned optical-illusion toys—and my spending quality time with Bridge (because God knows, he doesn't). It means I'm putting aside science, my career, but I must remember to call him at the appointed times. If I suggest we see my friends (*our* friends, really; I realize I don't have my own anymore. They've been cut off so subtly—*Not really our kind of people, are they?* and *George is very loud, don't you think?*), he frowns. Don't I understand I'm not ready? *For fuck's sake, Jo, you're fragile.* God knows what I would say in front of them.

And I see this, fuck, I see this now only because I have been other Jos, many Jos, who are not married to a controlling narcissist dickbag. It makes me feel more pathetic, even more contemptible and useless. Maybe I am fragile and unstable, someone who doesn't know what she wants. Maybe I am the worst of all the Jos.

I find a man on the internet in Germany, Edward Balzer, who has a collection of optical-illusion toys and patterns and disks, and he is so pleased to find a fellow enthusiast that he scans them and e-mails them to me so I can print them out at Kinko's. I have talked to him about hypnosis and meditative states and shamanism, and I asked him if he knew of anyone who used them for this purpose. He did not. "But please, you will keep me informed?" he said in his formal English. I don't have a second language. Unless you count science. And desperation.

"Who is this German guy you've been e-mailing?" Dave asks, which tells me he's reading my messages, which makes me even more squirrelly, more secretive.

"For the zoetrope. Do you want to try?"

"It's really fun, Daddy, you should try it, you feel really funny and dizzy and whoosh and then you're in a whole other place! And you're you, but you're also not."

"Your mother's not letting you have too many cookies, is she?" But the look he gives me says: *I will be very disappointed.*

"We're playing. Bridge likes it, and it's not video games or TV."

" 'The man who has no imagination has no wings,' " Dave says.

"Is that Steve Jobs?" I struggle to remember his favorites. "Soros?"

"Muhammad Ali." Dave ducks down and jabs at Bridge—left, right, hook—and although I know he would never hit her, or me, I flinch. She giggles and throws punches back, and he takes the time to show her how not to tuck her thumbs, how to propel herself from the hip. Bear barks and jumps up, trying to join in.

"Not on these pants! Goddamn dog." And then he's angry, sulky, as always, withdrawing to some arctic place where we can't follow.

Are you ready to face reality? No. Not yet. Not this one. Not until I find the sickness and cut it out. Then I'll make a plan to leave him. The caveat: I have to do it without losing Bridge.

It's terrible, I know. I am a terrible mother, like Dave says. But I can't leave her alone with the other Jos. If I had friends, I could ask them for help. But I don't. I could go to the university, show them, but my sample is being eaten away. No longer a spindly carrot; soon it will be a green bean.

So I do Bridge first, leave a note for her alter self: *Welcome to your dream, you can play with any toys you like!* And then I drug myself, enough that the other Jo will be calm and drowsy. Dave's doctor (what happened to mine, to Dr. Moosa?) has prescribed benzos by the fistful for me to help my anxiety, as if I am a fifties housewife with bad nerves. I leave a note for my otherself as well: *This is a dream, it won't last long. But you have to answer one important question. Do you have brain cancer? Can you draw on this piece of paper where the tumor is?*

I am impeccably careful about the timing. It lasts as long as it takes the zoetrope to spin down. I am always back before Bridge is. Is this the right way to do things? I don't know. I'm trying. I document everything in cryptic notes that I keep in my music book, where I know Dave won't look: which otherworlds I've been to, the results. I have a system.

And maybe I'm not the worst Jo, because there are a lot of dead ones. I learn to recognize it early, yank back from the absence.

It's not unlike trying to quell a seizure before it starts: deep breaths, a mantra. I use my daughter's name. This daughter, here, in her room next door. The only person who matters. The one I'm doing this for, because I need to live, for her. *Your child needs you.*

I realize I have to do this alone. She can't come with me or go on her own. It might be dangerous. And the supply is dwindling. Dwindling every day.

She's mad about it, stamps her foot. I take to locking myself in my room for "Mommy alone time." Two minutes, five minutes. I can't risk any longer. I slide the key under the door and tell Bridge she can let me out only when I give the secret knock; it's a game. And I make treasure hunts to keep her occupied while I'm gone—or here but someone else.

Sometimes I think I'm mad. What the hell am I doing? But then I am somewhere else and someone else, and it is the most real thing I have, apart from my kid. We start writing notes back and forth to each other, me and the otherselves.

Please help me, I write.

Stop doing this to me.

I'm sorry, I don't have a choice. I scratch that out. *This is my best chance. Please.*

I don't have cancer. Leave me alone.

Are you sure? You should check.

It's too late, it's terminal.

But where? Where is it? Can you draw a diagram for me?

Wow, this is a stupid dream.

The absurdity of these telegrams across space-time. But I also use my words when I am there: *Am I sick, can I see my charts, can I talk to my doctor, it's very urgent.*

I am a scientist, or a high-school science teacher, or I'm working at a big pharmaceutical company, or I'm living in a tiny apartment with cockroaches and a baby, and I'm married (but not to Dave), or I'm divorced from Dave. In some otherworlds, I don't have a daughter or any children at all. In one, I have two boys: gentle, doting, not like my wild ruffian girl. And even though it's only two, three, five minutes, I miss her so terribly in those worlds where she doesn't exist that it feels like I have been cut open, that I'm on my knees with my insides spilling out.

One time, Bridge is mad at me and won't slide the key back under the door.

"It's not fair, Mom! It's not fair that you go without me."

She tells her father, and I have to explain that sometimes the medication wipes me out, that I need to lie down. I use my get-out-of-jail-free card: "To stop a seizure coming on." This makes him start talking about moving down to Florida to be near his parents so they can help his poor invalid wife. In-valid. But he also tells Bridge that she needs to help me, she's a big girl, and he's counting on her. The contempt for me barely veiled.

And finally, finally, success when I am down from a green bean to a string of the dreamworm; Jo from HA writes to me: *It's in the motor cortex. It's hard to find. I drew you a picture. Tell them to look here.* And I am saved, and if I'm saved, I can leave. I need to live to leave. And now I can. I am standing back in my bedroom looking down at the piece of lined paper, the doodled scrawl of a brain (she draws as badly as I do), and the arrow to the dark spot between the lobes.

* * *

I am coming back from my doctor's appointment to schedule the scan, and Bridge meets me at the door, gulping with sobs, and it's something about the dog, and she's so sorry, she didn't mean to. She drags me to the kitchen, where Bear is sitting, happily panting, next to the island Dave put in so we could entertain while we cooked—which happened only once, for his boss, and he oversalted the pork and wouldn't speak to me for a whole day because it was my fault for distracting him.

"It's okay, baby, Bear's fine." I whistled. "Hey, Bear, c'mere, girl." But the dog kept sitting, panting, blank. "Bridge, what happened?"

"You wouldn't let me go with you, so I told Bear we could go on an adventure together."

There's a chair pulled up to the kitchen counter so a kid could climb up, reach the cupboard above the microwave where I keep the lentils and dried beans that no one in the house eats except me, and then only because Dave said I was putting on weight. The perfect hiding place, I thought. I didn't think Bridge knew it was there. But now the cupboard stands open. The wrap Mina gave me is unfurled on the counter alongside the mbira Bridge has been learning to play, the zoetrope.

I whistle again, click my fingers in Bear's face, and she turns her head toward me, an automatic response. But her eyes are unfocused. Empty. Like she went out and didn't come back.

Nodoggy home. I choke a laugh at the sacrilege, but it's partly a sob too.

Because, oh my God, this could have been Bridge. I'll have to lie to her, tell her none of it was real, it was all a game, but we can't play it anymore. I can't risk her going out ever again.

BRIDGE

Murder Wall

Her head's still spinning from all the other lives. *Keep it together*, she thinks. It's her imagination that she can still feel them, a ghost flutter at the edges, other thoughts overlaid on hers. It's all a lot for a human brain to absorb.

"All right, interdimensional jet-setter." Dom directs Bridge to the table in Jo's living room. "Sit down. We're having more takeout, and you're going to defrag and tell me about your day. All your days. But let me get you caught up on where we are with the investigation."

The lists of things to keep/sell/donate have been taken down, the boxes shoved aside. In their place, Dom has tacked up a series of new white poster boards, and there's string and stickies.

"Our very own murder board?" she says, trying for upbeat. She's exhausted but itching to go back.

"We're going to do this right. So, I've had a big day with some big revelations, especially regarding an e-mail from Haiti and a certain artist who was murdered only weeks after Jo was there."

"What?"

"And also what really happened to your dog and why your mom never told you about the worm, let you think it wasn't real. You have some catch-up reading to do. I also dropped off some specimens with the grad student who helped your mom when she got in trouble in Argentina, and she's very kindly going to be doing some complex science-y analysis for us. And we need to talk about parasites too."

"What?" Bridge says again.

"We'll come back to that, but I didn't want to bury the lede. Let's start at the beginning, shall we?" Dom goes to the poster on the wall and writes *1987* in large print. "It's 1987, Reagan is in charge, AIDS is a new big scary thing. Cold War, Chernobyl."

"That was '86."

"In the shadow of Chernobyl, then. Jo runs away from home—she's fourteen years old—and ends up in a squatters' house where this Rabbit guy, real name unknown, introduces everyone to the dreamworm."

"But we don't know where he got it."

"Maybe from Haiti." They write *Haiti* on the other side of the poster, top right. "As your mother observed, there are a lot of Haitians in Louisiana. It's worth trying to find out the provenance of Rabbit's worm. I've tried to get hold of Mina Remington, the witchy food-artist lady, but she hasn't replied to any of my e-mails, and the phone number listed on her artisan-cuisine website—which it doesn't seem to have been updated for years—is out of service. No sign of anyone by that name on Lifebook or Photoco or any other social media. She's dead or she's missing or, less morbid, she gave it all up to play housewife with a brand-new last name in a small town somewhere in upstate New York."

"Does it matter where Rabbit got it?"

"Well, it does, because even though I'm rationing it, we are going to run out. You took a lot today."

"I know." She's still reeling. "Caden said Jo would come back with major dislocation. She'd be incredibly clumsy, drop things, be unsteady on her feet—but that sounds a lot like her normal post-seizure symptoms."

"Are you experiencing anything like that, auras, tingling? Because I am going to kill you if this turns out to give you epilepsy and brain cancer after all."

"No, I don't think so." Ghosts of other lives, though, stacked on top of each other, those brief snippets. An uneasiness: Is she really here? What if this universe isn't actually hers, and she isn't her, and Dom isn't them? No, she can't get paranoid. But if she closes her eyes, even for a second longer than it would take to blink, she can see other places, otherworlds, through her otherselves' eyes. You could go mad from this. Maybe that's what happened to her mother: Jo completely lost her hold on reality, and this whole search is in vain.

Dom is talking about scarcity: "I just gave Caden his cut. I'm using drug terms because that's what it feels like right now. As if this is some premium-grade world-bending heroin."

"Fair point. Put sources on the list." She's trying to concentrate on the here and now, to shut out the frayed glimpses of otherselves.

Dom writes down:

Ushuaia—source?

And then Xs it out.

Writes:

Man in Sacramento???

"Okay, back to our timeline. In 1987, Jo B, let's call her, in universe B, with dreamy Damien, was dying of a brain tumor. So Jo, your mom, in our universe, let's call it A—"

"Very imperious of you to assume we're the primary universe."

"You let me know when you have a better name, but for now it's universe A. The place where we are. Jo comes back here, she goes to a doctor with all these symptoms and these big words she's learned from Jo B, and everyone is very skeptical, but she's right, she does have a tumor, and undiagnosed epilepsy that's related and has been going on for months (ergo, she couldn't have caught it from Jo B). They cut it out and everything is fine. For a long time. She marries your dad, has you. Things are complicated at home."

"Understatement." She remembers that during the divorce, her mom tried to talk to her about some of these things, but she yelled that she didn't want to hear it, it wasn't fair. *I'm no-man's-land, okay?* They got together at Christmas under strict cease-fire terms, but it still felt toxic, and for the longest, longest time, Bridge blamed her mom. The difficult one, the crazy one.

Dom writes down *2006* and circles it. "So, 2006. Your mom is sick again, but no one, including the doctors, believes her about the tumor, even though she is most of the way through her master's in neuroscience, and maybe, ya think, she might have a clue as to what she's talking about. But they can't find any trace of a tumor, so they decide it's psychosomatic."

"*Somaticized* was the technical term, I think."

"A-plus for paying attention to the boring medical stuff. But she knows it's not because, like you with your free will and your instinct that she's still out there somewhere in the multiverse, she *feels* it. But she has no way of proving it. Unless... she goes back to find the dreamworm so she can travel to another universe where maybe one of the other Jos (not Jo B, because that poor kid was terminal way back) might have the solution. And to be fair, she has a precedent for this."

This is important, Bridge knows, but she's chafing to cut to the important part—the universes where Jo might still be alive. Where *her* Jo might be trapped or lost or frightened or waiting for her or just hangin' out. She swerves around another alternative that she's not ready to acknowledge yet. About intent and choice.

"And Mina had some worm left over, but Rabbit got murdered along the way. And then I get this e-mail back from Jacques—your mom's fixer in Haiti—who says Olivier was also murdered. And that's two people directly connected to the dreamworm who have been killed and their remains incinerated."

They hand over their phone so Bridge can read it, but the e-mail seems to say that Olivier was murdered because Jo gave him all that money and he was flashing it around. This is horrible, but she's still struggling to connect with Dom's big *I've gathered you all here today to reveal the killer* energy.

"This is awful," she manages.

"I'm sure we'd find the original e-mail exchange in Jo's inbox, which is probably worth checking."

Bridge nods. "Did you send Jacques money?"

"Of course," Dom says. "I zipped fifty bucks over, and he's going to send me the photographs he has of your mom and also of the dreamworm."

"I'll pay you back."

Dom nods, grateful. She knows that's a lot of money—for either of them. "Anyway, back to chronological events. Mina gives Jo the worm, and Jo uses it for the same kind of blitz you did. But for some reason, she decides to bring her small kid into it."

"Maybe she was looking for a better place for both of us."

"Sure. Or maybe she wasn't thinking right because of the whole tumor thing. Or maybe the dreamworm makes you *want* to get other people involved because it's a parasite and that's how it spreads."

"A new theory enters the ring!" Trying to be playful, but she's not feeling it. If your only tool is a hammer... If it was a parasite, her mom would have said something. Warned her.

"And she swaps with another Jo who has the answer at last, and she draws the site of the tumor on a piece of paper, like we're doing now. And, same as last time, Jo goes back to her doctors, and voilà, there it is, the little fucker, hiding in the thalamus, and this time they do very good 2006 medicine and nail it."

"Except they didn't. It came back."

"Getting there. But there's been another casualty along the way." They write up:

NODOGGY HOME

From the most recent diary entry Bridge read this morning, the upsetting stuff about her dad, the chilling bit about Bear, the dog.

"Your pup goes out and she *doesn't come back*. And this, frankly, is what scares the fuck out of me, more even than people getting murdered and burned."

"But this entry proves it—she wanted there to be somewhere for us to go together, she was looking for a place, another life. She wouldn't have just left me."

"Can we focus on the dog that was empty? Bear ate a piece of the dreamworm and got lost, and your mom was terrified the same would happen to you. So she tells you Bear had a stroke, and she decides no more experiments on you, and she's going to let you think none of it was real."

"Which leads to all the therapy and almost two decades of thinking I made it up or there was something wrong with me."

"Which is awful. You're going to need some expert baggage unpacking when we're all done here. Jo divorces your dad, goes back to her career—"

"Neglects her kid." But did she? All that time she spent working, studying long into the night—how was that different to her dad's constant trips?

"Gets her PhD, yadda-yadda, maybe she's trying to forget all about the dreamworm too. But then this article comes up on this artist Olivier St. Juste who has painted it exactly the way she remembers it. So she goes to Haiti, meets Olivier, pays him too much money for some strands, has a seizure at the airport, Customs confiscates the worm, he gets murdered—"

Bridge interrupts. "That was more than a decade after Rabbit, in a different part of the world. What was the homicide rate in Haiti in the twenty teens before the reparation payments? Or New Orleans in the early 2000s? Isn't that still one of the most violent cities in America?"

"Same MO."

"Have you seen the police reports?" Bridge challenges.

"You think I didn't go digging? The problem with New Orleans is that so many of their records were lost in Katrina. I'm practically still on hold with the police department, who do not have time to help me find a case file from almost twenty years ago. A whopping two hundred and sixty-four homicides in 2004, dropping to two hundred and ten in 2005, holding steady around a hundred and sixty for a few years. I did find a two-line report from 2002 on an 'indigent' John Ravet who was stabbed to death or burned to death or both in an abandoned house. And Ravet is close to Rabbit."

"People die. It doesn't mean it was because of the dreamworm. What, you think there's someone out there hunting down and murdering people to keep it hush-hush? So why didn't they come for Jo in all the years she's been switching?"

"I don't know that part yet. But I know her cancer comes back, terminal this time, inoperable, and she's so desperate, she throws away her relationship and her career to go get scammed in Argentina. She does not come home with the worm, not this time. But somewhere along the way, she does get her hands on it, maybe from the man in Sacramento. I have not found that VIP diary entry yet, by the way. Suddenly it's game on. She's got the worm, but she needs to find the right world, like she did before, because maybe there's a reality where they have a fix for this. And she's really desperate now because she doesn't have much time left. She recruits Caden, and she starts doing all these switches."

"Doesn't tell her daughter, leaves only mysterious clues and the dreamworm."

"And by the time you get here, it's too late and she's out of her mind in a hospital bed. Which brings us pretty much up to speed, and now I want to talk about behavior change and parasites and what the dreamworm is exactly." They switch to a red pen, write down *parasites* and *life cycle?!?!* Circle the words repeatedly and turn back to her, waiting for—what, applause?

"Just because you spoke to a neuroparasitologist doesn't mean it's a parasite."

"But it might be and the point is we don't know, which is why we need to do more research."

"She wouldn't have put me in danger. I know you're hung up on this," speaking in a rush over Dom's disapproval, trying to be reassuring, trying to be patient with them. "And we should definitely do more research, follow all these leads, this *investigation*. But in the meantime, I can just go and find her."

She stands up and takes the pen from Dom and chicken-scratches.

17 Uncertain
9 Promising
2 Definite

Under this last category she writes:

XN: Bathroom Bridget

"Her mom's social media profile was active two days ago."

WV: Religet

"This is the one where you spoke to Jo, who is still alive in that world," Dom says.

"Yeah, last one of the day. First one I'm going back to tomorrow."

Dom opens their mouth, snaps it shut again.

Bridge continues. "And there were two promisings I have strong feelings about." She writes down:

ZC: Teen-mom Bridget

"Is that the would-be lamp-clubber?"

"Yeah. And the children." And the man's voice on the phone, she does not mention. "But I should go back and check. It's the one that was the first file listed on my mom's computer and maybe that's significant? Low down the list, though."

"What did she say when Caden talked to her about your mom?"

"We hadn't worked out that was what we were supposed to be doing yet. I left her a message, a voice note on her phone, and the idea was I would go back. So I'd like to go back to her specifically. And also here." She scrawls:

SG: Yachty Bridgette

"I got bounced before her boyfriend could tell me about Bridgette's mom, so it's a real possibility. And I have a good feeling about it."

"You sure it's not because you like being a seafaring bae?"

"I like her. I trust her. It's hard to explain."

"We are in the realm of the inexplicable. But how about these seventeen unknowns and the other nine possibles?"

"Dom, I have two, maybe three really good candidates." Both of them are frustrated.

"But you don't actually know what you're doing or where you're going, and we have a finite resource. Also, it could be infecting you, and then there are the murders and lost dogs, and maybe parasites, even if you don't want to hear it, and I don't want you jumping back into the fray until—"

"It's not about what you want," Bridge says, so cold and brutal that Dom flinches. "I'm sorry. I have to do this. I'm going to do this. Now. For as long as it takes. However many switches, until I run out of dreamworm or find my mom."

"Now? It's ten at night."

"You can leave if you want to. I understand. It's not going to change our friendship." It's not meant to be an ultimatum, but a matter of fact. She feels so terribly tired, and so very certain.

Dom clenches their fists into tight knots at their sides, blotchy. "You selfish cabróna," they snarl.

Bridge nods, sad, exhausted. She deserves this.

"You stubborn dickhead," Dom continues. "You rat-bastard idiot. You think I'm going to leave you to do this alone?"

BRIDGE

Reborn Reborn

Dom is sitting beside her in the bedroom. No cable ties, they insisted. Headphones on, holding up the iPad so she can see the video. So she can continue that conversation with Jo, *who is alive.* Alive. This is the one. She's certain. The colors are whirling faster, falling, rushing.

Bridge can understand how she got to be Religet. She can imagine the branch point in this reality where she spun off to someone else—she can imagine most of them, actually, the moment she could've become that photographer in a luxe apartment or that adventurer girl sailing around the world. So much of being young is auditioning for who you think you should be.

Those Christian summer camps she begged and pleaded to attend until her dad ponied up the cash, and all the trouble with Tim Walters when lust arose instead of faith. He'd made his interest clear when he'd swum underneath her during the raft-building challenge, grabbed her dangling legs, and yanked her into the deep and the dark of the lake. Bridge came up choking and sobbing in a full-on panic attack. She's always been afraid of water where you can't see the bottom, which makes Bridgette's seafaring even more admirable. God, if she could be that brave.

Kissing her bully behind the shower block was a way of

reclaiming her power, except of course they got busted, and she received a lecture about letting the devil put his hands on the steering wheel.

And here she is now, behind an actual fucking steering wheel on the freeway at night, and it is so unexpected, she takes her foot off the accelerator, cueing a concert of honking from behind her as she slows to thirty in the fast lane. Shit. She waves her hand—*Sorry, sorry,* uselessly—jabbing the accelerator down. Her nose is clogged and she's struggling to breathe, a snorting piggy hitch, her eyes swollen from sobbing. And she has no idea where she is or where she is going. Not a sinking migrant boat, not even close, but fuck, yes, it is dangerous to make the leap into the unknown.

Bridge looks down at the wheel to see which lever is the turn signal. See, she's already learning how to drive someone else's life. She hopes Religet is okay. At least Dom is going to be honest with her. They should try to time things, work out a custody schedule that's more equitable and consensual. *This is when I'm taking your life, and you can have mine.* Future goals.

She guides the car across the freeway, one lane at a time, heart racing. *I feel you,* Bridge thinks as a truck blares past her. There's an off-ramp coming up ahead, and she takes the turn and drives until she spots a big-box store called Target and pulls over in the parking lot next to an SUV covered in stickers for a political candidate she doesn't recognize. She's given herself longer for this jump. A whole hour to do what she needs to.

She raises the gold cross around her neck to her mouth, an automatic gesture. One of Religet's mannerisms, surely? *You could lose yourself in other people,* Bridge thinks. She clicks open the glove compartment, roots around for wipes. Religet is surely that kind of person. There's gum, bills, and, yes, wet wipes. She cleans her face as best she can. Takes deep breaths. Scruffs her fingers through her hair. She's pretty sure that's her unique anxious tic, but maybe this girl does it too. She doesn't know her.

She scrolls down the phone to MOM and hits Video-Call.

The phone rings and rings. Declined. She phones back, again and again. Until finally the woman picks up. The front-facing camera shows a big theater door swinging shut behind her. She's got a lanyard around her neck, and she's wearing a blue blazer with a little red scarf like a knife slash at her throat, very French, very unlike Jo, but also so very much her mother that Bridge's whole body jerks.

"I'm at a conference, like I told you, and you're making me miss the keynote," her mom—but not-her-mom—snaps. "You're not calling to tell me about your demonic possession again, are you?"

"No. It's me." Her mouth is dry. "The possessor, I guess. Nondemonic. Real girl. Not your daughter, not here, but Jo's my mom in another...place, and she died, but I think really she might be lost." She could have rehearsed this, said it better. It's the shock. *Her mother's voice.* Not her tone. But Jo. Or Not-Jo. Not her mother. Unless it is. She keeps on, hoping to force some coherence through the spill of nerves. "Has she been here? My mom, I mean. Not you. You would know. If she's been you."

"Oh." Not-Jo's whole demeanor changes; she's laser-focused. Her voice drops lower: "Where are you? Can you come to me?" She pushes through another set of double doors and out onto a balcony where other people with lanyards are smoking, and she finds a spot away from them. The sky is dark behind her; there are palm trees strung with lights. Dom was right—she should have waited till morning.

"I don't know where I am. In a parking lot? Outside

Walmart?" She glances at the clock on the dashboard. One twelve a.m.

"Cincinnati?"

"I'll look it up on the map. Hold on." Thumbing through the unfamiliar apps. "Yes, the outskirts. Where are you?" Her heartbeat a kettledrum.

"No, that's no good. I'm in Honolulu at a neuro conference. I'll fly you out. We need to talk about this."

It's happening so fast, and she's still not sure. "Mom?" Bridge says, the splinter of uncertainty. Of hope.

The woman sighs. "No, I'm sorry. I don't think so. But if this is real, we need to talk. She *was* here, a couple of times. I should have put it together, Bridget's possession and what happened to me. Two, three weeks ago now? There was a video game with animals, an experiment I absolutely *knew* I hadn't agreed to participate in, but the young man who claimed to be a scientist, so full of shit, insisted I had and that it would be over soon. And it was, and I was back in my life, except someone had gone through all my things. My computer, my desk drawers, my e-mails and research. What was she looking for?" And then, with a casual hunger: "How does it work?"

"It's, um, complicated." Not sure how much she should be telling her, caught between the ache of recognition and the knife twist of the unfamiliar. Bridge rubs at her arms, another mannerism she's not sure belongs to her. There is a mosquito bite or something, a little scab on the inside of her wrist. *Parasites,* her dumb brain says. She pushes the thought away. "She had brain cancer. She was looking for the cure."

Not-Jo lights a cigarette, something her own mother never did for fear of aggravating the cancer or acquiring a whole new one. She exhales. "You know, she did this before, years ago, in 2006 or 2007. Hijacked my body. I found myself in a bedroom, the doors locked, picture frames turned facedown—as if I wouldn't pick them up. Photos of my ex-husband. That did my head in. And when I woke up, she'd left me a note, not in my handwriting. Almost a threat, saying I might have a tumor. I thought it was all a side effect of the new anti-epileptics I'd started, but I went for a full MRI, had to pay for it out of pocket. I still go every five years or so. She really scared me."

"I'm sorry."

"No, none of that matters. You need to come see me. *You,* not Bridget. What's your name?"

"Bridge...et." She adds the *t* sound at the last minute.

"She safe? My daughter?"

"Yes, my friend is looking after her."

"How do you do it? Is it technology? Magic? Satan taking your soul out of your body, like my daughter thinks? Or are you swimming through the collective unconscious, picking a mind to surface in? Was that crazy bastard Jung right?" She laughs, rueful, annoyed at the thought, another mannerism that is painfully familiar.

"I don't understand it myself." She feels terrible, but she can't handle the questions, the implications. And this isn't Jo, not *her* Jo.

"It must be complex. We can figure it out together. And find your missing mom. I have access to excellent equipment, funding. I'm a neuroscientist, in case you didn't know."

"I guessed. My mom was too. But if she's not here, I need to keep looking. I can't stay."

"Can you come back?"

"Maybe." Bridge feels like an insect in a specimen jar. "Maybe after I find her. If I can come back. But I have to find her first."

"I can help you, if you'll let me. Come back soon and let's talk again. We can run tests."

"I don't know if Bridget would like that." Squirming. Bridge doesn't like the steely focus; worse, she recognizes this from her Jo. Single-minded, ambitious. Not quite the same, though. Her mom was never like *this*.

Was she?

"I have to go."

"Please don't hang up. There's this awards dinner in half an hour, but I can get on a plane. This is important. For both of us. For your mom. You need to come to my lab so I can run tests."

"I really can't."

"She left a note for you."

"What?"

"The same way she wrote one for me. I'll show you, but you have to come here." Wheedling.

"Can't you tell me?" Bridge doesn't dare believe her. "Was it a code? Two letters?" That would be so fucking helpful, a direct-dial.

"I'd have to find it." Not-Jo drags on her cigarette. "Does anyone else know about this?"

"Sorry, I really have to go." Bridge hangs up, and the phone immediately trills with a call back. She declines it. It rings again. She switches the phone to Do Not Disturb mode.

Who else might know, here? Who might be able to tell her more? She searches Caden Lyall, but there's no one by that name that she can find. Her dad, Dave Harris? But that's laughable. He'd definitely have her committed. She looks up Dom Serrano, but there are hundreds of people by that name, and not one of them in her contacts list.

It's wrong. She's in the wrong place. There is nothing for her here.

And then a text message comes through from MOM.

> I'm sure you're overwhelmed by all this. I'm sorry if I alarmed you! I know I can help you, and as a gesture of good faith, let me share what I remember. She'd written all over a page, scrawled notes. But I remember a word: *Bird*. Or *Birdie*. I hope that's helpful. Please do come back. I'm probably the only person who can help you.

Birdie? She's trying to remember what that might mean. Coming up blank. Thanks a lot, Mom.

DOM

Demon Slaying

The banging and screaming from the bedroom has stopped for long enough that Dom thinks maybe Religet has worn herself out. All that hate has to be exhausting: Screaming at them that they're a gender traitor and a satanic pervert and a demonic influence trying to corrupt her soul. Dom thought comic artist / human rights lawyer was an ambitious combo, but Religet obviously sees so much more in them. They tried talking to her, explaining what was happening without being patronizing. And yes, it's technically kidnapping, so they understand why she's so upset—especially because they did this to her earlier, and now it's happening again, and Religet is convinced she's possessed by a demon.

But then she called Dom a disgusting piece of shit and threw a pillow at them. They noped out, locked the door behind them, and hoped she wouldn't damage anything. They've removed all breakables from Jo's bedroom, locked the bathroom door. She could still smash the window, though.

It's tempting, considering Dom grew up Catholic and is a super-horror-nerd besides, to go in there with a makeshift cross blazing and stage an exorcism, but their Latin is up to shit and Religet is already convinced they are the devil anyway.

Instead, they're in the living room. They can't find the bit on the man in Sacramento in any of Jo's papers, so now they're digging around on the internet looking up parasite conspiracies. And yes, fine, they don't have a stitch of evidence that's what the dreamworm is, but they would very much like to eliminate the possibility. They found something called Tomesians, although it seems mainly to be a psychological response to skin disorders, dust mites and bad diet and bedbugs attributed to alien fibers. They're willing to believe the dreamworm might be alien, interdimensional, but the description of the fibers is not a match. Red. Not yellow or gold in the right light. Here's a video of a sadly delusional lady with long hair and a baby voice. She is pretending to pull Tomesians fibers from the ear of her grumpy-faced gray cat, but they're obviously actual red threads from a sewing kit. It's sad and awful. But Dom posts a comment on the video and also messages on some of the forums, just in case, asking if the fibers ever manifest in other colors and if anyone has had out-of-body experiences.

And in the meantime, a certain cool young scientist pings them a message.

Hey.

Hey yourself. How's the hot sciencing?

A yell from inside just when they were beginning to worry about the ominous silence: "Hey, you fucking psycho! Are you still there? Let me out. Let me out or I swear—"

Dom bangs back on the door. "You can't swear, Jesus doesn't like it."

* * *

It's pretty hot. But actually, I need to show you. I've been dropping some of the banging tracks you sent me and the results have been really, really cool. Can you come? Bring Bridge, and you said you had a music friend who composed the songs for Jo? If they're available, ask them to come on down too. I wanted to show you first, but there might really be something here.

"You satanic whore! You tiny-dick jerkwad!" Religet screams. "You can't keep me here!"

"You are out of order," Dom calls back, banging on the door, glad they're texting with Tendayi, not voice-noting. "We need to talk, about a lot of things, really, but especially how it's no one's business what's in anyone's pants and also about gender-based slurs and shaming people about the size of their body parts, which they have no say or control over. Also, Jesus was all about loving sex workers."

That shuts them up.

"What?" Religet says after a moment of silence and in a normal voice.

"I can come in there and we can have a real conversation if you like and if you promise to stop yelling. But you have to give me a minute." Turning back to their phone.

Super-keen. Let me check when Bridge is available. She's a little...

Preoccupied with screaming about demons.

busy right now. Caden too (composer guy, although he can be a dick). Can you wait before showing other scientist types?

If you can bring me more specimens, I definitely can!:)

When is good for you?

Tomorrow? I know it's Sunday, but I'll be here working, because I have no life apparently! And this is fascinating. Really, really fascinating.

Dom unlocks the door warily, expecting something else to come flying at their head. But Religet is kneeling next to the bed, praying.

"You all right?"

"No." She looks up, hair plastered to her cheek from crying, and Dom feels terrible. "I want to go home."

"You will. In about..." Dom checks their phone. "Another eighteen minutes. Do you want to watch TV in the meantime?"

"No. Do you want to pray with me?"

"If it will make you feel better."

"I'm sorry I called you those things."

"Wasn't very Christian," Dom says, and adds, "I'm sorry we hijacked your mind."

"It's a dream. A bad dream. I'm going to wake up any minute now."

"You will."

"It's been making me sick, you know. I got a rash. My skin is crawling. I can't sleep."

"I'm sorry." Making a mental note. Do no harm, that's a satanic tenet, right? "Any other symptoms? Anything that looks like eggs, maybe? Or fibers?" They're going full Tomesians right now.

"It's the stress from the breakup. Eric's just so..."

"You can say anything to me. I'm an agent of Satan, remember? I don't care, I'm not judging."

She smiles, a wan glimmer that reminds Dom of *their* Bridge. "Boring. Really boring. He's got no inner life. It's football and

World of Warcraft, and every weekend we do the same damn thing. We go to church—he's in the band—we visit his parents, we go for barbecue with his boring friends. I'm so bored, I could die. It's always the same. But he broke up with *me*!"

"I've endured relationships out of spite and pride," Dom says. "*How dare you break up with me? I'll show you how amazing I am.* But when I convince them to get back together with me, I'm only hurting myself."

"Do you do that a lot?"

"Couple of times when I was younger. I'm over myself now. What do you want?"

"Honestly, a conversation about anything other than sports or video games or church." She lowers her voice. "His band is terrible. The worst. They're called, wait for it: Souled Out." She spells it out.

Dom has to laugh. "I can't. What the what, now?"

"They're sooo bad." Religet is smiling. "And they're planning to tour next year with Samson's Haircut."

"You're making these names up."

"I'm not. And you know the worst of it? *I* sing and play guitar better than he does."

"Did your mom teach you?"

"Yes, but we don't speak much..."

Her posture changes and her face takes on a whole other cast. How to explain it? Dom thinks. A different intelligence in the eyes.

Bridge is back and Dom is relieved, but it was starting to feel normal, bonding with Religet over her terrible boyfriend. Less like a kidnapping. Less like something morally wrong.

"Are we...praying?" Bridge-actual says, looking down, confused, at where she's on her knees, hands clasped.

"Hey, you do what you have to on the other side, and let me do my thing here."

Bridge gives them a puzzled look, and gets up, dusting off her knees. "Yeah, sure. But I'm really close. So close. I spoke to her! I mean it wasn't her, but she knew about it."

Dom trails after her into the living room, with the posters stuck up for their active-investigation wall.

"Bridge, I think it's enough now. That version of you was very unhappy to be here. I don't think we can keep doing this."

"I'm so close, though," she says, scanning the wall. "Jo was there. My Jo. In Religet's reality. Back in 2006 and again a couple of weeks ago. Right after the diagnosis."

"But she's not there now."

"No, but Not-Jo had a message for me. Well, maybe not for me, something Jo wrote down when she was there. A word. *Birdie*."

"*Birdie* what?"

"Just *birdie*."

Dom looks at the notes on the wall, the scrawls and links, still cryptic, unsolved. "Does *birdie* mean anything to you?"

"Not a damn thing. We already have a Rabbit, so this is adding to the menagerie."

"A person? Could be a cute nickname for a grandmother?"

"Everyone at the squat had nicknames. And there were chickens."

"And didn't the food artist lady Mina have dead birds in her studio? I think this is pointing us back to New Orleans."

"We haven't had any luck tracking Mina Remington down, right?"

"Not as yet, but I'm carrying the journals wherever I go so I can dip in when there's an opportunity. Did Religet's mom have anything else useful to say?"

"She wanted me to come to her lab so she could run tests, try to help me understand what was happening. I don't think

I want to go back there. It's not my mom, and she was giving me bad vibes, like I could be her prize lab rat."

She gives Dom a flash of a smile that is supposed to reassure them. It does not. Her tone is too jokey, the comment too throwaway. As if this otherJo might actually kidnap her and run tests. They've read that comic book too, seen that horror movie.

"Or, hear me out," Dom counters, "we could go see our own friendly scientist right here in Portland in Reality A. No human subjects involved. Tendayi is pretty excited about the results of different music on the dreamworm."

"Uh-huh." Bridge isn't paying attention. She's examining the poster boards, the sticky notes.

"I thought..." Dom knows they're going to regret this. "We should invite Caden too. Get in the music expert and really science this."

"Yeah, okay," dismissive, "but I need to figure this out. What or who the hell is Birdie?"

"Seagull? Your sailor girl?"

"Maybe." Bridge taps the bit of card with Bridgette's name thoughtfully. "Only one way to find out..."

"It is now almost midnight. Bridgette is probably sleeping, or it's ungodly early in the morning wherever she is in the Mediterranean, and you'll be waking her up." Finally, they seem to be getting through, and Bridge's perma-hunched shoulders relax, oh, ten degrees. "I don't know what the dreamworm does to your brain in the long term, but sleep deprivation has many well-documented side effects. It can wait. I promise you, it can wait."

DOM

Cesspools

Bridge is making snuffling snores in the bed beside them, but they've still turned their screen down to the dimmest setting. They never thought it would come to this, back here in the cesspools of the internet, dredging for gold among the shit. Bridge would kill them if she knew they were doing this. But they've got a few things they'd like to take her to task about too, like pursuing this in spite of how dangerous it is, and why can't they find any of the other people from Leftfield, and hey, maybe it *is* some kind of parasite and there's a whole ugly life cycle they don't know about that is going to turn Bridge into a sex-crazed cicada werewolf who runs toward cat piss and is more likely to get into car wrecks. Or, ya know, get stuck in other universes.

But here they are, deep in the Tomesians message boards. See how far they're willing to sink for their friends?

Private chat window: THREADS/OTHER?

BlackOwl*#: Hi, wormholierthanthou, nice name. I saw your post on the Tomesians group asking about different color threads.

Wormholierthanthou: Hi, yes, the name is inspired by a new religious friend. But anyway, do you know if the threads come in other colors?

BlackOwl*#: It's possible. I might have some important information on this. But I need to know you're the real deal.

Wormholierthanthou: Trying to prove who you really are on the internet. Always a fun time. I can send you the link to my Photoco account?

BlackOwl*#: I would appreciate that. What color are your threads?

Wormholierthanthou: They're not mine. I haven't seen them coming out of anyone. But I read this article and it sounded a lot like Tomesians. Also saw this painting, which I can send you a link to. I think my friend might have Tomesians, but her side effects are wilder than the ones described online. Not sure if it's adjacent or something else entirely.

BlackOwl*#: I think I should talk to your friend.

Wormholierthanthou: So it's back on you. Can you send me proof of who you are? Why do you know so much about it?

BlackOwl*#: I don't like social media.

Wormholierthanthou: I mean, fair. Apart from these dark corners obviously.;)

BlackOwl*#: Anonymity is important if you understand what we're dealing with. I need to make sure we're talking about the same thing. The true Tomesians, not the pretend ones the wannabes believe they're infected with. The *real* threads are charcoal, slightly powdery when you pull them out.

Wormholierthanthou: Shit. No, sorry to waste your time. Different thing. Thanks anyway.

BlackOwl*#: I was testing you. They're a kind of dark gray-green, like mold. Or dead things. But they're not dead, they're very much alive and they can do things to you, or for you.

Wormholierthanthou: Still nope on the color. But say more about the last part?

BlackOwl*#: They change you, interrupt you. Make you see things very differently, but from a familiar perspective.

Wormholierthanthou: Yes. Seeing yourself in a whole new way.

BlackOwl*#: What color are your friend's?

Wormholierthanthou: They're yellow.

BlackOwl*#: Sunflower yellow? Bright?

Wormholierthanthou: Paler, more sickly-looking. Like someone with bad teeth. She says they're gold, though. As if she sees them differently.

BlackOwl*#: Only the one? Or a cluster?

Wormholierthanthou: A cluster. Wrapped together.

BlackOwl*#: Where did you get it?

Wormholierthanthou: I'm not ready to share that information.

BlackOwl*#: We need to meet as soon as possible. Where are you?

Wormholierthanthou: Again, not comfortable sharing that.

BlackOwl*#: We can meet in a park. Would you feel more comfortable then? I'm a woman btw if that helps.

Wormholierthanthou: Public is better, but I'd rather we communicated here.

BlackOwl*#: There are things I can't say over the internet. I think you know what I mean. We need to meet in person. I'll come to you. I'm in Reno.

Wormholierthanthou: Portland, Oregon. See what I mean, easier to chat here.

BlackOwl*#: I'll fly out. Tomorrow.

Wormholierthanthou: Easy there. I know all the scams. So if you're about to ask me to send you crypto to pay for your flights...

BlackOwl*#: This isn't a scam. I don't have time to waste. This is serious. I am offering to help you, to come to you with real answers that can help you and your friend.

Wormholierthanthou: And you're not going to charge me any money?

BlackOwl*#: Absolutely not. Is Overlook Park close to you?

Wormholierthanthou: I'm sure I can find it.

BlackOwl*#: I'm five foot four, white, sixty years old. I'll have a yellow backpack.

Wormholierthanthou: Five nine, brown, dark hair, undercut. I'll wear pineapple earrings.

BlackOwl*#: Man or woman?

Wormholierthanthou: Yes.

BlackOwl*#: Don't do anything until I get there.

BRIDGE

Colors from Outer Space

Dom was right. Sleep is the best. It's barely nine in the morning on a Sunday, middle of summer—good reasons the whole college feels like it's post-Rapture. They've seen a handful of other people: a man striding toward the admin building, a couple of study-birds holding hands as they head into the library, a groundskeeper sweeping the abandoned quad between the sputtering arcs of the sprinkler. But it's still eerie, the architecture looming and pregnant with all that knowledge—and only some of it forbidden.

Caden is "still half-asleep" he says, flushed and tousled from the bike ride over, even though Dom offered to pick him up. Bridge wonders if he doesn't feel exactly the same as she does: itchy and irritable and hungover, if that's the word to describe the aftereffects of mainlining too many lives in one day. Too rooted in *here*. Where she doesn't want to be. Her and Dom and Caden. *We three,* she thinks. *Strange witches. Bad science.*

This visit feels like a giant waste of time, but Dom has been so happy about doing this *their* way, with proper research and real science and, oh, yeah, a new online friend they're meeting later, because that's exactly what they need: more people involved. Dom can sense her impatience, and they nudge her while they're all standing around outside the very locked main reception doors of the science building.

"I know you want to get back, but it's okay, I promise. Nothing is going to happen. If Jo is out there, she's *still* going to be out there."

Easy for them to say, but Bridge feels the constant tug of it, the widening expansion of who she is through all those other lives that also has the effect of making this one seem ever narrower. The side door swings open and a young Black woman with a lush smile waves them over and beckons them in.

"Hi, sorry! I don't have a tag for the main entrance." She props the door open a crack with a brick. "In case anyone needs a smoke break later."

Caden puts up his hand, groggy behind his sunglasses. "Do you have any coffee?"

"Yes, there's a faculty kitchen upstairs, but we only have instant. Budget cuts. Are you Bridget? I'm so sorry about your mother."

Bridge says thank you, because she's supposed to and she'll never get used to hearing those words, is already heartily sick of them. She hopes that's the end of it. Itching to go back. To not be here. The building hasn't changed since the last time she was here in November, only it's more deserted now, eerie without students clattering around. Pale light filters in through windows wearing the dusty fingerprints of old rain. Their sneakers *squeak-squawk* on the tiles all the way to Tendayi's lab, which is an echo of her mom's down the hall, now locked up, her name no longer on the door. *A compatible,* she thinks.

"Shall I go make some coffee for everyone or—"

"Why don't we go ahead," Dom says. "It's a recording, right? So we can watch it a first time and then replay it after liberal doses of caffeine."

"I brought my laptop," Caden says. "More music samples to play around with."

"Amazing, thanks." Tendayi dips her head, smiling hopefully, revealing a gap between her teeth as if to remind Bridge she's human and imperfect and trying her best.

Ugh. Fine. "Hey, thank you—Jo would have been happy we're here," she manages.

Tendayi beams. "Of course! I'll pull it up, hang on." She turns on the external monitor and clicks through to a file with yesterday's date while Caden flicks the lights off. And is he being more quiet than usual? He's looking at her with a strange intensity.

"Mike helped me prep the sample. Don't worry, I didn't tell him what it was. We put it under the confocal microscope, totally unstained, and, well, as you can see..."

She clicks "play" and Bridge tenses in anticipation. But it's a scan thingie, not a zoetrope. She has no idea what they're looking at. A rounded head, a bit like an elongated dick, floating in a galaxy of striated lines and nebulas. Green, blue, red.

"It autofluoresced!" Tendayi says triumphantly as if she thinks they know what they're looking at. "You get some plants that do that, but not like this."

"It glows? From the chemicals?"

"Sorry, I'm not explaining clearly. No, I didn't stain it with any markers. Confocal microscopes use a limited range of lasers to simulate and emit light, specifically red and blue and green. You should only be able to see those specific colors, but here, as you can see..."

On the screen, there are shades emerging in that Magellanic cloud, purple and yellow, like an old bruise, and another color Bridge can't describe, one she's seen before. She goes to tug her hair, finds herself rubbing her arms instead.

"So it's showing other colors? Um, nonnatural colors?" Dom says, staring at the screen.

"Yes, colors that shouldn't be possible. It's literally out of the range of the lasers. The machine shouldn't be capable of doing this."

"Which means..."

"I don't have a clue. We need to do more testing. I've never seen anything like this."

"So it's alien?"

"As in foreign, not natural," Tendayi cautions. "Not as in outer space."

Unless it is, Bridge thinks. Or otherspace. The spaces between.

"Now, you said music was important," Tendayi goes on, "so I started playing it a selection of different songs, from Run the Jewels' 'Thirty-Six-Inch Chain' to the Andante movement from Mozart's Piano Concerto number twenty-one."

"Supposed to be great for studying—alpha waves, right?" Dom says.

"And my nephew playing the recorder back in Harare—pure torture. None of which had any effect on the worm or the fluorescent proteins, as you can see on the recording. And then I hit on this." She grins and plays another video of the dreamworm up close on the confocal microscope and, tinny in the background of the recording, the opening violin wail of Britney Spears's "Toxic." The response is immediate. The colors flare brighter, coruscating like disco lights through the strand of worm.

"It goes especially weird on the Bollywood parts and—wait for it—here! The fuzzy electronicky-feedback bit."

"That's the Hendrix chord," Caden says, but he looks impressed. "As in Jimi, who could actually play the feedback distortion and control it. You realize, out of all the Western pop canon, this song, very unusually, *does* play with dissonance and microtonalities."

Tendayi shrugs, grinning, enjoying herself. "The sitar also had an amazing response, no surprise there, lots of fluorescents." She shows them that video. "And then I had time, so I started getting really weird. Tibetan throat singing, vodou drums, Jon Hopkins music composed for ketamine trips, something called the Brain Dead Ensemble, where, like Hendrix, I guess, they've got all their self-resonating instruments plugged in together. What can I say? Major rabbit hole." She shrugs again. "You'd never guess I have a paper to edit. Most productive when I'm procrastinating. And then, hey, neuroscientist, I couldn't resist. There's a Stanford professor who developed a brain stethoscope that turns EEGs recorded during seizures into dope tunes. Check this out."

She clicks on the file. The music is not dope. It's awful. It's a high-pitched squiggle, increasingly frantic, over something like the unearthly tenor of a didgeridoo. On the video, the fluorescent proteins stutter, turning white, then dimming. "See how it thrashes and seems to shrivel?"

Bridge feels the sound corkscrewing into her brain with every squeaky tremor, pitching up, up, faster and faster. It climbs into her bones, sets her jaw buzzing.

"Whoa." Dom notices her distress. "Are you okay?"

"No, stop it, please." The spit is thick in her throat, like she's going to vomit. Her whole body's clenched like a fist. And then, mercifully, Tendayi stops it. The relief is instant. Caden also looks shaken.

"What was that?" Dom says.

Tendayi is making big eyes. Probably worried about her grant, about being disgraced and thrown out like Jo was, losing her student visa, being deported.

"I'm fine," Bridge quickly counters. "I haven't eaten. Sorry."

"I got you." Dom digs in their bag and hauls out a banana. But Bridge knows it's not hunger or a hangover or that horrible sound that would set anyone's teeth on edge. It's not wanting to be here. They're wasting time.

Tendayi frowns. "The specimen didn't like it either. It shriveled right up. No fluorescent proteins on that. Let me show you the video."

Dom stops her, gently. "How about we take that coffee break?"

"I could use a cigarette," Caden says. "Bridget, you wanna join me?"

"She doesn't—" Dom starts, as if they are the health patrol, as if they know everything about her. But they don't. Not all of her, not every iteration, not how she's feeling right now, reeling and nauseated and in desperate need of a cigarette, which she can already taste in her mouth, not sure if it's a memory or an echo.

"Sure."

They're sitting on a bench at the edge of the quad overlooking the campus, which is no more populated than it was an hour ago. The weather has changed, clouds rushing in.

"You felt it too?" he says, lighting her cigarette off his. "That track, the brain scan song."

"Didn't feel good." She shades her eyes against the light. The sky is migraine blue against the green, green grass, the humidity already thickening in the air. By lunchtime, it will be a breathable broth.

"Something's happened," Caden admits. "I didn't want to say in front of Dom. You know what she's like."

"They."

"Sorry, yeah. I didn't want them to overreact. Maybe it's why we're feeling off today..."

"Here I thought it was that white-hot brain-seizure remix Tendayi played in the lab."

"You were feeling shitty before that, though, weren't you?"

"Overexposed," Bridge says. "Like I can't shake it from my head, all the other realities, the other lives."

"Lucky you. I couldn't reach them. Barely any. I tried seven yesterday; I would have done more if Dom hadn't been so fucking miserly with the doses. Yes, okay, I know they're your friend and you don't want to hear a bad word, but they don't get it. They haven't done it. But *we* have."

"What do you mean, you couldn't reach them?"

He takes a long drag. Somewhere a raven creaks, harsh as the tobacco. "I started falling away and then bouncing back here. Like the doors were closing."

"Or like maybe you didn't exist on the other side? I felt that a couple of times—the dead air."

"Six out of seven times? That doesn't seem very likely. They're all realities I've been to before. The only one I could get to was SG, and I've got a theory about that."

"Maybe someone's mass-murdering you, personally."

"That's not funny." He takes a long drag; smoke curdles from his lips. "The doors are closing. Maybe there's a limit to the number of times you can use it? Or there's, I don't know, cosmic radiation from sunspots interfering? Or..." He lets it dangle. Takes a long drag. "Jo's closing them."

"That's not funny either." She's so sick of all the talking, the questions. The answers aren't here. Bridge squeezes her eyes against the bright rain clouds, wishing she had sunglasses, and in that instant, she catches a glimpse of a different sky, a different view. She blinks hard against the effect, which is gone, if it ever existed.

Caden doesn't notice. "You've got her journals," he says. It's a statement of fact, not an accusation, but she feels guilty anyway.

"Yeah, but she didn't write anything about closing doors."

"She didn't mention a device?" Dangerous-casual.

"A device? Not in anything I've read. But her notes are a shambles." She raises her chin at him. "What device, Caden? Is she alive? Where is she?"

"You think I know? You want the GPS coordinates? I have helped you every step of the way. I opened my home to you, showed you how the whole setup works, babysat while you went tripping fantastic on some crazy quest to find Jo, but she left us, Bridget. Both of us. She found a way to get out. And she left us here without anything, and now the doors are closing." He stabs out the cigarette on the edge of the bench, between the calcified white splatters of pigeon poop, then takes her wrist and turns it over. "Have you—" he starts.

It's the lightest scrape of his fingertips, rough from guitar strings, across her skin, but she recoils, out of proportion to the touch, yanking her arm back. "Ticklish," she says by way of apology, but she flashes to Religet's rash on her arm.

"Sorry. But something really weird happened in SG after you left. That's the main one I go to. It's a music-producer version of me. Aiden, not Caden. And when I got there last night—shit. I don't know if you're going to believe this."

"Really?"

"He had this old PC out, running Cool Edit, this really old software, but it has a brain-wave synchronizer in it, and he was playing a loop of Tibetan throat singing, which has all these shifts in timbre and pitch against a stable base."

"I believe you." She gestures impatiently. Not more theory.

"I'm getting to it! He's sitting there—no, *I'm* sitting there, with electrodes on my head, attached to the brain-frequency simulator, and my arm is outstretched and I'm bleeding because the crazy bastard has cut his arm open, and there is something moving inside there."

"In his arm?" Suddenly she's paying attention.

"And it's coming out, sort of waving around, like he was snake-charming it out of there with the music. That's where it comes from, Bridge. *It's inside us.*"

"But"—she examines her own wrists, which don't show any marks—"I've never..."

"Me neither. But at least one of my otherselves has. And imagine. Imagine if you could just summon it out of you. Maybe if we had the right tune, the right frequency—"

"Or maybe it's a parasite that lays eggs." She doesn't like where this was going, the manic look in his eyes. The horror thought she doesn't want to admit that maybe Dom has been right. It can't be true. It's absurd. She doesn't want to believe it. She doesn't have to. *They're wrong.* All of them. Worms spun from your veins?

"Uh, sure. But do you know how we find out?" His tone turns coercive. "We need to experiment. With music in my studio, not this rainbow-injection fluorescent stuff with Britney fucking Spears. But I can't, not while Dom's holding all of it. You have to ask them for me." Exactly with that addict fervor, Bridge thinks, and then immediately: *But* I *need it.*

"I'll ask. I will," she soothes. But her brain is churning. "After we're done here. We'll do the hard science, make Dom happy, and then go back to your studio together." All these people she has to please, entertain all their wild ideas. When all she wants to do is go back. She only has to say the right things, placate them all long enough until she can.

He searches her face, but he doesn't know she's an amazing fucking liar, has been since she was a kid, one of Jo's gifts to her. "And I'll share the journals with you," she continues. "You're right, we should have been pooling information. And you'll do the same, okay? If Jo told you anything about where she is."

"Sure," he says, only just meeting her eyes.

"And do me a favor?" She's sure of one thing, at least, about Caden's new grand theory or delusion or whatever, that Dom will freak the fuck out. "Don't mention any of this to Dom. Not yet."

DOM

Online Friends, No Benefits

Bridge comes back up to the lab looking pale and crumpled and reeking of cigarettes. Caden also looks like shit, but Dom isn't worried about him, unless his condition has something to reveal about Bridge's. Brain damage from all the jumping, for example.

"Is that coffee?" Bridge perks up.

"Freshly brewed, finest-quality supermarket instant." They hand her a mug featuring a cartoon of a cell with stickman arms holding up a phone above the witticism CELLFIE.

Tendayi is prepping a fresh specimen—the regular kind—for the microscope. No inexplicable coruscating colors, because the confocal requires other experts to help them with stains and things, and Dom would prefer to keep this on the down-low. Tendayi would too, they get the impression. Her curiosity is bursting, but there's the whole unauthorized-by-the-university thing, which they have studiously avoided talking about. Plausible deniability.

Caden is setting out his laptop, chatting to Tendayi about the process. Normally this would be a million times Dom's jam, but they have an appointment with BlackOwl*# approaching. "You feeling okay?" they ask Bridge, reaching to touch her forehead. "Because if you're experiencing any symptoms I need to worry about—"

"I'm tired is all." She flops down on one of the desk chairs under the overgrown Swiss cheese plant. The way the leaves and roots unfurl behind her head makes her look like some kind of flora Medusa. "Do you mind if I don't come to meet your online friend?"

A twist of disappointment in their stomach. "Of course not. Do you want me to drop you at home? We can postpone the experiment."

Tendayi looks panicky at the thought. Strike while the scientist is hot, Dom figures. Before she has second thoughts. Before Bridge does.

"Nah. I'll hang out," Bridge says, "see if I can be useful. Tendayi has gone to all this effort and I'm curious."

"Okay." Dom studies her face, uncertain. "I'll be an hour max. Maybe an hour and a half."

"It might be important," Bridge agrees. Maybe it's the cigarette, but she seems calmer, more together. "You've been doing the most and I know I've been a difficult bitch."

"Take your time, everything's under control here," Caden says, not looking up from his laptop. But why do they feel like it's not? Everything at a precipice. A grand uncertainty. But they love her and they trust her and how much trouble can she get up to in the lab anyway?

The sky above Overlook Park feels heavy and swollen with the threat of rain, gray clouds above the gray river, and the curve of the Fremont Bridge's in stark relief like it's been cut-and-pasted in a bad PrintMaster job. From here, you can see the railyards, port-land indeed, dozens of tracks running together and apart, and Dom can't help but think of them as worm trails.

There's no sign of their rendezvous, but then they are five minutes early, so they park themselves on the bench by the picnic area to wait. They've got some of Jo's journals in their backpack, a little light reading, and they're not expecting anything, skimming the pages when they snag on a date that jumps out at them from mere weeks ago, and a name, "Rabbit." The words "alive in California."

Shock and revelation, Dom grins, they can't wait to tell Bridge, but they don't get any further in the reading, because a woman is hovering nearby with the jittery nerves of someone on a first date.

"Wormholierthanthou?" she tries uncertainly. Her voice seems familiar, somehow, or maybe it's just that middle-aged-white-lady fry. She's exactly as described, with a bright yellow backpack, leaning on a rolled-up umbrella. Older than Dom had pictured, mousy hair cut too short in an unflattering style, body practically square under her raincoat.

"Dom, please." They shove the journals down into the backpack, while standing up to shake her hand. "BlackOwl-star-hash?"

"Amberlynn. It is So Nice to meet you." Her grip is delicate. She has a strange clipped way of saying her words, the capitals clear.

"Thanks for the outside meet. You never know with strangers online."

"I heard this podcast about Russian scammers on online dating sites who string lonely women along for months and months, saying they're working on the oil rigs in far-off places, and then of course something goes wrong, a missed salary payment, and they need money to fly out to meet them."

"I think I caught that one too. But really, you should start a podcast about whatever we're dealing with here."

"Well, I do YouVids about Tomesians with my little cat, Mr. Toe Beans, because animal videos get more likes."

"That was you?" Of course. More singsong and she looked different. "But your hair..."

"A wig. I also put on the voice. It's a lure, you see, to find the real sufferers. Like you."

Dom catches on that word *sufferers* and the peculiar fatalism in her tone, like she's talking about terminal patients in the cancer ward. "It's not me, though, like I said. It's my friend."

"I can tell," Amberlynn says mysteriously, and *Christ, please let this not be a giant hoax,* Dom thinks, trying to tamp down the excitement, the relief, of finding someone who might actually know about the world Bridge has catapulted into.

"Shall we walk?" As in away from people who might overhear. The clouds have darkened and fine drops are starting to spit down. A picnicking couple are gathering up their blanket, their sourdough loaf and assorted spreads. Cyclists are veering back toward the main drag, and even the people at the dog park are leashing up their pups. It's a slow-motion evacuation.

"So...how can you tell it's not me?"

"I'm also a Carrier. But I have it Under Control."

"What is *it*?"

"You tell me," says Amberlynn. "You've seen it. Used it? I need to check we're on the same page. What does it look like? What does it do?"

"Well, yellow, gold in some lights, we've already established that. But I haven't seen any individual threads or worms or whatever they are. Not under the skin, like with Tomesians."

Amberlynn raises her eyebrows but doesn't say anything.

"The thing we have...I'm going to call it a conglomerate form, dozens of them wound together like a spindle, and you can unpeel them into individual threads. And what it does, uh, well, it lets you switch, if you know what I mean." Fumbling in the dark here. "I mean, I don't want to feed you the answers either. For all I know, you're a Russian romance scammer." Or a North Korean agent, Dom thinks, or, hell, the alt-right or dubious forces in Kamala's government. But it's hard to imagine this woman with her cheerful yellow backpack pulling out a syringe full of Novichok and lunging at them.

"Realities. Minds. Bodies. But only for a short time."

"Yes, fuck. Thank fuck. That's it." They wilt with relief. Amberlynn is the real deal. Finally, someone who might actually know what the fuck is going on around here.

"It's very dangerous, Dom." Her voice falters.

"Yeah, well." They shrug. What are they going to do? Take it away from Bridge? "I've tried to tell her it's a terrible idea. It's complicated." The rain is coming down harder now. Fat splats of it. "Maybe if she heard it from you?" They've already decided she's not a serial killer. "Could you come talk to her? Out of the rain?"

"This friend of yours? How many times has she switched?" She's struggling with her umbrella, and Dom opens it up to cover both of them, and they head toward the Grand Am. They've already decided to bring her into the circle. Bridge might be pissed, but here is someone who actually knows what they're dealing with.

"A few." Sixty-seven, to be precise. "Dozens, maybe. She thinks someone got lost in between. Her mother. She's the one who had the dreamworm originally. That's what she called it. Her mom used to give it to her when she was a little girl."

"What was her name, the mother?" Amberlynn has stopped dead and is staring out across the park at nothing. But she's not dazed or dreamy or unfocused. It's as if she's seeing into somewhere else right now. Same look Dom has seen on Bridge in the instant before she makes the switch. They're torn between giving away too much information and giving too little. But fuck it, sometimes you have to trust people.

"Jo Kittinger, a neuroscientist. Do you know her? Maybe her name came up?"

Amberlynn's attention sweeps back around to Dom like a lighthouse beam. "No. It hasn't." Crisp. "We don't know her."

"We?"

"I work with other people. This is dangerous. Bad things can happen. Very bad. People could die. I drove here right through the night. It's that urgent. We have to deal with it immediately."

Dom has the terrible feeling that they're communicating *at* each other, using different bandwidths and technologies, Morse code to fax machine, and trying to transmit the whole damn library of Alexandria.

"Some people have already died, which I'm worried about. Bridge doesn't think it's connected. An artist in Haiti, Olivier St. Juste…"

"You sent me the article with his painting," Amberlynn says.

"I thought there was another death, but I just found out he's alive, or was a couple weeks ago." Add that to the murder board. It must be the man in Sacramento, Dom thinks. Everything is coming together. "And Jo, of course," Dom continues, the words tumbling out, but fuck it, they're all in now. "She wasn't murdered. She died of brain cancer, but Bridge is worried she is lost out there, that her consciousness or her soul or whatever makes the switch—"

"The Transgression."

"—didn't come back, and maybe she's still out there and Bridge is looking for her. I know it sounds like wild ravings."

"I believe you," Amberlynn says, and isn't that what Dom

has been waiting to hear this entire time? The wholly unraveling relief of being heard, understood.

"I had to come. Dropped my kitty with a neighbor, drove eight hours to get here. I had to come and help you. You don't know the truth about this."

"So what is it?" they ask again. *Not gonna lie, feeling pretty freaked out right now.*

She reaches into her coat pocket, takes out a small slim case, and opens it to reveal a tender yellow strand. "It's a monster. You think you can control it, but you can't. No one can. It lays its eggs inside you, the worms hatch, you can't pull them out fast enough. Your mind becomes infected, so you do what they want, which is to help them spread and infect other people."

Dom staggers. They didn't want this to be true. It can't be true. BlackOwl—Amberlynn—was supposed to be the voice of rationality against their half-baked conspiracy theories. But they knew, didn't they? Like Bridge did about her mom. This is real.

Amberlynn's voice starts to rise, the pitch of a doomsday prophet: "Eventually you are not a person anymore but a tangle of worms writhing under your skin, through your nervous system. What did you call it? A conglomerate? We've seen the Hatching. The threads tearing through the flesh.

Dom feels sick with panic. "No. Look, I don't know where you got that. I haven't seen any worms. No one's been getting worms under their skin. That's not what's happening here." They push the slim case away, but really they want to shove her to the ground, scream *Liar* in her face. "I mean, that's why I only followed up on Tomesians now."

Amberlynn gazes at them with pure grief. "Then maybe your friend is the Source. And she's been infecting everyone else."

BRIDGE

Dark Water

She waits a good eight and a half minutes after Dom leaves before asking Tendayi if there's somewhere she can lie down quietly for a while. Not feeling well, you see; she gets migraines. She needs a dark, quiet room, white noise on her headphones. This is a lie. Tendayi and Caden are ready to start the experiment, and Caden looks unhappy, but she doesn't give a shit if he knows what she's up to. She scoops up Dom's backpack holding her mom's laptop—and the Tupperware—and Tendayi leads her two doors down to her supervisor's office.

"It's Professor Fonseca's. He took over from Jo when, uh..." Tendayi looks sad and mad and guilty, and Bridge nods.

"This is perfect," she says, looking around at the immaculately organized room, so unlike Jo's scrambled decor. Rows of slick white filing cabinets to match the desk, with one inbox, an ergonomic chair over by the window, and a small two-seater baby-shit-brown leather couch. She goes to close the blinds even though she already knows she's not going to stay here. She wants to be far away from even the possibility of interference.

"Can I get you anything? An ice pack?"

"I'll be fine." Bridge winces, eyes scrinched up in pretend

pain, willing Tendayi to go away and leave her alone so she can go back. She needs to go back. Now. Especially if Caden is right, and the doors are closing. "Probably half an hour? I've taken my meds, so..."

"All right," Tendayi says, still reluctant, but Bridge is already lying down on the couch, recovery position, knees tucked up, her sweater pulled up over her eyes, earbuds in. "We'll be just down the hall if you need anything."

She waits, so fucking patiently, listening to Tendayi's sneakers squeak down the corridor, hears the clack and latch of the lab door, and then she's on her feet and padding down the corridor to find somewhere farther away where she won't be disturbed. Like this, say: the Museum of Surgical History.

It's unlocked and Bridge slips inside, closes the door behind her, and moves into a room of grisly photographs, old-timey paintings of dissections, and glass cabinets containing jars with fetuses and preserved stomachs and brains and a huge tapeworm that fills almost a whole wall, softly rotting in formaldehyde. The worst is the display of things they used to cut and slice: bone saws and scalpels and hand drills and screws and clamps.

Yes, this seems appropriate.

Bridge sits down on a wooden bench with a little plaque announcing that it is dedicated to the memory of one Frank Pieterse. Well, she hopes Frank likes interdimensional travel. She takes everything out of the backpack, pops the Tupperware. The damp fleshy squidge as she pinches off a piece of the dreamworm. Props the laptop on her lap, opens to the correct file. SG again, for seagulls? The music starts, the video, the colors and the howling wind, only now it feels joyful and familiar instead of scary and then...

The briny confines of a cabin.

She is back inside the lean, mean ocean queen who is, right now, curled up on the bed, watching some rom-com on Homecinema or whatever it is called here, and Bridget wonders if it's okay to despise yourself a little if it's not technically you. Even propped up on the pillows at rest, Bridge can feel the easy grace and strength in Bridgette's body. She examines her arms—maybe there's a bird tattoo among the snakes and flowers? She's still looking for Birdie.

Where did this iteration of her find her easy-breezy attitude that has her sailing around the world and streaming the adventure? Why doesn't she share Bridge's thalassophobia which has her freaking out about swimming in lakes let alone setting off across the deepest and darkest of waters? Where is her angst, her only-child perfectionism that should have paralyzed her, preventing her from achieving anything? Did her parents stay married here; was Dave the best dad; was Jo present and involved? Was that all it took?

Bridgette's boyfriend walks in with mugs of coffee spiked with whiskey, judging from the smell, and clocks her—Bridge, that is—right away.

"Oh, crap," he says, resignation mixing with an undercurrent of wariness. He retreats to the main cabin, sets the mugs down, and gets out his phone, turning away from her.

"I'm sorry," she says, getting up to touch him (a flash of his mouth on hers, the soft friction of his beard, and was that her memory from the first time she was here or Bridgette's?). "I had to come back."

He gives her a pained smile that really isn't a smile at all, holding the phone to his ear. "It's all right, she said you would."

"Who said? Bridgette? Who are you phoning?"

He ignores her, climbing up the ladder onto the deck. "Hello, Agent Drew? You were right, she's here."

Who the hell is Agent Drew? Bridge thinks, moving to follow, but she is brought up short by the sight of a glass jar on the table. The gold lid is screwed down tight above a half-peeled label advertising apricot compote. But it doesn't hold any kind of fruit concoction now. *It could be anything*, she thinks. *It could be a slender twist of orange peel.* But that's marmalade, not apricot, she knows from being a broke-ass student, from living on a diet of instant ramen and white toast and jelly. Where's that innocent kid now?

She knows. She recognizes it immediately. It's calling to her from across the cabin. A magnetic attraction. Bridge inside Bridgette picks up the jar and holds it to the light. A golden glinting strand, brighter than she's ever seen it. *Fresh.* She realizes that her wrist is itching. There is a tiny raw pockmark on her skin, like when you scratch off a zit, just below one of the snakes on her tattoo, so it looks as if its tongue is flicking out to lick the tiny wound.

"Yes, right now. Two minutes, maybe?" Ben's voice drifts down from above. "Can you come?" A whine in his tone. As if she's dangerous.

"Ben—that's your name, right? Listen, it's cool, I just need to ask you something," she tries as she clambers out onto the deck too, trying to put in a little hint of that sea-breezy herself. She's still holding the jar. The night sky is a dark blanket over the sea, pockmarked too, but with glinting stars. Are they still in Tunis? The time zones would make sense. The water slaps-slaps against the boat, against the floating wooden walkways, what are they called? Jetties? The yachts are all the same ghostly color in the moonlight, all rocking lullaby on their moorings.

"Ben, hey, wait. Who are you calling?"

He's lowered his voice, moved to the far side of the boat, close to the jetty, watching her. "Yeah, of course, thank you."

It's deliberate, she realizes, him getting between her and the way out. He wants to prevent her from leaving before this other *person* gets here. And maybe this Agent Drew can explain, maybe she knows where Bridge's mother is, how to find her. But that's not what his body language says. He's tensed like a feral cat.

"It's okay, babe," he says, faking it. "Grocery delivery for tomorrow. Amir's bringing us fresh figs from his garden."

"Cut it out. Who is Agent Drew?"

"You misheard me. I'm really worried about you, babe, you've been having these episodes, you're confused."

"So, then, what's this?" She rattles the jar at him, more of a half-hearted wiggle, and to her horror, the dreamworm inside curls up on itself. A trick of the light, surely.

"It's..." He falters in whatever lie he was going to concoct. "Okay, I know who you are," he admits. "I know you're not her." Sweet, honest Ben. A reminder of Sam, what could have been. She feels sorry for him. Ben's not a bad person. But neither is she and he's treating her like one.

"Did this come out of her?"

"Yes. That's what happens when you mess with this stuff, Agent Drew says."

"Who is he?"

"She."

"Who is she, then? How does she know about all this? What else did she say?"

"That you'd be back, and that you should wait for her. She's U.S. government, not CIA, some other agency that deals with *this*. You'll see. She's on her way. She's going to help you."

"What makes you think I need help?" She's trying to be tough, but she can feel tears pricking at her eyes. Crumpling bravado. *Doesn't* she need help?

"Look, I just want my girlfriend back. We don't want to be involved in all of this. I'm sure you don't either."

So reassuring, but he's still blocking her from getting off the boat, shoulders squared, making himself wider, as if he's not big already.

Here's the thing about boats, though. He might be standing between her and the gangplank or whatever the fuck it's called, but when you're on the water, every way is an exit.

"Okay." Bridge smiles—her own smile, not Bridgette's. "We'll wait for her." She perches on the railing of the yacht, sitting opposite him, on the ocean side. She would never be able to do this in her normal life. Never, ever, ever. The water is pitch black below. It's only her imagination that she can feel the chill of it at her back.

"Great, that's great. Really." He's pleased but still tense underneath, a wire through his shoulders. "We'll sort this out, don't worry."

"Ben, I don't know about any agency. I'm not working for anyone. I'm trying to find my mom. Can I ask, while we're waiting, about Bridgette's mom?"

He flinches. "Oh, boy, I'm really sorry if this comes as a shock. She died of a brain tumor."

The loss is as shattering as it always is when she's faced with it. That bleak whirlpool of grief, again. This is not the one. "When was this?" is all she can find to say.

"About a year ago. This trip was so we could scatter her ashes. Bee said Joanne wouldn't want us to stop living our lives."

Bee. Not Bird or Birdie. Wrong species, Bridge thinks, but she's also processing it all over again. Her mother died here too. Poor her. Poor Bridgette.

"We picked up our boat in Mexico, headed for the Med. And then you came and derailed everything." He scratches at his beard, sad and tired, growing agitated. "Why are you here? What do you want? You can't do this to people."

It's all been such a waste, Bridge can't help thinking—all these trips back here, the worm she used up making them. She knows it's not fair, because Bridgette also lost her mom, and then she notices a woman silhouetted against the lights of the yacht club threading her way toward them across the walkways.

"Benjamin?" a voice calls out. Confident, husky. The woman is about her height, but wide. And something in her tone twangs a note of recognition.

Bridge doesn't have a good feeling about this.

"We're here," Ben shouts back, euphoric. "Hang on!" He activates the flashlight on his phone, raises it toward the woman—Agent Drew—to show her where to go. He turns back to Bridge, but in that moment of inattention, she has done the unthinkable and has slid off the side of the boat, crashing through the rainbow slicks of diesel across the water's surface, and into the vanta-black below rushing up to swallow her.

"Hey!" he shouts as she comes up gasping, terrified, trying not to make a sound. "Hey, come back." He's above her, shining the light right onto her, exposing her. She squints against that spotlight. She's not a strong swimmer, but it's the thought of what's moving under there, the things she can't see. *Carcharodon sirenia,* she thinks, *shark mermaids,* and nearly laughs out loud.

"She's here!" Ben shouts.

No choice. She closes her eyes and dives under. The water is cold, although not Northern California cold, not the kind to stop your breath, climb into your bones. But cold enough. She feels blindly ahead of her, brute-forcing her way through the rising panic. Her hand brushes against a rope and the slimy swaying fronds of algae and she moans into the water, despite herself. She can't afford to pull away. She clutches it instead, uses it to yank herself along, her lungs burning. *There are no sharks in the harbor, no eels or lampreys,* she keeps telling herself. No bloated dead bodies floating under the pier, or wearing concrete shoes at the bottom, shedding bits of flesh like those museum exhibitions another whole life away.

Her fingertips brush against wood and she transfers her grip to that, a thick support pole. She surfaces as quietly as she can beneath the walkways. Barely ten yards away from where she started and how is that possible? She wants to scream in frustration, but she's too frightened of the things in here with her.

The dreamworm, a vicious part of her brain chimes. But she means the water, the sharks and the eels. *Holy shit, keep it together.*

"Where is she?" Agent Drew is yelling at Ben. "How could you let her get away?"

"I didn't expect—" He sounds so upset, so worried. Bridge feels for him. She does. She won't let anything happen to Bridgette if she can help it. *Keep it together. Come on.*

The lights of two phones are strafing the water. Bridge pulls farther back into the shadows. She doesn't want that agent to get her hands on her, grab her, haul her out, dripping, struggling. Something in the woman's voice says *No mercy.*

Bridge holds her breath, continues to tug herself along, breathing between her teeth that are starting to maraca a chattering accompaniment, so loud she's amazed they can't hear her. The black water licks against the support poles, the underside of the pier. Light reaches between the wooden slats, casting traitorous stripes. She tries to crocodile, swimming with only her eyes above the water, but she's gasping for breath; the ocean slap-slaps into her mouth, her nose all salt and diesel burn. Feeling in the dark and the cold for something to hold on to, recoiling at the feathery slime of the algae clinging to the mooring ropes, the chains on the buoy, trying so hard to stay silent, to move quickly, trying not to scream as something smooth and sinuous brushes her foot. *Not a dead body.*

She's concentrating on one move at a time, aiming for the next thing to cling to, fumbling in the dark, the voices receding behind her. She's never been good at this, being in the moment, only looking at what's right ahead, but it's the only thing keeping her sane.

At last, minutes probably, although it feels like hours, she has made her way to the other side of the network of jetties and docks, where the boats have thinned out and there's hungry ocean stretching far and wide, and a twinkle of lights of a town strung along the horizon. They'll be expecting her to have been heading for civilization—the buildings by the harbor master and the yacht club. And she will, eventually.

Looking back, she sees only the burning white star of a flashlight all the way on the other side of the marina. Bridge hauls herself as quietly as she can up the back of a boat, but her weight sets it rocking, fresh waves smacking against the wood to announce her presence. It's followed by the thud of rubber soles on wooden planks. They're running toward her now.

Bridge tries to jump onto the dock. But she misjudges in the dark, especially after the blinding flashlight beam catches her face. She slips, falls, smashes her chin on the wood as she slams back into the water. Blood in her mouth, mingling with the brine and oil and a hard chip of something against her tongue. A tooth, she realizes with horror, fragments of one of her teeth.

And then the woman has her, is yanking her out with two firm hands under Bridge's arms.

"Where's Ben?" Bridge says, struggling. He won't let Agent Drew hurt Bridgette.

But there is no sign of Ben, and she is a bedraggled bird, waterlogged, limp and helpless against the planks, and so far away from the buildings, from the chance of someone hearing her call for help. She's fucked up. Shit, she's really fucked this up.

"Who is with you?" Agent Drew shouts at her, holding her down, flecks of spittle around her mouth. "Who else is with you?"

But no one is. No one... but with the woman so close to her, on top of her, she feels like there is something crawling under the skin of her arms.

DOM

Amberlynn and the Hellshriek Box

Coño, Dom swears at the traffic and the one-ways, at a forced diversion onto a whole other section of the highway, because they can't swear at the woman sitting next to them, holding on to her yellow backpack and her umbrella, staying remarkably calm, considering the way Dom is being forced to drive. But goddamn it, they wish they could yell at her that she is a crazy old lady who doesn't know what she's talking about, who hadn't pulled an antique box from her pocket to show them her dreamworm that she says she "harvested." It looks like the real deal, and Dom wishes they'd never come to meet her. Because then none of this would be true. They wouldn't know there was a *real* possibility of "infestation." They would be innocent and ignorant, and isn't that life goals?

And of course no one is picking up their damn phones, not Bridge or Tendayi or Caden, although they keep trying between listening to Amberlynn. It's confusing, the way she sometimes talks in the plural and sometimes in third person, using I, we, she interchangeably, and also they have to concentrate on the road, and most of their headspace right now is preoccupied with getting back to Bridge and with what might be happening to her. The image of worms beneath her skin, tangling up inside her, like that disease that ossifies your tissue, turns your entire body into a cage of bone grown from the inside. And "the Hatching," whatever the fuck that really means. They have a sickening vision—thank you, horror movies—of the threads unraveling Bridge's whole body like a cheap tapestry.

It's okay, though, because it's not actually possible. Caden would have shown signs, right? Jo would have for sure. Unless she hid them? There was no mention of it in her diary. But why would she do that? And why would she expose her daughter? Amberlynn is wrong. She has to be.

"We had a friend in the army with us, Chris Beck," Amberlynn says. Dom sneaks a look at her, sitting with her backpack in her lap. She's staring out past the windshield, the fat plops of rain, the metronome swish of the wipers. They didn't take her for a veteran, but she picks up on their confusion and explains. "Amber's friend, not mine, you understand. Amber's the first. I had friends of my own in the army, but no one like Chris. He was a scrawny Algerian American son of a bitch, but he always had her back—when Parker tried to climb on top of her. And when the truck flipped and the whole damn convoy was caught in the worst dust storm we ever saw, sand that would flay the skin off your face, waiting it out for rescue, Chris was cracking jokes. He was the only person she could talk to afterward. We have that in common, all of us. No one understands what it's like coming back. Everything is banal and empty, people getting upset about their team losing or someone stealing their parking spot. Give me a break. Talk to me when you've killed someone."

"In the war, you mean?" *Just to clarify,* Dom thinks. *No, but really. What is going on?*

"We all did," she says, still staring out at the road.

"All the versions of you?" They can't believe they're saying these words.

Amberlynn twists her mouth, a flash of irritation. "Yes, of course. But only one of us was exposed to the dreamworm, and she brought it to the rest of us."

"The original Amberlynn."

"Amber." She looks uncomfortable, hands stroking the backpack. "But yes." Amberlynn goes quiet, so Dom probes.

"Was Chris the one who told you—uh, her—about it?"

"He didn't have to say anything. She could see for herself. His whole personality would change, but only for a short time. The Bad Chris, she called him. He threw a kettle of boiling water at me. I still have the sc—" She starts to pull up her shirt as if to show them. "Oh. No. It wasn't me. I wasn't there." And Dom *really* hates this, because it tracks, doesn't it. With what they know already. Bridgette looking for her ink on Bridge's never-seen-the-inside-of-a-tattoo-parlor arms. Their fear of reality collapsing, eclipsed by the fear of their friend never coming back, changing. Hatching.

"It went on for weeks. We didn't know what was happening. The doctors at the VA hospital said it was PTSD. But everything is PTSD and phantom symptoms when you're a veteran." A bitter snort. "Stubbed your toe? It's PTSD. Bad shrimp? PTSD. Friendships falling apart, gambling debts, car accident? PTSD. But it wasn't that. It was the Transgression."

She closes her eyes and taps the heel of her palm against her temple like you would if you'd been stupid-stupid-stupid.

"The switch, you mean?" They glance at the map on their phone because it's just updated their route. Extra traffic outside some kind of sports arena nearby, plus the storm. Fuck's sake, surely people in Oregon can drive in some rain?

"The Transgression," Amberlynn insists. "The Bad Chris was Christopher Bacque. The Dictator. He only told her because she offered to help him, which gave her the chance to talk to him, try to understand what was happening. He said he was rich and powerful. It sounded like a fantasy."

"But it wasn't."

"He wasn't the Dictator anymore. There was a coup. The soldiers threw him in prison, beat and tortured him. The first Transgression, Chris found himself on the floor of a cell that smelled like shit and sweat. His ribs were broken, he was spitting out blood and teeth because the guards had kicked him in the face. The Dictator would do that, would plan it so *he* wouldn't have to be there for the torture. Chris told her how the guards would yell at him in French, electrocute his genitals. He didn't understand French, couldn't speak it. But here, on this side, Bad Chris did. It's how we knew it was real, because how can someone suddenly speak fluent French and then forget everything half an hour later? The doctors at the VA hospital couldn't explain that, although they tried, didn't they? They said it was—"

"PTSD."

"That we were imagining things. That it was some vocabulary he'd picked up, maybe from TV, mixed in with made-up words. They didn't believe us."

"Por dios," Dom says. But they're thinking about Jo and that first brain cancer diagnosis. How she knew things she couldn't possibly have known. "How did he make the swit—ah, the transgression—if he was locked up in a cell?"

"He was cunning. An evil, cunning man. He convinced the guards to let him keep some toys that had belonged to his five-year-old son. A kaleidoscope, a thumb piano with metal tines, and the threads, hidden inside the hollow of the gourd. They mocked him about his baby toys, about playing music to himself like a simpleton. But he was using them to walk through other worlds. To try on other lives like they were his designer suits or leave someone else to get tortured.

We know he was doing it to other Chrises as well. We had to go find them." She shakes her head. "Our Chris would come back crying, running his tongue over his teeth. His poor mouth. He thought it was karma for what he did over there, in Iraq. Even though it wasn't worse than anything any of us had to. What were we supposed to do? They told you, drilled it into you: *The Iraqis use women and kids as decoys and suicide bombers. You have to be prepared to run them down.* And you did it, not because they drilled it into you and made you stab dummies with your bayonet, yelling, 'Kill!,' or repeated the chants so many times they lost their meaning." She chants a refrain that makes Dom feel ill:

"What makes the green grass grow?
Blood, blood, bright red blood
What makes the pretty flowers bloom?
Guts, guts, gritty, grimy guts."

"No," she goes on. "You did it because you were not alone out there. Your unit was your family and you would do anything to protect them. Anything, like now." She tucks her chin to look at Dom, coquettish somehow, which makes it worse. "Do you understand me?"

"War is fuckery," Dom manages, shell-shocked. They're trying to stay calm, neutral. "I'm sorry you had to go through that, both—all of you. Chris didn't deserve that. What happened?" Concentrating on the road. Seven miles away, twelve minutes. Finally back in the leafy suburbs en route to Everard.

"The doctors drugged him. Antipsychotics. He took more than he was supposed to because he wanted to be numb, and he would sit staring at the TV. It didn't matter what was on or even if it was just a blank screen. He used to work in people's gardens as a landscaper. That's how he got the war out of his head, digging in the dirt, planting things that grow.

But after the Dictator started coming, she would visit him every day, cook for him, wait for him to emerge. Some days he didn't. His mind was under the surface, like a drowning man who didn't want to come up for air. Chris messed himself the one time. She had to clean it up. She never told him because she didn't want him to be humiliated, but maybe he realized, because he stopped taking the pills. But only after Bad Chris stopped coming."

"How many times did Bad Chris, uh, transgress?"

"I wasn't there. Not yet. I didn't know. Ten times? Twelve? The worms started after the second Transgression. Under his skin. Making him itch. He would scratch until he bled, and one day she saw a thread come out. She took him straight back to the doctors, and they gave him more pills, for deworming and psoriasis. They said there were diseases and parasites out in the desert that Western medicine didn't have names for. But Chris didn't catch this in the war. He got it from *him*."

"Bad Chris."

"When he came into Chris's mind, he brought the infection with him. It laid eggs in his thoughts and hatched inside his body. We could see them moving in the thin places, his wrists, his throat. She would use tweezers to take them out for him, leaving little scars all over."

"So what the fuck is it? Where does it come from?"

"Does it matter? Where does Ebola come from? Or cancer? I know it does Terrible Things."

"Ebola has a biological precedent," Dom argues. "It's within the rules of our universe."

Amberlynn laughs at that, a sharp unhappy sound. "The Disciple might have known, but he's dead now."

They don't even want to ask who the disciple is. This was a fucking terrible idea. They thought they were prepared for the worst, but this is about fifty levels higher on the wacky-conspiracy-meter than they could even have imagined.

"We found him," Amberlynn continues. "Chris told us where after we... convinced him."

Against their better judgment, they ask, "The disciple?"

"Yes. The man who gave the worm to the Dictator, who showed him how to use it, control it. The Disciple uses it to move between worlds and brings the worm with him and gives it to people so it can spread further and further and further. He has a box that controls it. The Frequency Machine. We found him, at least Amber did, and she... forced him to show her how to make it. It's not that hard to replicate. It was too late to save Chris, but now we can control our infection, we can share our thoughts, and we can"—she looks out the window—"*help* others."

"Okay, I am going to need you to start making actual sense before we go any further," Dom says, pulling into a parking spot on a quiet street and turning off the ignition. Because they might be bringing hell to Bridge's doorstep and they can taste bile in their throat. They need time to think, to figure this out.

Sitting in the sudden silence, the engine tick-tick-ticking as it cools down, Amberlynn gives a small nod, the resolution of a self-negotiation. "I can show you." She reaches into her backpack and takes out a sateen drawstring pouch wrapped around a shoebox, and for a wild moment, Dom thinks they're going to pull out a fresh pair of kicks. But it's a wooden transmitter of some kind, something between a theremin and a Geiger counter, low-tech, DIY, with two metal knobs and a meter and a speaker. She sets the backpack down at her feet, nests the box in her lap, and clicks it on. The needle jumps to the middle then goes back down as she tunes the dial, finding its equilibrium at last, needle vibrating near the top range of the meter in twitchy accompaniment to a high-pitched mosquito whine right at the edge of Dom's hearing. Barely audible, but they can feel it in their teeth.

"If you were infected," Amberlynn says, matter-of-fact, "you would now begin Extruding." That word, *extruding*, is almost as awful as the malarial screech. Dom puts their hands over their ears, trying to block it out.

"Okay, so you have a demonic sound box," they manage. "Can you turn it off now?"

"I can't turn it off, because there's something I need to say. That I don't want the others to hear."

"The others?"

"All the other Amberlynns and Ambers and Embers and Ambyrs and everyone I've ever been." She pats the box like it's a dog, thoughtful and... frightened? Whispering, now: "I should have looked harder. Don't tell them. She'll kill me. I tried, but I didn't reach him in time, couldn't *take care of* him. Not in this reality. I didn't do my duty. I'm a coward."

"Who? Who didn't you reach?"

"The Disciple. Jon. Jon Coello. He calls himself Rabbit."

It feels like cold water is flushing down their spine, turning each vertebra to ice.

"I told the others I couldn't find him. They're inside my head. Amber is inside my head. But I did, finally. In the facility."

"In California?" Dom can't help it.

Amberlynn gives them a strange look. "Yes. He was arrested for murder. So I couldn't reach him and I was so tired... of all this. Of everything we've been through." There's a clipped specificity to her words, the searing focus of her gaze, as if she's leaving spaces between the lines for Dom to figure out. But they're not so much gaps for subtext as yawning crevasses, and Dom's stranded on this side without a nice ladder. That appalling shriek of noise is unbearable.

"And he's where Jo got the dreamworm?"

"It's where Chris got it. But Jon swore it was over. He wasn't infected. I should have checked. I should have—"

She suddenly remembers the box and turns off the dial, killing the maddening hellshriek and making it very obvious that Dom's phone is buzzing like a murder hornet on bath salts, and has been for a while, with an incoming call from Tendayi.

"Hold that thought." Dom pops in an earbud.

"Are you okay?" Tendayi gets to the question before they can, urgent, worried. "I have like thirteen missed calls from you."

"A-okay," Dom tells her, although they are most definitely not. Rarely have they been this un-okay, in fact, and this close to tears. "Why weren't any of you answering? Where's Bridge?"

"She had a migraine, so she's recuperating in my prof's office. Do you want me to get her? I'm so sorry we didn't hear you calling. We've been cranking the tunes for the experiment. You won't believe—"

"Can you go check on her? It's important. And can you ask Caden if…he's noticed anything…under his skin?" They feel sick saying it.

"Sure, hang on. Like what?" Her muffled voice calls out the question. They can hear Caden in the background, asking her to repeat.

"Threads, worms. Yellow or gold. Under his skin."

"They won't be extruding," Amberlynn mutters. "Not if they are the Source."

"What?" Dom glances over at her. There is so much utterly batshit info to hold.

"I told you already. The Source infects *other* people."

"Is that your online friend?" Tendayi says.

"Yeah, we're on our way. Ten minutes." They start up the car again. "I think it *is* a parasite." But then why didn't Jo show any signs of infection, why hasn't Bridge? *The Source,* they think, *like the tapeworms and the primary and intermediary infections. Eating of the forbidden worms rather than infected pork.* They're trying to get it all in order.

"Wow—" Tendayi starts to say something, and Caden interrupts, loudly, sounding cagey. But when does he sound any other way? "Tell Dom I'll talk to them when they get here."

Impossible to keep this four-way going. "I'll be there soon, will explain all. Can you wait for me before you do anything else? And let me speak to Bridge."

"Of course, hang on." The sound of a door opening, sneakers on parquet floors. A polite rap on the door. "Hey, Bridget?"

And then Tendayi says, "Oh," in a way that makes Dom's heart plummet forty floors.

"What?"

"She's not here."

"Shit!" Dom bangs on the steering wheel. They never wanted to be right. Not about this.

Jo's Diary

July 31, 2022

Alive. All these years. In California. Practically around the corner. I could have saved so much time.

I found Rabbit's missive by accident, in my message requests folder on my old Chatter account I barely touch anymore, sitting waiting for me for eight months. Almost a pregnancy. He was hanging out in a mental facility called Oakdale, recently downgraded from Atascadero, the maximum-security psychiatric facility in California for violent offenders.

I don't think I ever knew his real name. He knew mine, though. Would have gotten in touch sooner if he'd known how, but they don't give you social media access in prison. He got fifteen years for aiding and abetting a man called Chris Bacque in a double homicide. Rabbit says he wasn't there for the murder, but Chris came to him for help in covering it up.

I looked the story up later, found an article with scant details on a site called DirtyHarry, a breathless listicle of "Wildest Excuses for Murder." Sandwiched between Son of Sam's psychic dog and a woman who cut off her son's head because she believed he was the reincarnation of an ancient Jewish demon, you had Chris Bacque, who believed he was from a parallel dimension where he was a rich dictator, the king of Algiers-France, with a twenty-two-year-old ballerina wife. But in this reality he was an army vet who worked as a landscaper. And the ballerina wasn't his wife, didn't know him at all, and unsurprisingly didn't want anything to do with a middle-aged guy who was obsessed with her. She got a restraining order after he tackled her boyfriend. So he killed them both and, with Rabbit's help, tried to hide their bodies.

A variation on Capgras syndrome, the writer speculated, part of a group of misidentification and delusional conditions caused by physical brain injury or neurodegenerative disease, and it was all so tragic, and also, wow, what a freak show! Chris Bacque was found dead in the ashen remains of his home before he could go to trial. Both he and the house were burned in suspicious circumstances, the body identifiable only by the teeth. The writer did not mention dreamworms.

I would have gone sooner, but between new bouts of useless chemo—survival theater—and dealing with the abrupt loss of Stasia, I've been confined to bed, weak and stupid. The house is haunted by loss. Her cooking implements, the Le Creuset ceramics, the good knives, that damn spatula, marks on the carpet where her favorite armchair used to stand—a hideous thing inherited from her parents, dark green velvet, overstuffed, the arms threadbare from all the people who'd sat there before. I hated it. Hate it more now that it's gone and taken her with it.

She transferred to a university in Baltimore. Blocked my number after our last call, when I told her she should be the one to stay in the house, seeing as I'd be checking out any day now. She said that was cruel, so fucking cruel, and then I couldn't hear what she was saying because she was crying too hard. Radio silence since then. It's been brutal.

Bridge is angry with me too. The exasperation in her voice, sympathizing with the woman who left me to die alone: "You can't blame her, Mom." We talk on video chat. I tell her I'm trying an experimental treatment, that I'll tell her all about it when she's here in two weeks. She says she has some huge assignment due, but I don't know if I believe her. I think she's dropped out again, too embarrassed to tell me or her father. He's paying my rent at the moment, which is humiliating.

I flew down to California on Thursday, got the airport wheelchair treatment, people fussing over me. I wanted to tell them cancer is inevitable if you live long enough. *It'll be you one day, if all the other deaths don't get you first.*

The facility was depressing, somewhere between a prison and a strip-mall old-age home. Rabbit and I sat and talked in the visitors' lounge. I hadn't expected him to be so old, didn't realize there'd been such a big age gap back then. He must have been in his late twenties in 1987. An *old* sixty-four, with prison tattoos on the skin hanging loose on his bones, old-man jowls, a turkey wattle.

He called them the "god threads." He said he'd lived alternate lives through all the worlds, told me about the people he'd shown the way—a kind of guru, he said. He became a wealthy man. He never expected to end up back here.

Chris Bacque was one of them. Rabbit still referred to him as "the Dictator." Back in the other reality, Rabbit said, the Dictator lived like royalty. A huge mansion with servants, a chef, a fleet of million-dollar cars. But then there was a bloody coup. The wife and adult sons faced the firing squad, but Bacque got a life sentence. His enemies wanted him to suffer, not knowing he had the dreamworm.

I extended my trip so I could go back to visit several times. Rabbit wouldn't tell me where the dreamworm comes from. He says he makes it, spins it from his own flesh and blood, which is total bullshit. If that was true, I could homebrew my own. But he did show me how he made the box for the Dictator. He showed me how to get out. To stay.

BRIDGE

Bummerland

Bridge comes up gasping for air. But not out of the water, not beached on the dock. It takes her a moment to orient herself. She's not in Jo's living room or Caden's apartment but in the museum at the university, surrounded by dead things and sharp implements. The wooden bench beneath her butt. The sonorous tick of a clock. She can hear Tendayi calling her, but she can't wait around. If Dom gets any hint of this Agent Drew who is hunting her, they'll never let her go out again. And she doesn't know what happened to Ben. And fuck. She can feel Agent Drew's fingers digging into her arms, warm spit hitting her face.

She feels drowned. She should stop. She should stay here. Figure things out. But she is so close. She stares at the morbid display in front of her. There are animal fetuses, pickled in jars, in various stages of development. A piglet, a dog, a bird—they all start out the same, blobs that become little alien shrimp curled up on themselves, taking on form, identity as you run your eyes down the row. She thinks about the rubber fetus on her mom's bookshelf. *This is your baby! This is what you're killing,* the pro-life protesters would have said. There's something here, she thinks, something emerging.

She goes to examine the succession of jars containing a chicken. Blob. Shrimp. Shrimp with poky stick legs. The features getting more pointy, beaky. And finally a chick, still alien, undeveloped, but recognizable, beak and feathers. A little chicken. A birdie. Someone called her that. When she was a kid, one of the otherselves. She closes her eyes. The party, chocolate cake, her mom with her hair in waves. *My little birdie, budgerigar.* She had cool toys. A dollhouse. A plush octopus. A scar where she'd fallen out of the tree and broken her arm. Didn't the little boy in the supermarket have a raggedy octopus?

It was the first file on her mom's computer. As in, the last played. The Bridget with the two little kids and the fake identity and the man shouting at her on the phone, the one with a scar on her arm. The obscured identity must be because she's on the run from Agent Drew and her crew. She gulps down a sob-laugh at the rhyme. *But okay, okay. Think this through.* If that Bridget is in hiding, then maybe Jo is with her. Maybe she knew about these hunters, this agency, and she was trying to get everyone to safety. It still doesn't make sense, but it's what she has. The best hope. She twirls her hair through her fist and yanks, too hard. She hears Tendayi calling for her, voice echoing in the corridor.

"Hey, Bridge? Bridget? Dom's on the phone for you."

She doesn't want to bring them into this. If anything happened to Dom... this is her mess. She has to solve it.

Bridge moves deeper into the museum and tucks herself away down an alcove right at the end that's devoted to syphilis. There are photographs of a man with his head bowed, displaying raised Klingon coils on his scalp, "tertiary syphilis affecting the skull," a midwife's chancred finger, a metal nose replacing one that fell off, and X-rays of misshapen and scoured tibiae. She presses her back to the wood paneling below a yellow Soviet-style poster: stylized profiles of young men wearing navy outfits and factory hats and the slogan: MEN WHO KNOW SAY NO TO PROSTITUTES. Well, friends who know the real dangers will say *no* to dreamworms. She stifles a giggle. Not hysterical. Desperate. Scared. Excited to *see her mother.*

She cues up the file, sets the playback to two hours, and watches the colors coruscate and flow together as the music carries her away, away, into somewhere else. Again.

Pounding music. The TV is turned up too loud, set to some shitty nu-metal channel, angry long-haired boys in leather and camo prowling the stage, and there's a shrieky barking, not from the speakers but from a small fluffy dog losing its mind, its front paws over the edge of its carrier basket. And there's a woman bent over the coffee table in front of her, saying something, but Bridge is struggling to orient herself, to hear.

Also: She is tied to a chair, expertly, as if this otherself was expecting her and upgraded from cable ties. Actually, she can't move her body *at all*, only her head. Her limbs have turned to sticky tree sap.

"—be finished and gone before your children get back from their day camp," the woman says in a voice only too fucking familiar. Bridge shudders—Agent Drew, already here. Which means—she is trying to piece this together—the woman is *also* a traveler between realities? Panic is like a blanket thrown over her head; her breath is coming hard.

"It's very considerate of the school to offer a vacation day camp. What a blessing for you. And for me, with no one to interrupt us." Agent Drew goes to pick up the little dog, stepping over discarded plastic toys, that same threadbare stuffed octopus. "What's got you all riled up, Mr. Floof II?" she says in a baby voice.

Everything is hyperreal, dialed up: the blue logo on the woman's polo shirt, ORINOCO BOWLS CLUB, the wig on the back of the couch, the slink of sunlight through the gap in the curtains, not quite closed against the outside, meaning there *is* an outside, and someone could look in. *Someone could help.*

The kitchen is a mess; bright melamine plates piled up in the sink. Books and toys are scattered across the floor, over the couch, which is cheap and worn, like something dragged in off the street. But she keeps coming back to what's on the coffee table, which she can't take in. Her attention is like a buzzing fly, alighting anywhere but there, or only for a moment, before whipping away from the equipment Agent Drew has set up so carefully. A strange little box, like a handmade radio. A seventies kitchen tray with a stylized marigold motif—she's seen it at a million flea markets. And on the tray, neatly laid out, a variety of sharp implements that do not match the cheery floral print. Not at all.

A scalpel.

A fucking saw.

She concentrates instead on the woman's back as she hefts the dog into her arms and rubs its ears, soothing it.

Bridge tries to shift in the chair to establish how tight the ropes are, how much wiggle room there is. But she's the amazing gelatin girl. She could scream for help. Draw someone to that slice of daylight between the curtains to get a look inside, see what the hell is going on here. But the music is turned up too loud, and there's the dog.

It has calmed down to resentful yips over Agent Drew's shoulder as she strokes its head, keeping up the cutesy patter. "Is it that someone new has arrived? Is that what it is, my baby? Yes, it is, yes, it is." She turns to Bridge with a knowing leer. "You're not supposed to be here." The dog yips again as if in affirmation. "But I'm so glad you came."

"You're Agent Drew," Bridge manages, her tongue thick, but she can still talk. "From Tunis."

"Ah." That nasty smile deepens and the dog gives a

resentful growl as she sets it back in the basket. "I know who you've been talking to." She fiddles with the radio, turning the knob, head cocked as if she's listening to something, but there's no sound Bridge can hear. "I'm not Agent Drew. That was one of my others. It was her cover story to get close to Bridgette. Like I told Budgie here—that's you now, dear—I was her new neighbor, Mrs. Cassie Green."

Budgie. Birdie. Little bird. She's in the right place. This *is* where Jo is.

"I might have suggested I could be interested in babysitting. I brought iced tea. She just drank it down. She shouldn't be so trusting. Especially when she's been so very hurt by her ex-boyfriend, Franco. He's a piece of work, isn't he?"

"I...I don't know." Thinking about when she was last here. The phone call. The man purring insults down the line.

"But no one expects a little old lady with a sweet doggy to drug them." She twiddles the knob again, and now Bridge can hear a sonic echo of the howling from when she falls between worlds. It registers in her jaw, and her joints, through the gelatin. Not just her joints. Something stirs inside her.

"My real name is Amber."

And why would this woman tell her that unless...no, don't think about it. She can still get out of here. If she can live through this. The woman, Agent Drew, Amber, whatever the fuck, leans forward and takes Bridge's jaw between strong fingers, gazing into her eyes, to really see *her.*

"It's nice to meet you at last. The one who's been causing all the trouble."

"But I *know* you." Bridge does, she feels certain, now she's really seeing Amber back. Not from the docks or another reality but from a long time ago when she was a kid. When Jo first took her out into her dream life. The memory is blurry, but she's trying to pull the focus. There was a party, a big house. *This* woman, sitting with her feet in the pool. "You have an alligator scar," she remembers.

Amber sighs and releases her face abruptly. "I should have taken care of you then. Not you, but this one, the little girl you infected. But she wasn't extruding yet. And then it stopped suddenly, and I didn't follow up. I really should have." She gestures at the room. "And now look where we are. All the mess you've made." Singsong to the damn dog: "Who is going to have to clean it up, my baby? It's me, isn't it? It's always me."

She turns the dial some more and *the sound* seizes in Bridge's syrupy muscles like an electric shock. "Did you think it was a game? That you could go hopscotching all around with no repercussions?"

"I haven't. I didn't." Her chest is tight, like her lungs can't fill up all the way. It's the drugs in her veins, or fear. Both. She tries to avoid looking at the tray arranged with all the things that cut. The sonic torture device, and something rippling inside her, twisting, something that is not supposed to be there. "I didn't hurt anyone." How lame she sounds, how desperate.

Amber reaches for the tray, picks up a scalpel. "Don't worry, Bridgette won't be making any more of her videos."

What does that mean? Bridge's mind skitters. She's signed an NDA? Been paid off? She laughs, a small choking sound, because she knows. *She knows.* But she can't think about it. Despite the evidence here. The sharp things. An echo of Dom's warning. *You don't know what's on the other side.* And the horror that she dialed in for two *hours.* Which is more than enough time for... *No, don't think about it. You can't think about it.* Or what has happened to Bridgette. To any of her otherselves.

"I don't know what I did. Please, please don't hurt me." She could try to headbutt her, but Amber anticipates this and keeps her distance even as she digs the tip of the scalpel into Bridge's arm, sharp and deep. A ruby swell of blood.

Bridge moan-shrieks, a shameful sound, tries to twist away, but her limbs are so heavy, so liquid. *You used to do this to yourself,* Bridge thinks, when she was an idiot teenager, wanting to let the pain out. *It's not so bad.* She still has the faintest scars crosshatched on her inner thigh. Sam used to trace his fingers along them, and she'd push his hand away. But she stopped cutting herself. *I stopped.* And this woman isn't going to.

"Every time you Transgress, you take the eggs with you," Amber explains, intent on her work, a bright red line blooming in the scalpel's wake. "They hatch inside the consciousnesses you have infected."

Bridge gasps, not in pain, even though it's searing, slicing, every nerve end singing, but at the sight of Amber's own bare arms, thick and strong and speckled with age spots—and with twisting things beneath her skin. Bridge can't help it; she pisses herself. The hot, humiliating flush of it in her lap, soaking through Birdie's or Budgie's jeans, and this feels like the worst thing of all. She's sobbing. "Please. Don't. Please."

Amber expertly flicks up the scalpel tip, bringing a long yellow thread with it. "Do you see?" The scalpel is poised in front of Bridge's face, the dreamworm, gold and squirming, alive in the air. "How could you not know this?"

"I didn't know. I didn't know how it worked." She nearly says something about Jo, her research, her notes, but she bites her tongue for real. To keep herself quiet. Keep herself sane. The blood is running from her wrist into her palm. Something else moves inside the wound and she has to look away or go mad. She *is* mad.

"How many have you visited?" Amber puts the worm inside a small metal box.

"I don't know. Three. Three. That's all."

"Liar," Amber seethes. "Lying little creep. Who else used it? Did you get it from Aiden?"

"No, I don't know anyone called Aiden. Please, I don't know anything about this."

"What about the first time? When you were a little girl?"

"I don't know! Wait—" Reaching for fictions, laced through with just enough truth: "It was…a friend of my dad's. He said it would make my life better, that my parents would get back together. They were getting divorced and—"

"Dom?"

"Yes. Dominic. Yes, but he's dead now." Any lie will do.

Amber slaps her, a light smack, contemptuous, and Bridge wants to laugh at her own stupidity, might laugh if she weren't paralyzed and drip-dripping blood onto the floor with dream-worms in her veins—and she's here for *two hours.* The dog is barking again, little snarling yips, like it would eat her face if it could. Limp Bizkit on the TV. Why is *that* one of the compatibilities? She's going to die here, to Fred fucking Durst.

"It's all right, my boy." Amber softens for the little dog, tutting. "Look at what you've done. You've got him all riled up with your lying mouth."

"I'm not lying! Please."

Amber's palm glances across Bridge's cheek again. Humiliatingly light, more a casual flap. "That's funny, because we're with Dom right now, heading to you and your friends. Dom told us about your Great Big Quest for your mother, the scientist. Where is she? Think carefully."

"She, fuck, she, she…" Bridge hangs her head, no fictions to save her, her glib tongue as useless as her muscles. "I don't know. I was looking for her. I didn't know this would happen. Please don't hurt Dom. They didn't know, they told me not to do any of this."

Amber catches the head of another thin yellow dream-worm with a pair of tweezers. "You cause all this trouble, all these Transgressions and Infestations, leaving Nests wherever you go...you realize I'm going to have to find every single one of them and take care of them?"

Over the clamor of the music, the fucking dog going wild, there's something else: pounding on the door. Thank God, *the neighbors.* A prayer to the nu-metal gods.

"Budgie! I know you're in there!" A man's voice, raucous. "Open up. It's me, Franco."

Amber raises the scalpel, a warning to shut up. As if she's not going to kill her anyway. "Shhh. Or you won't see your children again. Well, she won't—Budgie. You'll be taking that away from her. You want that on your conscience too?" She turns off the torture box, and Bridge's muscles release all at once. She slumps in the chair, the rough ropes biting into her skin.

But the banging intensifies. He's not going away. "Budgie! Bridget. Open up."

Amber goes to the front door, slides the latch chain so it opens only a crack. Bridge can't see beyond her, but she can hear over the television.

"Are you looking for someone? You're making an awful ruckus, young man."

"Is she here?" he says. "Budgie, Bridget. She's my girlfriend. Mother of my children. Wife-to-be."

"I'm afraid it's only me and Mr. Floof II. You gave him quite the scare. The lady who used to live here—"

"Help!" Bridge yells, loud as she can. "It's me, Budgie! Help me, she's insane!"

The man smashes his shoulder into the door and the little chain snaps like a twig; the swing knocks Amber sideways, enough for him to bum-rush through. *Thug-punk gym rat,* Bridge thinks, short-cropped hair and stubble, wearing his own snarl. She's never seen him before, but maybe there's a glimpse of him in Budgie's children's faces? Who are not here, thank God, but she's bleeding and she's tied to the chair and he can see that, along with all the torture implements laid out, and he halts in consternation.

"Jesus Christ, what the fuck, Budgie?"

"Behind you!" she yelps and he turns to see the woman, swinging at him with a shiny new aluminum baseball bat—the kind a single mom might keep beside the front door. He dodges, so it thwacks him across the shoulders instead of catching him in the head. He roars with anger, turns and wrenches it out of her hands, raises it to club her. But Amber feints, ducks, and stabs him in the leg with the scalpel. "Fuck!" He goes down, clutching at his thigh. "You bitch!"

She launches at him, slashing at his face. He gets his forearm in the way, presses forward, and uses his momentum to push her up against the wall; he pins the arm with the blade. The dog is going insane, worrying at his jeans. He kicks at it.

"You crazy—"

She grabs his forearm, stronger than she looks, twists away out from under him—military moves, Bridge thinks—but he moves with her. Maybe he's army too or Krav Maga; he looks the type. He rabbit-punches Amber in the side of the head, again and again, so she staggers, and he wrenches her wrist until she drops the scalpel.

"Get out of here, you crazy cunt!" He feints with the baseball bat held out in front of him like a shield. "Or I'll knock your fucking head off."

Amber spits on the ground, but she is backing away, calling the dog to heel. Bridge is weeping with relief and adrenaline.

"Get out! Get the hell out of this house."

Her eyes skip to the radio box, her torture tools. "Every Transgression," she yells at Bridge. "I'll find you. I'm already there."

"Get the fuck out of here, you cunt!" Franco slams the door. "What the hell is all this, Budgie?" He moves toward her, unties her. She collapses into his arms because she still can't move, and he is holding her face in both hands, kissing her with tenderness. His breath smells of beer. "Can you stand up?"

"She drugged me. I'm bleeding."

"Shit. Yeah. We've got to get you to a hospital. Where are the kids?"

"At day camp." At least, that's what Amber had said. "At the school." Will the monster go after them? Oh God, she's in so deep. She's now weeping from the pain, her poor ruined wrist, the bright spots of blood on the shitty carpet, one spatter marking a plastic dog wearing a police uniform.

"What the heck, Budgie? I leave you alone and this is what you get yourself involved in, you dum-dum?"

"I have to get back," she says, pushing herself up, dizzy, uncoordinated, every movement like yanking herself up through wet sand, but she's getting the feeling back in her body.

"Budgie, you're bleeding all over the place."

"I have to get back."

"Coo-coo-ca-choo, tiger," he teases. "Get back where?" Sharp edges, like the ease of his violence. Muscle memory. "Let's get you patched up, huh?" He scans the room. "You got a first-aid kit around here?"

She must; Budgie's a good mom, Bridge is sure of it. And he doesn't know, so that means he doesn't live here. Playing detective. His voice on the phone, screaming at her. The way he barged in. Bad life choices coming back to haunt her. Her own Rescue Ranger and also a whole other problem.

Bridge has to get back. She has to find Dom. Stop Amber. But she doesn't know how she's going to do that.

But maybe Jo will. And Jo is here. She has to be.

BUDGIE

The Caged Bird Screams

She was honestly worried it was Franco at the door. Had the baseball bat down low, ready to swing when she cracked it. He'd been calling and calling and calling. When she blocked him, he'd get a new number, call again. It was a relief to see a middle-aged lady holding a little dog. But she wasn't paying attention, preoccupied with the *episodes* she's been having.

Number one: Finding herself in the dark bedroom with a stranger, locking herself in a bathroom while they swore at her in Spanish. Suddenly back, outside the supermarket, and a staff member berating her for trying to abandon her kids and making noises about child protective services.

Number two: Waiting outside the school, then suddenly cable-tied to a bed, fighting to remove a virtual-reality helmet that was playing a cartoon with a talking deer and another, different stranger telling her to calm down, it would all be over, then snapping back to the park with Jess clinging to her.

Number three: Marlon showing her where someone had written over his *Frozen* coloring book, and there was a message on her phone she didn't even finish listening to because the woman was saying absurd things *in her own voice.*

It's possible that all these things mean she is losing her mind, which means she might lose custody. Not to Franco;

no sane judge would let him have the kids. But she'd screwed up before, *because you're a stupid little fucking pigeon-brain*, and she'd nearly lost them, and they'd gone into the foster system, which had led to that whole battle with *her own mother*, which ended with Budgie telling Joanne how and where to get fucked.

But lately she's been reconsidering all the choices she made, not about leaving Franco, that was the best thing she could have ever done, up there with getting clean and sober, but maybe the things she said and did when Joanne was trying to help, trying to make her see.

And maybe that's partly, deep down, why she chose Colorado—because her mom lives in Denver, and there might be a chance to repair the harm done. Maybe her mother was only trying to steal her children because she *was* a worthless junkie who kept going back to the asshole. She's in recovery now. But also maybe going mad. The out-of-body experiences. The dislocations. She can't lose them. She can't.

All of *that* was going through her head when she opened the door, which was why she wasn't thinking that 5 to 7 percent of serial killers in the U.S. are women, that their preferred method of killing is poison. And she drank down that iced tea until she was slurring her words and "Mrs. Cassie Green" was propping her up and then tying her down with nylon towrope like a real professional, the dog watching calmly with its beady little eyes. And prattling that it was *For your own good*, which has to be the most evil phrase on earth, along with *You're making me do this.*

She was terrified. Trapped. But now she's somewhere else again.

Number four: She's not chained or tied up. Not this time. Sitting on the floor of a darkened room. There's a laptop in front of her playing a loop of horses running, old-fashioned animation in black and white. There's unworldly music through the headphones, like in the dark bedroom, she remembers. She removes them carefully and stands up, back against a glass cabinet. She's in a dimly lit chamber of horrors but nothing like as bad as where she's just come from. Some kind of museum, maybe? Showcasing grotesque medical photos and surgical instruments, like the ones "Mrs. Cassie Green" was laying out for her on her own coffee table.

There's someone calling her name.

"Bridge? Bridget?" But no one calls her that, and she doesn't recognize the voice of the woman calling her. So not a fuck is she answering.

A glimpse of herself reflected in the glass cabinet. She looks away. Doesn't want to be reminded of last time, when the face looking back in the locked bathroom with the steam rising from the shower and the stranger banging on the door was her—but not. The girl in the mirror didn't have the scar from when Franco smashed her chin into the sink and she'd had to drive herself to the ER because he was too messed up, and they made her wait outside in the parking lot with the kids in the back seat because of COVID while the blood soaked into her mask. She'd needed six stitches.

The voice again, closer. Paused in the doorway. Budgie can feel the pressure in the room change, see the amorphous blur of a human shadow stretching across the linoleum sheen. "Hey, Bridget? Are you in here?"

She shrinks back, casting around for a weapon. The laptop? But it's not heavy enough.

The young woman's shadow wavers there for long, terrible seconds. Talking to someone else. On the phone? "I don't know, sorry." The shadow retreats, taking her voice with it, echoey in the empty corridors. "Maybe she went to get a snack?"

Budgie has to stifle a little grunt of disbelief. She could do with a bite herself, she thinks as her stomach rumbles. But more important: a weapon. A real one.

AMBERLYNN

The Reluctant

Dom is swearing under their breath as they pull into the university grounds. It's not hard to grasp the pronoun, Amberlynn muses. Plural, because they contain multitudes. But not quite like she does, with the Ourmind. She wishes she could turn it off. She knows she is marked as a troublemaker, a weakling, one of the Reluctants. But she nearly went to jail for this, for them, over ten years ago now, over the suspicious death of a junkie chef in New Orleans, what was her name? Minnie? Marina? Mina? But there wasn't enough evidence and Amberlynn was a former police officer so no one pressed her too hard, and it was ruled a drug deal gone wrong, and the dealer shot her. Her arms were gouged already by track marks. (Only they weren't, Amberlynn knows, and the poor woman had been clean for years, but people want to believe the easiest stories that back-up their ugly preconceptions.) The husband tried to kick up a fuss, she remembers, but the poor don't get a voice.

She should have taken care of the Disciple years ago, copped to him being out of her reach instead of lying to the Ourmind. Most recently, she's been berated for her inability to locate her version of Aiden Lyleveld but it's not her fault she can't find him. Maybe he doesn't exist here.

But she's found Dom, and that's something. Maybe that's everything.

She shouldn't have shown them the Frequency Machine, shouldn't have said what she did. But Amberlynn is old and tired; they all are. In another reality she is aware of two bodies, a young man and a woman, being arranged to look like a murder-suicide in the cabin of a boat called the *Golden*. Somewhere else, a woodworker is screaming as another Amber uses his own tools to gouge open his arms, but the router is grinding too loud for anyone to hear him.

And Amber the First, the original, with her dog, is incandescent with rage, flooding through all of them. She's been attacked, and the girl got away. They have to find her—or Amberlynn does. Because it seems that *her* Bridget Kittinger is the Source, and it can all end here, right now, maybe for good.

It's all on her. And if she can't do it, Amber will do it for her. Like the first time, killing Chris Bacque, who was awaiting trial for his own double homicide. Her own Chris, but a stranger to her. Or in Haiti, where she was posing as an art collector, Amber had to hold her hand, force it, really, to kill the slender artist and his wife. She came in like a black fury, took control of her mind, seized her muscles, guided her through the murder like a puppet. She never wants to go through that again.

Dom parks the car on a red line outside the neuroscience building, frantic. "¡Vamos!" they say, spilling out the door. "I have to find Bridge."

Amberlynn is still unclipping her seat belt. She reaches under her jacket. Her Glock, her own weapon of choice, is hard and solid against her rib cage in her holster, a reassuring weight.

One last time. Maybe this will be the end of it. Make it quick.

BRIDGE

Frying Pans

Franco hoists her drooping weight to the bathroom, limping from where Amber stabbed him in the meaty part of his thigh. There's an angled rip in his jeans where you can see pale skin and hair and a runnel of blood.

"Got to patch you up before we go anywhere, baby doll. Still don't know how you going to your mom is supposed to help, though."

"I told you, I hid the drugs in my mom's shed, she doesn't even know." It's a trick to get him to take her there. "If I can get them back..." Leaves him to fill in the blanks. Let him think Amber's some heavy intent on recovering a stolen stash. More credible than the truth. Luckily, he's not interested, or not in that detail.

"How much we talking?"

"Enough." Trying to remember every narco show she's ever watched in any universe, guessing how much it would take to get him interested. "Fifty thousand."

He whistles low, admiring. "Holy shit, Budgie." Too much, fuck. He would probably have been eager if it had been a tenth of that. Look at him—the gauntness in his cheeks, his skin sallow and pocked, the bad teeth.

He helps her sit down on the edge of the bath. There's a mat in the bottom with sticky pads to keep little kids from slipping. A jury of rubber ducks in silly hats are all lined up along the edge, judging her. "Didn't think you had it in you." He kisses her and it takes everything she has not to shrink away. She lets him do it for as long as she can bear, his hot mouth against hers, his tongue flicking at her lips, then pulls back.

"I'm bleeding really badly," she says. If he hadn't noticed. "And I need to change my pants."

"Yeah, yeah. I got you, Budge." He opens the bathroom cabinet and, yup, between the sanitary products and bottles of no-tears shampoo, there's a first-aid kit in a bright red bag. Bridge dares to look at her arm. It's hard to see how deep the cut is, if it's down to the bone, but, most important, there is no glint of gold. But she's still bleeding, and that woman was going to kill her. And maybe she's killed other Bridgets, and she's going after Dom, and it's all her fault. With a choking sob, she covers her face, releasing a fresh wave of tears.

"Aw, my little dum-dum. You have to be strong. It won't hurt that bad."

She fights it down. There's no time to feel sorry for herself. If there's a worm still in there . . . if she's *making* them, can she use the dreamworms to get back to Dom? She doesn't know the tune. Doesn't have a zoetrope or a video file. But Jo will. She has to get him out of the room so she can excavate her injury. "Can you look for superglue?" she says. "I can use it to seal the wound. It's probably in the refrigerator."

He looks affronted.

"Please, Franco."

"All right, bossy boots." He gets up reluctantly. "I'll be right back. Don't fall and smash your head open." Like a threat. She's going to have to get away from him too.

She lays out Neosporin, wipes, gauze, bandages, a pair of tweezers. The wound is not as deep as she thought. It might be okay with pressure, bandages, except she's digging around in there. Bridge catches herself making a keening sound at the back of her throat, trying to imitate the radio transmitter. Lure it out. *Come on, you fucking bastard, come on.* But there's only the inside meat of her, and it hurts terribly. Which is when she remembers the torture radio Amber left behind. She can hear Franco coming back; it will have to wait. *Dammit.*

"No superglue, but I got this." He clacks a red stapler like a crocodile. She's tying off the bandage one-handed.

"It's all right. Can you pin this for me? And you should clean that cut of yours."

He manages to jab her with the safety pin — on purpose, maybe. She's avoiding his eyes in case she betrays herself.

He dabs at his stab wound half-heartedly with one of the wipes. It's definitely going to get infected. She hopes it won't become her problem. Trying not to think about Budgie's kids, if they're waiting at the school gates for their mother, whether *Amber* has already swooped in to get them. *She wouldn't, though,* Bridge tells herself. She knows about Jo. She's probably on her way there.

"We gotta get going, baby doll. Hit up your moms before that bitch finds her."

"What if she's waiting outside?"

"Got this bat right here and old trusty in the truck."

"Will you drive us? You know the way, right?"

"Been a while, but yeah, I think so. Remember when we smeared shit on her windshield? That was hilarious."

"So funny," Bridge agrees, feeling sick.

His eyes narrow. "Fucking cunt. Trying to take our kids. Hey, this better not be some kind of setup, with cops waiting over there for me."

"You think I got a woman to tie me up and drug me and

cut open my arm to *set you up*?" Bridge can't believe she has to rely on this human shitbag, but maybe stupid and fucked up is better than smart. Maybe she can work with that, slip away when she has to.

His face darkens, a whole weather system she doesn't know how to read; she doesn't have a handle on the history. And then the clouds clear, and he gives a raffish open-mouthed smile, like a dog (a hurt dog, a mad dog, a dog that will bite your face off), pulls her tight to him, gives her a noogie, really grinding his knuckle into her scalp. "Who knows what crazy shit you'll get up to, dum-dum."

AMBER

Shadow Life

In and out of focus, visiting the other Ambers while she waits, sitting hidden in the back of the anonymous white panel van she picked up at the Denver airport, looking out the rear window. Waiting for this Bridget—Budgie—to emerge from her poky apartment in a row of poky apartments, all alike in a four-story building with chipped paint and cheerful curtains.

No one has *hurt* her. Not since Christopher Bacque threw boiling water at her, laughing, twisting her arm. Wearing her friend's face.

She would like to feed Bridget's baby daddy to the alligators. Tie him up and drag him behind the boat through the inlets, but be careful not to let him drown. Not until she's got the gators circling. It's a fantasy that they will take casual bites out of him, rip off an arm. They're not sharks. But one will take him in the end. Or she could cut off chunks of his body as he watched and screamed, feed them to the animals like they do on the tourist boats with catfish.

She's nursing revenge fantasies but also checking in on her Reluctant, Amberlynn. It would have to be *her* reality harboring the Source. Right now Amberlynn is riding up in an elevator with this Dom—who is frantic, jabbing the button as if that will make it go faster—and a young Black woman who apologizes over and over. Amberlynn, wretched with nerves, keeps pressing her elbow against her side to feel the gun strapped against her ribs. Amber is worried she is going to have to step in when she has a messy situation of her own to deal with.

She's shaken up herself, but she would never let that leak into the Ourmind. She knows how to keep things to herself, be disciplined even when it hurts, like holding in her urine in the desert like so many of the female soldiers, so she wouldn't have to pee, because the toilets were disgusting and there were enemy insurgents and the rapists in your own unit who would lie in wait. She had constant UTIs, they all did, but that was the price you paid.

She doesn't know why she's thinking about the war so much. Maybe because she never left. She's been at war against the worm all these decades, and this feels like a defining moment. Or maybe because now they all need to hold fast, hold together, the same way you do in battle. Amberlynn needs to do her damn job. They all do.

And here come the wounded lovebirds, Bridget leaning on him heavily as they emerge from a door like all the other doors in this block, looking wary. Descending the stairs, one at a time, careful, careful; he's dangling the bat from his wrist, looking around. They clamber into a busted-up Ford pickup with a cracked windshield and snowboarding stickers on the back. She'd clocked it already. Easy to follow. But she doesn't have to.

She already called in a favor from one of her buddies still in the force. Advantages of being an ex-cop. The truck is registered to Franco Zachariah Reed, age thirty-seven, on parole for possession and domestic violence, with two restraining orders against him, one issued on behalf of Bridget Kittinger-Harris, age twenty-four, former partner and mother of his children, and, separately, one on behalf of Joanne Kaye for destruction of property and threatening behavior. The address is 449 Calder Avenue, Denver, Colorado. Forty minutes away.

DOM

Sonar Radiation

The elevator is taking too long. They're bouncing on their heels as it climbs; Tendayi is still stammering out apologies, and Amberlynn is smiling politely, but she's clearly uncomfortable, arms across her chest, hands tucked into her armpits.

"I'm so sorry, she said she wanted to lie down, she had a migraine."

"She doesn't get migraines," Dom says, trying not to snap, because it's not her fault. Bridge is gonna Bridge. "She lied to you because she wanted to go back. Because she knew I'd make her wait."

"It's dangerous," Amberlynn mutters, which makes Tendayi even more freaked. When Tendayi opened the door for them downstairs, Amberlynn looked at her intently and declared, "You're not one of them." It pinged weirdly for Dom, somewhere deep and dark, but of course Amberlynn would know, right? Who was infected and who wasn't?

But in the cold light of elevator LEDs, they're suddenly seeing her through Tendayi's eyes: some batty old conspiracy crank with her hair cut too short and her bright yellow backpack. And Tendayi hasn't even learned about the hellshriek box or how the magic worms can eat their way out from under your skin. And isn't this exactly like when Dom was young and running on self-loathing, and they fell down the worst rabbit holes in all the internet? Crazy. This is crazy.

"I think that when you find her, you should probably go," Tendayi says. "I shouldn't have brought you in here. I want to help, especially after Jo, but..."

"Of course," Dom says. "I'm so sorry, we shouldn't have—" Despondency is despair's less dramatic little sister.

"No, it's okay." Tendayi tries to smile. "Maybe another time when things are less hectic." Tries to mean it.

"I'll find her and we'll head out. No stress."

The elevator doors open and disgorge them onto the sixth floor, where there's no sign of Bridge, but Caden is skulking in the doorway of the lab.

"You won't find her," he says. "I told her the doors were closing. She's doing what she has to do."

"You smug ass-wipe," they say, and Caden cringes—as if they would ever insult their fist with his face. Or anyone's. They're generally the one breaking up other people's fights.

"Oh," Amberlynn says. "It's you."

"Bridge?" Dom calls, striking out across the corridor. She'll be somewhere quiet, somewhere she wouldn't be disturbed—offices, kitchenette, maybe a faculty lounge or grad-student hangout? The library, obviously, but it's not private enough, and they suspect she hasn't physically left this building. It would take too much time.

"You shouldn't be here," Amberlynn says behind them, with resignation. Second ping on their sonar. But it's the alarm in Tendayi's voice that gets Dom to turn—"Hey, no, put that down"—and see, utterly confused, that Amberlynn has materialized a label printer gun from somewhere under her jacket and is holding it in both hands. No, it's not plastic, they realize, scrambling through the shock. It's dull metal, heavy and solid. It's an actual fucking gun. This isn't goofing around, and they're cursing themselves for being so damn stupid. This is America.

"Hey, Amberlynn, there's no need for that." They use their reasonable voice, calm, warm even, as they move toward her, but the air has thickened, and they're too slow to react, too slow to stop her.

Shots burst out, one-two-three. Loud as lightning strikes.

Someone screams, and screams.

BRIDGE

Getaway Girl

She keeps looking back to see if they're being followed. There had been a suspiciously anonymous white van in the parking lot of Budgie's apartment block, but it pulled away by the time they got to the ground floor. Franco hauled her like a human sack over to his pickup. A dark blue Prius behind them seems to have made all their turns for the last few blocks, and she can't see the driver's face behind the glare of the sun on the windshield. Or see if there is a little dog with its feet on the dash.

"I'm watching," Franco says, like they are in this together. "You think that's your psycho cunt?" He reaches down, takes a gun—a gun!—from under the seat, and lays it across his lap.

"I can't tell." Staring at the gun. The gun, the gun, the gun.

"One way to figure it out," he sneers and swerves two lanes over without hitting his blinker and onto the highway on-ramp, setting off a blister of horns. The Prius doesn't break pace; it cruises past, and Bridge looks back to see a young Black man head-bopping to the radio, utterly unaware of them.

"Is this the right direction?" she says. *Through the woods to my mother's house.*

"Drugs did a number on you, huh?"

"I'd feel more comfortable if we could use navigation." Quick to add: "Not that I don't trust you."

But the phone in her hand gives her something more urgent to do. *Call Dom.* No, the photograph of Budgie's kids staring up at her. Serious Marlon and goofy Jess wearing cat ears. She has to phone the school, make sure Budgie's kids are safe. She owes her that. Many things, but especially that.

"Who you calling?" An edge in his voice.

"The school," she says. "They're at day camp." She should have told him before she dialed, she realizes. Franco doesn't like surprises; she has figured this out about him in the short time they've known each other. It rings and rings and finally a frazzled voice answers.

"Hi, this is—" Shit, what was her fake name? Thinking back to a hundred otherlives ago. "Jess and Marlon's mom," she manages.

"Ms. Ainsley, yes?" the woman says.

"I've had, uh..." She hesitates, intensely aware of Franco listening in, thumbing the steering wheel to a song in his head. "A family emergency. I can't come pick them up. But it's very important that you don't let them go with anyone else."

"Ms. Ainsley, is this about"—the woman lowers her voice, but not softly enough to keep Bridge's chauffeur eavesdropper from hearing—"the restraining order?"

"Yes." Less to explain—to the school, anyway—she just hopes she can deal with Franco. "Yes, thank you for understanding. I'm so sorry. Can they hang out for a bit? I'll be there as soon as I can."

"We can keep them till five, but then you'll have to make another plan."

"Okay, thank you, that's great. If anything happens—"

"I'll call you. Don't worry." The kindness in her voice might just fucking undo her. "Ms. Ainsley, wait, take my number. If you can't get here by five, I'll take them home with me. I know what it's like."

"There's no need, really," she says, glancing at Franco. She can't see his eyes behind the knockoff Oakley sunglasses, but there's a knot at his jaw. She pulls a face and twirls her finger, as in *Talky-talky, crazy-crazy, can you believe this bitch*, and he grins. She mimes taking down the number, jabby-jabby on an imaginary phone, rolling her eyes. Memorizes it. She will write it down as soon as she can for Budgie, for when this is over, when she's gone.

"Whole school knows, huh?" Franco says as soon as she ends the call. Thumbs tap-tapping the steering wheel.

"I'm sorry." *Careful, Bridge,* she thinks. "I made a mistake. I wasn't thinking."

"Damn right you weren't. You didn't think I'd find you, huh, dum-dum?" He reaches over and slaps her. Hard, not like Amber's contemptuous flap. Black sparkles and shock. "That was for being stupid. This"—he grabs her face, kisses her hard—"is because I love you. You're forgiven. Don't do it again."

"I won't. I'm sorry."

"We'll make it right, baby."

"We'll make it right," she repeats and sinks down into the seat, half flopping against the window. "Oof, what the hell did she give me?"

"You all right there? Used to be able to hold your shit better than that. You've gotten soft, Budgie, baby."

"I know." She attempts a half laugh. "I think I need food. Can we stop somewhere? We can get it to go."

"Chili fries."

This seems like part of a routine she doesn't know the accompaniment to. "You know it," she says. He doesn't notice that she's ad-libbing, lost in reminiscing.

"Taco grande. Margaritas. When was the last time?"

"Sounds like a celebration."

"Sounds like a Wednesday, baby." He glances over, a lopsided smile, showing his teeth. "You think your bitch mommy has the guts to move *the merchandise* herself?"

"She has no idea it's even there," she says, trying to match his jeering tone. Bridge doesn't know where Jo is. And she needs to know. "Give me the address again, I'll put it into the navigator. We don't want to get a speeding ticket on the way to a drug run, right?"

"That's my girl. See, you do have smarts." He grabs her hand and kisses the back of her knuckles. "Shit, what was it? Calder Avenue, but I can't remember the number. Put that in, it'll get us close enough. Did they miss me, the kids?"

"So much," Bridge says. "They're going to be so excited to see you." Almost as much as she is to see the gas station coming up under a silver and blue logo she doesn't recognize above one she does. Compatible but different. "Hey, pull over here," making her tone light, "I can grab some Twinkies to tide me over."

"If you're lucky, they'll have a whole corn dog."

He jumps across the lane, again not putting on his turn signal, which is just how he drives it seems. He pulls in to one of the bays in front of the 7-Eleven attached to the gas station chain she's never heard of. He nods his head at the doors. "Grab me a pack of Marlboro Reds too, huh?"

Bridge laughs so as not to cry, so as not to reveal her heart ready to drum itself out of her chest. She makes herself as small and floppy and pathetic as she can. "Baby, I can't walk."

"You left your wallet at home too, I'll bet?" That dark cloud looms.

"I'm sorry, I'll make it up to you. Margaritas on me."

He drums his thumbs on the steering wheel, gnawing on

his lower lip as if he's wondering if she did this on purpose. "Okay," he says, relenting. He unbuckles his seat belt, opens the door, and swings his long legs out, tucking that gun back into his waistband, under his shirt. He hesitates, and for a moment she's terrified he's going to take the keys out of the ignition, which will fuck up everything. Or he's decided he's tired of her and she's never going to learn and he's just going to shoot her here and now and be done with it. But he's getting his wallet, battered black leather, from the plastic holder by the handbrake. He wags his wallet at her as if she has been a naughty little girl.

"But you're only getting Twinkies."

AMBER

Ding-Dong-Ditch the Witch

The nice suburbs, like McDonald's, are comfortingly all alike. The sketchy ones, the not-yet-gentrified, are all distinct, unpredictable. She's relieved that Joanne "Kaye" lives out past the tree-lined neighborhoods populated with clapboard bungalows and ranch-style houses with double-wide garages and oversize pickups parked outside and sprinklers flickering over the lawns. Behind those cheerfully painted windows, Amber knows there are bored housedads and work-from-home wives ready and waiting to post on one of the neighborhood-watch groups about the white panel van that has been parked outside *for a little too long, don't you think?*

K-for-Kittinger, hardly a genius fake identity, Amber thinks. But then her would-be-son-in-law doesn't seem like the type to figure it out.

Amber drives out past the Whole Foods store and the slick new developments of Highland, past the Costco, into what she thinks of as Dollar-Store-Land, the kind of neighborhood where the high schools provide easy pickings for army recruiters offering *a better life than this, son.* Like hers was.

She drives still farther, into the scrub hills of whatever former mining shanty this once was, now absorbed into the city sprawl. It's a mix of historic row houses that have yet to experience the magic wand of redevelopment, although give it five, ten years and a booming economy, and these will be selling for upwards of half a million. But this isn't where Joanne Kaye lives either.

"No, she doesn't, Mr. Floof II," she tells the little dog in her lap, watching the road.

He yaps as if to say *Well, where does she live, then?*

Amber turns into Calder, finally, a long street to nowhere, parallel to the highway for ease of commute, where the ticky-tacky houses are newer and all built the same, cheap and quick and already worn out, worn down.

"Has to be one of these…" Watching the numbers ticking up toward the cul-de-sac. Fake gray clapboard or vinyl or whatever they use these days. Not exactly eco-friendly, but better than asbestos. Built like a strip mall around a parking lot, identikit homes, two-story, each with its own wooden patio, high canted roofs. This is what she likes about this kind of neighborhood: Cheap housing, but not *a community*. No overly friendly deli owner or local landmark who sits on the stairs in his suit and smokes and watches the Goings-On, no gossips all Up in Each Other's Business or teenagers lurking in packs. People here keep the hell to themselves and expect you to do the same.

The lawn of number 449 is overgrown, threaded with dandelions. No one answers the doorbell, but no one pokes a head out from any of the other town houses to look either. She rings again, follows it up with three firm raps. A shadow materializes beneath the door, darkens the peephole. Amber holds up her police badge, long since defunct, and puts on her best sorry-to-bother-you smile.

The front door cracks open and a woman with hollow cheekbones pulling a sweatshirt over her sports bra says, "Help you?" She's in her early fifties, long brown hair scraped back in a messy ponytail, black workout gear, barefoot: One times out-of-work lady. But she has a presence to her. Confident. This is someone who is accustomed to being listened to, like a teacher or a traffic cop. Amber feels no squirm of recognition inside her. Not infected, then.

"It's about your daughter, ma'am. May I come in?"

"Which *one*?" the woman says, as if this is a good joke. Maybe she has several.

"Bridget Kittinger-Harris. Although I believe she also goes by the name Bridget Ainsley? It's about her ex-boyfriend, Franco."

The woman sags. A flash of anger. "Of course it is. Come in," she says, then looks past her to the lot where the rental van is parked, inconspicuous among the other tenants' cars, and Mr. Floof II is curled up on his blankie in the back with water and the windows cracked. "Where's your vehicle?"

"My partner dropped me off. He's following up on something related." And this is enough to satisfy her.

The town house is in the process of being packed up, boxes everywhere, and no pictures, no ornaments, no indications of a life. An in-between place. The couch is well worn with cat-scratched edges but no sign of a cat. A yoga mat and twenty-pound kettlebells on the floor—ambitious for such a scrawny woman. The one indication of luxury is a faux-fur throw chucked over the sofa next to a brand-new laptop. The bed pillows on the floor, beside a grease-marked pizza box, make it seem like this is where she sleeps. *What's the matter with the bedroom, hmm?*

"Is she all right? Bridget?"

"Fell asleep at the wheel. She's in the hospital, minor injuries, but I wanted to talk to you about her parenting, regarding custody."

"I'm really not involved," she says, too vehemently. "I don't want to be involved. It's not my fight."

"Just moved in?" Amber says casually. There's something wrong here, setting her on edge. She reaches out again for that special connected feeling of the worm, but it's a dead line.

The woman looks around as if seeing the apartment for the first time. "Hoping to move out, actually."

Amber takes a notebook from her jacket, flicks it open. Props are reassuring, especially if it's As Seen on TV. "To confirm, you are Joanne, mother of Bridget Kittinger-Harris?"

"Joanne Kittinger, no Harris. Divorced so long ago I barely remember. Oh, no, wait. It's Kaye now. I changed it. There was an issue with Bridget's boyfriend, Franco. There's a restraining order."

"It's in your records." Giving the message *Here to reassure, ma'am.*

She folds herself onto the couch beside the laptop and motions for Amber to sit in the dark blue armchair opposite, also ripped up by sharp scrabble claws once upon a time. There are fine white hairs marking the armrest.

"Your kitty around?"

"I'm allergic," Joanne says. "*I* always preferred dogs. Used to, I should say." She smiles as if at a private joke and then frowns. "So what's happened to *Bridget* this time? Are the children all right?" She pulls down her ponytail and runs her fingers through her hair. A nervous gesture. It's shot with gray, matches the wrinkles, a knot of worry between her brows, lines tugging at the sides of her mouth. A heaviness weighing her down just under the surface of that quicksilver confidence.

"I take it you're not close?"

"We were once, I think—" She cuts off the sentence. But Amber can wait through a silence. She's very comfortable with it, and finally, Joanne twitches. "Do you want some tea, coffee?" She nudges the pizza box at her feet with that knife-slice of a smile. "Leftover pizza?"

"I'm fine, thank you."

"Forgive the mess, all the boxes. I've been very depressed. The kind where you want to lie down and die. But I'm working on it, getting fit again, fattening up." She raises the edge of the sweatshirt, pinches at the loose skin on her belly from too much weight loss too suddenly with that same flicker of impatience and frustration. "I'm sorry, I'm not used to company."

"Related to your family problems? The depression?"

"Oh God, yes, the custody battle, Bridget's drug use, her boyfriend. It's been physically and emotionally exhausting. I wiped out my savings, lost my job. Only as a high-school science teacher, total dead-end, but you can imagine." She gives a bright laugh, like glass. There's something like contempt in her voice, a disconnect, as if she's talking about someone else. "There were days, weeks I wouldn't get out of bed, couldn't bring myself to eat. Lying there with the curtains closed, waiting to die. I stopped feeding the cat. I think she ran away. Or he." She laughs again, full of jagged edges. "I didn't check."

"You seem to be doing better."

"It was such a *waste* of a life. But yes, I had a change of perspective, though it's still an adjustment. Work in progress. I'm trying to get strong again, look after myself. So no, to your question. Bridge-et"—she corrects herself—"and I haven't been close. Maybe in another life." Another little self-pleased smile, because she doesn't know Amber is right in there with her on that joke, even if she hasn't figured out *how*. "It was really ugly with Franco. The drugs, the harassment. She—*I* had to change my name, move out here to get away, and they found me anyway. I'm a little hazy on that time, forgive me."

"I can see that would be tough."

"My daughter tried to reach out to me a couple of weeks ago, but I could hear it in her voice that she wasn't ready. She still didn't sound right. Are you a parent?"

"No."

"Then maybe you won't understand. I want my little girl back. The way I knew her."

"Do you mind if I look around?" Amber gets up.

"I'd rather you didn't." She stands up with alarm to follow her. "Excuse me, do you have a warrant? Are you sure Bridge is all right?"

No *-et* that time, Amber notices, also the way she's talking around the subject, the vagaries, as if she knows Bridget has been infected. With any luck, if she's still Transgressed, she'll be heading over here for a family reunion. It would be the most convenient way this could play out. Maybe she could get Joanne to summon her over a little sooner, phone her with directions. She moves toward the bedroom.

"That's private." Joanne tries to take Amber's arm, stop her from going in, but Amber forges ahead, pushing open the door into a room that's been usurped for another purpose. The double bed and mattress are up on their sides against the wardrobe, leaving space for a trestle-table bench covered in a variety of tools: a soldering iron and screwdrivers, an Arduino board, and a peculiar lamp with a circular shade cut with slits. No, not a lamp. A children's toy, the spinning one.

"What is this called?" She holds it up.

"A zoetrope. It's a craft project, for my depression." Joanne is hovering, trying to get between her and the table and one item of special interest, the one that explains why Amber is not having a Reaction.

She flusters. "You really can't be in here. Sorry. Now, how can I help you with Bridget?"

"And this?" Amber reaches past her, picks up the box, which has been emitting this whole time—Joanne's very own Frequency Machine. And now where did she get a thing like that?

Amber experiences a surge of adrenaline. It takes her a second to realize it's echoed, not hers, from another iteration in the Ourmind. Amberlynn.

Gunshots in an empty college building.

She's torn between checking in and staying in the moment. Amberlynn will have to handle it, Amber decides. There is something new here, and she needs to get to the bottom of it.

"It's very fragile. Please be careful. It's part of my research."

"What does it do?" Amber lets her reclaim her box, a shoddy imitation. She's enjoying the luxury of letting this play out.

"It's for my epilepsy," Joanne says, taking it back with her to the couch, putting it down beside her like a pet. Her missing cat. "I have epilepsy, my whole life. The box emits a particular frequency that helps control the seizures. I really can't have anyone touching it."

"How strange," Amber says. "What a *giant coincidence*."

"What is?" Joanne puts one hand on the box as if Amber is about to try and snatch it away.

"I also had a brain injury," Amber says. "When I was tiny. We all did. That's why it's different for us. It must be why it's different for you."

She's suspicious. Only now, poor thing. Trying to be polite, but you can hear the hook of apprehension in her voice. "Could I see that badge again, please? Which department did you say you were with?"

"What do your daughter and her friends call it? The *dreamworm*."

Joanne has deer eyes, wild and wide. "How do you know—" And then realization. "Where is she?"

Amber takes the combat knife out of her jacket pocket and unfolds it. It's a vicious-looking thing, freshly purchased this morning from a hunting shop downtown because she couldn't fly to Colorado from North Carolina with a gun in her luggage. It's menacing, black, with a tip tapered for jamming home between someone's ribs. "You tell me."

DOM

There's Been a Shooting

Everything's unreal—high-pitched, slow motion; they're only able to latch onto snapshots. The hellshriek machine is ringing in their ears. No, it's the gunshots. Their hands are tingling, numb. The elevator doors are closing only now—that's how quickly everything happened. Amberlynn is holding the gun in both hands, like a soldier would, to steady it. They can smell the acrid bite of gunpowder.

Somehow, they jab their heel into Amberlynn's knee as hard as they can, and she staggers. They grab Tendayi's hand. They are running, Tendayi gasping alongside, whining hitches and pops of breath. She'll need to cut that out, Dom thinks. Someone is still screaming. Who is screaming? Are *they* screaming?

Caden can't scream. They glance back. Caden is leaning against the lab door, but "leaning" suggests agency. Suggests he's still alive, that his brains are still in his head and not splattered against the door, mixed with bits of skull and broken glass and splintered wood, and Dom is still screaming. Howling and running.

Another shot, a roar of the world ending, eardrums bursting. Dom ducks. Like you can dodge bullets. A dull rip of flesh, blood sprayed across the corridor. They skid, nearly tumble. Their least favorite trope, the fleeing victim who keeps falling down.

Dragging on Tendayi's hand. Pulling themselves up. Tendayi is shoving the handle of a door down, but it doesn't budge. You need a key. Dom swallows. Their mouth is so dry. Who got shot? Whose blood? Brains on the wall in the neuroscience lab. Seems appropriate. Don't laugh.

But this is the bad dream, the worst kind, where you can't run away fast enough and all the doors are locked.

Dragging Tendayi along, tugging on door handles, and Amberlynn is walking toward them, lining them up, double-fisting that gun. They're trying to talk to her, talk her down, but every sentence is punctuated with a nervous hiccupping hitch of breath.

"You don't want to do this, Amberlynn." Hic. "It was an accident. It went off." Hic. "It's okay. We're friends, remember?" Such good times in the car.

"Where is she?" Amberlynn yells. "Where's Bridget?"

They are propping up Tendayi, pressing their back against her to shelter her, both of them up against the wall and these useless doors that go nowhere. Like Caden said. Oh God, Caden. They're not going to let that happen to anyone else.

You Kevlar, now, come mierda? Big fucking hero? Maybe they said it out loud because Tendayi moans, her breath hot against their neck. The back of Dom's shirt is soaked through. Cold sweat.

"That's a good point," they say to her, glancing back over their shoulder, trying to smile, stay calm. They could defuse this whole situation if they had the chance. If everyone could just stop and give them a moment to think. *Their fault. They brought her in here.*

Tendayi's eyes are wild. There's something wrong with her neck. Hic. They turn their attention back to Amberlynn, going for placatory. "Bridge must be around here somewhere. We should go find her." But they sound desperate, manic, even to themselves.

"Where is she?" Amberlynn shouts. "I don't want to hurt you." Her hands are shaking, her lips pressed thin.

"Cool. Cool-cool-cool!" Dom yells back. "Then *don't* hurt us."

Tendayi is slowly sliding down the wall behind them. They can't hold her up and negotiate with their own personal psycho killer. *Qu'est-ce que c'est?* The tune catches in their head. *Stand on your own damn feet, they think*. She's making a rasping, bubbling sound right in Dom's ear. And oh. Oh no.

"Don't," they say, turning to catch her. It's blood, not sweat, soaking into their shirt. And where is it coming from? Foamy red on Tendayi's lips. Blood where it's not supposed to be. A Rorschach spreading from under her ribs. Her throat jutting at a weird angle like she swallowed part of a coat hanger. Tendayi gasps, her eyes imploring. Dom is trying to remember their first aid, what this means. Bullet must have punctured a lung. It's collapsing, the pressure yanking her trachea out in that horrible angle. But doesn't have to be fatal. Please.

"Uh-uh," Dom says, desperate. "No way. No te me mueras, puñeta. No te me mueras que te mato. You hear me? You stay alive. Tendayi, no te mueras.

"Hey," Dom calls back to Amberlynn without really looking. "Hey, she's hurt." No shit, Sherlock. Run, run, run away. Can't look. Because she's not going to help, is she? She's going to pull the trigger. Dom holds Tendayi's face, blinking, gasping, pops of blood on her lips. Jackrabbit breaths. Praying to a god they don't believe in: "Por favor diosito por todo lo que tu quieras, no te la. Jesus, don't you dare fucking let her die."

They hold Tendayi's glazing eyes: "It's okay, you're going to be okay." They don't turn around.

BRIDGE

The Sign at the End of the World

Looping around Calder Street for the third time while her phone buzzes with another call from an unknown number. She's too afraid to answer it. It could be Franco, borrowing a stranger's phone at the gas station after rattling off a sob story. Or worse, the school. *There's been an incident.* She ignores it. Let Franco think she drove his car off the road, that she's dead in a ditch.

Bridge threw *his* phone out the window on the highway in the direction of a freight truck, hoping that it would be chewed up by all eighteen wheels so he couldn't track it, couldn't find her. As if he doesn't know exactly where she's going. *Throw* is a strong word. She opened the window and dropped the phone out, so she doesn't actually know if it was splattered into so many component parts, rendered useless. Unfortunately, she's only two steps up from useless herself. Everything feels limp and heavy, and it takes all her focus to manage the pickup. Thank God it's not stick.

She also has no way to know which of these tatty houses is supposed to be her mother's, absent a neon sign flashing on the lawn or an interdimensional wormhole swirling above one of the low-rise apartment complexes. She could get out and ring every doorbell or stagger down the center of the street, still feeble, still bleeding, shouting Jo's name like a girl in an apocalypse movie. It feels like everyone might be dead. There's no one on the street, barely any other traffic.

Calder isn't that long, maybe two miles end to end. If she drives slow enough…and then she spots it. A white delivery van. It's parked in the lot of a town house complex styled to look like mountain cabins, two-story cookie-cutter in gray clapboard. There must be a million white vans. A literal million. But there was one in the parking lot outside Budgie's apartment, and this is the closest thing she's gonna get to a darkened sky, a luminous vortex, a neon sign.

The phone starts vibrating again. But this time the caller ID reads MAYBE: JOANNE KAYE, and Bridge pulls over to answer it, even as she spots something hanging from the eaves of a porch: a square Chinese bell.

Her hands are tingling; she nearly fumbles the phone. *Joanne Kaye*. It must be. It has to be, after all this. She needs it to be Jo, *her* Jo, so desperately. Her *mother*. The longing is a shining spear through her panic, the lingering dizziness, making her gasp.

If it's really her, what will that mean? It's too huge to wrap her head around. She wants Jo to brush aside her hair, kiss her forehead. Make it okay. Because Jo can help—her mom knows how this works, she *wanted* her to come here. She'll know how to fix everything.

She answers the phone, tries to find the saliva to speak. "Jo?" It's hard not to hear the yearning in her own voice. The need.

"Bridget, this is your mother," she says in a strange stilted way, but Bridge recognizes the particular intonation. Maybe. Maybe she's fooling herself. But the woman on the other side hesitates, hearing it herself.

Incredulous: "Bridge?"

"Jo." Alive. Holy fuck. Here. She's crying with relief and

shock. "Mom. Yes, it's me, I'm here. I came to find you." And a flush of anger. "Why didn't you tell me?"

"Tell her the address." Sotto voce, but she recognizes Amber, and her heart free-falls through her body. How much time does she have left?

"You need to get away!" Jo shouts. "Bridge, you need to run as far as you can."

"I can't, Mom. She's going to—"

The sounds of a scuffle. Amber suddenly on the line. "You come here now, girl, four forty-nine Calder. You know what I'm capable of."

"Don't. Don't come!" Jo yelling. There's the sound of a slap, a real one, and an involuntary whimper. "Don't come here!"

The line goes dead.

But she is already here. Right outside. Her hands on the steering wheel. She's come so far. And Jo is in there. Her *mother* is in there.

She grips the steering wheel with white knuckles and screams as loud as she can, burning her vocal cords, digging her fingernails into her palms. Sits there, shaky, furious, taking stock. There's Amber's torture box in the stained Whole Foods tote bag at her feet. The baseball bat is on the back seat.

Where else is there to go?

BUDGIE

Emergency Exit

Budgie slipped off her shoes at the first gunshots. *All the better to escape, my dear.* She'd done the same when she first left Franco. She'd wedged herself out the window, barefoot, in an oversize Care Bears T-shirt and blue cotton panties, picked up the bag of clothes she'd left beside the trash can, sobbing with relief that it was still there. The kids were at a sleepover, so they could have a "date night," like they used to. He didn't think to question it. She was pretending, faking the time when they were so in love and couldn't get enough of each other, devouring. Love-bombing, she knows now. Give the man an Oscar, a Golden fucking Globe. He wanted to try for another baby. She wanted to get the fuck away. Like she intends to now.

The door to the fire escape is right there, other side of the elevator. She is specifically *not* looking at the man lying slumped in the doorway opposite, missing half his head, with blood pooling around his hips, like an extension of his red hoodie.

She just has to make it across the hall, behind the gunwoman's back. And, yeah, she knows exactly who it is. Amber, aka Mrs. Cassie Green. Different clothes and this one has a gun, not a hunting knife. No little dog. Some disguise, bitch. The one who tortured her, who was going to cut her open and kill her and *harvest* her. She scrubs at her arms involuntarily, but there are no pockmarks here, no signs of anything beneath her skin. *Focus, dum-dum.*

Will the fire escape door be alarmed? She's going to have to take that risk. Hope that Amber is kept occupied with the other two cowering and bleeding all over the floor, one propping up the other, a young Black woman who is in a bad way. A real bad way, worse than anyone she's ever seen, even worse than her own face in the bathroom mirror at that painfully clean shelter a year ago, with her missing teeth and both eyes swollen to slits, black and yellow around her broken nose. This was after the fifth time she left Franco, which still wasn't the last. Dum-dum.

That young woman needs someone to save her.

The way no one ever tried to save Budgie.

Not the neighbors Mr. and Mrs. O'Donnell, who only ever filed noise complaints. Not the landlord, who took Franco's money and a little extra for the trouble, *You know what women are like.* Not her. Trying to fight back. Trying *not* to fight back, because it only made him angrier. Trying not to scream when he dragged her by the hair into the bedroom because she didn't want to wake the kids, didn't want them to be frightened. Trying to be quiet. Trying to be good so she wouldn't provoke him.

She hadn't even tried to save herself.

Not until she caught Marlon watching from the bedroom door, his big eyes peeking through the crack. Not until she saw him with his little sister, heard him telling baby Jess, "You better be quiet or you know what happens, fuckhead," and raising his chubby little fist over her head. She grabbed him, too hard, hard enough that he started wailing, and scooped up Jess. The next night she left. For good. Sixth time. Above average for DV. It usually takes seven tries.

Not to her mother's, because she'd burned that bridge. Napalmed the shit out of it, blown up the struts. She had *helped*

Franco torment Joanne. The human shit through the mail slot, the golf club to her car windows, the threatening notes he'd leave on her windshield, also smeared with shit, when she parked outside the court trying to get the injunction, custody of her grandkids. And didn't that prove, Franco had told her, that her mom was trying to destroy her, them, their little family?

It's not true that *no one* helped. There'd been Noelene X, who ran the shelter, chain-smoking clove cigarettes and making licorice tea, dabbing at Budgie's broken nose with antibacterial wipes. And the social worker, a whole series of social workers, even the police officer who was resigned to her going back to Franco again but helped her file the restraining order anyway.

The secretary at the school who was so kind and understanding, like she knew.

Her mom.

Even after everything. That was the worst of all. How do you live with forgiveness when you don't deserve it? She'd tried to reach out a week ago, but Joanne was cold, disinterested. But when she gets out of this shitshow, she'll try again to un-napalm the bridge. They can be there for each other.

If she can get out of here alive.

Amber is looming over the pair. The one propping up the bleeding woman won't turn around, won't look at her, but they're begging. "Please don't, please." Budgie knows how well *that* works. "Anything you want. You want the dreamworm? I have it right here in my bag. Please, I need to get her to a hospital."

Amber is shaking her head as if there's a bug bothering her. Or to express her regret—she really is sorry, but she is going to have to shoot them.

And Budgie remembers. Yes, there were people who tried to help her *afterward.*

But in the moment, the brutal moment—when noses were

broken and ribs were cracked and children saw things they should never have to see—no one was there.

Except her.

And no one is here.

Except her.

And she has a weapon, lifted from the museum, with all its gleaming metal tools, bone saws and trepanning drills, hammers and scalpels and a lobotomy punch, thick and dull as a screwdriver.

It's heavy in her hands.

The weight of what needs to be done.

All those should-have-dones in the past.

Budgie hoists the fire extinguisher and races up behind Amber on bare feet, and maybe she's yelling, she can't hear through the whine in her ears, because Amber half turns. Too late. The fire extinguisher connects with the side of her head and knocks her down, and the gun goes off again, but Budgie can't worry about that.

Amber is on her knees, looking up at her in utter bewilderment. There is blood coming from a gash along the side of her head, and she says, "No, don't," but Budgie has already heard all the words she ever wants to from this pure evil. Threatening her children. Holding her hostage. Drugging her, planning to cut her up.

Metal-y-plasticky scuff on the linoleum. Amber's grasping fingers have hooked the gun. She's bringing it up. Teeth bared. "You made me do thi—" she starts.

But Budgie has heard *those words* too many fucking times and she succumbs to the rage. A wave breaking over her, searing white and blank as the sun, as a new page, as napalm. Obliterating. She's screaming and crying and she smashes the fire extinguisher down again and again and again and again and again and again. And again.

BRIDGE

Where We Find Ourselves

There's still a glitter of safety glass in her hair as Bridge edges up the side of the cabin holding the baseball bat in one hand and an awkward squirming, snarling bundle against her chest. She's feeling calmer than she has in her entire life. Inevitability of death, maybe. Maybe she's died before, and the other Bridgets are lending her strength, even though it's her fault, her stupidity that got them into this situation.

No one came out when she smashed the van window or even so much as twitched a curtain as she yanked open the door and threw her jacket over the dog's head. Too early in the day, or just that kind of neighborhood. The tote is slung over her shoulder, the torture box banging against her hip with every step. The dog is yelping and struggling, trying to bite her through the layers of denim. She hopes the little asshole doesn't suffocate.

The cabin backs onto a communal stretch of yard overlooking a forlorn basketball court, tufts of grass poking through the cracks, like a nightmare chia pet. There's a rusted barbecue anchored in the weeds and drifts of plastic ephemera, laundry flapping on the lines, and, in the distance, sharp-etched against the sky, the mountains.

Bridge sidles up to the door and risks a quick glance through the window. The kitchen is small and narrow with janky wooden cabinets. One is hanging from a hinge, which might be useful for slamming into someone's face, but it obscures the sight line to the living room. The dog is hard to hang on to, and its squirming has reopened the wound on her arm—she can feel blood seeping through the bandage. But she can hear voices from inside—Amber, mocking. And then, abruptly, a thin scream unstitches the air.

She can't manage everything at once, the dog and the baseball bat and the door handle, trying to shove it down with her elbow. "Mom!" she yells, panicky. She can't be this close and lose her, not now.

The handle jerks suddenly, and the door swings open, and *her mother* is standing there in front of Bridge.

Or maybe not-her-mother.

The dog spills from the denim jacket and lands with a whuff on the ground. Bridge is aware of its hard-scrabbling claws on tiles as it bolts past Jo's legs into the house, where the scream has turned into a wailing.

She can't tell. Her mom (maybe?) is barefoot in sweatpants, hair drawn up into a messy ponytail. She looks so thin, and older, somehow. Sadder. She's searching Bridge's face, the same way Bridge is doing, both of them holding their breath.

"Jo?" Bridge says in the smallest voice, all her hopes and fears in that one short syllable, and her mother exhales.

"Bridge, Jesus." She reaches out and pulls Bridge to her. She drops the baseball bat, and it lands with an aluminum thunk; the tote slips off her shoulder. She hugs her mom tight, like she might never, ever let go. The immensity is too much to bear; all the words she wanted to say have fled like startled birds. Sobbing against her mother's—her *mother's*—chest.

"I'm sorry," Bridge manages. "I'm so sorry."

Jo pulls back, strokes her hair, gives a half laugh of disbelief. "Oh, Bridge. Bridge, why did you come *now*?"

The wailing is still coming from inside and they both look back. She can see that Amber is curled over on her knees, hitting her head with her fists. "No. No, no, no. Shut up, shut up, I can't hear myself think."

"Mom, get in the car, we have to go, now. You don't understand how dangerous she is." Still trying to compute what Jo just said.

Her mom shakes her head. "Come, we need to handle it." She nods at the bat and Bridge scoops it up, follows her into the living room, where Jo picks up a huge and ugly black hunting knife from the counter, most definitely not a domestic item. "It's hers," Jo says. "Don't worry."

But Bridge is very much worried, Amber is still collapsed on her knees on the floor, still wailing, "Shut up, all of you, I need to think." Her awful little dog paws at her, whining, trying to lick her face, but she shoves it away.

Jo goes down on her haunches, holding the knife in front of Amber's face. "Get up," Jo says. The dog growls. Amber shakes her head as if trying to banish the voices in her mind. Maybe that's exactly what she's doing.

She lunges for the knife and Jo rocks back. Bridge has the bat in hand, ready to swing it. "I'll knock your head off," she warns

"*You* killed her," Amber snarls at Bridge. "Amberlynn."

Jo looks at her askance.

"She means the other me," Bridge says. But in which reality? *Not hers.* Please not hers. Not where Dom is. She doesn't want to know. The not-knowing is the only thing holding her together. She's sick and shaky, a ringing in her ears, too high-pitched for her to hear properly.

Jo tilts her head at the kitchen. "Tape in the second drawer, scissors. Bring the dish towel."

It takes Bridge a fumbling moment to realize it's an instruction. She finds only packing tape, a bright green pair of kitchen scissors.

"Hands behind your back," Jo tells Amber. "Don't try anything."

"Shut up," Amber mutters. Not to them. "I can't do anything if you don't let me think." Who *is* she talking to?

Bridge winds the tape around and around her wrists and through and around again. "Are we going to call the police?" That word snaps Amber's attention back to them.

"Yes. Call them, tell them you murdered one of us."

"Mom?" she says, wanting her to make it okay, take charge.

"Hold this." Jo presses the knife into her hand. Bridge's fingers close instinctively around the smooth handle. Seductively easy. Maybe she does have it in her. All those video games Dom loves to play, Bridge curled on the couch watching them take out zombies with flowering fungal heads, trying to get the kid to safety. Isn't that what Bridge is trying to do here—get them all to safety? But who is she kidding? As if she would be able to hurt the dog, much less a person.

Jo rips off a section of the tape with her teeth, grim, focused.

"Ask her about the box," Amber says, seeing her future coming, and then she can't say any more because Jo has rammed the dish towel into her mouth and is taping over it, grimacing, her teeth bared.

"It's your fucking box!" Bridge yells at Amber. "I only have it because you used it to torture me."

But Amber is shaking her head fiercely, yelling vowels through the rag. Jo hauls her up, and marches her to the bedroom, the dog yipping and dancing after them, worrying at Jo's ankles with its sharp little teeth. She pushes Amber inside, nudges the dog in after her and slams the door and locks it.

"Whew," her mom breathes. "Do you want to tell me what's going on?"

Bridge doesn't even know where to start. Her lip is trembling. All of her is trembling. The knife is wavering in her hand.

"Come here," Jo says.

She drops the knife onto the carpet, between the boxes, and throws herself against Jo like she used to when she was a little kid, and her mom was the whole world, the whole universe, slamming into her with her full weight, because that was the only way she knew how to show her the vastness of her love.

Jo grunts with the same whoof and slings her arms around her, squeezes her tight, so tight she can't breathe. She never thought she'd hug her again, the raw physicality of it. It's what mothers do: they hold you, contain you. Bridge nuzzles in harder, a little animal again. Crying and shaking. She never wants Jo to let her go. The whole scope of their relationship, from her kid zeal to the teen resentment, forging herself against Jo in the fire of contempt. The phone calls she cut short, the visits she didn't make, the trips she bailed on, the things she didn't say. Because Jo had always proved to be immortal. Even at Jo's bedside, even when she was dying, and Bridge was angry and frustrated and bored, she didn't really believe... and she was right, it wasn't Jo. It was another iteration, an otherself. Because she got lost out here, stuck in this body. And it's not her fault and Bridge is so happy she found her, that she was able to follow the damn cryptic clues, the tangle of her journal entries, to be reunited.

But Bridge has seen the box sitting on the couch. A cousin to the one she has in her bag. Different color, a different configuration, handmade. The source of the pitch just out of range, the crawling feeling in her vertebrae. *Literally* crawling. And how *did* Jo get stuck here?

She shouldn't ask. She should let it be. She has everything she wanted. But she can't help it. "Mom, what is that?"

DOM

Desperate Measures

Cacophony. Bridge is slumped against the wall, bloodied hands over her face, keening like a broken kettle. Tendayi is still bleeding and gasping, that awful crook in her throat and they're pressing down on her chest. The fire alarm is screaming because Dom set it off, and the 911 operator is on speaker on their phone on the tiles, and they're trying to keep them apprised of what's going on, which is difficult because they don't know and they're counting down the minutes until the ambulance gets there. Too long. It's too long to wait. Nine minutes. Tendayi's breath is hitching and they haven't been able to find a plastic bag like the operator said to tape over the wound in Tendayi's chest, to stop the air from leaking out.

They really need Bridge to snap out of it. To help them out here. They're pretty sure Amberlynn is dead. They hope Amberlynn is dead. Dom threw a jacket over her face so no one has to see. They need another jacket for the fire extinguisher. Mute, dented, bloody witness. They can't look at Caden. It's too late for him.

"C'mon, I need you. Bridge, I need you here," they yell at her. "Snap out of it. Come back to me. I can't do this alone. Hey, Bridge!"

"Stop," Bridge says between her teeth, behind her hands.

"Make it stop. Please. I did it. I saved you. I fucking did it, and now I want to go home. I want to see my children."

"You're not her," Dom says slowly. "Look at me. You're not Bridge. Not *my* Bridge."

The otherself lowers her hands and they can see it in her eyes, the wild terror, a special ferocity.

"Coño." How are they going to explain this to the cops? Does it still count as murder if your otherself did it? If you weren't in your body at the time? "Who are you?" they demand. "Where is she?"

"Hello?" the 911 operator says from the phone on the floor. He's a supremely calm dude. "Are you still there? Can you tell me what's going on?"

Dom ignores him.

"Budgie. I'm Budgie." Snot and tears. "I had to. She tried to kill me before. She was going to kill you all."

"When did she try to kill you? *This* woman? Amberlynn?" As in the corpse over there.

"In my apartment," notBridge sobs. "She tied me up, drugged me. She was cutting them out of me, the yellow threads."

"Now? She's there now?"

"I don't know. Because she's here, isn't she?"

Oh, shit. Shit fucking fuck. Fucking shit fuck. Shit. "Okay," Dom says. "Okay, you're going home, I promise. It's going to wear off any minute now. Do you know where the laptop is? Where were you when you—when this happened?" They can't say the word *transgressed* again. It's thick with guilt in their mouth, because they're the one who brought Amberlynn here. This wouldn't have happened if they hadn't been such a naive idiot, hadn't trusted a stranger after all their arguments to Bridge about the potential dangers, the trail of murders and disappearances. It's their fault.

"Museum," Budgie says and nests her head down again and keens, an awful sound in the back of her throat.

"Hello? Ma'am? Sir? I'm going to need you to talk to me."

"Snap out of it!" Dom yells. "I need you. Come here. I can fix this. Maybe, but I need you to help me look after her."

Budgie crawls over and Dom takes her hands and applies them to Tendayi's chest. The young scientist's eyes are hazed behind the pain and shock. She barely notices the change-over. "What am I doing?"

"Here. Press down here, keep the pressure on. You have to tell me your phone number."

"What?"

"You—Budgie—your phone number. I'm going to need to be able to call you." Even though there's no guarantee, right? That they're friends there too. That they're even in the same city or state or continent. "The police and the paramedics are going to be here soon. The door's still propped open so they can get in." Racking their memory if that's true, if they have to tear downstairs and prop it open themselves. Yes, it's right. When Tendayi came down to get them, she replaced the brick. "But I need you to look after Tendayi. Can you do that? Keep the pressure on?"

They pick up the phone, tell the operator, "Hey, I'm handing you over."

"Where are you going?" the operator says, alarm in his voice. "You have to stay with the victims."

"It's all right," they say, pressing the phone into Bridge-Budgie's hand. "I need you to handle this. I have faith in you."

"What?" she says.

"Take the phone." It'll give her something to do. "Talk to the man. Do what he says. Just keep talking."

"Hello?"

"Ma'am, can you give me your name, please?"

"It's Budgie—I mean Bridget—Ainsley. No, Kittinger."

"Just keep talking. Tell them to take the fire door, come up to the sixth floor. You've got this."

"The sixth floor," she repeats numbly into the phone. "The fire door."

"They're seven minutes away, Budgie. Give me your number."

She says it numbly, blood welling between her fingers, already blood-stained, and Dom repeats it back three times.

"Bridget," the operator calls. "Where is Dom? Can I talk to Dom?" She looks over at them, but Dom is waving, *You got this*, running for the surgery museum, and they're digging in their backpack for the Tupperware and hoping to all the saints they do not believe in that the laptop is still set to the same universe key when they find it.

AMBER

Missing in Action

The howl is ongoing through the Ourmind. All the voices, every iteration. The shock. No, surprise. *Outrage.* The void where Amberlynn should be.

They've lost Ambers before. The one who let the worms grow into a whole city—they cut her off. They had no choice. Another to a heart attack—they all felt the fist clutching inside her chest. A car accident. A mugging. Each time, they felt the suffering, the pain, the fear before they died. But those worlds were lost; they have no way of knowing what happened, if the worm spun itself across the whole universe. It's part of what makes their work so important.

So, yes, they've lost Ambers before, but never like this. And now she will have to be an avenger, yet more mess to clean up, scales to balance. The interfering mother with the knife—as if she'd dare. Coward. *Thief.* The way they taped up her wrists with sloppy enthusiasm rather than diligence. The idiot daughter misunderstanding what she was telling her. Unable to face the truth.

Mr. Floof II is beside himself. He's still trying to nudge his fluffy head up under her palm, looking for comfort. Licking, licking. What she needs him to do is bite through the tape.

Amber presses herself against the door to hear, twisting her hands, backward and forward, backward and forward.

She's going to kill them. And then find and kill every iteration of both—mother and daughter.

I can't, someone says in the Ourmind. *Oh, I can't.* As if she did not inject fentanyl into Aiden's arm yesterday and set him on fire beneath the underpass.

It's enough, says someone else, Amber 5, as if she had not faked a murder scene on a boat in Tunis after Amber had helped her through the dirty work.

Cowards, she thinks back. *Cowards! All of you. We have a duty.* As if she is not also afraid, confused. *Don't you remember?*

Summoning up the image of Chris scratching at his raw and bloody arms and the threads spiraling out of him, thrashing in the air, reaching out, hungry and blind.

Remembering the first time she took it and found the others. Aligned, bound together across realities—a fighting sisterhood.

What makes the pretty flowers bloom. Guts, guts, gritty, grimy guts.

If she lets them go, this mother and daughter, what has it all been for? The sacrifice, every time she killed Chris, her friend, her brother in arms, even in those universes when he hadn't yet been infected. She has to save the world. They all do.

War makes monsters of us all.

BRIDGE

Truth and Reconciliation Commission

"Mom, what is that?" Almost too soft for Jo to hear, nudging her head into her mom's shoulder like a small burrowing animal. It's everything she wanted, to be held close, to hug her mom. One more time.

"You took so long," Jo says, acting as if she didn't hear the question. Maybe she didn't. She's tangling her fingers in Bridge's hair, like she used to when she was a little kid. "To get here," she gives a rueful laugh. "I've been waiting. I thought you'd be here sooner." As if she hadn't had to search dozens of worlds to find her, Bridge wants to chirp in protest, but Jo is holding her tight, stroking her hair.

"I'm sorry," she says instead.

"No. I'm sorry I had to leave without telling you. I wanted to. But I couldn't wait. She was going so fast."

"In the hospital? It was terrible. She was so confused, Mom. The doctors said it was dementia from the chemo and I thought…I thought it was you and I didn't get to say goodbye."

"Oh Bridge. You poor thing. I never wanted you to go through that. You didn't find the instructions?"

"Instructions? What do you mean?" If only, Bridge thinks.

"I left a letter on the kitchen table about rat-fooey, which file to use. I knew you'd get it."

"It wasn't there," Bridge protests. Why wasn't it there... how could she have missed it? The break-in. Caden. He must have taken the letter. She's going to punch that asshole in the face when she next sees him.

But really, now, for the first time, she's thinking: Why the trail of bread crumbs, the frozen assets? She didn't get the instructions, but why would Jo have written them in the first place? Unless... she knew somehow. And there's that damn box she can see out of the corner of her eye.

"Mom," Bridge says, pulling away, "how did you know you were going to be trapped?" *Nodoggy home.* But Bear was a dog, and dogs don't know how dreamworms work. Jo, however...

"Oh, Bridge," Jo says. Bridge can't help it, her attention is drawn back to the little DIY radio. The counterpart to the one in her bag. The one Amber wouldn't shut up about.

"How *did* you get trapped, Mom?" she asks again. She has to. Searching her mother's face.

"It's complicated," Jo says, sad and also faintly irritated. "I wanted to explain in person."

"I'm smart. I found you. You can explain it to me now." Explain it like she's seven, and her mom is bundling her into the car for a *big adventure*, aka a kidnapping. Or locking her out of her bedroom while she goes on one of her trips, or winding up the zoetrope and ruffling her hair as the horse starts to run in circles and the sky comes up to meet her and she, Bridge, is falling away... "What is it? What does it do?"

"You have to understand, baby. She didn't want to live."

"Who?" Bridge's voice is flat, because she knows, of course she knows. *Why won't you let me go home?*

And Jo knows too. Her tone has turned defensive. "She wanted to be released from her pain, Bridge. You don't know what she was going through. She was suicidal. I came in the one time, and she had a tab open on her laptop about how to connect a hose to the muffler, seal the windows. It would have been such *a waste*, Bridge."

"Suicidal ideation isn't the same thing! It can be a call for help." But what she's thinking is: *The one time.* Jo revisiting those realities, the otherJos. It wasn't a cure she was looking for, all this time.

"She wanted this," Jo insists. "This was the best way I knew to help her."

"Did you get it in writing?" The magnitude of it is starting to overwhelm Bridge. Jo playing God (playing doggo) with other lives—including her own daughter's. The 1987 diary, brooding-chicken lovestruck Jo wishing there were a way to stay with her teenage boyfriend. The experiments. *We're looking for somewhere even better.* It's impossible. Absurd. That her mom would even be capable of this. She couldn't be. Surely she couldn't, wouldn't do this to someone? Bridge dips into sarcasm, a smoke screen for the roiling inside, the rising sense of betrayal. "Did she write you a note, Mom? Put up an ad on Craigslist? *Hey, not using this life, first come, first served.*"

"Look at this." Jo gestures around the dreary apartment. "Look at how she's been living. She wanted to die, she was done"—as if by saying it again, it would carry more weight. "She didn't *want* to live. She wouldn't get out of bed most days, would lie there hoping she would just stop breathing."

"You don't *know* that. You weren't inside her head."

"That's the point, I was. I came back again and again. I saw. She kept a journal too. I'll show you. People have the right to die."

"Did you ask her?" Bridge is yelling. "Did you ask her if you could steal her whole fucking life? Did you make a deal? Did you tell her how much dying of cancer would suck?" *You're not my daughter.* "It took her days to go, Mom. Do you know what she said to me as she was lying there, facing the wall and sobbing because she didn't know what the fuck was happening to her? She said, 'I want to go home.'"

"She wanted to *die*," Jo snaps. "I gave her what she wanted. It was mercy."

"But did you ask her?" Bridge sits down heavily on the couch, tears coming again. What do you do when your whole world collapses? When the closure you thought you needed tears the universe apart? When your mother isn't the person you thought and maybe never has been? Our parents are supposed to disappoint us, but Jesus Christ, not like this.

Jo closes her eyes, tilts back her head. "No," she says finally. Anguished. "I didn't ask her. I didn't think I needed to ask her. It was so apparent. And I wanted to *live*."

Bridge has mistaken her expression. It's not anguish, it's pity, because Bridge doesn't understand, and why can't she understand? Wouldn't she have done the same? Sophie's choice, but both babies are Sophie and so are you. And if it's true, if otherJo really wanted out, the two could have come to some kind of fucked-up agreement... but *she didn't know*. Because Jo didn't ask. And she didn't tell Bridge either.

And her plan this whole time was—what? That Bridge would follow the clues and come here and steal Budgie's life, and they could play happy families and raise the grandkids together? What the fuck. "Fuck."

"I know." Jo sits down next to her, takes her hand. Long fingers, good for magic tricks and science and gently stroking her daughter's hair. "It's going to take some getting used to. I didn't want it to be like this. But I had to, Bridge. You understand that?"

"You *left* me."

"But you're here now. You found me."

"You left her to die in your body."

"Bridget," she says, wrapping her ponytail around her hand, "I know it's difficult."

"And Amber!" Bridge gets up as if yanked by a string, stalks the room. "Did you know about her?"

"I've never seen her before. I didn't know."

"She's going to kill every other Bridget. She's already started. There are people who are dead, Mom! *I* might be dead." She's thinking about the way Agent Drew was spitting into her face. "You have to send me back. You have to tell me how to stop her. Will that box do it? Is that the secret? Do you realize she used one of those to torture me?"

"You have to calm down."

"Calm down? That murderer is hunting me in every conceivable reality! Did you know? Did you know about the *extruding*?" She starts unraveling the bandage, which is soaked through again. Peeling it away reopens the wound further. "Did you know about this?" She jerks the bleeding gash at her mother's face. "They're *inside* me."

"The dreamworm?" Jo is puzzled, intrigued, leaning in closer.

"No. Don't you understand? That's why she's hunting me and all the other Bridgets. Because when you switch, you infect the other you."

The dog is howling in the bedroom. And Bridge's—Budgie's—phone is ringing. Ringing and ringing and ringing.

"No," Jo says, a mix of horror and fascination on her face. "It's never happened to me. Not here or anywhere I visited."

"Congratulations for being fucking magic, Mom. It happens to everyone else. Caden, me. The Haitian artist guy, Rabbit. We can't find any trace of Mina Remington either."

"Not Rabbit," Jo says.

"Sorry to break it to you, but yeah, around 2002, John Ravet. Cut up and burned, like Amber was cutting me up."

"That's not his name. It's Jon Coello. He's in a step-down psychiatric facility in Oakdale. I saw him a few weeks ago, before I...left. He said he grew the dreamworm inside him, but I didn't believe him. He showed me how to make the box."

"This box?" Bridge picks it up.

"Be careful!"

"That psycho used hers to torture me, to draw out the worms! What does yours do, Jo?"

"Amber said she had a brain injury." Jo is pacing, calculating, tugging at her ponytail. "It doesn't affect her the same way. She doesn't make them—what did you call it, extrude? And me too. My brain. Maybe—"

"I don't care, Mom! What does the box do?" She moves to turn the dial.

"Don't!" Jo yells with such terror, Bridge understands exactly what it's for. If she felt sick before, this is worse. Worse than she could have imagined.

Jo sinks onto the couch, forlorn and guilty. "It lets you stay."

DOM

Echoing

Dom-dom-dom, they're thinking, a horror movie riff. Feeling a little mad. They're sitting on a memorial bench, the laptop balanced on their knees, surrounded by the evidence of dozens, no, hundreds of what were previously considered "wild experimental procedures." And all that turned out okay, right? Apart from the lobotomies, and the boiling oil used to cauterize gunshot wounds, and the leeches applied to the cervix, and the malformed rickets bones broken to try and straighten them…

But hey, can't get worse than it already is.

Dom-dom-dom. Luckily, or unluckily, for them, the file is still open, playing in the window, on a loop. Two hours? What was Bridge thinking? If only they could just hit Pause and prematurely eject her back here, into her own body. But it doesn't work that way; it's something in the frequency, the brain waves it stimulates. Caden would know. But Caden… Nope. Eject. Don't think about it.

The file is ZC, and they pull up their carefully plotted spreadsheet on the laptop that listed all the universes and *ding-ding-ding,* we have a match! Budgie, the young mom with two kids. They weren't sure if Jo was alive in that universe and maybe she isn't, but Bridge is there, Dom's Bridge.

The only thing left to do is *the thing.* Here is the dreamworm, squelchy yellow rotten spaghetti, chew it down.

They don't know who they'll be on the other side. That's what's terrifying, even more than the idea of worms hatching inside their veins, spiraling through their body, eating their way out. Dom has fought so damn hard for *this life;* why would they be interested in any other? What if they've failed? What if their sisters, their parents, have died somewhere along the way? What if Dom is boring? Or small and broken inside, still in denial and self-hate? If they haven't found their them.

Swallow it down, baby. Tune in, drop out. ZC_12m. That's twelve minutes. They can always go back if they need more time, but they need to be here when the cops come, probably a whole SWAT team by now, to try and explain. Oh, Christ, how are they going to explain? But they can't dump that on otherDom. They hope they don't hate them too much, that they don't hurt themselves or get too frightened.

They've left them a note from *The Hitchhiker's Guide*, a smiley face and the words *Don't Panic* in friendly letters. *Please let them be a sci-fi geek too.* And more:

> *Read this! You've swapped realities. You're safe as long as you stay here. It'll last twelve minutes. There's a timer on your watch. Don't go anywhere.* I know this museum is creepy but it's the safest place. Trust me.*
>
> *I love you*
> *- Dom*
>
> **Except if the cops arrive, then stay calm and go out slowly with your hands above your head.*

They settle the headphones over their ears, click on Play in the window. They're so afraid.

The video starts. Old-fashioned animation, the zoetrope.

A horse galloping. Faster and faster and faster, until it's no longer a horse, only light, and it's warm on their face, like lying on the beach—or the heat death of the universe. And colors. Like seeing the inside of their own brain, filigree veins, electrochemical signals, dropping down into pink crenellations, and see, they knew, they *knew* it was just a trip. But then it turns to the gray static of an old television screen, giving way to fractal swirls spinning wider and wider, a *Wizard of Oz* twister into neon blues and greens and blossoming parabolas of mathematical flowers, because everything is math, and this is what is happening inside their brain, inside everyone's brain all the time, this is consciousness, all of us flying alone in these hallucinating meat cages, so of course we try to reach out to other minds, to other stars in the firmament, wide and deep and greater than all of us, spanning the universe, and every universe, every self, and oh, wow, holy shit, how high are they right now? The tornado is back. Howling wind; they remember Bridge describing it.

And then.

Then Dom is in bright sunlight. On a beach. Sand between their toes. Board shorts and a T-shirt. The ocean is an unreal aqua, like a hair dye they once tried, so bright and blue, and their sister Lur is lying on the towel next to them, belly-down, her bikini top popped open to even her tan, reading a celebrity magazine Dom didn't even know still existed.

"Am I? ¿Estoy dead?" It feels so real. And even though they thought they knew what to expect, it's something else when you experience it.

"Por dios, Dominga." Lur arches her eyebrows behind her sunglasses. "Te dije que dejes de leer tanto cuento de horror." A book beside them, also splayed on its belly, *Mexican Gothic*. But this isn't Mexico, they don't think. It's Puerto Rico. Why are they here? Has something happened to their grandmother?

"Y Lita—¿está bien?"

"Why wouldn't she be?" Lur lowers her shades, gives them an evaluating glare. "You high? No seas jaiba, si tienes hierba, prende y pasa." She makes a grabbing motion for them to share. But they haven't been smoking. They don't think.

"Lur, préstame tu celular."

"¿Dónde está el tuyo?"

Good point. Dom casts around, finds their own phone stuffed inside one of the yellow Crocs beside their towel—and that's taking things too far, they think. Greatest-fear stuff: Of all the bad decisions they were worried this person might have made about their life, what kind of *them* would wear Crocs? They grin until they remember who they really are and the shitstorm waiting for them at home. Eleven minutes, maybe ten.

"Ahorita nos vemos," they say. They stand up, make it two steps before realizing how hot the sand is and returning for the butt-ugly Crocs. They walk away down the beach. They don't want Lur to hear the call.

"Si pasas por la barra," she yells after them, "agárrame un mojito y dile que esta vez no sea tan miserable con la menta."

They give her the thumbs-up, but they are not going past the bar. No time for cocktails. Dom wrote the number down on their arm. But of course, this isn't their arm. Memorized it too, luckily, repeating it like a mantra as the video started up. Plus 1 to dial the mainland. They punch it in. The sun is beating down, hot on their skin. Why don't they do this more? Head to Arecibo, visit Lita, have a vacation.

An ice cream vendor is making his way down the beach; someone else is selling knockoff designer sunglasses, woven fedoras, and beach hats. They wriggle their toes in the hideous shoes and listen to the phone ringing. End call. *Shit.* Again. No answer. Again. How many minutes has it been?

A flash of a hallway pooled with blood. What awaits them when they return? It's tempting to think about coming back here to explore this other life, this Dom's choices, but then they remember that they might have infected them already, and they have to find a way to put a stop to all this.

They type a message:

Bridge, it's me. I came to find you. Call me.
Or I'll keep trying to call you. Answer please.
It's so fucking urgent.
—Dom

The phone rings almost immediately and Dom nearly drops it in the sand.

"Dom?" Bridge's voice, incredulous, but also heavier.

They can't help it, they let loose. "¿Cómo tú me haces esto, canto e cabrona? Estaba tan preocupada. No te puedes ir así de la nada. Estás cabrona." Almost sobbing in relief. "Sorry, I'm sorry, I was so fucking worried." Looking out across the beach, the colorful umbrellas, Lur jerking her thumb as if to say, *Hey, bar's that way.*

"Something bad happened, Bridge. Something really bad."

BRIDGE

The Choices We Make

She's still holding the box. She could destroy it, hurl it to the ground, fetch the baseball bat, and smash it to smithereens. She *should.* But what would that solve? Would Jo stay here, since Joanne has already died, trapped in her body? Would Jo die, would she move on, to... somewhere? Joining the flow, the lights and patterns, a universal collective, or the afterlife. Or another life, again. If consciousness is transferable, that must mean it can transfer elsewhere.

Maybe Budgie's mom is waiting in the wings, ready to pick up from her understudy if she would just get off the stage. Or maybe she would just be extinguished. Two dead mothers for the price of one. Or would Jo simply vacate the body, like Bear did, leaving behind a blinking breathing husk?

Budgie's phone is still ringing. It's hard to think, and the box is doing something to her, to the worms inside her. *The worms. Inside her.* That's a pressing fucking problem. And all the other Bridges and Cadens and Ambers and who knows who else is out there and Dom, in her universe, and whatever has happened in her absence. And the damn dog, howling.

Her phone double-bleeps petulantly with a message, and Bridge takes it out of her pocket, on autopilot, to check it. She should turn it off, she thinks, but it might be the school calling about the kids, and what if it is Franco on his way here? And that's a whole other thing they're going to have to deal with.

But it's not Franco. It's Dom. Her Dom. And that's obviously apparent on her face, because Jo, who has at least stopped making excuses, pipes up again: "Who is it?"

Bridge ignores her. She calls back right away, on video, to make sure, to see for herself. And there they are, looking frightened and exhausted in a pink flamingo-print T-shirt against the flare-out background of bright sunlight. A beach, maybe? Shaved head. She doesn't even have a chance to say anything before Dom launches into a hot stream of Spanish—swearing, she's pretty sure—and then they tell her that something bad has happened. Really bad.

"What is it? Dom, you shouldn't be here. You shouldn't have come. You need to go back. The dreamworms infect you—"

"I know, that's why... is that your mom? Your real mom?"

Bridge glances back, Jo is standing behind her, raising one hand to say hi. "Yes," she says. Unfortunately, yes. She wishes it weren't. Wishes she hadn't found the dreamworm, tried the dreamworm, come to find Jo, set off all the ripples.

"I know. That's why I'm here." A deadness to their voice. "Puerto Rico, not wherever you are, but same universe."

"Listen, you have to get out of there. There's this woman, Amber, she knows where you are."

"I've already met her," Dom says flatly, holding it in. "Fuck, Bridge." Their voice cracks. "She, fuck, there's no way to say it."

"Am I dead?" Reeling.

"No. You would have felt that, wouldn't you? No, you're okay. Budgie is okay, that's how I got your number. But... this is probably too much, more than you need to know right now, but I want you to be prepared—"

"Amber said I killed her," Bridge interrupts. "The one here. So Budgie..." Willing it not to be true. It can't possibly be true.

"Yes," Dom says, unable to meet her eyes. "It was self-defense. She—you—saved my life. Tendayi's too. I think. Hopefully." They are getting frantic. "I don't know if she's going to make it. The ambulance is coming. I don't have time. The cops are going to be there, and I'm the only one who can explain. Although how—"

"Caden?" Bridge asks.

Dom shakes their head. It's enough. And, oh my God, how is she going to go back to that? She can't bear it. Suddenly she can almost understand Jo's decision. The box means she never *has* to go back. She'll never have to face Dom, knowing it was her bad decisions that got them here. If she hadn't been so insistent on using the dreamworm... Caden's dead. Tendayi's hurt, maybe dying. It's all her fault.

She could stay. She could walk away. She could be a young mom, probably a better one than Budgie, from what she's seen. Rebuild her relationship with her mother. Make different, better life choices than the ones in all the other lives she's experienced.

She could abandon someone else to her fate, her bad decisions, the repercussions. Budgie would plead insanity. Get off with six months probably, depending on the definition of *self-defense.*

But it's not a life. It's not *her* life. She couldn't do that to someone. Not to a total stranger, and not to herself. Which means she has to fix this somehow. She can be the mad scientist's daughter, if that's what it takes.

"You didn't come to tell me that? Risk getting infected for that?"

"No," Dom shakes their head. "I did it because I think

there is a way to kill it. Do you know about the noise box? Amberlynn, that's my one, told me they use it to control the parasite and harvest it, using different frequencies."

"I have one here," Jo says, her voice flat and dull. "I built it." She glances sideways at Bridge. "So I could stay."

Dom looks confused at this confession, but Bridge has caught on. "The video Tendayi played in the lab. I felt sick hearing it. There was this overwhelming nausea, like something was wrong inside me. Really wrong. I honestly wanted to run out of the room. And she said it made the sample shrivel up."

"I think, hang on." Dom shakes their head—*No, thanks*—at a woman offering to sell them a hat on that beach. "I'm trying to get this right. Amberlynn explained you're a source, the carrier, which means you don't breed the worms inside you, but there must be some egg or larval form inside you. If there's a frequency that activates it, there must be one that can kill it or stop the spread."

"It was the mystery when I found Rabbit," Jo says. "He claimed he spun the worms but I didn't."

"Do any of the Jos? Have you ever encountered it?" Dom says. "There's no mention of it in your journals."

"No. Not once in all the switches."

"Is it because of your brain cancer?" Dom says. "Because the video Bridge had such a strong reaction to was a musical interpretation of a seizure."

"It's the epilepsy." Jo is excited, on the case. Bridge remembers this, the late-night moment at her desk when Jo would jump up, fizzy with delight at solving a difficult problem. The memory is shadowed with everything she knows now. Was Jo always like this? Or was it all the switches, the dreamworm changing her behavior, like Dom said parasites do? She should have listened to them. Story of her life.

Jo is pacing, scruffing the fingers of one hand through her hair. Bridge quickly releases her own ponytail, which was bunched in her fist. A quirk of genetics or learned behavior. But she doesn't *have* to be her mother's daughter. She could be anyone, or simply herself.

"It works using frequencies and images, so this is credible," Jo says. "Consciousness is emergent, a translation of physical signals and information into thought, so if the seizures were interfering with the worm's propagation, then it's very possible that a video that replicates the frequency would also interfere with the life cycle, maybe at all stages, which is why you felt so sick, Bridge." She stops pacing. "Amber told me she had a brain injury when she was a child." She rolls her eyes. "Right before she pulled out her knife."

"She kept disappearing when she was torturing me," Bridge says. "Checked out of her face. But it wasn't like a switch, it was more as if she was visiting somewhere else. Projecting."

"Maybe it works differently on her," Dom says, "because maybe, like Jo, she has a differently wired brain."

"We could ask her." Jo looks toward the door. The dog has stopped its whining.

"So can we play the seizure music video and... kill it? Or will it kill the host, the source, as well?"

"It died in the lab," Dom points out. "You stepped out for a smoke after the seizure song. But Tendayi showed me the video recording and the worm withered right up on the slide. Stopped fluorescing."

"So now what?" Bridge says. "We get a boom box and go play the magic seizure song in every universe outside every infected person's window? What if it kills the host?"

"My understanding is most parasites explicitly don't want to do that," Dom says. They glance at the top of the phone, checking the clock. "I'm running out of time. I found the video online, there must be a version in that reality too. You need to figure it out. I love you. Come home."

"To a murder charge?" Bridge feels everything inside her tense up. "Fuck."

"We'll fix it. I promise. I got you. I have to go. I still have something I need to do here."

"Yeah, me too. I love you too." *The family we choose*, feeling it so deep, so hard. How could she not go back when Dom is waiting for her?

Jo has already found a variation of a seizure song online. She looks grimly at the bedroom door. "We need to test it."

And maybe she is her mother's daughter, after all, because Bridge agrees with her. After everything Amber has done, she deserves it. And maybe this will make it stop. Make *her* stop.

AMBER

Disconnect

No. She's heard everything, she knows what they're going to do, and she still hasn't managed to free her hands, despite all her training, all her willpower. The tape has pulled thin, but she's not as flexible as she used to be, can't hook her hands under her feet, bring them around in front of her, use her heels to break the tape.

The door opens and the girl hauls her out, steering her toward the living room. Amber twists and struggles, setting off Mr. Floof II, but he's exhausted, poor thing, tail between his legs, and it's easy for her to close the door on him. The howling starts immediately. A heart-stricken lament. A funeral dirge.

And inside her head, the chorus of the Ourmind is out of tune. Discord in the ranks. There's a swell of exhaustion across the Ambers. Disgust. Fear. But mainly…relief. *Let it go,* someone says.

Fuck you, she thinks.

But what if all this, all her hunting, *was* unnecessary? There might have been another way all along. But how could she have known that the box could be tuned to other frequencies that could exterminate it as well as share minds? All the killing they've done.

But we didn't have to.

We didn't know, she reminds them, herself. And even if it is true, even if this works, who will carry out their duty? Who will ensure the worms don't fester in other minds, find a new way to spread? They still have work to do. Vital work. Work only they can do.

Bridge is guiding her to the couch, pressing her down. Firmly but without real strength. Bridge thinks she's defeated. She's not.

Aren't we?

Jo is crouched down by the coffee table, setting up her laptop. "We're going to show you a video," she says. "It might cure you. Or it might do nothing."

Amber shouts into the dish towel, struggles against her bonds. Muffled inchoate fury, accompanied by the tragic howling in the room next door.

"Mom, we should let her—"

"All right." Jo is unhappy about it, but she peels the tape from Amber's mouth, taking a layer of skin with it. Amber spits out the towel, licks her lips, tastes blood.

"You can't do this. I'm the Protector, the Guardian. You don't know what I've had to do."

"We have some idea," the girl says, angry. But it's *her* fault. She chose to dabble with the devil. They are all here because of her. No, her and her mother—the Life Thief. Exactly like Christopher Bacque, who stole her Chris. Monsters, all of them.

"I'm sorry." Jo is avoiding her eyes. "We have to."

"I'd rather you killed me."

"Yeah, well." Bridge's mouth tightens.

"I won't listen. I won't watch it."

"Don't make me tape your eyes open," Bridge says. Both of them know if the roles were reversed, Amber would simply cut off her eyelids.

"This makes you as bad as me."

"No, it doesn't," Bridge snaps. "It really fucking doesn't."

"It'll affect you too. They'll die inside you. Do you know what will happen then?"

"Do you?"

"You'll die. You'll be trapped here in this body and their corpses will rot inside your veins and slowly poison you. You'll die in agony." She has no idea if any of this is true.

"Mom?"

Jo shrugs, helpless. "If it works like a garden-variety parasite, there's a chance that any matter it leaves behind will cause an immune response."

Bridge jerks away. "No. I might be trapped here. I need to go back. I can't stay here. Sorry, I can't watch it. I'll wait outside."

Jo looks bewildered. "But here, you'd be with me." She reaches out to touch Bridge's hair, hesitates halfway.

"I can't, Mom. You know I can't—"

"You can't fix it," Amber interrupts, taunting them. "You're broken. You did this. There's no going back." It's the wrong thing to say. Bridge replaces the dish towel in her mouth, and the tape. She screams into the cloth.

It's worse inside her head.

I've found it, someone says.

Me too.

Joanne and Budgie are going to the front door. Maybe they've changed their minds, decided to abandon this reckless stupidity. They're talking in low voices, and in the locked bedroom, Mr. Floof II is still howling, disconsolate.

What? What have you found?

But she can see through their eyes even as she's wrenching against the tape around her wrists with renewed fury, screaming against the dishrag. It's the video, or whatever variations exist in their realities, recordings of seizures mapped into music. They're watching it; all of them are *choosing* to listen, to be cut off. She yanks her mind away from theirs so she doesn't have to hear, doesn't have to see. Wrenching against the tape around her wrists.

One by one, the stars inside her start winking out.

BRIDGE

Ruby Slippers

Jo steps out behind her onto the porch and closes the door. The Rockies have faded into a haze. It's humid. Budgie's kids must be waiting for her. Inside the faux timber cabin, the little dog is howling in grief. Bridge can hear Amber mumble-screaming against the gag. But Amber is wrong. About her and Jo, anyway. They probably *could* fix things, find their way back to each other, make amends, figure shit out. The possibility is thick in the air between them as they stand outside the front door. It feels like the last door in the world. There's a dread finality.

It must be close to two hours now. Home time. Bridge is sickened at the thought of what's waiting for her. It's like passing a traffic accident: Keep your eyes on the road, away from the blood on the asphalt, the crumple of metal and human bodies. Can't look too closely at what is happening here either, the reality of what Jo has done. Both of them murderers of a kind, and the really fucked-up thing? She still loves Jo. Loves her with that little-kid heart, deep and true, because she's her mom. Despite everything.

"You could come back," Jo says. "After it's done and she's gone."

Bridge leans her head against her mom's shoulder, wanting

to feel her closeness. "People are dead, Mom. Because of me. And you. And her."

"But *we're* not," Jo protests. "*We* have a chance."

"You *are* dead. Where I live. Which isn't here. I can't stay. I can't do that to someone else." She pulls away.

Her other life, her *real* life waiting for her. All the bad choices she's made, some she hasn't. One big one. She has to go back, show the other Bridgets what to do. Pray that Amber isn't still out there in other worlds. Hope that Budgie doesn't go back to Franco, that she gets some grade A therapy to deal with the trauma Bridge has put her through—accidentally, yes, but still. Bridge imagines the tug of all the otherselves she feels responsible for, especially the dead. She needs to fix things as best she can. But she can't live their lives, only hers.

The keys to Franco's truck are clenched in her fist, the teeth biting into her palm. A bird sings like a cricket somewhere in the trees, sharp and trilling. A lawn mower grumbles. She's vaguely aware that the little dog has stopped howling somewhere inside.

Jo winces, opens her mouth to explain all over again. But Bridge stops her. "I can't. I don't want to hear it. I love you." She really does. She squeezes her hand, lets it go, and Jo chokes. She seems so small, so fragile. There's such utter misery on her face, but it's not her face. Not quite. *Was it worth it?* she wants to ask her, the love and anger all knotted up. There are things she could say. Like: *I love you, but Jesus. Look at what you've done, Jo. Look at who you are, who you chose to be.*

But instead she says: "Maybe you can look after Budgie."

She reaches up and double-taps the doorway to show respect for the dead. Or to say goodbye.

AMBER

Roadkill

She's picking her way across the grass behind the complex, the tape, snapped at last, dangling from her wrists and the bag with her own Frequency Machine slung over her shoulder. Mr. Floof II is clasped in her arms; she's holding his mouth because he needs to be quiet. She needs to regroup. She'll come back and take care of this.

She has to find the others. Reconnect with them. There's a gathering darkness inside her head, a terrifying blankness. She hasn't been alone in forever, not since the first time she took the worm and felt them all swarming in. What's a queen bee without the hive? Dying in an empty palace of rotten honey, she thinks.

They can't *all* have watched the video. She still has a freezer compartment at home with the worms she cut out of Aiden. She can use those. It can't be that just one frequency, one little video of an epileptic seizure, would deworm them all. She'll be able to reinfect herselves.

Not *reinfect. Reconnect.* She's the parasite killer, the deworming pill, the hunter of monsters. She doesn't *infect.*

The mother is shouting for her out the back door now, but Amber is behind the laundry lines hung with pale blue sheets, crouched down beside the rusting barbecue grill overgrown with weeds. *That's a fire hazard,* she thinks.

She wonders if the mother is going to watch the video. Unworm herself. Unwoman herself. If she'll die.

She expects the others to chime in. But there is only the emptiness and the dark.

Amber will take care of it; alone, if she has to. She waits the mother out and eventually the woman goes back inside. Probably won't call the police. How would she explain? Amber laughs to herself, and Mr. Floof II shakes off her hand and licks her face happily.

"I've got you, haven't I? Yes, I have, my baby. You and me."

She creeps along the side of the cabin, takes the risk of glancing in the window, through the bedroom, the open door. Jo is sitting on the couch, stricken, her head in her hands. But the movement outside alerts her and she looks up.

Their eyes meet. The stealer of lives and the exterminator.

She could go in there now. Use the knife. Joanne might welcome it. Or maybe it's enough to let her live with it all.

Again she reaches out for confirmation from the Ourmind, but no one is there.

She can always come back. Take care of it in the future.

Joanne raises a hand—*Wait*—but Amber is already moving, limping around to her van, fast as she can. A blue confetti of broken glass where the girl smashed the window. She's going to have to explain it to the rental company. Awful, a wrong turn, a bad part of town, these thugs came out of nowhere. She was lucky to get away; of course she understands there will be a deductible to pay. Amber could explain all the deductibles *she's* going to be dealing with—all the people who are going to have to pay once she's back to herself, the others.

She can come back for Budgie too. Later. She has all the time in the world.

She brushes the broken safety glass off the passenger seat

into the footwell, so that Mr. Floof II has somewhere to sit. He curls up and thumps his tail hesitantly.

"It's all right, my baby," she assures him. It will be.

The engine fires up right away. Denver airport, she thinks, to return the rental. Then back to North Carolina. Back to her little house, her freezer with the worms.

But as she's driving away, racing for the highway, she spots a man walking on the other side of the road, thumb out, hitchhiking. He has a swagger and a storm on his face that means no one is likely to pick him up. Shaved head, bad attitude—the boyfriend. What was his name, Franco? Two hours ago, they were grappling, trying to inflict maximum damage on each other. He actually *hurt* her, and the outrage fills her again. She does a U-turn, floors the gas pedal, intending to run him down, smear him all over the road. Pity the gators won't get to chow down on him.

But reason floods in even as she accelerates toward him. Maybe she can make this work for her; he's sure to lead her to Budgie, and then it'll be another neat murder-suicide. With his record and the restraining orders, no one will wonder about it or question the open slice on the girl's arm. Two birds—ha, one of them a budgerigar—with one stone.

She pulls up alongside him, keeping pace, rolls down the window.

"Get in," she says. "We need to talk." This always works. The secret knowledge she has to share. She knows how to play people.

But he jolts at seeing her, teeth bared. "You!" Hostile.

She can calm him down. She knows what to say. "I can get you to Budgie, help find your kids—"

But his eyes are wild, and he is drawing a gun out of the back of his jeans, and it's pointing right at her face.

"You fucking bitch!"

And he pulls the trigger.

BRIDGE

Rest and Restitution

"Well, it's a definite upgrade on jail," Dom says, both of them sitting outside on the bench of Cedar Peaks Psychiatric Facility. They're under a huge oak tree overlooking the swimming pool, where a young Black man is leading some of the other women inmates—sorry, Bridge should say *clients*—in a water aerobics class. "Think your dad would put me up too? I have a whole lot of unprocessed trauma. We could be roomies."

"You're only saying that because you haven't tried the food," Bridge says.

"Bad?" Dom says.

"Goddamn terrible. Practically not food. Unfood."

It's been two long months of talking on the phone and e-mailing between Cedar Peaks, outside Seattle—so her dad can keep an eye on her—and Austin. But that's not the same as in-person, and after the first crushing hugs in the reception area, they've both been a little tentative, feeling each other out. Bridge runs her hand over her shaven head. It felt necessary, a break from who she was before. And another clear sign of her breakdown.

Her dad's lawyers think she'll walk entirely. Self-defense is one thing, but acting in the defense of *other people*? Especially against someone who turned out to be some kind of serial killer? The police are still collecting and collating, but there's previously unidentified DNA linking Amberlynn Damron to several other deaths over the last three decades, including an ex-vet, called Chris Bacque, presumed to have died by his own hand while awaiting trial for the murder of a young woman and her lover, as well as one Wilhemina Hilburn (neé Remington) in New Orleans, much missed by her husband, Angelo Hilburn, who always maintained she would never go back to drugs, a Belgian tourist who took a suspicious dive off a bridge, possibly others. After Bridge tipped them off, the police are working with the Haitian authorities, looking into a trip Amberlynn made over there in 2017 according to the stamp in her passport, which they discovered at her modest house in Reno, along with various illicit drugs, weapons, tools, and surgical implements as well as a tarpaulin with blood spatter, video equipment, and an elderly cat, Mr. Toe Beans, who has been adopted by a neighbor. She also suggested they talk to a Jon Coello, who was at a mental facility in Sacramento, and tied to Amberlynn's victim Chris Bacque, and that double murder. But he's checked out, literally, his term served, and disappeared into the world. Maybe Rabbit is still Discipling, finding new teenage squatters or dictators to share the communion of the dreamworm. She hopes not.

The point is, no jury alive would convict Bridge. Not in this or any other compatible universe.

Her dad paid her bail, so she spent only two days in the local holding facility. There is a part of her that wants to be punished and wishes he hadn't. Doesn't she deserve to be doing time behind bars, even if it's only in the lead-up to the trial? Which could be in another month or a whole year, depending on when the DA decides to throw the whole thing out. *If*, she should say. She doesn't like to count on anything these days. Except herself.

Dom eyes her cautiously, evaluating the fine fuzz on her scalp, and reaches out to stroke her like a cat.

"Man, I could have told you this wouldn't suit you. I could have told you that you, Bridge Kittinger-Harris, have a funny lumpy head."

"It goes with my funny lumpy personality. Besides"—she indicates Dom's own hair, the undercut growing out and dyed back to their natural dark brown—"hello, corporate!"

"Don't remind me." Dom looks glum. At least their clothes are still very of-them—pastel-yellow dungarees today and arm warmers they must have stolen from an eighties exercise class.

"How's the internship going?"

"I have learned many things. Like I do not ever want to be an architect. Sorry, Papa."

"It's just because your boss is a dick."

"No, he's fine. And buildings are…fine. But I want to make comics, you know? Or be a lawyer. Especially after…"

"Wouldn't want to die an architect, I get it. But you *could* afford more beach holidays."

"And designer Crocs," Dom agrees. "One of my favorite artists is doing portfolio reviews at Powell's Books in Portland, and I thought I'd drive down for a day or so, show him what I've got. Maybe you can help me pick out the best ones."

"You know I'm here for a rage-in-the-cage art battle."

Dom grins and hesitates before saying anything else. Bridge knows there's another reason they're in town which has nothing to do with her.

"How is Tendayi?" she nudges them.

"Yeah, sorry, I never know if you want to hear about it." As if Bridge doesn't understand Dom is never going to forgive themselves for what happened. Tendayi spent eleven days in ICU with Dom by her side. Not family, but one of the heroes, so the hospital made an exception, especially when the family had to fly out from Zimbabwe. Bridge was Dom's emotional-support animal that time, as much as she was allowed to be on her phone in the facility.

"Of course I do. How is she?"

"The physical therapy is going well. Grueling months of it still. And the university's health insurance covered most of the medical bills. You wouldn't believe—"

"I believe. I saw the HelpFund page you set up for her. That was kind."

"Yeah, well. Generally, she's doing good. Still needs to get that trauma counseling. I've been encouraging her to go."

"You should go with her."

"Don't worry about me. I'm going on a family vacation in a month or two. Tendayi might come if she's feeling better. See my lita, explore PR together."

"Sounds romantic," Bridge teases and Dom blushes furiously.

"Yeah, well," they grin. "Let's see. We're taking it really slow. And you? How's the macramé or whatever they have you headcases doing here?"

"Hiking club is more where it's at. Lots of group sessions. I'm not allowed to talk to the media, for my own sake."

"We should make a comic. The dreamworm bible."

"I've been doing a writing course, so, yeah, maybe. But I think I'm pretty interested in—don't laugh—studying psychology."

"Haven't you already had several lifetimes' worth of climbing into other people's heads?"

Bridge laughs, delighted. "I think that's why. I mean, I wanted to do documentaries, but I've become extrasuper-plus interested in other people's lives lately, can't imagine why. I'm interested in our choices, how the stories we tell about ourselves shape who we are. Who we could be."

"Yes, that does sound very much like good psychology and introspection and... future planning?" They raise one wicked eyebrow. "Are you sure you're *my* Bridge?"

"Not historically my strongpoint," Bridge acknowledges. "But I'm trying. Taking it slow, like you."

"So, no comic, then? We're never going to be the dynamic duo? Flying around the world to all the cool cons? Obviously I'd be the real talent."

"Always have been."

They sit there listening to the leaves rustling above their heads, the water aerobics instructor's encouraging instructions: *Lift those legs, use the resistance of the water.* There will always be resistance, Bridge thinks. To what she has to say, when she's ready to say it, about what happened. To warn others. And hey, maybe it'll have the opposite effect, get the wrong people interested. There's resistance inside her too. The internal pressure, the fear of making the wrong choices. One of the therapists here told her that it's all about keeping the kite up in the air; you need enough tension in the string to let it fly, but not snap. She's trying.

"Speaking of goddamn terrible unfood..." Bridge says.

"Your favorite." Dom takes out a bag of sour gummy worms. The bag has been carefully doctored by someone with an artist's eye so it looks like it's never been cut open, never had some additions slipped in between the confections. But if you really look, you can see them, the pale yellow ones, dusted with sugar to blend in. A few strands only. Not much left. She hopes it's enough.

"You sure?" Dom says, not quite giving it to her. Not yet. Bridge will have to submit it to the warden for assessment to ensure it's not CBD or LSD or some other drug that can be boiled down and mixed with gelatin. But she won't be looking for dreamworm, won't know how to test for it.

"I have to." She has her headphones and a series of video files stored in the Cloud, carefully marked, carefully calibrated with Dom's spreadsheet. At night, she'll dream another life, long enough to warn them, to tell them how to stop it. Sixty-seven. Minus the dead. She saw Jo once. RealJo. Playing in the park with the Marlon and Jess. Which meant Jo had probably already told Budgie what to do, showed her the video. She left instructions with her otherself anyway, stayed only long enough to record the voice note. Didn't say hello to her mom. There's nothing to say. But she hopes they're all okay. She hopes they're happy.

Dom is still holding the bag out of reach. "But you come back, you hear?"

"I will." She takes it from them. "Always." To this life, these choices, the ones she's made. "Because you're here."

"Damn straight," Dom says. "Damn fucking straight."

Postscript

October 26, 2023

Cher journal,

Words from another life. A person I used to be. I'm trying. I really am. It doesn't suit me. Fighting through the chemistry of Joanne's depression. Being a grandmother. I'm too impatient, too preoccupied with the possibilities. I think I've made the wrong choice. This life is too small and too narrow, a box that cramps me.

The children are too loud, and Budgie, that ridiculous name, is so sad all the time, even with baby daddy in prison where he belongs. He tried to claim that he was defending Budgie, that the woman he killed had been torturing Budgie, that he saved her.

But Budgie wasn't here, or not really. She couldn't say what had or hadn't happened or who cut her open. I told the police she was in shock. He'd hurt her, like he had all those times before—check the history—and she'd stolen his pickup and come running to me for help.

The truth is that Budgie *did* come running to me. Came back to herself only three blocks away, behind the wheel of Franco's truck. It was a miracle she didn't crash it. She showed up incoherent, sobbing that she'd killed someone in a hospital or some science building. It must have been Amber. The other one. In the reality I left behind.

Her arm was still bleeding, and I helped her re-bandage it and called the police, who were already in the vicinity, attending to a shooting on the stretch of road two miles away.

I watch the kids sometimes, try to do the best I can. I know Bridge has been back. Budgie told me about the voice note. I could have encouraged her not to listen to it. Told her it was part of her mental illness, another episode, waited to see if she spun any more worms from under her skin. But I'm not evil. I'm not going to keep my daughter as some kind of dreamworm breeding ground.

I already have the one I removed from her arm when I was bandaging it. When she was out of her mind, thinking she'd killed someone, weeping on the couch. A simple matter. A pair of tweezers. Three inches of worm. It won't get me far, but it might be far enough.

To the other Joanne, the one who isn't a failed science teacher, bankrupt from trying to get custody of her grandchildren and paying for rehab for her fuckup of a daughter. Joanne the scientist who gives talks at international conferences.

I have the box. I know how to build a new one and I have been experimenting with other frequencies.

I'm going to burn this now, cher journal. So no one will find me. No one will come looking. I've learned.

People can change.

Acknowledgments

I'm so grateful this book gave me an excuse to hang out and talk to the most fascinating experts on neuroscience and parasitology and music and medicine and police work and more. I have taken huge liberties with all of these subjects, and any mistakes are mine.

Some of the very useful books I read for background include *This Is Your Brain on Parasites* by Kathleen McAuliffe, *Parasite Rex* by Carl Zimmer, Rosemary Drisdelle's *Parasites: Tales of Humanity's Most Unwelcome Guests*; *The Lonely Soldier: The Private War of Women Serving in Iraq* by Helen Benedict, *Shoot Like a Girl* by Mary Jennings Hegar; *The Big Truck That Went By: How the World Came to Save Haiti and Left Behind a Disaster* by Jonathan M. Katz, Tracy Kidder's *Mountains Beyond Mountains; Being You: A New Science of Consciousness* by Anil Seth, and Adam Becker's *What Is Real? The Unfinished Quest for the Meaning of Quantum Physics.* On that note, Understanding Music's YouTube video essay on "Understanding Toxic" was influential, as was *Radiolab*'s episode "Bringing Gamma Back," on how certain light frequencies applied to rat brains can destroy plaque caused by Alzheimer's disease.

The people I spoke to were more important than anything I could have read or listened to or watched.

On the brain stuff, my dear friend and neuroparasitologist Dr. Hayley Tomes at the University of Cape Town let me hang out in her lab and showed me all the equipment and workings, explained tapeworm life cycles repeatedly, and invited me to take home a slice of (uninfected) rat brain of my very own. (Obviously, I said yes, and his name is Pinky.) She also read this manuscript over and over, and the plot was hugely shaped by our conversations.

Likewise, neurosurgeon Dr. Sally Rathemeyer sat at my dinner table and explained epilepsy, drew diagrams of where Jo's tumor would have been, and how it would have been treated over the decades and wrote Jo's physician's report. I'm grateful also to her colleague Dr. Graham Fieggan, to Professor Joe Raimondo, who allowed me to borrow some of his bio for Jo's own studies, to Dr. Anil Seth, who sent me a copy of *Being You* before it was published and talked consciousness and invited me to try out the Dreammachine experience he worked on. I'm eternally indebted to immunologist and helminth expert Dr. Bill Horsnell, who literally saved my life and someone else's. You know how.

Huge thanks to Twitter friends Dr. Alastair McAlpine, for giving me real medical advice for novel ailments, to former Chicago cop Joe O'Sullivan, for talking me through the intricacies of army training, police work, and corpse disposal (and the indelible image of Shrimp Head Man), and to Scott Hanselman, for walking me through Portland.

I learned so much about music theory and resonances from award-winning composer, musician, and forensic musicologist Simon "Fuzzy" Ratcliffe and from getting to hang out in the studio of Mr. Sakitumi, aka Sean Ou Tim. Anil Seth introduced me to Jamie Perera, whose work explores social issues through music and sound, including the Holocene, COVID deaths, data privacy, consciousness, and making a soundtrack out of guns for Amnesty International. He also introduced me to Alice Eldridge, a "reader of sonic systems," who makes feedback music designed to induce altered states both on her own and as part of the Brain Dead Ensemble but focuses mainly on eco-acoustics, which involves listening in on ecosystem health, about which I could write a whole separate novel.

Thanks to Nica Cornell for inspiring me to go to Haiti in 2015 and to Richard Morse at the Hotel Oloffson, especially for putting me in touch with the houngan Anis, who plays bass in his band. Anis spent three hours talking vodou with me in his home and was kind enough to give me a reading and laughed when I mistook the young woman doing her physics homework in his basement for a mambo-in-training. Thanks to Jojo Maislin, whom I met while crashing the U.S. ambassador's party, and architect Nathalie Jolivert, who showed me another side of Haiti and took me for dinner with her mom and sister. Lee Hirsch gave me excellent introductions in general, but especially to Patrick "YouYou" Payin, my wonderful fixer, guide, and interpreter. Both Patrick and Nathalie were kind enough to read over the Haiti chapter to ensure the representation was respectful and accurate. Any mistakes or misinterpretations are mine.

I am hugely grateful to my friend and comic writer Vita Ayala for sharing their awesome life stories, Puerto Rican perspective, and lived nonbinary experience to help me understand Dom. Pablo Defendini, Erynn di Casanova, and Leila Rodríguez helped me with the use of Puerto Rican Spanish. Thank you, too, to my careful sensitivity readers. Again, any mistakes are mine.

I'm grateful to Chris Denovan for inviting me to share his studio space and watch his new exhibition come together at the same time as this novel did, and our upstairs neighbor Caro Jesse, whose studio inspired Mina's. Thanks to Paige Nick for her sea views, to Juanita de Villiers, who helped me out in between doing their own cool projects, to Page Wicks for expert life-running, to Sarah Lotz, forever and always, and Charlie Martins, who helped me to change worlds. I miss you, friend.

Thank you to my editors Josh Kendall, Jessica Leeke, Fourie Botha, Helen O'Hare, and Catriona Ross, and my ace copyeditor, Tracy Roe—and, of course, to the passionate teams at all my publishers, as well as my agent Oli Munson.

This book wouldn't have been possible at all if not for my first and best readers, Sam Beckbessinger, Tauriq Moosa, Hayley Tomes, Sam Wilson, Dale Halvorsen, and especially Helen Moffett, my longtime editor and coconspirator who, like a dreamworm, is inside my head. Helen, you know I couldn't have done this without you.

And finally, thanks to my daughter, Keitu, in every world, every life.

About the Author

Lauren Beukes is the award-winning and internationally bestselling author of *The Shining Girls*, which has been adapted by Apple TV+, as well as *Zoo City, Moxyland, Broken Monsters*, and *Afterland*. Her novels have been published in twenty-four countries, and she's also a screenwriter, comics writer, journalist, and award-winning documentary maker. She lives in London with two trouble cats and her daughter.